DIGGER

DIGGER

Joseph Flynn

BANTAM BOOKS
New York • Toronto • London • Sydney • Auckland

DIGGER

A Bantam Book / October 1997

Grateful acknowledgment for permission to reprint "DEROS: My Soul"
by Steve Mason from *Johnny's Song*. Copyright © by Steve Mason.

Book design by James Sinclair

Map by Jeff Ward

Library of Congress Cataloging-in-Publication Data
Flynn, Joseph.
Digger / Joseph Flynn.
p. cm.
ISBN 0-553-10524-8
I. Title.
PS3556.L872D54 1997
813'.54—dc21   96-50948
CIP

Published simultaneously in the United States and Canada

Bantam Books are published by Bantam Books, a division of Bantam Doubleday Dell
Publishing Group, Inc. Its trademark, consisting of the words "Bantam Books" and the
portrayal of a rooster, is Registered in U.S. Patent and Trademark Office and in other
countries. Marca Registrada. Bantam Books, 1540 Broadway, New York, New York
10036.

PRINTED IN THE UNITED STATES OF AMERICA

BVG   10 9 8 7 6 5 4 3 2 1

This book is dedicated to Mom, Dad, Mary
and in memory of John,
the four best parents I've ever known.

These people helped to make this book possible:

Catherine and Caitie, who make all things possible by filling my life with love and joy, and who encourage me in my writing and everything else I do.

Anne Dougherty and Marlene Carls, Congressional staffers and *essential* government workers; Scott Murphy, attorney-at-law and former 11-Bravo, 25th Infantry (Tropic Lightning); Loren Larsen, Chief Deputy (Ret.), Sangamon County, Illinois, Sheriff's Department; Richard A. Daniels, Assistant City Engineer, Department of Public Works, Springfield, Illinois; Kevin Mulroy, who predicted big things and then helped them to come true; Jim Latz, electronics engineer; Laura Hammond, RN, MSN; Susan McIntyre, RN, MSN; Chris Peterson, demographic consultant; Virginia Witt, one-woman focus group; Joseph Bacher, jewelry consultant.

David Vigliano, agent extraordinaire; Kate Miciak and Nita Taublib, my editors at Bantam, for their wisdom and hard work; and Amanda Clay Powers, editorial assistant, who kept the machinery running smoothly.

My thanks to one and all.

Author's Notes

While central Illinois has been the site of several protracted—and even violent—labor disputes in the past few years, and is home to many Vietnam veterans, the town of Elk River, all its inhabitants, and the events described in this book are completely imaginary.

There is no secret system of tunnels around here—as far as I know.

The puzzle solution, from page 177.

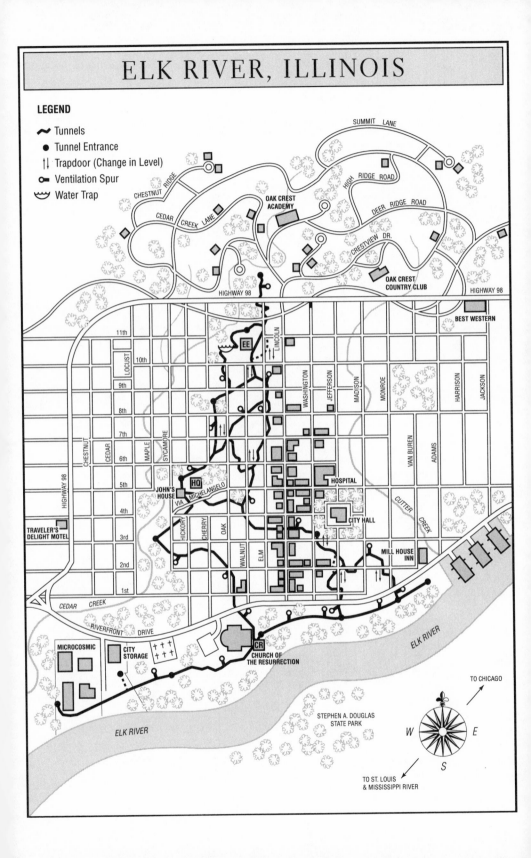

Part One

My soul just did
what most souls did.
Just disappeared one afternoon
when I was in a firefight.
Just "walked away" in the scuffle
like a Dunhill lighter
off the deck of a redneck bar.
                    —Steve Mason
                    DEROS: My Soul

1 The church was dark until John Fortunato struck the match. The point of light revealed rows of votive candles in red glass sleeves. John touched the match to a wick.

"God keep you, Jamie Doolan," he murmured.

He blew out the match and watched its wisp of blue smoke curl upward.

The vast blackness of the church seemed to swallow the flicker of light from the candle. But as a cloud passed away from the moon, the stained-glass figure of a resurrected Christ was illuminated high above him.

John had intended to light the candle and go. Now, cradling the camera he'd brought with him, he took a seat in a pew and regarded the image of the risen Savior. He never tired of looking at it. The mosaic of leaded glass was what he held on to: his image of God.

Of redemption.

His grandfather, Michelangelo Fortunato, had created the window. Had built the Church of the Resurrection. Then the immigrant artisan had gone on to construct a fair part of the town of Elk River around the limestone church.

John had likewise left his mark—not upon the town, where all could see, but somewhere none would ever know.

John stepped out of the church.

Another cloud bank rolled in, drawing a curtain across the moon. The loss of its light didn't bother him. Darkness was an old friend. But he felt a sudden chill, a sense of menace, in this night that made his heart beat faster. To his surprise, long-dormant combat instincts came bristling back, and he wished he had his M-16 in his hands again instead of the Nikon around his neck.

John knew his hometown as well as he knew the lines in his face and the scars on his soul, and every instinct had told him that something was very wrong that Sunday night.

He began to walk east from the church. He stayed on the park side of Riverfront Drive. The expanse of Riverfront Park on his right was dark and peaceful: a chorus of cicadas provided the respiratory buzz of a landscape at rest.

But to his left, toward town, something was definitely wrong. A predator was waiting out there . . . waiting to spring. As he drew even with Lincoln Avenue, the town's main commercial street, John stepped behind the statue of the Great Emancipator that dominated the park.

From behind its pedestal, he let his eyes follow Lincoln's bronze gaze out over the sleeping town. He didn't see a soul on the street, but still his uneasiness grew.

In any normal time, he would have felt foolish, peeking out from shelter as if he expected to be attacked. Elk River, Illinois, was Heartland America, the kind of picture-postcard small town where you could walk the streets at night and not be afraid.

Or it had been until just last week.

Now, the town was entering the second week of a strike against its major employer, Pentronics Systems. Over 3,500 workers, 95 percent of the company's workforce and a fifth of Elk River's population, were off the job and on the picket line. Negotiations had broken off the first day of the walkout and showed no signs of resuming. If anything, the dispute promised to become uglier. The possibility of violence was on everyone's mind, had people on edge, watching their backs.

Staying in the shadows, John continued on to the next street, Washington, then turned north, quickly crossing Riverfront Drive. His destination was the storefront office of the Brotherhood of Manufacturing Workers, Local 274, at the corner of Washington and First, and the closer

John came to the union office, the stronger his feeling of foreboding became.

The Pentronics walkout was being led by Tommy Boyle, the president of Local 274 and John's closest relative. John was on his way to talk with Tommy about creating a photographic record of the strike. Even though it was late, he knew Tommy would still be on the job.

He was edging up to the corner of Washington and First when he heard a voice curse.

"Fuck." A male voice. Angry. Maybe anxious, too.

John stopped dead in his tracks.

He heard a door being rattled forcefully, and another curse. Then soft footsteps moved off to the west along First Street. John stole a look around the corner.

A large man dressed in dark clothes was moving toward Lincoln Avenue. The man walked swiftly and silently, turning his head from side to side as if looking to see if he was being followed. John was sure that the man had been trying to get into the darkened office of Local 274, but he didn't know why. Or which side he was on.

John ducked back around the corner just before the man turned to look behind him.

Tommy would want to know what he'd seen, John knew. So he turned and made his way back toward Riverfront Drive. Since Tommy wasn't at the deserted union office, John thought he'd have to be with his picketers on the line outside Pentronics Systems.

The plant was a half mile west of the Church of the Resurrection. He'd have to retrace his steps. But just as he'd turned onto Riverfront, John heard the sudden mechanical roar of an engine. He knew it was a car, but the image that immediately came to mind was of a Cobra attack helicopter coming in for a strafing run.

Ahead of him, the man he'd seen walking away from Local 274 came running out of Lincoln Avenue, turned the corner onto Riverfront, and headed straight for John. Just behind the man, like some dark, snarling monster torn from a nightmare, a lights-out black sedan raced out of the soft April night.

John did the only thing he could. He flicked on his flash unit and its battery pack, and heard the capacitator whine as it powered up the unit. He pulled off his lens cap, and raised his motor-driven Nikon to his eye.

The car overtook the runner with predatory ease, veering up onto the sidewalk to block his path. The runner desperately reversed his direction, dashing back the way he'd come. The car slammed to a stop with an assist from the brick wall of Riverman Savings. Before it stopped rocking, the back doors flew open and two hulks pounded after the runner.

No one had yet noticed John. If he went now, he could slip away unseen. Except he'd never be able to explain flaking out to Doolan.

He tripped the shutter. To his ear, the Nikon on full automatic screamed as it drove the 1000 ASA film through the camera. A fusillade of searing white light erupted from his flash unit. He caught one of the hulks cutting the chase short with a silenced handgun. The weapon's noiseless flash left the runner writhing on the ground.

John wondered if he'd captured the moment when a man was murdered. A movement at the edge of his lens drew his attention back to the black sedan.

The front window on the passenger side was sliding down, and the first thing—the only thing—John saw was the barrel of the gun pointed at him. He aimed the Nikon at the car, keeping the camera stationary while he ducked down and to the left. His flash unit popped off another series of electronic firecrackers.

The idea was to draw the gunfire to the light and blind the shooter at the same time.

Some idea. The SOB shot the flash unit off his camera. The Nikon spun from John's grip, but the strap looped around his arm and he pinned it at his elbow.

The next two shots missed. Badly. The shooter *had* caught the glare from the strobe. John sprinted across the street toward Riverfront Park. Behind him, he heard heavy footsteps followed seconds later by car doors slamming, the snarl of an engine, and screeching tires.

Now, he'd become the runner.

But he was into the trees—and the sheltering darkness—before the car could catch him. He heard footsteps crashing through the bushes behind him, and shots were fired blindly, some of them coming chillingly close.

He needed a hole in the ground, and he had one. He raced down a path to a shadowy stand of trees and shrubs where he bent down. Even in the dark his fingers quickly found the release that secured the camouflaged lid to the tunnel entrance. He lifted it, slithered into the hole he'd dug years before, and lowered the lid from below.

He was safe—as long as his tunnels stayed secret.

2

The sniper lit up Davey Morowski.

One minute poor little Mo was walking point, and the next you could see daylight through him. Seemed he never should've been able to stand up to so many rounds for so long. That fucking machine gun just kept hammering him, and Mo just stayed on his feet, jerking and dancing backward. Like he could bow away from death.

Platoon Sergeant Jamie Doolan didn't know why the sniper had been dumb enough to light up the point man instead of waiting for more of the squad to come into view. He didn't know why the sniper stayed with Mo so long when he had to be dead after the first few rounds, even if he was still upright. Doolan didn't know and he didn't care. Stupid or just plain green, the fucking dink had given the other seven men in the squad, all bunched up behind Doolan like dumbasses, time to dive into a gully and save themselves.

"Doolan, hey, Doolan," Sp4 Timothy Washington whispered, "what's this crazy fuckin' cherry doin'?"

Doolan didn't take his eyes off the tree line. He was looking for the machine gun that had just smoked poor Mo, and Washington was asking him stupid questions. Shit, there were three cherries in First Squad—that's why he was humpin' with them—but he didn't have time to baby-sit them now.

But Washington wouldn't give up.

"Look at 'im, man."

"Who, goddamnit?"

"Johnny Fortune."

Fortunato? Of the three cherries, he was the last one Doolan figured would flake out. He turned to look and was surprised to see Fortunato right next to him, right between him and Washington.

He was sitting there with his back against the gully wall and his eyes closed. Peaceful. Like he was taking a nap, didn't have a fucking care in the world. All the others were looking around everywhere, eyes bugging out, heads jerking back and forth, expecting to get their shit scattered any second now. And Johnny Fortune was taking a snooze. Jamie Doolan was dumb-founded.

He didn't see any blood on Fortunato, hadn't thought the sniper had hit anyone except Mo. Still, he asked.

"You hit?"

"He freakin' out, that's what," Washington said.

Johnny Fortune didn't open his eyes, didn't say a word. He just pointed, and that's when Doolan saw it: a trip wire running through the grass. Seven guys had dived into the gully and they'd been out-the-ass lucky enough not to trigger it. The sniper hadn't been dumb. He'd just thought he'd explode their asses for them.

"Don't move," Doolan hissed down the line to his men. "Look around for trip wires and mines. Just point if you see anything."

Elston and Burnside pointed. More booby traps. Fuck! Diving into these weeds, this gully, not setting anything off, they'd been luckier than a busload of gimps getting cured at Lourdes.

Washington was still staring at Johnny Fortune.

"You jist happen to notice that wire while your ass was divin' for cover?" he asked. "How the fuck you know that thing was there?"

Doolan stuck to the point.

"Better question is how the fuck do we get outta here? We call for air support to blast that sniper, who knows what shit Charlie pulls on us while we're waitin'?" A small shudder ran through him. "Got no fuckin' choice on this one. Tim, you watch the trees for the muzzle flash. I'm gonna shag my ass back onto the path—for just a second. Try to get that fuckin' dink before—"

Fortunato silenced Doolan by placing his index finger to his lips. Neither Doolan nor Washington could believe it. They gaped at him. Fuckin' cherry, still sitting there with his eyes closed, looking more unconscious than ever, telling them to shut the fuck up.

Like he shouldn't be disturbed.

Then before they could say a word Johnny Fortune popped up, whirled, fired the clip from his M-16 into the tree line, and was back in the gully before they heard the sniper's shriek.

"Fuck me," Washington murmured, "he dinged the dink."

Doolan stared at Fortunato. The cherry was only now opening his eyes. The platoon sergeant was sure he'd fired with his eyes closed. Then Johnny Fortune popped up again and was out of the gully and sprinting for the tree line.

When Doolan caught up with him he was taking off his goddamn pants. Fuckin' guy even shushed him again before he could get the first word out. Then he pointed to a hole in the ground that Doolan hadn't even noticed, he was so charged up.

The dink who'd gone down it hadn't had the time to pull the trapdoor closed.

Well, maybe he hadn't been able to; there was an awful lot of blood leading down into that hole. By now, Washington had crept up and, to Doolan's surprise, was giving Johnny his 16. Fortunato had already put his own rifle down one of the legs of the pants he'd removed. He put Washington's down the other. Then he tied his boots to the pant legs.

He'd made a decoy. Before he lowered it into the hole, Fortunato gestured to Doolan with cocked fingers that he should be ready to shoot.

Then he lowered the decoy into the hole in the ground. No sooner had the empty boots touched bottom than out popped a blood-drenched dink who slashed the crotch out of Johnny's empty pants with a bayonet.

It was hard to say who was more surprised, the dink or Jamie Doolan. They just gaped at each other.

"Fire, fuckhead!" Fortunato yelled.

So Doolan did.

Goddamn Johnny Fortune had done it again. He'd known the dink was waiting there ready to ambush the first grunt dumb enough to jump into that hole. He'd known it without any way of knowing. After he'd somehow been able to shoot the guy with his fuckin' eyes closed.

Platoon Sergeant Doolan intended to get some answers to this shit right goddamn now.

But, again, Johnny Fortune was too fast for him. He yanked the dink's body out of the hole, grabbed a .45 from Washington, and disappeared into the tunnel.

Doolan looked at the small, inky-black hole that had just eaten Johnny Fortune alive, olive drab underwear and all. It made him shudder.

Which was too fucking bad, because Doolan's pride wasn't going to let him do anything but follow Johnny Fortune right inside.

3 The striking worker spat.

"Look at that prick up there." The man on the picket line outside the Pentronics Systems plant shook his head sourly. "Anthony Tiburon Hunt. Mr. High-and-Mighty. Makes me wanna puke."

Tommy Boyle, president of Local 274, Brotherhood of Manufacturing Workers, said nothing. He was already looking at the figure silhouetted against a window on the top floor of the executive office building.

"Lookin' down on us like ants he can't wait to step on," said another picketer.

"Bastard," a third added succinctly.

Tommy Boyle leaned his tall, hard frame against the front of his car and thought what a wonderful target Hunt made all backlit like that up there in his window. You couldn't miss him. Any marine who'd ever made it through boot camp could drop that sucker with his first shot.

He certainly could have.

"Don't worry," Tommy assured the dozen men on the picket line, "he'll get his soon enough."

"Hey, Tommy," another asked, "you bring us anything? There's gettin' to be a nip in the air."

Tommy grinned. "Don't I always take care of you?"

He walked to the back of his car and popped the trunk. Inside was a battery-operated coffee urn, a five-pound can of coffee, bottles of water, paper cups, and a box filled with packets of sugar and artificial cream.

"You're the best, Tommy," a picketer said, and began unloading the supplies.

"Hey, Tommy, didya bring a little somethin' special to spice that coffee?"

Tommy Boyle smiled again. "There's a bottle or two in the back seat. Help yourself." But before the man could move Tommy stopped him, speaking loudly enough for everyone to hear. "Hey, all you guys, listen up. You picket, you drink your coffee, you carry on expressing your legitimate labor grievances. But you don't get drunk, you don't get loud, you don't even *litter*. In short, you don't give the assholes one little excuse to call the cops. Got it?"

They got it.

"Good," Tommy said.

Before pulling up to the plant's chain-link gate, he'd parked a block up the street and watched for an hour. A Sheriff's Department patrol car had cruised by the picket line every ten minutes. The cops were keeping a tight orbit. They hadn't stopped, but they always gave his men their hard cop stares, looking for any reason to kick ass.

Maybe not, though. Maybe it was just in the nature of cops to stare. Either way, Tommy liked it when his people stared right back at them. Didn't say a word to the cops, but didn't lower their heads, either. That was important. He didn't know for sure where Sheriff Orville Leen was going to come down if—more likely when—the shit hit the fan, but he'd never met a cop yet above the rank of sergeant who was a friend of labor.

Thinking of cops, Tommy headed over to the gate that barred the entrance to the plant. The company security guard standing behind it was Ben Harrison. Tommy'd known him for years. Ben was a decent guy and a neighbor to three of the men on the picket line.

But as Tommy approached the gate the expression on Ben's face wasn't neighborly. The security guard looked alarmed, angry that Tommy was coming his way. Unconsciously, Ben's right hand strayed to his hip. It settled on the butt of his shiny new gun in its shiny new holster.

Since the beginning of the strike, eight days before, Anthony Tiburon Hunt had armed the plant's security force for the first time. The weapons were scant comfort. At least for Ben Harrison. As soon as his fingers touched his gun, they nervously flew away again. Then, indecisively, they crept back.

Tommy leaned against the gate and smiled. "It's okay, Ben. I just wanted to ask if you'd care for a cup of the coffee the boys're making."

The guard shook his head.

Tommy looked up past Ben to Tony Hunt's shadowed form. He stared for a moment before returning his eyes to the guard.

"That jerk-off has you scared, huh?"

Ben's face turned stony.

"It doesn't have to be that way," Tommy said. "You guards could join our union. Strength in numbers, you know."

Tommy's pitch on the benefits of organized labor was interrupted when the phone in his car rang.

Tommy Boyle ran into the emergency room at Community Hospital. The ER nurse who had called him, the wife of one of his men, sat in a glass-walled cubicle where preliminary treatment was done. She looked pale and shaken. Tommy knelt in front of her.

"What happened, Ellen? Who got hurt?"

"Do you know a man named Phillip Henry?"

Tommy nodded.

"Does he work at the plant?"

"No, he works directly for the union." More precisely, Phil Henry worked directly for Tommy Boyle. He was a private investigator, an old marine buddy who'd done a stint with the Naval Investigative Service, and Tommy had hired him to snoop on Tony Hunt.

"He's been shot."

"Is he dead?"

"No, he's in surgery. When he was brought in, he was calling for you." Ellen started to cry.

"Is he going to make it?"

"Yes, he'll survive."

"Then what's—"

"Whoever shot him also broke his thumbs . . ."

"What?"

"And they . . . cut off the end of his tongue."

The nurse's tears streamed down her cheeks; Tommy's face filled with rage.

"The poor man kept trying to speak. He was in terrible pain, but he kept struggling, making these awful gargly noises. He wouldn't let us take him to surgery until we understood him, and finally I recognized your name."

She smiled through her tears, and for the first time, it registered in

Tommy's mind that her pale blue uniform was splattered with drops of blood.

"That was what did it," she said. "When I promised him I'd call you, he finally let us get an IV line in him. We put him under and took him straight into surgery."

Tommy gently took her hands in his. She shook her head in bewilderment.

"Who would do such terrible things?" she asked.

Tommy could have told her, but he didn't.

"What kind of town are we becoming?"

That, he honestly couldn't say.

When Tommy got back into his car the cellular phone rang again. He picked it up.

"It's me," John Fortunato said. On a family tree, John was Tommy's nephew. Anywhere else, they were brothers. "Something happen to one of your people tonight? Something bad?"

"Yeah, how the hell did you know?"

"I photographed it," John said.

Tommy was dumbfounded, and then greatly excited. He wanted to see the pictures immediately, but John told him he hadn't processed the film yet.

"What were you doing out?" Tommy asked, knowing John's social life was nil.

"Lighting a candle for Doolan."

Goddamn Johnny, Tommy thought. Lighting a candle every day for a guy who'd been dead twenty-five years. He could never just let go of someone. His mom. Doolan. He was worse than an old lady.

Of course, there were a lot of people whose memories Tommy could have honored a little better himself. The thing was, there always seemed to be a fight going on right here and now that took all his attention. Still, because of Johnny, he might have something useful in the fight against Tony Hunt.

"Pictures be ready in the morning, Johnny?"

"Eight-by-tens," John answered.

Tommy clicked off the phone. Normally, he'd've gone to John's house and waited right outside his darkroom for those pictures. But at the moment, he had someone waiting for him, and if he didn't get back to her pretty soon she might deck him.

He turned his engine over and sped to the Traveler's Delight Motel.

4 From the pinnacle that was his office, Anthony Tiburon Hunt looked down at the twelve men outside the front gate of his plant. Tony Hunt was just under six feet tall. He wore his dark hair brushed straight back. His gray eyes shone with the feral intelligence and predatory resolve of a hunting wolf.

He'd just seen Tommy Boyle drive away, his tires shrieking loudly enough for Hunt to hear through his plate glass window. As if in response to the melodrama of their leader's exit, the strikers put down their coffee and resumed marching in a tight circle with their signs held high.

At one in the morning. For his benefit, no doubt. Hunt laughed and murmured, "Little men, you have no idea of what you're up against."

Hunt had led the raid against Pentronics Systems at a time when hostile takeovers had largely gone out of fashion. Outside analysts couldn't understand what he wanted with a smallish defense contractor whose post–Cold War prospects were iffy at best. Let them wonder, Hunt thought.

Because Tony Hunt hadn't wanted to take over just a company; he'd wanted his own town. And since the Pentronics Systems payroll, its ripple-effect spending, and the taxes the plant paid constituted two thirds of Elk River's economy, he'd gotten one.

"I own you chumps," he said, looking down at the picketers. "I've got you by the balls . . . and it won't be long before you know it."

There was a knock at his door.

"Come in," Hunt said.

He listened to the door open and close. The overhead light went off and the barometric pressure in the room seemed to drop, as if a storm front had just blown in. Hunt turned from the window. Through the gloom, he saw the tall, wide, menacing shape of Krieger.

Hunt smiled inwardly. All Krieger needed to complete the likeness to Frankenstein was to have electrodes sticking out of his neck.

He waited for Krieger to speak. When he did, it ruined his monstrous image. Krieger's voice was maple syrup in sunlight. He could have sung duets with Streisand—as long as you didn't have to look at him. But the fact was that Krieger believed in pain, not music.

Which brought Hunt back to his original point of view: Krieger had the morality of something assembled from parts stolen from a graveyard.

Not unlike himself.

"We caught him," Krieger said.

Hunt merely nodded.

"Then we dumped him."

Hunt bided his silence. Power meant people gave you everything before you gave them anything.

"Alive," Krieger said.

Hunt sat down behind his desk. He didn't say anything, but Krieger could tell Hunt was losing patience with his piecemeal delivery.

Krieger never kidded himself. He knew that he was subordinate to Hunt. Or he would have been sitting in Hunt's place, instead of wondering how to get there.

Over Hunt's dead body was one way, but he hadn't figured out the right way to do it . . . yet. So, Krieger told Hunt everything that had happened that night.

Hunt's first response was one word.

"Pictures?"

"Bad luck." Krieger shrugged. "We hit our man clean as a whistle. And right then some dipshit with a flash camera is putting us in pictures."

Krieger waited for a comment. But Hunt didn't bite.

"I think I got my arm in front of my face before he got my picture," Krieger added when Hunt remained silent.

"But you didn't catch him, so you don't really know." No hint of emotion burdened Hunt's voice.

Krieger never made excuses, either.

"No."

"Why did you let your target live?"

"Because maybe Mr. Flashbulb *did* take my picture. I'll do a lot less time this way than if I whacked the guy."

The prospect of Krieger's doing *life* didn't faze Hunt.

"But Tommy Boyle might find out what I don't want him to know." Now the ice in Hunt's voice was cold enough for even Krieger to feel.

Even so, Krieger shook his head.

"I said I let the chump live," he told his boss. "I didn't leave him in any shape to talk."

5 The town of Elk River came into being as the result of a government giveaway. In the early years of the nineteenth century, Congress offered free 160-acre tracts in the region to all noncommissioned officers and soldiers who had served in the War of 1812. As with all free offers, there were catches.

The government's generosity had not been ratified by the resident Sac and Fox Indians; no funding was provided for travel to the frontier territory; and guarantees of safe passage were neither expected nor given.

Nevertheless, a company of two hundred and ninety eligible pioneers was formed at Pittsburgh in 1818 to take advantage of the opportunity. Boats were built. Provisions were purchased. Muskets were loaded.

Most important, a solemn compact was made: The company would survive. If need be, any man, woman, or child would be sacrificed for that survival.

This principle was based on necessity. Over the course of the preceding year, while they were making their preparations, bloodcurdling tales had reached the pioneers, stories of attacks on settlers who had dared to sail west on the Ohio River. Indian raids and worse were becoming commonplace.

The redskins would lie in wait in the trees along the banks, and when they spied boatloads of settlers approaching, they'd bring out white captives, often women and children. Then, in plain sight, they'd torture these unfortunates. When a rescue was attempted, the Indians would fall upon the pioneers in great numbers and butcher them.

River bandits, like the Harpe brothers' gang out of Cave-in-Rock, took a more direct approach. These brigands paddled right out to the pioneer flotillas to loot them. The river bandits would rape and kill for the sheer sadistic pleasure of it. They finished off their victims by slitting them open, filling them with rocks, and sinking the corpses in the river.

The company of souls that founded Elk River fought its way past both these scourges, losing twelve men, five women, and two children. According to local lore, they made the passage safer by dispatching thirty-five villains of black hearts and various skin hues.

When the settlers arrived at the land they'd been given, they had the opportunity of establishing their outpost on the mighty Mississippi as many others were doing. They chose to do otherwise. They moved east of the Big River and founded their settlement three miles up a tributary, the Elk River.

Town historians had long debated whether the pioneers favored this more remote location in the hope of safeguarding themselves from further depredations—a notion conceded to be one of wishful thinking—or if the settlers merely preferred the natural beauty of the setting they chose. Rolling woodlands rich with game swept gracefully down to the river, and the Elk, unlike the muddy Mississippi, was clear and congenial. With an average width of sixty feet and a surprising depth of twenty feet at its center, the river was well stocked with fish. And on a hot summer's day, there was no greater relief than bathing in it, and diving down to the riverbed.

As might be expected, the Sac and Fox Indians fought fiercely to hold on to such land, a place they had considered their own for generations beyond reckoning. They yielded only when they saw that the flow of arriving white men would be never-ending.

Scarcely had the battles with the Indians ended, however, than new fights began with other settlers across the Big River. Illinois was abolitionist, Missouri was slaveholding; Illinois was Union, Missouri was Confederate.

The fall of the South didn't bring peace, it brought economic competition. Trade on the Mississippi couldn't be bothered with a backwater like Elk River, not when great cities like St. Louis and New Orleans beckoned. The community was galled.

But little Elk River was also battle-hardened. If the townspeople didn't have what it took to attract business, by God, they would get it. The town fathers hit on the strategy of becoming the best poachers on the Mississippi.

They didn't steal game or fish, but they made off with the best marine architects and boatwrights, the best millers and brewers, even the best panderers and whores, along the Big River from Minnesota to Louisiana. If someone had a skill or talent that could draw business to the town, he was recruited.

The inducements to relocate to Elk River were a free house to be built in the best part of town, a lifetime guarantee that no part of a man's profits would ever be taxed by the municipality, and an automatic seat on the town council.

The newcomers helped the community to prosper and, except for the proprietors of the red-light district, they settled on the east side of town, where the streets were named after presidents. In time, these privileged merchants, businessmen, and politicians came to be called the Presidentials.

Those who labored for them lived to the west of Lincoln Avenue, the town's main thoroughfare. On this side of town the streets were named for native trees, and the residents were known as Hardwoods.

The town grew gracefully from the north bank of the river. The business district burgeoned to six square blocks. The residential neighborhoods stretched north, and beyond the last paved street the land rose among a stand of ancient oaks.

The linchpin of the town was Riverfront Park. A ribbon of green running all along the river, it was a retreat where all might picnic, swim, or idle on a Sunday afternoon. By an unspoken agreement, all were equal in the use and enjoyment of the park.

Life was good in the little town for many a year, and in 1920 Elk River once again reached out to a talented outsider.

This time all the way to Italy.

In the midst of unprecedented prosperity, the better elements in town decided that Elk River needed some monument to show how far it had come in the world. The mayor's wife suggested a church, something on a grandiose scale. That would not only show how thankful they were but how much they had to be thankful for. At a stroke, both morality and ego could be served.

The recruiters carried their commission to build the church to Venice. In addition to the traditional offer of a free house, they added the incentive of American citizenship. A bill providing that citizenship would be introduced in Congress by the state's senior senator. The recruiters returned from Italy with the man who wound up saving the town, Michelangelo Fortunato.

The Italian artisan was impressed that businessmen had chosen the site for the church so well. It was a grassy promontory at the western end of Riverfront Park. The river looped gently around it, and the site sat snugly between the town to the north and the forest across the river to the south.

But Michelangelo brushed aside the absurd notion of building a *cathedral* here. Something of that scale would dwarf Elk River. It wouldn't be a house of God but a grotesque celebration of Man's self-importance. He wouldn't do it.

His patrons insisted: Do as he was bid or find his way back to the Old Country. Michelangelo wanted to stay where he was, in America, but he was not about to give in.

So he calmly asked the swells of Elk River if they could afford to spend the *millions* of dollars and wait the better part of a *century* that a cathedral required to construct.

Then, before his patrons could answer and his commission was lost, he promised to build the most *beautiful* church they had ever seen, one where prayers would not only be heard but also answered.

Because very few people want to spend more money than they have to pay for something they'll never live to see, much less claim credit for, Michelangelo's alternative was accepted—with the stern caveat that his church had better be something to behold.

It was.

In daylight, its native limestone glowed like gold; in moonlight it was silver. The blue slate roof was the color of heaven. The stained-glass windows shone as if lit by God's grace. And when the morning sun climbed into the sky, the reflection of the church in the river rose to meet it.

But the church took eight years to complete, and by that time the prosperity in Elk River, as in the rest of the nation, had become a great deal shakier. A sense of dread infiltrated the manic mood of the day, people were getting very nervous about where they might be heading, and there was considerable debate about funding the last expenditure for Michelangelo's church.

In order that the interior be properly lighted, Michelangelo had insisted on electric lights and the best fixtures available. It was a tribute to what he had accomplished in the previous eight years that his argument once again carried the day. In November 1928, shortly before Thanksgiving, he traveled to the Modern Electric Company of Menlo Park, New Jersey, to contract for the job.

The president of the company was so awestruck by Michelangelo's renderings of the church he traveled to Elk River to survey the job himself. When he saw what Michelangelo had built, he *donated* the cost of electrifying the church. He swore that he would take no money for the job, that it was his great privilege to do it for free.

The man kept coming back "to see how work was progressing." He came again when the Church of the Resurrection was consecrated in the summer of 1929. In order to have a reason to keep returning to Elk River, the president of Modern Electric committed funds to build a plant adjacent to the church to manufacture lightbulbs and fixtures for the Midwest market. Despite the market crash of Black Monday of that year and the start of the Great Depression, construction of the plant went ahead for the simple reason that people never stopped buying lightbulbs, whatever other sacrifices they were forced to endure.

Finally, and while so many other towns and cities were suffering, Elk River had found its economic reason for being. Even so, it endured a schism, one that would change the basic character of the town. The arrival of the plant created a wealth of job opportunities for the Hardwoods. No longer would they have to depend on their Presidential betters for their sustenance. Why, some Hardwoods, as they rose through the plant hierarchy, came to make more money than the Presidential merchants who'd formerly employed them.

This reversal of Elk River's historical pecking order went largely unspoken, but it did not pass unnoticed or unresented.

Through the years, the Modern Electric plant became Althauser Industries, which became Pentronics Systems. Which Tony Hunt was about to change again.

The Church of the Resurrection, after losing its last pastor in 1983 and having no priest to replace him, was deconsecrated and sold to John Fortunato, the grandson of its builder.

6   Monday morning, Sheriff Orville Leen studied the unconscious man in the hospital bed. Deputy Billy Shelton stood close behind him. Too close. Billy was a crowder. He liked to get right up in people's faces. It wasn't a bad technique for quieting belligerent suspects, but the sheriff didn't appreciate anyone breathing down his neck.

"Gimme a little elbow room, Billy," he said.

The deputy backed off with a grunt.

Leen bent his stocky body forward to get a closer look at the assault victim. He'd been called about the matter soon after the man had gone into surgery but had been content to take the hospital's word that there was no point in coming to see him before this morning.

The sheriff scratched his scalp through his wiry gray hair and then turned his head toward the doctor who'd accompanied him and Billy into the private room.

"How bad was the gunshot wound?" Leen asked.

"Missed the femur and the femoral artery. Tore a nice hole in both his hamstring and quadriceps, though. He's looking at a lengthy course of physical therapy."

Leen examined the casts on the man's hands. "Broke his thumbs, did they?"

"Yes. Occupational therapy'll be needed there."

The sheriff straightened and faced the doctor. "You say they cut his tongue out, too?"

The doctor shook his head. "Approximately the anterior third of his tongue has been *bitten* off."

"Could his pain have made him do that?"

"It's possible," the doctor replied. "But if you look at the discolorations around his jawline and throat . . ."

"Looks like finger marks," Billy Shelton said.

The doctor nodded. "Exactly. That's why we think he may have been forced to extrude his tongue and then had his jaws forced together to sever it."

"Never heard of that one before," the deputy said.

Sheriff Leen forestalled any further comment from Billy with a look.

"Musta been a strong SOB," the sheriff said.

"And quick. And brutal," the doctor agreed.

"And despite being all tore up, this man calls for Tommy Boyle?"

The doctor shrugged. "I was just his surgeon. But that's what I heard from Dr. Roth, the ER physician."

Orville Leen sighed. He looked at the unconscious man's face—he'd suffered a pretty good pavement facial, too—and wondered how he'd feel when he woke up. Even if he was cooperative, it'd be tough as hell to get anything out of him. Someone had damn sure seen to that.

"What do you think, Billy?" the sheriff asked the deputy as they pulled away from the hospital.

"Union dirtball versus company dirtball. Company dirtball wins."

"Maybe," the sheriff allowed.

"You think the shit's about to hit the fan, Sheriff?"

"That would depend on why the man wanted to see Tommy Boyle, now, wouldn't it?"

The deputy shot a glance at his boss. "I could go have a little talk with him."

"No, Billy," the sheriff said. Not unless I go brain-dead in the next two seconds, he thought.

Like everyone else who knew anything about Elk River, Orville Leen was well acquainted with the fact that Tommy Boyle had been whipping Billy Shelton's ass on a regular basis ever since they were snot-nosed boys, including one time after Billy had tried to arrest him.

Making things much worse was the fact that the deputy's estranged wife, Bobbi Sharpes, formerly Shelton, had taken up with Boyle immediately after dumping the deputy. Billy felt certain his wayward missus had had some prompting in making her choices.

Comparing the deputy's hatred for the union leader to your everyday grudge, in the sheriff's estimation, was like comparing the Mississippi to a stream of piss.

Still, Orville Leen was of the opinion that every police force needed at least one mean mutt like Billy; he just intended to keep his on a very short leash. At least until this shitfire strike was over.

"We'll go see him together," Leen said.

7   The pictures came out.

John watched the ghostly images appear as he worked in the red glow of the safelight in the basement darkroom of his home. The house, too, had been designed and built by Michelangelo Fortunato.

He moved the prints from the developer to the stop bath to the fix to the rinse, then hung them up to dry. They were all good shots, but one of them was so shocking, so powerful, that he'd have to include it in a book.

John had published three volumes of his photographs.

Of course, the sheriff would want to see the shots, too . . . but he'd let Tommy decide about that.

"We want you to settle," Harold Noyes told Tommy Boyle that Monday morning. "Accept Hunt's offer and get your people back to work."

Noyes was the international president of the Brotherhood of Manufacturing Workers. A bigshot. *The* bigshot, as far as Tommy's union was concerned. The head of a local chapter was supposed to show him some deference. But with Noyes's bulbous nose and lumpy body, Tommy Boyle thought he looked like a tuber in a suit.

Tommy said, "Tell me, Harold, is Tony Hunt *paying* you, or just letting you suck his dick?"

The two men sat in Tommy's tiny office at the back of Local 274's storefront at the corner of First and Washington. There was no room for anyone else inside. So Noyes's attorney, Vic Kushner, hadn't heard the insult. But watching through the window in Tommy's door, he saw Noyes turn red and sputter.

"You sonofabitch . . . you do what I tell you or we'll withdraw support for you."

"Come on, Harold," Tommy said reasonably, "there's just the two of us here, so tell me. You on the take?"

Noyes's voice dropped to a menacing whisper. "You'd better do what the fuck you're told."

Tommy smirked. "Harold, you're a gasbag. You really think I'm worried about you?" He shook his head. "No. What I'd worry about is selling my people out. If I told them to go back for the slave wages and piss-poor conditions that Hunt is offering, *they'd* kill me. Except I'd kill myself first."

While Noyes sought a more persuasive threat, Tommy noticed a good-looking woman enter the outer office. She was blond. Medium height. Green eyes. Had a serious expression on a face that would look good with a smile. She wore a no-nonsense business suit and carried a briefcase. She seemed to size up the situation at a glance.

She had to be the labor lawyer he'd hired over the phone. Tommy liked the way she took a seat without introducing herself to Noyes's legal flunky, Kushner.

Turning back to Noyes, Tommy continued, "You see, Harold, what really worries you is that little Local 274 is gonna beat the mighty Anthony Tiburon Hunt. And you'll wind up with shit on your face because you've been selling capitulation for so long: a bad job's better than no job. Some fucking labor leader you are."

Tommy leaned forward. "We win, Harold, and *you're* the one looking for a job."

Noyes's face turned the color of prime rib. He shoved back his chair. "You're out, you bastard," he snarled, shaking with rage. "You just cut your own throat. You're a dead man."

Noyes threw open Tommy's door with such force its glass shattered. He stormed out of Local 274 so fast his lawyer had to run to catch up with him. Tommy stepped around his desk and nudged the larger pieces of glass out of the way with the toe of his shoe.

He smiled at his new lawyer.

"Ms. Baxter? Please come in."

. . .

Jill Baxter coolly regarded the devilish grin Tommy Boyle was giving her.

"That's a very nice smile you have, Mr. Boyle," she said. "Might be called shit-eating. Or even mistakenly thought of as lady-killing."

Tommy laughed.

"I'm not hurting for ladies," he said. "I'm just surprised is all."

"By?" There was a soft echo of Appalachia in Jill Baxter's voice.

"Well, you're Grady Baxter's daughter, right?"

"That's correct."

"I've read your father's book on labor organizing. He was a hell of a man."

"Yes, he was," Jill said.

"I've also seen pictures of your father. You don't look anything like him."

Jill Baxter bit the inside of her lower lip to keep from saying anything intemperate. The man sitting across from her was still grinning, but those cold blue eyes of his were deadly serious, and she could see Boyle was wondering if he'd made a big mistake in hiring her.

"I resemble my mother," she said tightly. "Perhaps you've read of her as well."

Tommy nodded. "Sure. She was the schoolteacher who taught your father to read. She was the woman who married a coal miner and made a labor lawyer out of him."

"She helped Daddy get to college. Labor law was his idea. He didn't see turning his back on his friends just because he had advanced himself."

"Like I said, a good man."

And now you wish you had another good man here instead of me, you bastard, Jill thought.

She said, "Let's speak plainly, Mr. Boyle. Is it my appearance that bothers you? Would it help matters if I'd had broken my nose a time or two?"

Tommy's grin widened, but his eyes remained calculating.

"I'm just trying to sort you out, Counselor. I'm wondering if you've got the goods, if you're up to dragging Tony Hunt in front of the NLRB and raking his ass over the coals for refusing to bargain in good faith."

"I see." Jill nodded. "Mr. Boyle, let me tell you something: A lot of people have underestimated me . . . but *nobody's* ever done it twice."

"I'll bet." For the first time Tommy's smile reached his eyes. "But even if you're tough enough to take on Hunt, you may not like working for me."

"And why would that be, Mr. Boyle?"

"This is a privileged conversation, right, Counselor?"

Jill nodded. "You've sent me a retainer check, and I've cashed it. You might as well get something for your money."

Meaning there wasn't a chance in hell she'd refund his money if he went with another lawyer. Tommy Boyle laughed. Even if he didn't wind up working with this woman, he was beginning to like her.

"Okay, Counselor, then listen to this . . ."

In the spring of 1984, Tommy Boyle, newly elected president of Local 274, Brotherhood of Manufacturing Workers, strode into the top-floor office of Robert Ruud, CEO of Pentronics Systems. Ruud, a tall, florid man, stepped out from behind his desk to shake the new union leader's hand. Talks for a new labor contract were scheduled to start soon, but this was a get-to-know-you meeting both sides thought would be helpful before the actual bargaining began.

Bob Ruud would never forget his introduction to Tommy Boyle.

The first thing he noticed was that Boyle always seemed to have a grin on his face. It wasn't that nervous, vacuous expression Jimmy Carter had worn throughout his presidency. It was more like . . . like he was going to eat you alive, and he was just waiting for the steak sauce.

Ruud retreated to his high-backed leather chair, behind the moat of his broad mahogany desk, and adjusted the armor of his three-piece Saville Row suit.

"Well, Mr. Boyle," he said, "I must confess I'm surprised to be meeting you. I thought I'd be dealing with your predecessor, Sam Crispman, as I had for so many years."

Boyle's grin grew more wolfish than ever, and Ruud had to make a conscious effort not to flinch.

"Life is full of surprises, Mr. Ruud," Tommy said. "And so few of them are pleasant."

Ruud cleared a sudden constriction from his throat. He decided he'd better state his position before things got out of hand.

"Yes, quite so, and I'm afraid an unpleasant surprise is just what I have in store for your membership, Mr. Boyle. What with increased competition, soaring medical costs, and other business considerations, I'm afraid the pay-and-benefits package I'll be sending with the company negotiating team won't be nearly so generous as in years past."

Tommy Boyle didn't say a word, just shook his head. The gesture let Ruud know that for once that bullshit wasn't going to fly. But the executive had yet to play his trump card.

"You are aware, of course, Mr. Boyle, that the political climate in the country has changed in recent years as regards organized labor. President

Reagan's action against the air-traffic controllers has clearly demonstrated—"

Ruud stopped dead when he saw Tommy reach inside his suit coat. For one bowel-loosening moment, he imagined that this grinning psychopath was reaching for a gun. Ruud almost went limp with relief when he saw Boyle's hand emerge with just a few sheets of paper.

Ruud continued, trying to regain a firm tone. "The PATCO situation demonstrated that *any* workers can be replaced these days. I'm sure you'll want to keep that in . . ."

The head of Pentronics Systems ground to another halt as Tommy casually handed the papers over to him. With more than a little trepidation, Ruud examined them. His face grew ashen.

"You've been a very naughty boy, Bob," Tommy Boyle said. "You and your top executives. Here you are, an important defense contractor supplying vital tools for the national defense against what your beloved Mr. Reagan describes as 'the Evil Empire,' and how do you get your business? The old-fashioned, true-blue American way, by providing the best product for the best price?"

Tommy shook his head again, and Bob Ruud felt like he might vomit.

"Unh-uh, Bob. You won contracts from the United States government, worth hundreds of millions of dollars, by kicking back pots of money to Pentagon procurement officers. Why, two of those former officers now sit on your board of directors. It's all there in black and white."

Pointing at the papers in Ruud's hand, Tommy Boyle laughed out loud. "You're a fucking crook, Bob."

"How . . . how did you find out?" Ruud asked anxiously.

"That'll have to be my little secret. The important thing for you to focus on now, Bob, is that you and your friends *don't* have to wind up in a federal prison."

A glimmer of hope arose in Ruud's heart, along with a fervent plea that this sadistic bastard wasn't just toying with him.

"No," Tommy said. "Nobody ever has to know about these little indiscretions of yours. And you know what else? I believe we can work out a new labor agreement right here and now. One that'll please everybody. I believe we can do that, Bob. Just you and me."

Robert Ruud heard the soft thunk of a bottle of steak sauce being set on his mahogany desk.

"You blackmailed him," Jill Baxter said.

Tommy Boyle leaned forward. "I told him we could live and let live . . . as long as *everybody* got a decent standard of living. After that, every time our labor contract came up for renewal, there were no problems. The cutbacks, givebacks, and the rest of the crap that have been killing other unions the past fifteen years, none of that stuff touched us. I kept my people on the job, with good pay and benefits."

Jill knew this was the test. He'd laid it out there for her in no uncertain terms: He was a man who would do whatever it took to make sure his people got a good deal. And getting that good deal was all the justification he'd ever need for whatever he did.

"Just so you know the rest of the story," Tommy said, "the way I got elected head of this local, I found out that Sam Crispman, the guy I replaced, was on Ruud's payroll. He never bargained quite as hard as he should have at contract time. When I worked at the plant I always resented that. So I decided to run against him, and I found proof of the corruption I'd always suspected. I blackmailed Sam, too, but I let him retire to Florida and save his skin. So, that's who you're dealing with here, Ms. Baxter, a lot of people with dirty hands all grabbing for their fair share. You got the stomach for that?"

"Do you have plans to blackmail Mr. Hunt?"

Tommy laughed. "Hell, that's the problem. When Hunt took over in a leveraged buyout last year, I lost my hole card. I haven't been able to get anything on him. I have to play this one straight." He stared at her for a long moment. "That's why I need a very smart, *very* hard-assed lawyer."

Jill needed time to think and to listen to what her gut was telling her. To buy that time, she asked Tommy Boyle about his negotiations, thus far, with Anthony Tiburon Hunt.

"What, in your view, constitutes Pentronic's refusal to bargain in good faith?"

"Hunt made us a take-it-or-leave-it offer. Hourly wages go from an average of fifteen dollars and forty-three cents to five dollars and fifty cents. Medical benefits go from comprehensive to nonexistent. No paid sick days. Four fewer paid holidays. No seniority considerations. And so on down the line."

"You made counterproposals?"

"Sure. I said we'd take ten dollars per hour. Keep full medical and dental. Split the difference on sick days and holidays. . . . But, in return for our givebacks, I want profit-sharing and an employee stock-purchase plan. If the company's bottom line gets fatter because of union sacrifices, then I want a spoonful of gravy for my membership."

"And Mr. Hunt's response was?"

"Shove it. He won't even talk to us again until we agree to all his demands."

"Will he submit to binding arbitration?"

"No."

Tommy Boyle was right, Jill thought: It was a clear case of refusing to bargain in good faith. She should have no problem bringing Hunt before the National Labor Relations Board.

She returned Tommy Boyle's stare and wondered how many people were depending on him. How many had been inspired to follow him by that cocksure grin of his? Whatever his flaws, this was a man who'd fight with no holds barred for the people who trusted him.

"All right, Mr. Boyle, I'll do whatever I can—within the law—to help your local. But the minute you try anything crooked, I'm gone."

"That's terrific, Ms. Baxter, but I haven't decided yet that I want you to be my lawyer."

"Oh, yes, you have. Or you never would have confided your criminal history to me." Now Jill smiled. "And you know you won't find a better lawyer."

Again, Tommy Boyle laughed, and he radiated such an enveloping warmth that Jill Baxter suddenly understood this man's power. At that moment, more than anything else, she wanted to please him, she wanted him to like her.

Which wouldn't do at all—feeling that way.

But made entirely credible his claim about not hurting for ladies.

Tommy Boyle stood and extended his hand to her; she rose and took it.

"Come with me, Counselor. There are some photos I want you to see."

8 John was laying out a dozen eight-by-ten prints on his dining room table when Tommy walked in without ringing the bell. That didn't surprise John. Tommy had a key, and he considered the place his home as much as John's. What surprised John was that Tommy had a stranger with him, a woman. A very good-looking woman.

Tommy noticed the photos immediately, but he remembered his manners.

"Jill Baxter, meet John Fortunato. Johnny's my little brother. John, this is my new lawyer." Tommy gestured at the pictures. "Johnny's a famous photographer, and last night he got some interesting shots."

That was it for the amenities. Tommy stepped to the table and began examining the prints.

Jill extended her hand to John. One of them must have picked up static electricity from the rug, because when their hands touched there was a spark. Neither pulled back.

With her modest heels, Jill was almost of a height with him. Her shrewd green eyes took in the dark hair, the steady gaze, and the strong, clean lines of nose, mouth, and chin. His handshake was firm, and his shoulders looked good under his T-shirt, but she doubted that he outweighed her by twenty-five pounds.

She wondered if *he* liked what he saw.

"Pleased to meet you," Jill said.

"My pleasure," John responded.

"I have to admit, I don't see the family resemblance."

Tommy Boyle glanced up and, appreciating the barb, chuckled.

"Tommy's actually my uncle," John said, content to let the inside joke pass without comment. "We just fight like brothers."

"Fight *for* each other like brothers, too," Tommy added. He looked like he might say more when a picture on the table caught his eye. "Je-sus Christ! Will you look at this?"

Jill stepped over to the table. Her eyes widened when she saw the photograph that had caught Tommy's attention.

The glossy image of the man firing the gun was stunning.

The muzzle flash blossomed from the barrel like the petals of a lethal flower; the dark blur of the emerging bullet its deadly center. Pointed right between the viewer's eyes.

As riveting as that element was, it took second place to the gunman. The glare of the gun's discharge and the flash from the camera combined to throw a hellish light on a grimacing nightmare face, features from the imagination of Mary Shelley and the palette of Edvard Munch.

"That shot took the strobe unit off my camera," John told them. "I'm calling the picture 'Face of the Killer.'"

Tommy shook his head. "Call it Egon Krieger."

"Who?" Jill asked.

"Hunt's chief goon. This is what we're up against."

Before the discussion could go any further, the doorbell rang and a voice came through the screen door at the front of the house.

"Mr. Fortunato, you at home? This is Sheriff Leen. I'm looking for Tommy Boyle."

John flashed Tommy a questioning look. Tommy nodded, but held his thumb and index finger an inch apart to indicate John should stall Leen for a minute.

While John went to the door, Tommy scooped up the photos. He walked over to a sideboard and opened a drawer.

"What are you doing?" Jill whispered.

Tommy slipped the photos into the drawer and closed it.

"You can't conceal—"

Tommy put up his hand to silence her.

"I'm going to let you decide whose side the good sheriff is on. Whether he might accidentally misplace these pictures, then come looking for the negatives. Use your best legal judgment, Counselor." Tommy grinned at her.

"Something funny, Mr. Boyle?" Leen followed John into the room. "I didn't expect to find you in such a good mood today."

Deputy Billy Shelton stood beside his boss giving Tommy a hard stare. Tommy smiled acidly at him.

"You forgot to zip up again, Billy," Tommy said.

Before he could stop himself, Billy checked. The bad thing was, the sonofabitch was right. Billy zipped up quickly.

"Maybe you need a woman around the house to help you get dressed," Tommy added.

A lifetime of rage flooded Billy's face. Leen grabbed the deputy's arm and hauled him out of the house before he did anything rash. When the sheriff returned, he shook his head.

"Why a man would want to antagonize a peace officer, I just don't know. Are you really that foolish, Mr. Boyle?"

Tommy shrugged. "What's more foolish, Sheriff? Me letting a lifelong prick know I'll never be afraid of him? Or you giving him a badge and a gun?"

Orville Leen's face turned to stone.

"You got a real gift for rilin' people, Mr. Boyle."

"Practice makes perfect," Tommy said casually.

Jill was about to enter the fray when she saw John shake his head. He seemed completely unperturbed.

Leen had nowhere to spit his bile, so he swallowed it.

"I'd like you to come down to the station, Mr. Boyle."

"Why? You arresting me for a bad attitude?"

The sheriff felt another surge of anger but restrained himself. Barely.

"Just a little discussion about what happened to Mr. Phillip Henry last night. I believe he works for you?"

"He does."

"Then you'll want to help us with our investigation."

Tommy turned to Jill.

She knew it was her call. Neither Tommy Boyle nor John Fortunato was going to say a word about the photographs. She decided she didn't trust the sheriff. Not yet, anyway.

She didn't have to say a word. Tommy understood. He turned back to Leen.

"I haven't forgotten all my manners, Sheriff. Let me introduce Local 274's new counsel. Jill Baxter, Sheriff Orville Leen."

Leen touched the brim of his hat. "Pleased, ma'am."

"Likewise," Jill said.

Jill knew that the introduction was Tommy's way of giving her the opportunity to look Leen in the eye and reconsider her decision.

"Would you like me to accompany you, Mr. Boyle?" she said, confirming her choice.

Orville Leen was no fool. He knew these two—three, if you counted Fortunato—were up to something. Talking right out in front of him, saying something he didn't understand but should damn sure know.

Unfortunately, they weren't people he could afford to bully. Not yet, anyway.

"Shouldn't be necessary, should it, Sheriff?"

"Up to you, Mr. Boyle."

Tommy turned to John. "Will you take care of Ms. Baxter, Johnny?"

"Sure."

Tommy extended his hand toward the door. "After you, Sheriff."

Leen asked, "You want to ride with us?"

Tommy grinned and shook his head. "Better not. I might say something to upset somebody."

9 Even as the end of the twentieth century approached, the town of Elk River continued to look as if it belonged to some earlier, mythical age of American innocence and isolation. The church, the river, the park, the tidy downtown, and the neat houses all seemed to be parts of an idealized image of the country that people had always yearned for but hardly ever found.

And even in Elk River the appearance was deceptive.

Just below the surface of Midwestern America—thanks to John Fortunato and, later, two of his friends—one of the most horrifying killing grounds of the Vietnam War had been recreated. The tunnels of Cu Chi.

During the Vietnam War, the Twenty-fifth Infantry Division (Tropic Lightning) had established its base camp on the site of a former peanut plantation near the town of Cu Chi, twenty miles northwest of Saigon. The base camp was supposed to be a bastion from which America would protect its ally's capital and carry the fight to the enemy.

The problem was, the Twenty-fifth found it difficult even to secure its own base. Acts of sabotage and sniping took place daily. The enemy seemed to appear and vanish at will. The army couldn't understand how this was happening.

Until one day somebody noticed Charlie popping out of the *ground.*

It wasn't long before the Twenty-fifth realized it had built its base camp directly over an underground world owned by the enemy. The tunnels of Cu Chi were part of a subterranean system that ran from Saigon to the Cambodian border. Hundreds of kilometers of tunnels provided the enemy with living quarters, storage depots, ordnance factories, hospitals, even theaters. Most important, the tunnels gave the VC a way to move undetected—the perfect means to prosecute a guerrilla war.

To fight the enemy in this almost incomprehensible labyrinth, the army turned to new specialists known as tunnel rats. But in a moment of candor a general admitted that the U.S. Army's tunnel warfare capability was in its infancy, and if the VC had wanted to be cagey about it the army might *never* have known their tunnels even existed.

The three tunnel rats who'd brought their hard-won skills home to America had been very cagey indeed.

At that moment, Darien Givens and Gil Velez were standing in a chamber called EE, beneath the baseball field at Eleventh and Elm, looking at something that probably even the Vietcong had never had in a tunnel. A righteous full-dress police Harley-Davidson.

Darien Givens was tall and black and skinny enough to hide *behind* a beanpole. His shoulders curved inward as if someone had once rolled him up and stuck him in a tube. Which someone once had. His broad muscular hands looked like they belonged on someone much heavier. Which they once had.

Gil Velez, at five-six, was eleven inches shorter than his friend. He was no broader, but at his height he looked wiry rather than emaciated. He had hard dark eyes, a bandito mustache, and a prosthetic right foot that had become so much a part of him he showed no trace of a limp.

Working with John Fortunato, the two men had invested a combined total of more than fifty man-years digging the tunnels of Elk River. John had been the first to start digging—by hand, the same way the Vietnamese had dug all of their tunnels. After Darien and Gil had joined the effort, manual labor had been abandoned in favor of power auguring and excavating equipment. Even with this advantage, the three diggers faced problems the VC never had to consider: namely, avoiding the complex underground infrastructure of a modern American town. Accidentally interfering with the electrical grid, the phone lines, the gas and water mains, the sewers, the traffic signals, or the cable TV lines would have brought immediate discovery.

To avoid all these obstructions, the diggers needed to know exactly where they were buried.

In most small towns, each utility had its own map. The drawback to this was that if something like a water main burst and involved, say, the electrical grid, crucial repair time would be lost while maps had to be cross-checked. The other side of the coin was that generating an integrated map for a town of almost twenty thousand like Elk River could cost half a million dollars, the kind of expenditure most small towns could never manage.

Elk River got around this financial problem because Pentronics Systems was a defense contractor. In a way, the tunnels of Elk River were made possible by the largesse of the diggers' old taskmaster, the Pentagon. The Department of Defense footed the bill for the town's integrated utilities map out of its pocket change.

As a public document, a copy of the map was available for a nominal fee to anyone who was curious.

Now—dug meter by winding meter, year after backbreaking year, threaded through every conceivable obstacle—the tunnels ran from Riverfront Park on the south to the exclusive enclave of Oak Crest on the north. From the town marina on the east to the Pentronics Systems plant on the west. Several branches at varying levels connected the main lines. There were three large storage chambers: one below John's house (HQ), one below the Church of the Resurrection (CR), and the one Darien and Gil presently occupied below Eleventh and Elm (EE).

Each of the vets had the most simple yet compelling reason for such a prodigious undertaking. They'd left the war, but the war hadn't left them. They sometimes joked among themselves about whether they were trying to exorcise their demons or exercise them.

For Darien, it was a simple matter of feeling safer in his tunnels than he felt anywhere else. Here he was protected, even from himself.

For Gil, it was the best way to remember the glory of being an elite soldier. He often said that what he'd done would have made Green Berets cry for their mamas.

And John . . . For John, it was guilt. He'd committed the two mortal sins of a combat soldier. He'd let his best buddy get killed, and he hadn't brought back his body.

"It's a beauty," Darien said of the Harley.

Gil nodded and laughed sharply. "Cops ain't never gonna find it down here."

Gil had stolen the motorcycle, taken it apart, and reassembled it in the chamber, where it gleamed in the light of a battery-powered lantern.

The chamber was three meters high and five meters square. On one wall, under glass, hung a VC flag that Gil had captured. Its red background had faded years ago, but the yellow hammer and sickle still glowed with malignant life.

Along another wall was an armory: a rack of Smith and Wesson revolvers; a quartet of M-16 assault rifles; cartons of cartridges, .38s for the handguns, .223s for the rifles; a stash of C-4 plastic explosive; and a case of fragmentation grenades. Gil had purchased the rifles, the plastic, and the pineapples on the Miami black market.

In fact, Darien thought, Gil had been buying enough stuff the past month or so to go to war. He'd been more than a little prickly about things, too. And now he'd stolen a police Harley.

Darien decided to take an indirect approach. "What was the weirdest thing you ever saw in a tunnel?" he asked Gil.

"Told you a million times, man. That M-48 tank. Fuckin' dinks stole it from the ARVN and got the whole thing down a tunnel, used it as a command center. I about shit when I saw that."

"That's a good one. Right up there with them howitzers John found." Darien hooked a thumb at the motorcycle. "So, you gonna dig a highway down here, or what?"

Gil smiled, more to himself than Darien. "I got plans."

Darien was curious, but instinct told him to hold off asking about Gil's plans. Instead, he said, "You wanna play some Charlie 'n' Joe?"

VC Charlie and GI Joe. Wargames in the tunnels.

"Sure, man. I'm always up for that." But a frown clouded Gil's face.

"What?" Darien asked, seeing it.

"Ah, nothin'," Gil answered. "It's just . . . you know, instead of just playin' tag . . . I'd really like to ding someone again."

That Monday after school, Ty Daulton was running for his life.

He stood five feet two inches tall, and at age fifteen weighed barely a hundred pounds. He had blond hair, blue eyes, and pink cheeks, and there was only one girl in his sophomore class who was prettier.

He was being pursued by Frank Murtaw and a bellowing pack of oafs from the school rugby team. They chased him through the woods of Oak Crest.

Ty's failure to keep pace with his peers' hormonal maturity was only one of the offenses he'd committed against the social weal at Oak Crest Academy. There was also the fact that he was far and away the smartest kid in the school. And in the status-obsessed cauldron of the Oak Crest high school corridors, he was the only scholarship student, the only poor kid, the only townie from down the hill—Elk River.

Ty stood out for all the wrong reasons. Now, as the predators howled at his heels, the boy cursed his father. This was all his fault.

Wesley Daulton was a brilliant man who couldn't make a passing grade as a human being. He was an alcoholic, failed Ph.D. candidate, deserted husband, itinerant teacher, and one-man term paper mill.

After Ty's freshman year at Elk River High School, Wesley had told his son he wouldn't allow him to remain there, calling it a prep school for convenience store clerks—even though he, himself, was on the faculty. This news greatly upset Ty, who had worked hard to achieve anonymity among his classmates. As a teacher's son, he hadn't been welcomed to their ranks, but he'd been tolerated.

At Oak Crest Academy, the boy knew he'd have no chance. So when Wesley had persuaded the headmaster at Oak Crest that his boy would help the school's academic cachet match its social standing, Ty was heart-sick.

Things went from bad to worse when Wesley decided that teaching and ghostwriting schoolwork were taking too much time away from his drinking, and volunteered Ty to run the family term paper business. He willingly acknowledged that his son's intellect was even more incandescent than his own, and told Ty he'd have no trouble with the chore.

The hitch in the plan was that Ty was also more intellectually honest than his father. The boy refused to go along. Wouldn't write a word that would appear below anyone else's name.

Because Wesley's physical stature was as slight as Ty's, there was nothing he could do about his son's intransigence . . . but Frank Murtaw, and several others of Wesley's erstwhile clients, who felt betrayed and were failing in the attempt to do their own work, were at that very minute trying to show Ty the error of his ways.

Ty had seen at least six of them pursuing him in the one backward glance he'd dared to take. He could hear them crashing through the underbrush behind him, grunting and laughing—enjoying the hunt.

Then he heard a call that shriveled his soul.

"Piggy!" Frank Murtaw yelled. "We're coming to get you, Piggy!"

His English class was studying *Lord of the Flies*. Ty hadn't thought these dullards were even doing the assigned reading, but now Frank was calling him Piggy. The boy in the book who'd been murdered.

They really were going to kill him.

Ty's head throbbed with every breath and stride he took. His heart felt enlarged to the point of bursting. His lungs were on fire, and his legs were growing wobbly. Fear was the only thing that kept him going, and he didn't know how long that would suffice.

The world started to tilt in front of his eyes. He didn't know if he was succumbing to exhaustion or terror . . . but he couldn't go on much longer.

Then, ahead and to the right, he saw a bush. It was thickly packed with leaves and it nestled tightly against a rise in the land. He lurched for it, squirming frantically between the bush and the slope. He silently prayed that none of the pack had seen him take shelter. He was in luck. He heard them hurtle past.

Ty squeezed himself into a tiny ball. He tried to quiet his breathing and his trembling limbs. He wished he could sink into the earth until the danger had passed.

Suddenly, the woods were still. No more crashing or cursing or whooping. In a moment, his ears picked up the sounds of labored breathing becoming more regular, whispered comments, and feet shuffling closer.

Then Frank Murtaw called out again.

"You're *hiding*, Piggy. And we're going to *find* you."

Ty desperately sought a solution. He tried not to yield to the panic that squeezed his throat shut. If they found him now, he'd die without being able to make a sound.

He heard them approaching. They were moving slowly, checking the undergrowth methodically. They were showing more intelligence than he'd ever have given them credit for; they were bound to find him.

From a level more primitive than fear came a spark of rage. If he had to die, he was going to make them pay. He'd make *Frank* pay. Put his eye out with a stick. Wait until the bastard moved the leaves of the shrub aside and ram it in!

Ty searched the ground for a suitable weapon, and that was when he made his discovery. There in the dirt was a groove an inch or so deep. His foot must have made it when he dived behind the shrub. Brushing aside the dirt, his fingers uncovered a sheet of wood, a *milled* sheet of wood.

Frank's calls were getting closer, the promise of capture more imminent. The hunters smelled blood. Quickly, Ty scraped away more dirt. He saw where the sheet of wood met a frame. Next his fingers uncovered a handle.

He'd found some kind of concealed trapdoor. He didn't care where it led or what awaited below, he yanked it open just enough for him to enter. That was all he could manage, anyway. The trapdoor was heavy. The bush had been planted so its roots extended through the sheet of wood into a container that was fastened below.

Ty squeezed into the opening and silently lowered the door above his head. He held his breath and listened. The voices above grew loud and then profane. They promised dire fates. But there was no response to sustain their fury, and the voices faded and then disappeared.

Ty had no intention of falling into a trap. He wasn't going to resurface anytime soon. He decided to rest at the bottom of his new hideaway. Except he couldn't find the bottom; he just kept going down.

Then he realized he'd found more than just a hole in the ground; this was the entrance to some kind of tunnel.

He climbed back up through the darkness to where he'd started and turned around so he could crawl down headfirst. He'd accidentally discovered some kind of subterranean world. And he intended to explore it.

In games of Charlie 'n' Joe, Gil and Darien were evenly matched.

Gil was the only *official* tunnel rat in the group—he'd been assigned to the First Engineers of the Big Red One and had gone through the army's Tunnels, Mines, and Booby Traps School. Gil was the pro.

Darien had been an Eleven Bravo, an infantryman, a grunt. But he'd been taken prisoner by Charlie and held in the tunnels of Cu Chi for two months before he'd escaped. Darien knew tunnels from the VC point of view.

Darien was playing Charlie this time. He inched along a jet-black tunnel, having to stop Joe from finding a cache of VC battle plans, or, failing that, kill him before he got back above ground.

The scenario was familiar, and today Darien had a hard time keeping his mind on the game. He wondered what was bothering Gil. When Darien had suggested recently that he take some time to go see his favorite ex-wife, Rayette, thinking that might cheer him up, Gil had looked like he was going to take a swing at him. And now he'd stolen a police motorcycle and was making cracks about wanting to kill someone. Something was going on in Gil's head, but what the hell was it?

Darien's musings were interrupted by a sharp bang.

Gil hadn't snuck up and shot him; it was worse than that. Someone had set off one of the booby traps they had strung throughout the tunnels. The charge itself was tiny, no stronger than a firecracker and not intended to cause harm; it was meant as an embarrassment if someone got sloppy. But Gil had been playing better than ever lately.

And John would never trip any kind of ambush.

Darien realized that for the first time they had an intruder in the tunnels.

Giving Gil the perfect excuse to ding someone again.

When the explosion went off in his face, Ty Daulton wet his pants, just peed his jockey shorts before he knew it. Now, even through the ringing in his ears, he could hear someone coming toward him. He started to crawl backward as fast as he could.

Ty cursed his stupidity. He should have known that anyone who could dig such a fantastic tunnel, with such an elaborate entrance, would have provided safeguards against idiots like him.

He was certain that if he was caught he'd be killed to protect the tunnel's secrecy. And since he was already underground there'd be no problem getting rid of his body. Tears stung his eyes and he cursed himself again.

Crawling backward fast was almost impossible. Whoever was coming after him had no such trouble with speed. Ty could hear a rapid, rhythmic scrape-and-slap of cloth and flesh against the hard clay floor of the tunnel. It wouldn't be long before he was caught.

There was no place he could hide even though it was pitch-black. The only way out, as far as he knew, was the way he'd come in, but he'd never make it back to the entrance in time.

He didn't even know how he could fight. He was on his hands and knees. What was he supposed to do, use his teeth? He didn't know *what* to do . . . but . . . but he knew he was done running. Maybe he didn't have long to live, but he wasn't going to run anymore. Ever. He stopped.

To his utter amazement, his pursuer stopped, too. He must have stopped. Ty couldn't hear him crawling forward anymore.

But he could *feel* him. Out there in the darkness. Not very far away, either. Ty could hear him breathing heavily. The chase must have been an effort for him. But why didn't he say anything? What the hell was the bastard doing—toying with him?

"Hey, fuck you, anyway," Ty yelled, "whoever the hell you are."

A light went on and blinded him. Ty felt certain that he was going to die. Then a hand reached up and closed around his neck. He was yanked downward through the darkness, through a trapdoor in the tunnel floor. Ty started to struggle, but something hit the back of his head.

He fell into a blackness even deeper than that of the tunnel.

10 John asked Jill Baxter if she wanted anything to eat or drink before he took her back to Local 274, and she said she'd like some coffee. They sat at his kitchen table, cups of decaf in front of them.

Jill said, "You and Mr. Boyle—"

"Call him Tommy. He'd prefer it."

"Very well. You and *Tommy* seem too close in age to be uncle and nephew."

John looked at her. There was something—an awareness—between them. Nobody was going to make any quick moves . . . but over the horizon forces were gathering.

"Tommy's the baby in his family. He's only two years older than me. My mom was his much older sister."

"Your mother's passed away?"

He let his gaze linger, surprised that she'd come right out with a personal question like that so fast. But she had, so he answered.

"Yes," he said.

"My father's dead, too," she told him.

Now, he understood: They were comparing scars.

"Were you young?" he asked.

"Very."

"Did he go hard?"

"He was murdered."

"I'm sorry," John said.

She nodded. "Was your mother's death bad?"

"She was struck by a car a Christmas drunk was driving along a sidewalk in Chicago. My father was with her, and he was blinded."

"What happened to the driver?"

"He hanged himself in the men's room of a bar."

"What?" she asked, not quite sure she'd heard right.

"He was caught and went to trial, but he was rich—he got off with a slap on the wrist. So my dad, my grandfather, and Tommy went up to Chicago to kill him."

John watched to see if he'd shocked her, but if he had she didn't show it.

"They took Tommy along to be with my dad while Grandpa Devlin did the deed. But they were too late. The guy must've had a conscience. Grandpa found him dangling by his necktie in the men's room of his favorite watering hole. Tommy told me, even though he wasn't supposed to."

Jill nodded and took a sip of coffee.

"He was eight at the time; I was six," John said. Then he asked, "They ever get the guy who killed your father?"

"No," Jill said.

She might have said more, but a voice called, "John?"

They turned to see Gil Velez standing in the kitchen doorway. With a gun sticking out of his pants. Gil seemed unaware of it. He stepped forward and extended his hand to Jill.

"Gil Velez," he told her. "I'm a friend of John's."

"Jill Baxter," she said, shaking his hand but offering nothing more.

He gave Jill a nod, then turned to John. "We need to talk in private for a minute."

"Can it wait?"

"No."

"Can't you tell me in front of Ms. Baxter?"

Gil's eyes narrowed. "We just caught a trespasser. In the *sub*basement."

That was all the explanation John needed. He stood quickly and said to Jill, "Will you excuse me for a minute?"

Jill got to her feet, too. "If this is a bad time for you, I can call a cab—"

"No, I'll be right back. Just give me a few minutes."

He wanted to hear about her father, and wondered what else they might have to talk about.

. . .

Darien had Ty in a set of Gil's fatigues and standing at attention by the time John and Gil entered HQ, deep below the house. The boy's posture was correct, but he couldn't keep from trembling. He was terrified.

Gil whispered to John, "I almost dinged the little shit. Now I think Darien wants to keep him for a pet."

The boy glanced his way, and Darien screamed at him to keep his eyes forward. The boy's head snapped back and faced front.

"All right, mister," Darien told him, "let's have your name and rank again."

"Daulton," Ty recited, "Tyler Garret, sophomore, Oak Crest Academy." The boy was worried sick, not knowing where this lunatic game with these madmen might lead.

Darien left him holding his rigid position of attention while he went to confer with his friends. Presently, John stepped in front of the boy.

"At ease," he said softly.

The kid assumed the proper stance. Darien *had* been busy.

John continued, "You found our tunnels by accident?"

"Yes, sir."

"But Sergeant Givens tells me you already have some ideas about them."

"Yes, sir."

"And they are?"

"You've got a whole system down here. A whole *world*."

John exchanged a look with his friends. Darien mimed *Smart*.

"What do people call you, son?"

"Ty."

"How do you know what we have, Ty?"

"I came down a tunnel that didn't branch, and I was caught from below. That means there's another level with a connection. Where there's one connection, another may be inferred. From the looks of this cavern, you've been in operation for a long time. That means you've had the opportunity to do a lot of digging."

Darien beamed, mimed *See?*

Gil pulled his two friends to the far side of the chamber. "What the fuck're we gonna do with him?" he hissed under his breath. "We can't just let him go."

Darien said, "I already told you, man. I done *drafted* him. He's ours now."

Gil rolled his eyes. "Just because you put him in some of my fatigues . . ."

John held up a hand for patience. In a normal voice, he said, "Ty, who are your parents?"

"My mother abandoned me the day I was born. My father's a drunk. If you're planning to get rid of me, don't worry about it. No one's going to miss me." The boy's voice was empty.

"Ain't *nobody* gonna kill you," Darien said. He gave Gil a stony look to emphasize his point.

John asked quietly, "Darien, you really like this kid?"

"He's about the same age as my boy. I've talked to him 'n' I think I can work with him. I make him one of us, then he's got a secret to keep, too."

John looked at Gil. "He's right. We're not going to kill the kid." Gil nodded, still uneasy, on edge. "You got a better idea?" John asked him. Gil shook his head. "Okay, then. Darien, he's all yours."

John had kept their secret for too many years not to share Gil's misgivings, but he wasn't about to murder a kid to keep it.

Made him wonder if you could keep things to yourself for just so long.

11

Tommy Boyle did a five-minute tap dance in Orville Leen's office at the sheriff's station and then he walked out. He left behind a few deliberately vague answers to questions about just what Phil Henry had been doing for him and the union, and who might want to harm him. He didn't care if the lack of cooperation ticked off the sheriff. Cops had a long history of being bought, and Tony Hunt wouldn't hesitate to buy them. Tommy was not about to tip his hand to anyone.

After he finished with Leen, Tommy went back to his office at Local 274. He was happy to see that someone had not only cleaned up all the shattered glass but had also replaced his window. He'd just sat down behind his desk when the phone rang. It was the hospital. Phil Henry had regained consciousness. Tommy said he'd be right over, but the doctor told him they had some tests to run and that he could see Mr. Henry at four that afternoon.

Tommy wasn't inclined to wait that long, but then his phone rang again, and when he answered it, he got the most surprising news of his life. It sat him right back in his chair. He was going to be a daddy. God*damn*, he was going to have a kid.

So what the hell did he do now? It certainly made a man stop and think, gave him a whole new fix on things, an entirely new set of priorities. Did he keep on the way he always had? Stay a small-time union leader? Did he remain the point man for this strike, with all that implied?

Yeah, he thought, he had to see the strike through. He couldn't give up the fight, if only because his people never would have gone out if he hadn't led them out. They'd have acquiesced to Harold Noyes and knuckled under to Tony Hunt. They'd have been screwed blue—be working for peanuts with no benefits—but they'd still have jobs. He was the one who'd told them to gamble with their futures, it would be worth it. He couldn't abandon his people now.

But later on, after they'd won . . . Tommy could see making some changes in his life. He didn't actually need his job. There was money in his family. Not big money. But enough to be comfortable until he got something else going. Something where he could concentrate on his new responsibilities.

Being a father. Jesus!

Almost as an afterthought, he realized this meant he'd have to clean up his personal life, too. That might result in an unpleasant scene or two . . . but, hell, it'd be worth it. Tommy couldn't remember the last time he'd felt so good about anything.

He got up and left word with the people in the outer office that he'd be out for a while. He got into his car and drove away, hoping with all his heart that the baby would be a boy, a son.

Billy Shelton watched Tommy Boyle from his patrol unit.

Billy was on lunch, and that time was still his own. He had decided to use it to try to talk Bobbi into coming home. She was still his wife, goddamnit. He was going to march right up to her and—

He never made it that far, never reached Bobbi's rental house. From a hundred feet up the block, he saw Bobbi and that sonofabitch Boyle standing on the front porch.

Billy pulled his unit to the curb. They hadn't noticed him, but what he saw ignited a spark of hope in his heart. Bobbi and Boyle were arguing. Yappin' and scrappin' like dogs over a bone. Bobbi shook her head vigorously, that long, shiny black hair of hers whipping back and forth.

"That's it, baby," Billy whispered, watching through his windshield. "Get him to hit you just once. I'll blast his ass into the next time zone."

Almost on cue, Bobbi smacked Boyle a good one, and Boyle raised his hand to return the blow. Billy was about to go ballistic when the scene and his world turned inside out.

Boyle didn't hit Bobbi. Instead, he grabbed her shoulders, pulled her to him, and kissed her. That would have been good enough for Billy, too, if Bobbi had fought him. But she didn't. She threw her arms around Boyle's neck and kissed him right back.

Then she wrapped her legs around him. Climbed right up onto him. Her dress riding up over her hips. Right there in public. Like a goddamn free porno show. Boyle walked her into the house right like that.

Billy was going to kill them both there and then. Except he still had enough cop sense left in him to look around, see if there would be any witnesses.

He spotted the big freak who worked for Tony Hunt, the one who looked like he'd stuck his head in a trash masher. The guy was parked in a black sedan on the other side of the one-way street a couple of cars up from Billy's unit. He hadn't noticed the deputy, either.

Of course, he hadn't. He'd been too busy watching the show. But what the hell was he doing here in the first place?

Following Boyle for Tony Hunt was what. Had to be.

That gave Billy Shelton an idea.

He'd kill Boyle later on—after he'd planned it out—and lay the blame off on Tony Hunt's thug.

Tommy Boyle walked into Phil Henry's hospital room that afternoon with a sparkle in his eye. When he saw how busted up Phil was, the sparkle hardened into a glint of rage.

There was a nurse in the room. She sat in a chair in the corner and looked up from the magazine she'd been reading.

"Would you leave the room, please?" Tommy asked flatly.

The nurse started to say something, and Phil made a thick burbling sound. Tommy didn't understand either of them. He turned to Phil.

"I'll be right with you, buddy." To the nurse, he said, "My friend and I need some privacy."

"Your friend gets extremely upset anytime I try to leave. So far I've been able to accommodate him only because the floor is quiet. I don't know if he likes my looks or just the way I changed the dressing on his leg."

The woman was pleasant-looking, but Tommy knew Phil had to have more than that in mind. He looked down at the battered investigator he'd hired to snoop on Tony Hunt.

"You want to tell me something and she's necessary?"

Phil nodded. The nurse looked puzzled. Phil inclined his head, gesturing them to him.

"Would you mind?" Tommy asked the nurse.

"What the heck, I'm curious, too."

They stepped over to the side of the bed, and Phil Henry used one of his casted hands to gently tap the nurse's right wrist. Tommy didn't understand until the woman raised her arm. Then he saw it.

The woman had abraded her wrist and it was healing. There were *scabs* on her skin.

Tommy looked at Phil.

"Hunt's bringing in scabs?" Tommy's voice went stone-cold. "He's going to try to break the strike?"

Phil Henry nodded.

12 By the time John got back to Jill Baxter, she had her mind on business, so he drove her back to Local 274. She wanted to talk with Tommy, but he'd left the office without saying where he was going. Jill learned this from the man who introduced himself as Marty McCreery, the local's secretary-treasurer. When Jill told him who she was, McCreery gave her the same kind of look Tommy Boyle first had: Could this dame really be our new lawyer?

Well, to hell with him, Jill thought. She'd explained herself to Tommy Boyle. That was enough. *He'd* have to see that his troops got the word.

John asked her, "You want me to hang around in case you need a ride somewhere?"

"If you don't mind."

Jill appreciated the offer, and knew that John was putting the implicit weight of his family behind her for the union official to see. Turning back to Marty McCreery, she told him what had happened that morning between Tommy Boyle and Harold Noyes.

The secretary-treasurer of the local had had no idea the international boss had even been in town. "So that's how Tommy's window got broke. Musta been something to see," he said. "Wish I'd been here."

"I'm concerned the international might try to cut off your strike funds," Jill said. "I'd like to know who I should call about preventing that."

McCreery's eyes narrowed with suspicion. He clearly hadn't bought this woman as someone who'd be working with the local, and certainly not as someone to whom he should speak freely. "Maybe we should wait till Tommy gets back."

"Why waste time . . ."

Marty started to turn away. John put a hand on his shoulder. "Tommy hired Ms. Baxter to represent the local, Marty. She was with Tommy and me at my house this morning. She's trying to do her job, but she needs some help."

"You know what's going on here, John?" Marty knew there was no one closer to Tommy Boyle.

"Not specifically. But I'm family, and Ms. Baxter is Tommy's lawyer. You can talk to us."

Marty thought it over, then nodded. "Come on into Tommy's office."

Marty sat behind Tommy's desk, Jill Baxter was in the guest chair, and John leaned against the door.

Marty looked at Jill. "You know the relationship between a local and an international union?"

A pop quiz, Jill thought. She couldn't believe this guy and his dumb question.

"Well, let's see," she said brightly. "One's bigger than the other?"

She'd said it with a smile, but Marty McCreery knew he'd just been called an asshole.

The union man turned to John. "The international grants us a charter, and, in turn, we send in our dues to the international."

"Out of which, should the need arise, the international provides funds for strike pay," Jill added.

"Yeah," Marty said, grudgingly conceding that maybe this broad knew a thing or two. "Only we won't get strike pay from the international because we haven't paid any dues for the past two years."

Jill was amazed. "Why not?"

Even in the privacy of Tommy's office, with the door closed, Marty was reluctant to divulge his secret. He looked past John to the outer office to see if anyone had an ear cocked, but nobody seemed to be listening.

"Tommy's got a theory," Marty whispered. "He thinks that the reason the international always wants its locals to settle rather than strike is they're looting union funds. If they had to come across with strike pay for any length of time, the jig would be up. So a couple of years ago he started withholding our dues."

"That's incredible," Jill said. But she immediately realized it was entirely consistent with the way Tommy Boyle had operated. An admitted blackmailer, he wouldn't worry about ignoring the international's dues-paying rules. "Did he have any proof?"

"I don't know if Tommy had anything on paper, but he told me the night before we went out on strike he got this phone call."

"And?" John prompted.

Marty had to drag it out of himself. "And he was told to send in all the money we owed and follow the international's orders . . . or he'd get two in the back of the head."

The union official formed his fingers into a gun and dropped the hammer twice.

"You intend to stay?" John asked.

"I'm thinking," Jill said. Then she looked at him. "I'm not a quitter, but . . ."

"You're wondering what you've gotten yourself into."

They were in John's car. He was taking her to her hotel, the Mill House Inn, known locally as the Nixon. Despite the dig, it was a step up from the Best Western out near the Oak Crest Country Club—and a giant step ahead of the Traveler's Delight on Route 98. Tommy had obviously thought that a big-time labor lawyer from Chicago deserved the best accommodations Elk River had to offer.

They'd waited an hour for Tommy at Local 274. Then Jill announced she wanted to freshen up and get out of the clothes that had the scent of Amtrak-in-the-morning all over them.

Jill asked, "How did you happen to have your camera with you when you saw that man with the gun?"

John braked for a stoplight. He looked at her and grinned. For the first time she saw a resemblance to Tommy Boyle.

"I really am a photographer . . . but I haven't done much lately. I've been living off line extensions from my books."

"Line extensions?"

"Marketing jargon for milking the heck out of a product. In my case, the photos from my books become calendars and posters, whatever my agent can dream up." He told her the titles of his books, but she didn't know any of them.

The light changed and he stepped on the gas.

"I'm sorry," she said. "I don't have time to read much outside of my field."

"That's okay. Anyway, I felt the need to get back to it, and maybe connect with the people around here a little more, too. So, I thought I'd see if there was a book in this strike Tommy's leading. Last night I was going to take some shots of the midnight picket line out at the plant. Labor's lonely vigil, something like that."

She looked to see if he was poking fun at the strikers—at her indirectly—but he wasn't.

"And instead you almost got killed."

"Yeah."

"And now we hear that the international has threatened Tommy's life. This is shaping up more like a war than a strike."

John had been coming around to the same idea. But hearing someone else say so made him uneasy. He looked over and saw she was looking at him. Looking *into* him, it seemed. He wondered if she'd spotted any of his secrets.

But she didn't say anything, didn't push. She was being patient, and he liked that. Instead, he asked the questions. "You remember back at my house when Gil interrupted us? Were you going to tell me more about your father?"

13 Tony Hunt was broke.

This appalling discovery was made by his investment banker, Carter Powell, only after financing had been provided to bankroll Hunt's new company, MicroCosmic, Inc., presently known as Pentronics Systems. In theory, Hunt had secured his financing for MicroCosmic by pledging shares of Hunt Enterprises as collateral. The problem was, those shares would be worthless unless Hunt's new business went through the roof.

Carter Powell had gotten greedy, precisely as Hunt had anticipated. The banker hadn't given the numbers in Hunt's financial statements a thorough crunching because he'd been afraid another bank would steal the deal if he didn't act quickly. Doing his homework after the fact had revealed the awful truth.

Even so, the spell of seduction Hunt had woven over Powell still held: Everything and everyone involved in the MicroCosmic deal would come out golden if Hunt's scheme succeeded. Because Anthony Tiburon Hunt had gotten his hands on the invention of the century: a superconducting microprocessor.

Its introduction would rock the world. At a stroke, every other microchip in production would be obsolete. Just the material from which the chip would be fabricated was worth a boundless fortune.

And Tony Hunt had the chip's inventor in his pocket.

A pocket Carter Powell had intended to have his hand into up to the elbow.

Now, Powell knew the prize would be theirs only if they moved fast. Before the fraud Hunt had perpetrated was discovered and they were both sent to prison as co-conspirators. Nobody would believe that Powell hadn't been in on Hunt's scam from the beginning. He couldn't be *that* stupid.

That's why Powell was so worried about the Pentronics strike dragging on. True, it had been going on for little more than a week, but there was no end in sight. The damn thing was going to kill them both. So he called Hunt with increasing frequency, urging him, pleading with him, to *do* something.

Tony Hunt got tired of listening to his banker whine. He said curtly, "Don't worry, Powell, I'm handling it."

In fact, Hunt had felt the first slight twinge of uneasiness himself. He'd mastered it at once, though, with the decision to send Krieger out to kidnap Tommy Boyle's PI. Having learned of the man's snooping, Hunt had to know if the investigator had discovered his secret.

He'd told Krieger only that he didn't want Boyle tipped to the fact that he was bringing in scabs, and in his own bestial way Krieger had solved that problem.

Krieger might even have eliminated the possibility that the investigator would be able to tell Boyle *anything* he'd uncovered. But Hunt felt comfortable only with certainties, not possibilities. He wished Krieger had killed the man.

Instead, the oaf had dared to exercise independent judgment, and that bore even closer scrutiny than Powell's weak-kneed whimpering.

There was so much for a busy man to do.

Anthony Tiburon Hunt was the son of a Boston bagman and the Cuban flower girl he'd met on a gambling trip to prerevolutionary Havana.

Tony's dad, Big Ed Hunt, collected the swag for the legendary political fixer, Irish Jackie Knowles. Irish Jackie had fascinated Tony from the time he'd given the boy his first lollipop. Through the years, Tony watched as men deferred to him, women fawned over him, and politicians curried his favor. Everybody who knew the man said hello with a wave and a smile. Irish Jackie had a big car, a bigger house, and a deep pocket that was always stuffed with cash.

How he managed all this was what intrigued young Tony, because Irish Jackie was just a nice little guy not much more than five feet tall. He had wiry ginger-colored hair, bright blue eyes, and a crooked smile. Whenever he saw Tony, he always ruffled Tony's hair and stuck some money in his hand.

He always gave Tony a little chuck under the chin, too. Made his teeth click.

One day when he was ten, Tony went to Big Ed with a question. Why didn't he just take everything away from Irish Jackie and run things himself? After all, he was much bigger and stronger.

His father gave him the oddest look the boy had ever seen. Then he took Tony out to the family garage and administered the thrashing of his young life.

"You're never to speak of such things again," Big Ed told him when he'd finished.

Tony's backside was afire, but he was stubborn. He demanded to know why. Why couldn't his father handle Irish Jackie? Big Ed was big enough to turn *him* over his knee, too.

Tony Hunt's father tore at his hair in exasperation. Another beating would serve no purpose. So he tried another approach.

"Do you like the money Jackie gives you?" he asked his son.

Tony said that he did.

"Well, so do I. But do you like the little chuck under the chin that comes with it?"

"No."

"But it's worth the money, isn't it?"

The boy was ashamed to admit it, but he nodded.

"Do you know why you don't like that chuck?"

"It's mean."

"It's more than that. It's a reminder of who's who. He's the one who's figured out the game and has the money. You're the plodder who feeds off his crumbs. When you like money and you take it from Jackie, in one way or another, you always get your chuck under the chin."

"You can't have one without the other?"

"The day you figure out how, we'll come back here and have another talk."

Big Ed didn't know it, but he'd just issued his son the challenge of a lifetime. Someday, Tony was going to outwit Irish Jackie . . . and everyone else.

Tony got top grades in school right through Harvard, but his real-life lessons came from planting himself at the knee of Irish Jackie. He knew instinctively that this was the way to accomplish his goals. He never asked Jackie for anything; he always asked if there was anything he could do for Jackie. Because he liked him. He didn't have to pretend, either, because he *did* like Jackie. He found the man to be smart, funny, and generous.

He might even have come to love the little bastard if he'd ever stopped chucking him under the chin.

As Tony grew older, Jackie took him into his confidence, told him secrets he wouldn't have confessed to his own priest. He told the young man he wanted him to go to law school and become his lawyer. He said Tony had a fine mind unburdened by any sense of morals whatsoever. He was a natural for the job.

By the time Tony graduated from college, he had enough on Irish Jackie to go to the state's attorney and get him locked up for life. Which was just what Tony would threaten to do unless Jackie made him not his lawyer but his partner. That would be his chuck under the chin for Irish Jackie. See how he liked it.

But Jackie escaped him. Never sick a day in his life, he was diagnosed and dead within a month. The last person he sent for from his deathbed was his protégé, Tony Hunt. He looked up at the young man and grinned knowingly.

"Had plans for me, didn't you, lad? As if I didn't know. Well, old Jackie slips away once more." He beckoned Tony closer, and the young man sat warily on the edge of the bed. "Don't try to overstep yourself," Jackie advised in a surprisingly firm voice. "You've many fine qualities, but you lack the common touch."

Irish Jackie tried to chuck Tony under the chin one last time, but Tony pulled away.

"Good lad," Jackie said, and then he died.

Tony Hunt left Irish Jackie's house that day with three hundred thousand dollars he stole from the bedroom wall safe, and an education in the use of power that was comprehensive but fatally flawed.

He never really understood, or perhaps accepted, that people had loved Irish Jackie even more than they had feared him.

Hunt had wanted his own town for his new operation because he knew it would be impossible in today's world to replicate the kind of urban fiefdom Irish Jackie had ruled. Big cities were too diverse now, too violent, and there were too many prosecutors looking to crown their careers by crucifying the men who really made things work in this country.

But in a small town, removed from the glare of predatory politics, regulation, and media, it was reasonable to think a man might carve out his own niche, be able to run things in a way that suited him, a way that rewarded him in proportion to the risks he took.

Hunt had anticipated the need to use scabs, and to house them he'd covertly bought the Traveler's Delight Motel. He sent Krieger to evict anybody who still held a room there. The scabs would be arriving that night after dark.

Krieger was not happy with his assignment. Next, he thought, that sonofabitch Hunt would have him taking out the trash. Krieger picked up the motel phone. He called room 166. A woman answered.

"This is the front desk," Krieger said. "You have to be out of your room in thirty minutes."

"Forget it," she said.

"Lady, believe me, you don't want to argue with me."

Not at the best of times, but especially now; Krieger did not need any sassy broad talking back to him. But she kept on coming.

"Is that right?" she asked. "You the baddest desk clerk in town? Or maybe you're the bellhop."

Krieger was about to go show her who he was when he glanced out the office window and noticed a motorcycle stopped in the parking lot. The rider wore a helmet. The motorcycle was not parked. Just stopped with the motor running. Right outside room 166.

"What, now I get your heavy breathing routine?" the woman on the phone said sarcastically.

Krieger didn't have a chance to respond.

"Listen, asshole, you think you're leaning on some poor little woman here? You know who rented this room? Tommy Boyle. He paid for it through the week, and that's how long I'm staying. So unless you wanta fuck with Tommy, fuck off."

She hung up on him.

And the guy on the cycle drove off.

Krieger put the phone down slowly, but his mind was racing. Had he just talked to the woman with all that long black hair he'd seen with Boyle on the front porch of that house? Sounded like about the same kind of hellcat. But why rent a motel room when you got a whole house?

Unless they found out that peeper cop was onto them. Krieger'd spotted that numbnuts in his rearview mirror, and he'd seen right away the cop had taken a personal interest in the grab-and-grope Boyle'd had going with the broad.

Had the cop been the guy on the cycle just now? Had he tracked down the lovebirds?

Krieger didn't know, but he certainly hoped so, because he'd just had a terrific idea. In this town, those pictures of him making the grab on that PI were bound to get back to Boyle. Now, if he could only get Boyle, the broad, and the cop all together in one room.

In the meantime, he had work to do. Forget about the phone, he'd go knock on doors. Anybody else who gave him lip about leaving their room would go flying.

14   That Monday night, "The News Hour with Jim Lehrer" was showing Orville Leen pictures of a famine so bad he couldn't even finish his microwave dinner.

What the hell was wrong with people? the sheriff wondered. Even the most dim-witted dictator in the world had to understand that if you didn't feed people, you had no one to boss around. He clicked off his TV set in disgust.

Leen thought of screwed-up situations and sighed. Look at what he had to deal with. The city manager had left a month ago to become the director of economic development for some sandbox county in Nevada, the town council was in a shambles, and who did people expect to hold the whole damn place together?

Him.

He wasn't entirely sure he wanted to do it, either. His idea of law enforcement was to provide a safe environment where people could go about their lives with peace of mind. That was all. It wasn't about taking sides in some goddamn labor strike.

He had the uneasy feeling, though, that was just what would be asked of him.

The doorbell interrupted his ruminations.

"Now what?" the sheriff muttered.

He opened his door and saw the solid, dark-haired form of Chief Deputy Ron Narder.

"What drags you out, Ronnie?" Leen asked warily.

"Sheriff, the head of plant security out at Pentronics called. He thinks they're facing a takeover attempt."

"What?"

"He said the union people were massing on the sidewalk, said it looked like the entire union workforce."

"That's thirty-five hundred people."

Narder nodded. "The man said they weren't smiling, either."

Leen grabbed his gun belt and his hat, and hurried with the chief deputy to the waiting car. "Lights and siren, Ronnie." A thought occurred to the sheriff. "How come Billy Shelton didn't come get me? He's supposed to be on call whenever I need a driver."

Narder kept his eyes on the road. "Dispatch couldn't find him. Didn't answer his phone at home, didn't respond to his pager."

That worried Orville Leen almost as much as whatever he might find at the plant.

Jill Baxter stood with John Fortunato on the hood of his car. It was parked up the block from the plant's main gate. All around them were milling union members, occupying the street, waving picket signs, and filling the night with the angry, ominous rumble of their voices.

John was taking pictures. Wide-angle shots of the crowd, and then, switching lenses, individual faces that caught his attention.

"This is not good," Jill said.

She and John had found out about Tommy's plan to march on the plant only after it was well under way. She'd have preferred working through the courts to try to delay the hiring of replacement workers. But Tommy had insisted on showing Hunt what he was up against.

Jill looked at the plant security guards. They were carrying shotguns. John followed her gaze, and took several pictures of the guards.

"This is not good," she said again.

Tony Hunt looked at the horde from his office perch.

"Fools," he said flatly.

The mob spread from the plant's front gate right across the asphalt to where the city's streets department maintained a facility. The site was a parking area for snowplows and a storage dump for road salt. Its location guaranteed that the plant never had any trouble getting its access road cleared. Now, with the arrival of spring, the plows had been parked and the mounds of salt were depleted.

Hunt picked up a pair of binoculars from his desk. He read a sampling of picket signs.

SCABS ARE SCUM, said one.

WE DON'T WORK, NOBODY WORKS, read another.

An unexpected movement caught Hunt's eye. It flickered across the tops of the lenses as he scanned the mob below. It came from across the street in the storage dump. He raised the binoculars to try to find it again.

He didn't see anything. He didn't know what he was looking for, and it was almost dark. Part of his mind told him it had been nothing, a passing bird or a small animal. But a more compelling area of consciousness nagged at him to identify what he'd seen.

Then a flame caught Hunt's eye. Someone had ignited a torch. He saw that someone was Tommy Boyle.

Hunt knew it was time for him to put in an appearance.

Tommy Boyle watched Tony Hunt walk straight toward him. Brassy cocksucker didn't even bring a guard with him. He even waved back the guards closest to the gate. They retreated.

Tony Hunt gave the impression of a well-dressed man with nothing more on his mind than an evening stroll.

"What the fuck's he doing, Tommy?" a voice behind the labor leader whispered.

Tommy didn't answer, but he knew. Hunt was showing them who had the biggest balls in town. The whole strike might be decided in the next few seconds.

Hunt hit a button on the wall near the gate, a motor whirred into life, and the main gate slid open. Nothing stood between the strikers and the plant owner. Nobody moved.

Except Hunt. He stepped in front of Tommy Boyle. The two men were separated by no more than ten feet. Tommy had to admit that Hunt had a lot of nerve.

Hunt was facing thousands of angry workers with torches in their hands and murder in their hearts. They'd pick his bones clean before his rent-a-cops got off their first volley.

Tommy handed his torch to someone behind him. This was going to be the fight of his life. The thought made him smile.

Hunt stared at Tommy coolly, then swept the crowd with his eyes. He raised his voice and said, "Pentronics Systems is dead! The new company doing business at this location is MicroCosmic, Incorporated!"

His announcement was greeted by silence. Then a voice behind Tommy yelled, "Let's get the fucker!"

Tommy felt the surge and heard the howls start at his back—all he had to do was let the stampede happen and Hunt was a dead man—but before anyone could move, he extended his arms and bellowed, "Stop!"

And everyone did.

Tommy continued, "We don't want anyone to say we're trespassing on this prick's property. We don't want to turn him into the good guy."

Reluctantly, the strikers heeded him; the roar for blood that had begun in a thousand throats slowly died away.

Tommy didn't even bother to look at his people. He kept his eyes on Hunt. As much as he hated him, Tommy respected the bastard's courage. He hadn't backed off an inch.

But the guards with the shotguns had crept several steps closer.

For the moment, Hunt paid no attention to the strikers, either. He seemed to meditate on the shine of his handmade shoes. Then he looked up.

"I have two thousand job openings," he said, "for anyone who doesn't mind working for a *prick*."

The man's gall was unbelievable. He'd come out to offer two thousand piss-poor jobs in place of thirty-five hundred high-wage jobs. To a crowd that wanted to rip his heart out. Boyle's anger flared.

None of the strikers said a word.

They waited for Tommy Boyle.

But Hunt had more to say. "As of tomorrow, the first group of new hires will start work . . . and then there will be nineteen hundred jobs available."

There were no shouts of protest, no curses; just guttural growls more suited to canines than humans came from the crowd. Tommy Boyle's was the only hand on the leash.

"You're never going to beat us," Tommy told Hunt. "You're never going to make this place work with scabs."

"No?" Hunt asked. "Why not?"

"Because we won't let you. Elk River won't let you. There'll be no place in this town for anyone who works for you. No place that will feed anyone who goes to work here. No place to buy a drink, a newspaper, or a stick of gum. No place to walk, no place to stop, no place to take a breath. You think you got it made because there are always people desperate to find work, right?" Tommy leaned forward, thrusting his face at Hunt. "Well, let me tell you something, you hand-tailored pile of shit, *nobody's* gonna be desperate enough to work in this town, not with the reception we'll give them. Not while I'm still breathing."

Tommy felt the bullet pass within an inch of his right cheek. A split second later he heard the flat, cracking echo of the shot. It had come from *behind* him. Without hesitation or thought, he threw himself to the ground.

He was surprised to see that Hunt was down, too. And bleeding.

Then came the surge of bodies as the strikers charged. Shotguns roared, punches landed, screams filled the night.

And, finally, came the wail of police sirens.

Krieger stepped outside of the motel office, listened to the earsplitting jangle of police sirens and howlers, and cursed. He knew that something big had to be going on at the plant, and whatever it was, it was wrecking his plans. Boyle wouldn't be coming now, and neither would the cop.

Krieger'd had a change of heart about taking the rap for his part in kidnapping Boyle's PI. His new career plans didn't include another stretch in the joint.

Boyle had to have those pictures of him.

And he was going to get them back.

"What's the charge against my client?" Jill Baxter asked.

Sheriff Orville Leen closed his eyes and pinched the bridge of his throbbing nose, wishing either that the attorney standing in front of him in his office were a man or that his upbringing would have allowed him to pistol-whip a woman.

His police station in the Fox County Building was bursting at the seams. The waiting line to book those who'd been arrested at the plant ran out the door and down the block. Leen didn't have the cells to hold even half of them. So he was letting most of these assholes go on a fifty-dollar bond.

The goddamn Illinois State Police, once he'd admitted the riot was over, had offered no help. Hadn't he heard about their manpower shortages?

Manpower shortages? Leen had forty-five deputies to police the whole goddamn county!

Oh, Lord, his nose hurt.

He'd waded into the melee and some sonofabitch's flying elbow had caught him smack on the honker. He'd bled like a stuck pig all down the front of his shirt.

The only real satisfaction he'd had all night was to lock up three bastards—two guards and a striker—he'd charged with murder. The guards, Dwayne Peevis and Arnie Colton, had been seen firing on unarmed strikers. Peevis shot his man in the back. The striker, Sam MacElroy, had taken a guard's shotgun away and turned it on him.

All three of the men had killed someone they'd known for years. Leen intended to transfer them to the jail over in Sangamon County before any morons could get the idea of storming his station to either free the bastards or lynch them.

If he'd had his way, he would have arrested *both* Tommy Boyle and Tony Hunt. But Hunt was in the hospital, with three dozen others, awaiting medical treatment. That had left Boyle as Leen's prize prisoner.

Except now this goddamn woman lawyer was chewing on his ass about him.

"Well?" Jill Baxter demanded.

Leen finally opened his eyes. "How about disorderly conduct?"

"Fine. Then you'll release him on a bond just like all the others."

The sheriff shook his head. "No, I won't, because Tommy Boyle *isn't* just one of the boys. He's their leader. I *might* decide to charge him with incitement to riot."

"You have no reason to believe that—"

"I sure as hell know there was a riot," Leen said heatedly. "I got proof of it all over my uniform."

The sheriff hadn't had time to change. Except for the three dead men, he looked worse than anybody who'd been at the scene. His eyes were blackening as he spoke.

"I also got six deputies in the hospital," the sheriff added. "So, I'll take my sweet time deciding the charges against Mr. Boyle."

Jill didn't practice criminal law, but she was smart enough to know you never argued with a pissed-off cop. Especially a sheriff. Just the same, she'd be damned if she'd let him flout her client's rights.

"Indisputably and regrettably," she replied evenly, "there was violence at the plant tonight, Sheriff. However, the fact remains there's no evidence to support any contention Mr. Boyle fomented violence. On the contrary, I personally saw Mr. Boyle *prevent* his membership from crossing onto company property."

"Not entirely, he didn't."

The sheriff put a stained handkerchief to his nose. It came away with glistening drops of fresh blood.

"Are you going to charge my client?"

"In due time."

"You refuse to allow bail?"

"Yes."

"I'll be back with a writ tomorrow."

"You do that."

"And I'll advise him about bringing a civil action against your office."

"That's what lawyers are for."

Leen *really* wished he could clip this woman a good one. Instead, he settled for speaking his mind.

"But I'll tell you this, Ms. Baxter. I'm going to stay right here, bleeding from my nose, and talking to as many people as I choose. People from both sides. Then I'll decide about Tommy Boyle. Now, I don't care if you got a personal friend on the Supreme Court, no judge, no writ, no *nothing* is gonna get him outta my lockup before I say so. Do *you* understand *me?*"

She must have, Leen thought. After one final glare, she turned on her heel and left.

Well, that was one less problem anyway.

The respite lasted two seconds. Chief Deputy Ron Narder, a shiner under his right eye, walked in.

"We found Billy Shelton," he said.

The sheriff tensed. Then he let his shoulders slump. He was too goddamn tired and sore to worry about Billy now.

"Where'd he turn up?"

"Hospital emergency room."

"Responding to the situation?"

"No. As a patient."

The sheriff just shook his head.

"You want to hear the rest?" Narder asked.

"Tell me."

"The sarge over there dragged it out of him. He'd gone to see his wife, tried to get her to come back to him."

"And?" Leen asked wearily.

"She said she'd stick with Tommy Boyle, and when Billy objected she creased his skull with a bottle of Scotch."

Jill Baxter slammed the car door. "Let's get out of here," she told John through clenched teeth. "Drive lawfully."

They were two blocks away from the station before she spoke again.

"Leen isn't going to let him out."

"Why not?"

"He's just conducting a thorough investigation, if you believe him. What I think is, he got his nose busted and he's taking it out on Tommy."

John didn't like it, but neither was he worried about Tommy's spending a night in the sheriff's lockup.

What struck him as peculiar was Jill's rage. He could feel it radiating from her. It seemed more than the situation called for, more than professional indignation. After all, only a few hours earlier, she'd still been undecided about staying on the job.

Jill saw him looking, gave him a hard stare, then turned her face away and muttered, "Damn."

"Is that for me or you?"

"Me. I messed up in there."

"How?"

"I pissed off the sheriff. If he wasn't on the other side before, I put him there."

"You call him a name?"

"No, but I practically said I'd sue him."

"Is that all?" John laughed. "You'd have lost your ABA card if you didn't do that."

She turned and saw him grinning. And again she saw the resemblance to Tommy. She smiled back . . . until something terribly sad overcame her, and the years fell away from her face to a time when she was a heartbroken little girl.

John stopped the car and killed the engine in front of her hotel.

"I don't know how much good I'm going to be around here anymore," Jill said.

"Why don't you wait and let Tommy decide that?"

Jill thought about it, then nodded.

"Who will he call first," she asked, "you or me?"

"Me," John said.

"Then would you mind if I wait at your house?"

"No problem," he said, starting the car.

"When we get there," she said, "I'll tell you what happened to my father."

Tommy Boyle was released Tuesday morning at four fifteen. On Orville Leen's personal instructions, Boyle was the last man let go—an hour after the sheriff had left.

In the sheriff's own words, "Let him stew till I'm home in bed."

Ultimately, though, Leen had been forced to free Tommy Boyle. Without charges. A dozen interviews with strikers and plant guards had made it clear that the whole stinking situation might never have come to grief if that first shot hadn't been fired.

Leen meant to find the bastard responsible for that shot.

Innocent or not, however, Leen still wanted to avoid Tommy. He couldn't take seeing that goddamn smirk of his again.

But Tommy wasn't grinning when he stepped out onto the sidewalk in front of the sheriff's station. He was thoughtful and serious, unsure what he should do next.

Helluva time to start having doubts, he thought.

He had to walk home because the impound yard was closed until seven and he couldn't get his car. He'd briefly thought about calling Johnny, but had reconsidered and decided to use the time alone to sort himself out.

Getting shot at had scared him. Having had the time to think about it, he knew that it had been a sniper shot. It had come from behind him. He'd been ready for the guards with their pistols and shotguns. He had not expected an ambush.

Tommy walked west on Third Street, crossed Lincoln Avenue with its commercial buildings and bright lights, and made a right onto Elm with its dimmer residential lighting.

Every house on the block was dark. Tommy wondered at the lack of insomnia. The people on Elm Street, like any other street in town, either worked at the plant or depended on the patronage of those who did. Were they all able to sleep soundly tonight?

Or were they just saving electricity, staring up at their ceilings in the dark?

Tommy turned off Elm and onto Eleventh. Here the yawning blackness of Dirksen Park loomed to his right. He was only a block from home now.

A chill passed through him. If he'd died last night he never would have seen his child.

For the first time in his life, Tommy Boyle wanted to walk away from a fight. The sad fact was, though, he just couldn't. Not when he thought about the families of the people who were counting on him. What would those kids do if Mom or Dad lost their jobs? Or had to accept ones that didn't pay a living wage?

He had to stick it out. He had to fight this one last time, and he had to win. But once he did, that was it. Then they could find somebody else.

He'd have his own family to take care of.

Tommy didn't hear the car until it rolled up right alongside him. Its lights were out. He saw the driver and started to speak.

He never got the chance.

The driver raised a gun and fired.

And didn't miss.

Part Two

A house divided against itself cannot stand.

—Abraham Lincoln

15 The police were never any help with holdups, so Tran Chi Thanh had made it his policy to shoot first, from concealment, and tend to the cleanup later.

Tran owned Convenient Liquors in Westminster, California. Before coming to America, he had been a highly decorated captain and a tunnel commander in the National Liberation Front, aka the Vietcong.

He'd wished to join the victorious People's Army in 1975 but had been told that he would have to do so as an enlisted man. Officers' billets were reserved for Northerners, or those who'd had years of indoctrination in the North. All Tran had done was to live underground for five years and kill Americans at every opportunity.

So, disillusioned with the Communists, he'd stolen a boat, loaded his family into it, and sailed for Thailand. As happened to many refugees, Tran and his family had been set upon by pirates. Unlike most others, however, Tran had been prepared. He'd brought an RPG and several AK-47s along with him—and the combat-tested will to use them.

As the pirate craft approached, one scorching afternoon on the South China Sea, ready for yet another episode of plunder, rape, and murder, Tran crouched on the deck of his stolen boat, barely visible over the gunwale. He spied the pirate captain in the wheelhouse of his craft. The man was smiling in anticipation. Every tooth in his head was made of gold—gleaming, evil testimony of a long history of pillage. Tran holed the brigand's vessel at the waterline with his first rocket-propelled grenade. He fired his second round at the wheelhouse, out of which the pirate captain was already diving.

As the pirate craft sank, Tran calmly used an AK-47 to pick off survivors. Sharks took care of the waste disposal. All except for the pirate captain. Tran fished his body out of the water. He meant to yank his fallen enemy's Midas smile tooth-by-tooth for the benefit of his family.

That decision proved a godsend for Tran and his family. The gold was taken as planned, but of far greater value was the treasure the pirate captain had worn around his waist in a webbed belt. Pulled from the belt's confines, glistening with sea water, sparkling in the blazing sun, were sapphires, rubies, and other precious gems—two hundred and eighty-four stones of varying sizes, shapes, and clarity. The pirates' ill-gotten booty became the Tran family's treasure. This fortune was secreted in the clothing of family members and was used to buy favorable standing in the relocation camp, and eventually passage to the land of Tran's former enemies.

It also helped to purchase the liquor store in California that three members of the Dream Warriors gang were trying to rob just before Tran closed for the night.

Convenient Liquors was anything but convenient to robbers. Directly inside the doorway of the small store a maze began. The six-feet-high walls of the maze were made of stacked cases of liquor bottles. The shape of the maze changed at random intervals, as did the location of the cash register. Observation of those who traveled through the cardboard corridors was made possible by the use of wall-mounted mirrors.

All of this was to Tran's advantage. Once he'd come to understand how rampant crime was in his neighborhood, and that the police were useless against it, he'd reverted to guerrilla tactics to operate his store.

Straight wide aisles, stock openly displayed on shelves, a fixed-position register at the front of the store—these things were madness to Tran. They were as suicidal as the base camps the Americans had used to fight their war.

An honest customer could always be given help to find what he wanted and to make his way to the checkout counter. But the three Dream Warriors who entered the store that night wearing Halloween masks and brandishing automatic weapons faced a much more difficult time.

As Tran watched the gang members approach the first turn, he hurried his wife, mother, and youngest son into the back room. There they would lock the steel-lined door and call the police—who, as ever, Tran knew, would arrive too late.

From under the counter, Tran pulled a fifteen-shot Beretta. A glance at a mirror showed him that the Dream Warriors had come to a cul-de-sac. A tremendous crash followed as the three criminals tried to defeat the maze by bulldozing their way through it. Their task was made a great deal harder by the fact that all the bottles in the cases had been filled with sand.

In frustration, two of the gang members fired their automatic weapons into the barrier. Cardboard, glass, sand, and shell fragments flew through the store. The din of automatic weapons fire in the enclosed space was fierce. But the fusillade was pointless, merely the temper tantrum of homicidal children.

Tran had seen the slashing devastation wrought by the miniguns of the American Cobra helicopters. He'd waited to be suffocated underground during the all-consuming B-52 raids. He was not about to yield to children who sought to rob him because he wouldn't pay their extortion demands.

Tran slipped through a trapdoor in the floor and disappeared into the dark crawl space below. His eyes adjusted quickly. Light from the store entered through small holes drilled in the floor. Tran had a space thirty inches high to crawl through—twice as much as he needed.

The first thing he did was scurry to a point below the front door and lock it by shoving home a bolt from beneath. The door, like the front windows, was fitted with panes of Lexan, a transparent but incredibly strong polycarbonate resin—in layman's terms, bulletproof plastic. The Lexan would not break or shatter under the impact of the small cartridges of automatic weapons. Neither would the robbers be able to flee through the rear metal-clad door.

Tran had trapped the Dream Warriors inside his store.

Now, he would hunt them down.

Overhead, he could hear their footsteps and their curses and, by now, he could even see dustfalls seeping through cracks in the floor. Silently, he followed along below them. The trio of robbers made their way to the middle of the store, where the cash register had been set up that night. Tran heard the cash drawer open. Juvenile laughter and boasts followed.

Tran popped up through a trapdoor—one of several in the store—and shot two of the gang members dead, the ones who'd been facing him from behind the register. He disappeared again before the surviving Dream Warrior could turn around.

Tran heard a scream of rage as the robber realized what had happened to his friends. A burst of gunfire accented the sentiment. But since none of it was directed into the floor, Tran knew that the fool had no idea where he was.

He heard the surviving gang member run behind the counter. The boy wasn't going back to his gang empty-handed. He was cleaning out the cash drawer.

Tran crawled as fast as he could to the area below the front of the store and took a small instrument out of his pocket. It was a dental mirror. He stuck it through a hole in the floor.

It took the remaining robber a minute to renegotiate the maze. The boy was agitated. Finally, carrying the weapons of his fallen comrades as well as his own, but with none of them at the ready, he appeared in Tran's mirror heading for the front door.

Tran popped up through a trapdoor. The Dream Warrior's mouth fell open as he skidded to a stop and fumbled to find the trigger of one of the weapons.

Tran blew off the top of his head.

The former Vietcong reached down and unbolted the front door. Then he vaulted out of the crawl space and closed the trapdoor behind him.

Only three minutes earlier, the robbers had entered the store. By prear-rangement, Tran's wife had given him a minute to make his preparations. So, the police had been called two minutes ago. Tran had to hurry to reconfigure the store. He didn't want to hint at his tactics or upset the fire marshal.

He'd shot all of the robbers from the front, so the killings were clearly in self-defense. The gang, of course, would swear vengeance. But Tran knew that if he could outlast the American army, he could outlast the Dream Warriors.

16 The Traveler's Delight Motel exploded into flames at four fifty-seven A.M. that Tuesday. The fire began with a great, crashing thunderclap that shattered every window in the structure. By concussion or panic, it dumped every scab out of bed and onto the floor.

Clutching meager possessions to their chests, men and women ran screaming from their rooms dressed only in their underwear and nightclothes. Barefoot and wailing, they fled across the parking lot.

Within seconds the entire southern wing of the motel was engulfed. Blue-yellow flames shot fifty feet into the air, illuminating a cloud of toxic black smoke.

Every piece of firefighting equipment in Elk River was on its way to the scene in minutes. The county's hazardous materials unit was summoned.

Shivering in the predawn chill, the replacement workers struggled into their clothes, watching the conflagration with awe. The miracle was that none of them had been killed, or even injured. Krieger confirmed this for the fire officials when he arrived and took a head count.

He wondered if the union had set the fire. He wondered, too, what had happened to Miss Mouthy in room 166. But he didn't say anything to anyone.

Since he was already up, Krieger got busy. He asked the scabs, "How many of you are ready to go to work?"

Ninety-four were. Out of a hundred.

Standing there in shock, burned out of their beds, not knowing what might happen next, ninety-four people still decided that they had to have these jobs.

Krieger thought maybe he had a thing or two to learn from Tony Hunt yet.

John and Jill spent the night in his living room, telling each other their life stories, starting small and working their way up to the important stuff.

John sat in his dad's old easy chair next to the fireplace. Jill was on the sofa. The only light in the room came from the embers of the fire that had been lighted hours ago. John didn't need the soft glow of the coals to know where Jill was. He'd stopped being sight-dependent a lifetime ago. He could smell her, hear her breathing, *feel* her presence and position.

He'd closed his eyes thirty minutes ago.

Jill asked John a question. "Didn't Tommy tell you anything about my dad?"

"No," John said.

She'd wondered about that. In fact, she'd gone so far as to think that maybe Tommy had hired her in the first place because her history meshed so well with that of John Fortunato. Like Tommy could get a lawyer and play Cupid for his "brother" John all at the same time. . . .

Jill said, "My father was killed in West Virginia when he tried to organize a group of coal miners."

"Was he a labor lawyer, too?"

"Yes, and before that he'd been a miner himself. That was why the mine owners all feared him: He could give the other men the idea that their own lives weren't hopeless, that they, too, could improve themselves." Jill probably didn't notice it herself, but John heard her slight Appalachian accent thicken appreciably. "People all across coal country, from Pennsylvania to Kentucky, took heart when Grady Baxter came to speak to them, told them how a union could improve their lot in life. And in a small way—for a group of people nobody ever gave a damn about—Daddy started rallying public opinion to the miners' cause. A professor from the University of Chicago even came to write a book about him and what he was doing."

"All of which made him a serious enemy of the mine owners," John said.

"Yes," she said flatly, her voice returning to normal. "My father's work

took him to West Virginia. A mining operation there was said to be forcing their men to work under horribly unsafe conditions. The mine owner
denied this vehemently. He said that all the trouble was being caused by
Bolshevik Communists and other outside agitators."

"Meaning your father?"

"Meaning my father. This bastard owner said his mines were safe, but
he wouldn't let anybody who didn't work for him inspect them. But
Daddy, being a former miner, wasn't afraid to have some union sympa-
thizers smuggle him down into the mines so he could see for himself what
conditions were."

"What went wrong?" John wanted to know.

Several moments passed before Jill could reply, and when she did her
voice was choked with grief for a man of whom she had no living memory.

"The way it was reconstructed—but couldn't be proved—was that the
owner had a spy, or spies, among the miners, and they found out what
Daddy was doing. Then, one evening, a farmer who was out in his field
saw Daddy's car pulled over on a country road—by the local sheriff."

Which gave John a very clear idea of why Jill Baxter hadn't turned his
photos over to Orville Leen when she'd had the chance and why she'd
been so outraged that the sheriff hadn't released Tommy.

"Daddy was taken away in the sheriff's car . . . and he was never seen
again."

"And the farmer who saw it happen," John asked, "was he bumped off
or bought off before he could testify in court?"

"Bought, with the bump undoubtedly implied," Jill said. "He soon
moved to a much bigger and nicer farm in Tennessee."

"And nobody ever found your father's body?"

"No . . . the conventional wisdom was that since Daddy had taken
such an interest in the condition of local mines, the sheriff had dropped
his body down an abandoned shaft."

John felt a chill go through him. He had more in common with this
woman than she could ever imagine.

Which was when Jill said, "Okay, John Fortunato, your turn to bare
your soul."

Where do I start? John wondered.

Maybe, he decided, with one of the hardest things he could ask her to
believe.

"You believe there are some things that just can't be explained?" he
asked Jill. "Not in any rational way."

"Like what? ESP?"

She'd said it jokingly, but she didn't hear him laugh.

"When my mom died," John said, "I wanted to be with her, and if I had to die to do it, well, that was okay with me. I was really young, and there was more comfort for me in the thought of being dead with my mom than alive without her. It was my Grandma Sophia who got me turned around. She said my mother would always be with me; her spirit would always be close to me. . . . And she said I had to stay right here and help take care of my dad."

Now it was John's turn to take a long moment of reflection.

"I took her words to heart, and that was when I started my night walks."

"Your what?" Jill asked.

"I told you my dad was blinded when my mom was killed?"

"Yes."

"Well, the way he got around the house was by memorizing where all the furniture was placed. So, in order to understand what he was going through, I thought I should practice doing the same thing. After Dad and Grandma and Tommy had gone to bed, I'd get up and carefully walk around with my eyes closed. Pretty soon, I had the layout of the whole house memorized and I could move around the house without using my eyes as easily as my dad got around."

"That was very compassionate of you," Jill said, "but anyone could learn to do that. What's so hard to believe?"

John said, "It's what happened next that might trip you up."

"What's that?" Jill asked hesitantly.

"One night when I was walking I *felt* my Grandpa Michelangelo enter the room."

"He lived with you, too?"

"He died before I was born."

Now John could feel her doubt, her sudden discomfort.

"If . . . if he was dead . . ." she began. Then the logical, legally trained mind of the lawyer took over, and Jill asked, "No, the question is, if he died before you were born, how did you know who it was?"

"I guess with ghosts you just know."

Okay, she thought, if he wanted to play it that way. "Were you frightened?"

"No, I never felt better in my life. He put his hand on my cheek and it was like being touched by an angel. For just an instant, I was completely at peace. I knew everything."

"What do you mean, you knew *everything*?" Jill asked uncertainly.

John sensed that he might lose her here, but he pushed on.

"Everything," he answered. "It was like being able to see with God's eyes. I knew that my grandfather had come for my grandmother. I knew that she had just died, but it was all right because she'd be going with Grandpa. The sense of omniscience passed quickly . . . but ever since that night I've been able to *see* in the dark."

He gave Jill an opportunity to respond, but she remained silent.

"Look, I know that sounds crazy," John said. "And when I came home from Vietnam, I had a lot of things to work through. A lot of guys did. Anyway, I went to see a shrink, Dr. Maryanne Risom, a former nurse with a field hospital unit in Korea. She'd taken her own hike through hell; she was someone a grunt could open up to. So along with a lot of other stuff, I told her all about this, too."

Jill asked, "And what did she—"

John cut her off in mid-sentence. Jill felt the flow of their rapport stop as if someone had stepped between them, and the word John spoke chilled her to her marrow.

"Tommy?" he said.

John wasn't talking about Tommy Boyle; he was talking *to* him.

"Oh, God, Tommy!" John cried with anguish. *"Now?"*

Jill strained her eyes against the slowly rising curtain of dawn to see if Tommy Boyle had somehow slipped into the room. All she saw was John sitting in the chair across from her. With his eyes closed.

Despite a sense of overwhelming dread, she couldn't stop herself from speaking.

"Is he dead?" she whispered.

John's eyes opened. And filled with tears.

17 The town was going to hell faster than Orville Leen ever would have believed possible. The sheriff hadn't had three hours of sleep before he was pulled out of bed.

And already he'd been to a burned-out motel that the fire marshal said was arson plain and simple.

And now he was looking at a bloodstained sheet that they told him covered the remains of Tommy Boyle.

Forcing himself to do his job, Leen squatted down, lifted the sheet, and saw that it was Boyle, all right. "Shit," the sheriff said.

Letting the sheet fall back into place, he rose and turned to Chief Deputy Narder, who was in charge of the crime scene. "Who found him, Ron?"

"Schoolteacher out walking her doggie." Narder pointed to a drying puddle of vomit a few feet away. "Apparently, she likes an early breakfast."

"What's this teacher's name?"

"Alice Wills."

The chief deputy saw the sheriff's face cramp up.

"What, you know her?"

"Yeah," Leen sighed. "You got her waiting for me in one of the cars?"

The whole street was blocked off, a half dozen patrol units sat parked at random angles on the asphalt and the sidewalk.

"No, she looked like she was about to faint. I offered to have Martinson take her to the ER, but she said she preferred to go home. She'll be there when you want her."

"Any physical evidence?"

"We found a shell casing. Nine-millimeter." Narder said it deadpan, but Leen felt the acid building in the pit of his stomach. All hell was about to bust loose, he just knew.

"You slept yet, Ronnie?" the sheriff asked.

"No."

"You got any energy left in you?"

"Some," the deputy said. "Not a lot."

"Walk me to my car."

As the two men headed to the sheriff's car, Orville Leen was thinking hard, as hard as his tired mind would allow. The murder weapon had fired a nine-millimeter round. As of three years ago, all Sheriff's Department deputies carried Berettas as their standard sidearms. The Beretta was a nine-millimeter weapon.

Billy Shelton carried a Beretta. Would that dumbass actually use his duty weapon to commit murder?

Boy, Leen thought, you talk about your self-answering questions. Damn right, Billy would do it. Especially after his wife had told him to get lost, she liked Tommy Boyle better. And rung his bell with a whiskey bottle to boot.

Both law officers got into the sheriff's personal car.

"You know what I want, don't you?" Leen asked.

"Arrest him, or just bring him in?"

"Tell him he's relieved of duty. For not being available when he was supposed to be. Then tell him to stop in and see me this afternoon."

"Relieve him of his gun and badge, too?"

Leen answered that one with a look.

"I'll get the gun to the lab first thing," the chief deputy said. "I'll take a couple backups with me, too."

"I'd be disappointed in your judgment if you didn't, Ron."

It fell to the sheriff to inform the next of kin. He didn't see John Fortunato taking the news too well, either. Which might be another goddamn problem.

Like any good cop, Orville Leen knew all the important people in his jurisdiction. That "everybody gets the same treatment" stuff might sound good on the TV news, but it was so much BS. Every cop in America knew you didn't fuck with the people who had money, power, or connections. If you did, you were apt to have a short, miserable career in law enforcement.

Cruising slowly through Elk River, the sheriff wondered how many of the houses he passed had been built by Fortunato-Boyle Contractors. Half? More than a quarter, for sure.

Michelangelo Fortunato, everyone knew, had built the Church of the Resurrection, and the story was the design had come to the old man straight from God. Never used a blueprint.

Of course, that was just the kind of colorful horseshit people liked to spread to make a neighbor seem like a real character. Which, by association, made the place where they lived much more interesting.

Still, the sheriff had to admit, it was as beautiful a church as you'd ever care to look at. Lovely enough to make that story about Michelangelo Fortunato last. More than lovely enough that plenty of people in town had wanted the man who'd built God's house to build theirs, too.

So, right from the get-go, John Fortunato had had local prominence and money behind him. Then he went out and made a name for himself.

Leen had made it a point to buy those picture books that had made Fortunato famous all the way across the country. The photos in his first book, *Moments of Truth*, were genuinely scream-for-Jesus scary.

That one on the cover, a goddamn lion bearing right down on him, charging full out, lips pulled back, fangs a-slobber—it made Leen go cold just to think about it. Now, a man who could calmly crouch down and take a picture of that motherfucker, all the while trusting that the guy behind him with the rifle wouldn't miss—or run—well, that man had to have a suicidal disregard for life and limb.

And that was just one of the crazy, gut-wrenching images that filled the book.

Then there was the fact he'd served in Vietnam. Which by itself didn't mean anything, but you put it together with some of those pictures, and who knew what Fortunato had done, or had happened to him, over there?

The biggest problem Leen faced, though, was that it looked like he himself might have had something to do with Tommy Boyle's death. He knew, and would swear to God, that he hadn't. But he couldn't deny the way it appeared.

He, Orville Leen, had refused to let Tommy go when there were still plenty of people milling around. Then he, Orville Leen, just happened to change his mind and let Tommy out in the wee hours when everybody'd gone home. Then Boyle just happened to get drilled with a nine-millimeter slug.

Sweet Jesus! He wouldn't blame Fortunato if he thought Leen had pulled the trigger himself.

The sheriff drove along Fifth Street to the point where it curved and for one block the name changed to Via Michelangelo.

Leen knew that old man Fortunato had been brought over from Italy with the customary promise of a house, and then had figuratively given the back of his hand to the town fathers by choosing to live among the Hardwoods rather than with his rich sponsors on the Presidential side of town. Still, he'd picked one fine site, and today the Fortunato house sat in what amounted to a private park, the only address on the street.

Leen stopped out front. The first rays of the sun were warming the day but not his mood. The sheriff got out of the car and hid his black eyes behind sunglasses. He crossed the front yard, climbed the steps, and knocked on the door. Tommy Boyle's lady lawyer answered it.

She looked at him like he was something you'd kill with bug spray.

"Is Mr. John Fortunato at home?" Leen asked flatly.

"No." Her tone was even more devoid of emotion than his. "He went to the morgue to claim Tommy's body."

The sheriff's jaw dropped.

"How'd he know?"

"Ask him," Jill Baxter said.

Then she closed the door on the sheriff.

18 Fifteen feet below the Fortunato house, in HQ, that Tuesday morning, Darien Givens and Ty Daulton knew nothing of what had happened above. The tall black man and the short white boy had spent the night touring the tunnel system.

And each of them was delighted to have discovered the other.

They ate MREs—meals ready to eat—by the light of an electric lantern. Ty was having the time of his life. As the boy swallowed the last of his prepackaged food, his nose wrinkled. "You know, it *smells* down here."

Darien laughed. "My man, this is a lady's boudoir compared to tunnels in the Nam."

"Well, why's it smell, here or there?"

"You tell me."

Ty thought a moment.

"Well, first of all," he said, "being underground, the air can't circulate much. No breeze."

"That's for sure."

"Just those small ventilation shafts you showed me."

"That's right, you only got so much air down here. You have an explosion, it can suck up all the oxygen in a section of tunnel. Means a body can suffocate even if he don't get fragged."

"That sounds awful," Ty said.

"Bet your skinny white ass it's awful."

Ty grinned. Darien's calling *anyone* skinny was a laugh.

"What else'd make it smell?" Darien asked.

"Farts." Ty smirked.

"You better not," Darien said. But he grinned, too.

"BO," Ty added.

"Yeah, well, that can't be helped."

"So, if you had a whole bunch of people . . ." Ty shrugged.

"You gettin' the picture now. War don't stop for no hot showers."

Then Darien told him about other things. Piss pots and shit jars that got buried only when they were full. Corpses and amputated limbs the VC plastered into the walls to throw off American body counts. The tangy funk of two desperate comrades tearing off one last piece of ass.

"There were women in the tunnels?" Ty asked, amazed.

"Women, men, kids, grannies, you name it. The dinks did everything down there. Even put on musicals you ain't never gonna see on Broadway."

Darien rambled on about the things he'd seen as a VC prisoner. To his own ears, he started to sound like some old fool, but this little white boy gobbled up every morsel like he was being fed pudding with a spoon.

Seeing how Ty paid attention to him made Darien feel proud. He'd been a righteous grunt. Had the medals to prove it, too.

"I best shut up," he said at last, "before I use up all our air."

Ty sensed the change in mood. "Can I sleep here?" he asked.

"Sure," Darien said, "I do it all the time."

He took two sleeping bags out of a footlocker and handed one to Ty.

"Zip yourself in good, conserve your body heat. These tunnels stay a constant fifty-eight degrees."

"Air-conditioned," Ty said.

He told Darien thanks for everything.

"My pleasure," Darien replied, turning off the lantern. "It's about time this outfit had some new blood."

19 Krieger stepped through the front door of Elk River Community Hospital, on his way to see Hunt, and saw someone else who made him stop dead in his tracks.

It was the guy from the other night. The one who took his picture. Krieger was sure of it. The guy stepped into an elevator and was gone.

Krieger hurried over to the elevator bank. The car he wanted was going down. There was a directory on the wall. It listed only one level below the ground floor. There were three departments down there: Maintenance, Radiology, and Morgue.

A nurse, tough-looking and gray-haired, came over and pushed the up button. She gave Krieger a glance, but his size and appearance didn't make her bat an eye. She just tapped her toe and waited for an elevator.

Krieger decided his man hadn't dropped in to turn a wrench or get an X ray. The guy had come to visit the morgue. Krieger wondered if he could get any information out of the biddy standing next to him.

"Pardon me," he said. He put a lot of honey into it. He knew what kind of voice he had. What kind of face, too.

The nurse looked at Krieger again, not exactly startled, but surprised. Like she wanted to say: *Hey, where's the ventriloquist?*

Krieger went on. "Did you see the man who just got on the elevator going down?"

"Yes," she said, fascinated. Wondering how he did it.

"Do you know who he was?"

"Yes."

Now she was trying to improve *her* voice, rounding out the tones.

"Can you tell me his name?"

"I could."

Coy. She wanted to keep him talking.

"Would you? I think he's an old friend, but if he's going to the morgue, I wouldn't want to bother him."

"What's your friend's name?"

"Elbert Niles." Not bad for right off the top of his head.

"Wasn't him. That man's name is John Fortunato."

"You sure?"

"I've known John since he had his tonsils out."

Gotcha, Krieger exulted to himself. He had the sonofabitch's name, and now he'd find him. Outwardly, he just held up his hands and shrugged.

The woman frowned, like she'd been cheated.

"You were right about one thing," the nurse said.

She didn't say what. It was a tease to draw him out. Krieger played along.

"What's that?"

"He is on his way to the morgue."

"Oh, yeah," Krieger said casually. "Who died?"

"His uncle," she whispered, like she was letting him in on a big secret. "Tommy Boyle."

"Tommy Boyle was that guy's uncle?"

"He was murdered. Shot in the head," she added.

Probably wasn't a secret in the place safe from this broad, Krieger thought, but he just nodded.

"You don't seem too shocked." The nurse looked disappointed.

"I'm not," Krieger replied with his wonderful voice.

Krieger walked into Hunt's private room as a young doctor finished taping a dressing to Hunt's left shoulder. Hunt's injury had turned out to be minor, but for appearance's sake he'd elected to spend the night in the hospital. The doctor told Hunt to limit his movement with the wounded shoulder, then he left.

"Why are you here?" Hunt asked Krieger. He never liked it when Krieger showed up unexpectedly. The brute was showing increasing signs of thinking for himself—and no good could come of that.

"Just came to see how you are," Krieger replied. "And to give you some news."

Hunt waited.

Krieger found that he didn't mind the silent treatment this time. It was an old trick by now.

"Tommy Boyle's dead," Krieger said. "How about that?"

Hunt finally responded to something. "Did you kill him?"

Krieger smirked.

"Funny, I was gonna ask you the same thing."

The morgue attendant opened a compartment and rolled out the platform. On it was a sheet-covered body. The attendant turned to John.

"We already have a positive identification," he said. Then he warned, "I'm afraid his appearance is rather shocking."

John stepped past the man and pulled back the sheet. The round had caught Tommy right between his eyebrows. The exit wound was a large hole in the crown of Tommy's skull. That meant the shot had been fired upward. Someone short? Or someone sitting? A drive-by.

"Are you okay?" the attendant asked.

John said nothing.

He stared down at Tommy's body. This would be a lot easier, Tommy, he thought, if you'd told me who did it. As long as you were stopping by to say you were dead.

He replaced the sheet, and the attendant rolled the corpse back into its compartment. John signed a form to claim the body, left the hospital, and headed for his church.

Now he had two candles to light.

20 "Johnny Fortune, meet Gil Velez," Doolan said.

John looked up from his cot in First Squad's hootch. Doolan had another sergeant with him, a little Tex-Mex guy from the Big Red One.

John was annoyed because he'd been reading a typewritten letter from his dad. He'd read it word-for-word three times and hadn't drained the last ounce of home from it yet. But he refolded it and put it in his pocket. He got up and shook the hand Velez extended to him.

Velez stood no taller than Doolan. He wore a bush hat instead of a helmet, and his uniform had a badge on it with a gray rat holding a .38 and a flashlight. Beneath the rat was a motto in Latin: Non Gratum Anus Rodentum.

" 'Not worth a rat's ass,' " Velez said. "Motto of the tunnel rats. I heard about you fakin' that dink outta his hole and then goin' in yourself. Nice work."

The tunnel rat paused so John could thank him for the compliment. He didn't.

"So, anyway, I came 'round to see if you'd like to take some tests. If you pass, you could get sent to the army's Tunnels, Mines, and Booby Traps School. Become a real tunnel rat."

The one place John wanted the army to send him was home. ASAP.

"Thanks, Sarge, but I only went down that hole because I was afraid the little people might have some more snipers in there who'd pop up and ding our asses—before we could call in one of you guys."

It was the same lie he'd told Doolan. John had really gone into that tunnel because he felt safer in the dark. Where nobody was going to sneak up on him.

Velez took the rejection with a shrug. "Suit yourself. We all gotta kill dinks our own way."

He started to leave, but when he got to the hootch's doorway, he turned.

"You got a point, though: us rats can't be everywhere. So, maybe you'd like the short course, just in case you gotta go down another hole."

What the fuck, John thought. He shrugged an okay.

"You mind if I sit in on this, Sarge?" Doolan asked Velez.

"No problem, bro. I heard you went down that hole, too."

"Yeah," Doolan replied.

He shot a glance at Johnny Fortune.

"And I'd like to know just how some-a this shit gets accomplished."

In fact, Doolan was dying to know how Johnny Fortune had done it. How had he shot the dink sniper who'd had them pinned down, and how had he known the SOB was waiting for them in that hole? He'd been trying to figure it out for weeks and it was driving him crazy. So one night when they were back in the field, on a night ambush in the same foxhole, he came right out and asked.

John wasn't surprised by Doolan's questions. He'd felt them building up inside his platoon sergeant. And since Doolan was teaching him how to be a first-class boonie rat, and was largely keeping him alive, he figured he'd better answer him the only way he could.

"I've got instinct," John said, not telling Doolan the source of that instinct.

He'd expected an argument, but he could almost hear Doolan smile.

"Sonofabitch," Doolan murmured. "Instinct. Only what you're not saying is yours has been sighted in."

In those few words, Doolan made the intuitive jump that explained the situation to John better than he'd ever explained it to himself.

"Well, I've got instinct, too, bro," Doolan told him. "And you just watch how I improve my aim."

John didn't know how Doolan was going to do that, but he soon learned.

. . .

GIs used flashlights when they traversed tunnels. The VC found their way with candles. When John and Doolan went down their next hole, three days later, they took a single penlight, and that was for emergency use only.

Their only weapons were knives and .38s. Doolan pulled rank and crawled point. He was eager to test himself and his instincts.

Since Charlie booby-trapped his tunnels with everything from explosives to punji sticks to snakes, it could be quite a test. Especially when you knew that, even using lights, half of all booby traps were found by tripping them.

John crawled slack. He maintained an interval of five meters behind Doolan without conscious effort. Several minutes later John felt his platoon sergeant stop. He waited. Waited some more. Until he realized Doolan was waiting for him. He crept forward.

The tunnel ended a foot in front of Doolan's nose, but that wasn't why he waited so patiently. The reason was that they had company.

Among the foul stew of tunnel odors, John could smell someone below them. Doolan had his fingertips on a trapdoor leading down to another level, and just inches away someone waited as patiently and silently as they did.

The thing was, that someone didn't smell Vietnamese. Unless the VC were getting into Afro-Sheen.

John stuck his face forward over Doolan's shoulder; Doolan felt him exhale. He was whistling, oh so gently, just breathing music out into the darkness.

"Sweet Georgia Brown." Ben Bernie.

Doolan didn't know whether to laugh or scream. Then the someone below whistled back.

"My Girl." The Temptations.

Doolan figured it was his turn.

"Love Me Tender."

From below, an American voice spoke up.

"Presley? You gotta be a white boy."

John and Doolan led Sp4 Darien Givens, all six-foot-five of him, out of the tunnel. Darien brought with him two clavicles that had been broken and had subsequently healed at horrifying angles.

He also had nine shriveled Vietnamese ears.

21 The pain in Deputy Billy Shelton's head, that Tuesday, throbbed in counterpoint to the insistent knock at his door. Knock—throb, knock—throb, knock—knock—knock, throb—throb—throb. The echo was enough to kill him.

"All right, already, goddamnit!" he yelled.

The effect of his own shout was so painful he almost blacked out. His head started to spin.

Knock—knock—knock! Throb—throb—throb!

Billy lurched from his sofa, in T-shirt and BVDs, animated by the desire to break the neck of whatever sorry sonofabitch was at his door torturing him.

He flung the door open and saw Ron Narder and two third-watch guys whose names he couldn't remember to save his life. They stared at him, not as friends, or even colleagues, but across the cold-eyed chasm of Us versus Them.

"Quite a goose egg you got there, Billy-boy," Narder said. "Looks like you're growin' a baseball outta your head."

Billy's hair had been shaved and his lump stitched. He'd removed the bandage because the adhesive made his skin itch.

"You look like fucking Rocky Raccoon yourself," Billy snarled. Both of Narder's eyes had blackened by this time.

Billy didn't care if Narder was the chief deputy. Today, he wasn't going to take shit off *anyone*.

"The sheriff sent us for your badge and your gun," Narder said bluntly.

"What!" Billy exclaimed.

Too loud again. He started to sway. Narder took his arm and sat him down on the sofa hard enough to make him cry out. Then Narder crouched down right in front of Billy's nose. The other two stayed on their feet flanking him.

"You're suspended for dereliction of duty, Billy. We had a riot on our hands last night, and you were supposed to be at the sheriff's side."

"You know where I was," Billy said.

Narder nodded. "Where you weren't supposed to be. And see what happened."

Billy thought that the bastard shouldn't be talking to him this way. He wasn't some goddamned lowlife.

"You do anything else last night you weren't supposed to do, Billy?" Narder asked.

That's when Billy finally understood. It'd taken him a while because of the nuclear war being fought inside his skull, but when he did it made him smile.

"Like kill that miserable prick Tommy Boyle?" he asked.

Now Narder's eyes got really cold.

"You want to make a statement, Billy?" he asked softly.

"Yeah," Billy said. "I'm glad he's dead."

Narder was reaching for the cuffs when Billy added, "But I ain't saying I did it."

Narder backed off with the cuffs.

"Are you saying you didn't?"

Billy smiled. "Why don't you prove me innocent?"

"If you didn't kill him, how do you know he's dead?"

"My loving wife called me and accused me of doing the deed. . . . That could be *one* way I know."

Billy was fucking with the chief deputy. Narder wanted to take Billy in and bounce him around. There was nobody he hated worse than a bad cop.

But Leen hadn't told him to bounce Billy around. So he'd get Billy's gun, take it to the lab, and if Billy turned out to be the shooter, he'd make sure he was in on the arrest.

"Let me have your badge and your duty weapon, Billy."

Narder thought that should have made Billy nervous, but the asshole just grinned and led them to a locked gun cabinet in his bedroom. He opened it to reveal six neatly racked weapons: a shotgun, a deer rifle, a derringer, an antique Colt revolver, and *two* Berettas.

Billy said, "Now, let's see . . . which one is it belongs to the department?"

"We can check the serial number," Narder answered.

Billy took the lower Beretta off its pegs and gently handed it butt-first to Narder.

"There you go, Chief Deputy. Lucky for me I have a backup weapon, huh?" Billy handed his badge over, too.

Narder said harshly, "The sheriff said you be sure to see him this afternoon."

"Sure," Billy answered. "Right after I get my beauty rest."

When Ron Narder got home Tuesday afternoon he was bone-tired—and almost as disgusted with life as he had been the time he arrested the choirmaster at the First Gospel Church for trying to get under his soprano's robes. His mood wasn't brightened when he saw his father and his Aunt Martha standing with his wife, Clare, in his kitchen.

"Dad, Aunt Martha," he greeted the visitors.

His father, a retiree from Pentronics Systems and a dyed-in-the-wool union man, disregarded the social graces and narrowed his eyes at his son.

"You know about Tommy's murder?" he asked.

The chief deputy nodded, not surprised that the crime was common knowledge already. "I was at the scene," Ron said.

"And have you arrested that bastard Hunt yet?" the old man demanded harshly.

"We don't have a suspect at this time," the chief deputy answered evenly. No way was he going to tell them about Billy Shelton. Not until he had proof.

The old man gave a bitter laugh and shook his head. Then he hugged Aunt Martha and Clare and said he had to be going. He didn't have another word for his son.

Aunt Martha hugged Ron and said she knew he'd do his best. This was a sincere expression of faith for a woman whose husband and two sons were on the picket line. Then she left, too—with three of the five bags of groceries that had been sitting on the kitchen counter.

Ron walked over to one of the remaining bags and plucked the receipt from it. The chief deputy thought it was a goddamn crime what it cost to eat these days. He dropped into a chair and rubbed his tired face.

"They needed help, Ronnie," his wife explained simply. "They didn't have anything to eat at their house."

"You did the right thing, Clare. Family takes care of its own."

"Dad cashed in one of his CDs to give Aunt Martha and Uncle Milt." Clare took her husband's hands and looked with concern into his battered, bloodshot eyes. Then she gently stroked the bruised skin on his face. "He'd do the same thing for us if we ever needed it."

Ron Narder rose and kissed his wife.

"I've got to get some sleep," he told her.

"Dad's just worried about what'll happen to everybody now that Tommy's dead. So am I, if you want the truth. But I'll talk to him. Tell him you won't let anybody get away with murder."

The chief deputy's sigh carried more than the weight of fatigue.

"You think he'd know that without being told."

Jill Baxter sat at Tommy Boyle's desk at Local 274. She was about to call Marty McCreery at home when Vic Kushner barged in.

He said, "You're fired, get out."

Jill calmly told the general counsel of the Brotherhood of Manufacturing Workers, International, to get lost. Then she tapped out the number for her call.

Kushner was a graduate of Columbia Law School and sixty-two years old, but he was a large man who still thought of himself as a no-bullshit New York kind of guy.

He reached over to grab the phone.

He got it, too. Jill popped up like she was on springs and jammed the receiver smack into his brow. There was an awful crunch, skin split, Kushner's right eyebrow divided into two parts, and blood spurted. Pain made the man's knees go weak.

A voice squawked out of the phone in Jill's hand. She brought the receiver back to her ear.

"Sorry," she said tersely, "I'll call you back in a minute."

She hung up as Kushner sat down heavily in the guest chair. While she waited for him to collect himself, Jill listened to the roar in her ears and felt her cheeks burn. Finally, Kushner glared at her from under the handkerchief he'd pressed to his wounded head. He's gotten off too easily, Jill thought. He's going to try intimidating me again.

"You don't know how much trouble you just bought yourself," Kushner muttered hoarsely.

Jill didn't say a word. She just picked up a letter opener from Tommy's desk. At the thought of what she might do with that, Kushner blanched.

Jill said, "Tell me, Counselor, how'd you know Tommy Boyle was dead? You wouldn't be here unless you knew."

A defensive look appeared below the hankie.

"A little birdie tell you?"

Kushner remained mute.

"You got a pipeline into the cops?"

That brought a reptilian flicker to the attorney's eyes.

"I heard about the death threat Tommy received," Jill continued. "You know, fall into line, pay your dues, et cetera, or else. Was that your idea?"

Kushner pushed himself to his feet. Jill stood, too. She twirled the point of the letter opener against the palm of her left hand.

Kushner edged toward the door. "You don't know who you're fucking with," he said.

Jill shrugged. "Thanks for stopping in, Counselor, but we won't be needing any help from the international."

John was the next person to visit Jill. He had to wipe off the bloodied guest chair before he could use it. She told him what had happened.

"The bastard just tried to steamroll me," Jill said.

He could see a vein throb in her throat.

"It never occurred to him I wouldn't submit. He was big. He was strong. He was a *man*. God, I hate bullies."

"Me, too," John said.

She looked at him and remembered he had troubles of his own. She slumped in her seat. Still, she had to ask.

"Why do they do it? Why do some people always have to behave that way?" If it were up to her, any form of bullying would be a capital offense.

John shook his head. "I don't know."

"Did you see Tommy?" Jill asked.

"Yeah."

"You want to talk about it?"

"I think we better," John said. "Let's get out of here."

22 They went for a walk in Riverfront Park. The day was mild, but the sky had gone overcast. They had the pathway along the river to themselves, and they walked all the way to the town marina before either said a word.

"Tommy was shot," John told Jill.

That's right, Jill thought, Tommy's ghost—or whatever the hell it was; she still couldn't understand it even though she'd been there—hadn't specified the cause of death.

"Somebody shot him in the head," John added.

Jill took his arm and said, "I'm sorry."

He nodded. They reached a park bench and sat down.

Jill chewed her lip. "How did you know to go to the morgue? That he hadn't just been dumped somewhere?"

Somewhere he'd never be found, John thought. Like your father.

"I just knew," he said.

And how could she respond to that? That people didn't know things without an empirical reason? She'd already seen that idea shot to hell.

"You know who did it?" Jill asked.

"No."

They lapsed into silence, each looking for solace, then Jill looked down and saw that they were holding hands. She couldn't say who had reached out for the other.

She said, "I had an idea when I was alone at your house this morning. It sounds crazy to say it out loud, but . . ."

"But a lot of things seem crazy around here," he suggested.

"Yeah. Crazy but inarguable. I tell myself certain things can't happen, and then they do."

"What's your idea?"

"You remember how you told me that your grandfather touched you that night and you knew everything?"

John nodded.

"Well, maybe that's how you *know* things. How you *feel* your way around in the dark. Maybe your grandfather gave you a gift. That *is* a crazy idea, isn't it?"

John gave her a searching look before he replied.

"I don't know. But it's the same idea my shrink, Dr. Risom, had when I told her that story. She said that extrasensory abilities were a matter of dispute, but if they existed, what could be more elegant than a supernatural source?" He smiled briefly. "I've been thinking about that. Maybe you read my mind."

"That's—"

"Crazy?" John finished.

Not wanting to chase after ghosts any further, Jill changed the subject. "Sheriff Leen came by your house, looking for you."

"He was still out when I got to the sheriff's station. But I got the bare-bones details from the desk sergeant. Tommy was released on a recognizance bond at four fifteen A.M. His body was found on the sidewalk a block away from his town house about an hour later by a woman walking her dog."

Jill's eyes filled with suspicion.

"What?" John asked.

Jill took her hand from his. She clasped it to her other hand in her lap. John waited for her to work out what she had to say.

"I know I'm hardly unbiased here," she said, shaking her head, "but this sounds just too much like what happened to my father."

"You think Leen killed Tommy?" John asked.

"Think about it," she replied. "He refused to let me post bail for him when you and I could have taken him home. Then he lets Tommy out in the middle of the night? When there's not a witness in sight. . . . There wasn't any witness, was there?"

John shook his head. "Not that the sergeant said."

"So no one was around. What better time to kill someone? And who arranged this convenient-to-kill release time? There could be only one man. I'd like to hear Sheriff Leen's explanation for what he did."

The look on John's face said he'd like to hear it, too. But he remembered that Jill, as she'd said, was not objective about such matters.

"What would the sheriff's motive be?" he asked.

"Money. Same as every other crooked cop."

"Who's paying him? Hunt?"

"Sure, why not? Murder's the ultimate bargaining tool. Kill Tommy and you kill the strike."

"What about Billy Shelton?"

"The deputy?"

"Deputy and cuckold."

A memory jostled to the front of Jill's mind. "That was what that crack was about? The one Tommy made at your house. About the deputy needing a woman to help him get dressed."

John nodded. "Everybody in town knows Tommy and Billy's wife had a thing going."

"Infidelity and public humiliation. Yeah, that could lead to murder," Jill admitted.

John leaned forward, thinking, then turned his head to Jill. "As a deputy, Billy also could've found out when Tommy was going to be released, no problem."

Jill conceded that, too, but there was less emotional satisfaction for her in thinking of Billy as the killer.

"Then you also have to consider Bobbi Sharpes," John said.

"Who?" Jill's brow furrowed.

"Billy's wife."

"But I thought she and Tommy were lovers."

"They were until a month or so ago. Tommy wanted Bobbi to divorce Billy and marry him. She refused; he broke it off. Said it was all or nothing."

"Tommy told you this?"

"Yes. He also told me she'd been after him lately to come back to her."

"He wasn't interested?"

"He was making a point of being seen with other women by then."

"Rubbing her nose in it," Jill said.

"And Bobbi can be meaner than Billy. More dangerous, too."

"So, where do we start?"

"Are you staying?" John asked.

Jill sighed and stared out at the river.

"This is a hell of a situation . . . and I know that with Tommy gone

I'll probably have nothing but grief from Marty McCreery and the other officials at the local . . . but, goddamnit, I've got a job to do here."

She stood up, put her hands on her hips, looked down at John, and defied him to say otherwise.

John didn't contradict her. He wanted her to stay. But he was sure that part of her resolve was rooted in the fact that she wanted the search for Tommy's killer to lead to the sheriff, and she wanted to be on hand if it did. And, just possibly, John thought, she didn't want to see him disappear from her life so soon.

John stood up. He wanted to take her hand again, but he didn't. He just started walking back the way they'd come, and she fell into step with him.

"You think maybe you can get a line on the labor angle?" he asked.

"What do you mean?"

"Well, you said it. You kill Tommy, you kill the strike. Seems to me Hunt wasn't the only one who wanted the strike ended. The international union did, too, and Marty McCreery said Tommy had received a threat from those quarters, remember?" He mimicked a gun with his fingers, as the labor official had.

"Oh, my God, you're right."

John shook his head. "Poor Tommy," he said, "so many enemies."

Now Jill took his hand.

"We stick it out, whatever it takes?" she asked.

He gave her the saddest smile she'd ever seen, and nodded.

"Whatever it takes."

23   That same afternoon, Sheriff Orville Leen sat with Alice Wills in her living room. Leen kept his sunglasses on to cover his black eyes. Alice was the schoolteacher who'd found Tommy Boyle's body early that morning.

"Well, of course, I called Bobbi Sharpes, Orville," Alice told the sheriff.

Leen and Alice had once been classmates about a hundred years ago, but he still didn't like her addressing him by his given name.

She hadn't seemed to age a day since they'd been in school, but that was only because she'd been born middle-aged. She still had the same frosted brunette hair, pinched mouth, and clumsily rouged cheeks. Even as a child, she'd been known as Alice "the Pill" Wills.

She stroked the Dalmatian pup in her lap and continued. "I was out so early walking Albert because I had an appointment to have Bobbi clean my teeth before school started. You think I was going to wait until she had a dental probe in my mouth and say, 'Oh, by the way, I saw your boyfriend this morning. He was lying dead on the sidewalk.'"

Bobbi Sharpes was Alice's dental hygienist. Alice had called Bobbi to tell her she'd be unable to make her appointment . . . and to blab about the murder. Bobbi had called Billy.

Which gave Billy all the cover he needed for knowing Tommy Boyle had been murdered.

Which didn't mean for a second that Billy couldn't also have known Tommy was dead because he'd pulled the trigger. But along with the deputy's goddamn second Beretta, it muddied the water.

Alice continued her story. "I remembered to call Bobbi when I was brushing my teeth because . . ."

Leen remembered the vomit at the scene.

". . . because they needed to be brushed."

The sheriff sighed. "How many others did you tell?"

"Well, I don't see—"

Leen lost all patience.

"Goddamnit, Alice, how many?" he roared.

"Eight," she squeaked, shrinking into her chair. "I had to call school to say I wouldn't be in; I had to give them a reason. And my mother. And I have a friend who—"

Leen raised his hand to stop her. He took a deep breath to calm himself.

"Did you see anything to suggest who might have shot Mr. Boyle?" he asked.

Alice shook her head nervously and cradled the pup.

"But if I think of something, do you want me to call you?"

"That'd be nice, Alice," the sheriff said. "That'd be just peachy."

Leen stood in front of the Wills house and did his best to ease the steel band that kept tightening around his head.

His men had canvassed the neighborhood where Tommy Boyle had been shot. Nobody had seen anything. Several people had heard the fatal shot, but none had gotten up to find out what had happened. A single shot always went uninvestigated, especially at night. It fell under the heading of "What do you know, I ignored it and it went away."

Leen's headache was getting worse.

He'd *fucked* himself when he hadn't let Boyle's lawyer bail him out right away. And then to order Boyle's release in the dead of the night. God Almighty!

There had to be some way out of this for him, but he was damned if he could see how. Shit. Maybe he'd just go challenge Billy to a showdown. Loser could take the rap for Tommy Boyle's homicide. Leen heaved a sigh and got into his car.

He felt anything but confident in his judgment at that moment, but he thought he was going to have to reinstate Billy. That might look like a cover-up, but he really had no choice.

If he didn't reinstate him, Billy would know he was gunning for him. He'd clam up. Or maybe show an ounce of brains and hire a lawyer. Or just leave town altogether.

On the other hand, if he brought Billy back on board, he could keep an eye on him. He could get the boy looking into whether that shit Hunt was behind the killing.

Wouldn't that be great, Leen thought, if Hunt did it? Because if it turned out that Billy, or *any* of the sheriff's deputies, was involved, that'd make it look like he was, too.

The more he gnawed at it, the more he liked Hunt for the crime.

"It wasn't me, Sheriff," Tony Hunt said.

He'd walked into Orville Leen's office unannounced and sat down like he held title on the building. Like he owned all of Elk River.

"What wasn't you, Mr. Hunt?" the sheriff asked.

"I didn't kill Tommy Boyle—or have him killed."

Leen sighed to himself. Aloud, he asked, "How do you know about Mr. Boyle's death?"

"From an associate who visited me at the hospital. He heard from a nurse that Boyle had been taken to the morgue there."

"Yes, he was," Leen said, massaging his temples, "and that morgue is doing a booming business lately. Four people, all connected with you in some way."

"That's why I felt we should talk, Sheriff. Understand each other."

"What do we have to understand?"

"That not only didn't I kill Tommy Boyle, but you're not going to pin his death on me, either."

Leen's face went stony.

Hunt didn't seem to care. He added, "I don't have time for distractions."

Leen did his best to keep control. It wasn't easy.

"Mr. Hunt," he said slowly, "you want to be real careful talking that way to a man in my position."

Hunt didn't back down. He'd come to play hardball.

"Sheriff, let me suggest that our interests converge."

"I seriously doubt that."

"You be the judge then. My associate—"

"Name?"

"Krieger. He told me an interesting story at the hospital."

Leen waited for it.

Hunt continued, his expression unchanged. "He saw one of your deputies spying on Tommy Boyle as he and a woman groped each other on the front porch of her house yesterday. Krieger couldn't hear what Boyle and the woman were saying, but words were hardly necessary. The woman wrapped herself around Boyle, and he carried her into the house."

The sheriff's heart sank. It was all he could do to ask the obvious question.

"What was this Krieger doing there?"

"Watching Boyle."

"For you?"

"On his own initiative. You see the possibilities, Sheriff? Your man, a woman, and Tommy Boyle. Of course, cops cover up for each other, don't they?" He sat forward on his chair with a hard look. "I just wanted to tell you personally—if you need a patsy, it won't be me."

"Why is it, Mr. Hunt, that an old football saying just popped into my head? I'm sure you know the one: The best defense is a good offense. Makes me wonder all the more if you didn't have something to do with Tommy Boyle's death."

Hunt smiled coldly. "Wonder all you want, Sheriff. Just so you know, you come at me, I'll come right back at you. And don't think your deputy hasn't left you vulnerable to a charge of covering up for a killer in your own department."

The two men stared at each other. Finally, Hunt broke the silence. Offered an olive branch.

"The thing is, Sheriff, we can be stuck with one another . . . or we can live with one another and get on about our business."

Hunt stood up. He extended his hand. Leen didn't take it. Unlike Hunt, he could see that John Fortunato was about to open his office door.

And Fortunato didn't look happy.

Hunt's hand fell to his side when he turned and saw the dark-haired man who stood in the doorway. He sensed immediately that this stranger was an enemy.

"Mr. Hunt here to pay a traffic fine, Sheriff?" John asked, his eyes flicking from Leen to Hunt. "Or did I interrupt something more important?"

"And you are?" Hunt asked John coldly.

"Mr. Fortunato is Mr. Boyle's nephew," the sheriff replied. "He's a famous photographer and a prominent member of our community."

Hunt kept his face blank as he met John Fortunato's eyes. Tommy Boyle's blood relation, and a famous photographer?

It was a short jump to figure out who would carry a camera around at night in this town—and have the nerve to shoot a kidnapping. Hunt watched Fortunato casually sit down in the sheriff's other guest chair, shrewdly assessing him. This was the man who'd taken Krieger's picture, all right, and he'd bet the photograph had come out just fine.

The sheriff and Hunt felt foolish standing while John sat, so they took their seats. It gave both of them the uneasy feeling that John was setting the agenda.

"Is there something I can do for you, Mr. Fortunato?" the sheriff asked.

"I'm here to talk about Tommy's murder. The circumstances are very disturbing. And they seem to keep getting worse."

He looked meaningfully at Hunt. Hunt blinked. Leen saw what was happening and didn't like it a bit.

"We'll talk in just a minute, Mr. Fortunato. I was just about to show Mr. Hunt out."

"Let him stay, Sheriff. I'm kind of curious to know just what the two of you were talking about."

"I'm leaving," Hunt said.

He started to stand, but John reached over and shoved him down hard into his seat. Hunt's mask of moneyed superiority slipped for just an instant. A look of pure murder flashed in his eyes. No one had laid a hand on him—had dared to try—since Irish Jackie had died.

Hunt's naked hostility didn't faze John. "No, you stay," he said, getting to his feet. "It was rude of me to intrude on your private meeting with the sheriff." Then he turned to Leen. "One of us is going to find out who killed Tommy. It'd look better if it was you."

24 Krieger was doing a walk-around, taking a look at Elk River. He knew you never really got to know a place until you saw it on foot. He'd gotten Fortunato's address from a phone book at the hospital, and the street map he'd torn from the book showed him how to get there.

He wanted to case the house. Play the percentages. If you went after a guy, you had to know him. Know where he lived. Know how he lived. Maybe know how he thought. Most important, know what he could do. Otherwise, *you* could be the one getting fitted for a toe tag.

Things got a lot more interesting when Krieger came to a bookstore. There was the guy's name. John Fortunato. Right there on a book in the window. A *picture* book.

The same guy? He'd bet on it.

The cover of the book showed this mother of a mountain. Sunlight, poking through a cloud, darted over the mountain, lighting up some parts, leaving others black as tar. Krieger liked it. The mountain, the rockiness, the light, the dark. It had muscle. The guy was right to do it in black and white, too. Color would have ruined it.

The only thing wrong was the book's title. *Natural Graces*. What kind of an airy-fairy name was that?

Krieger went into the store and asked the female clerk to see a copy. He started looking at it right there next to the cash register. Tough fucking pictures, all in black and white, every one with real style. Attitude. And the guy had to be a goddamn mountain goat to get some of them.

"This book is John's tribute to Ansel Adams," the clerk told him.

"My thoughts exactly," Krieger responded.

He didn't know who this Anselm guy was, but he picked right up on how the clerk talked about Fortunato like he dropped in for coffee.

"Have you seen John's other books?" the clerk asked.

"Can't say I have."

She pointed them out, and . . .

Was that a fucking lion? *Moments of Truth.* Now, Krieger liked that title. The other title, *Discord,* he didn't understand. But the picture on the front was a hoot. Some bag lady carting her load of shit past some glitzy jewelry store, and this rich, pickle-pussed biddy dripping diamonds just stepping out of the doorway, trying to hold her breath till she got upwind. The photograph made him laugh out loud.

When Krieger entered the store he'd thought he'd just leaf through the one book. Now he saw this was going to take some serious study.

"Would you like to buy one?" the clerk asked.

"I'll take 'em all," Krieger said.

First time in his whole life he ever bought books.

That Tuesday afternoon, while his father was still teaching his last class of the day, Ty sneaked back to the apartment where he and Wesley Daulton lived. He needed a change of clothes, and he had one other important matter to attend to.

Right now, he had on a pair of Gil's sweatpants and a sweatshirt of Gil's that said YOU TRY, YOU DIE. Ty felt self-conscious about the shirt.

Before he'd left John's house, he'd asked Darien, "You think it's all right, me wearing Gil's clothes? He doesn't seem too happy to have me around."

Darien had smiled. "It's cool. You just took us by surprise. Gil'll get his attitude adjusted. He's been cranky lately, is all. . . . Well, maybe a little crazy, too. Most times, though, ol' Gil, him an' Rayette are the life a the party."

Ty asked, "Who's Rayette?"

"Gil's favorite ex–old lady. . . . Ain't seen her lately." Then Darien mused, more to himself than Ty, "Rayette lives in Texas, but she's around most every spring. . . . Maybe that's why the horny little fucker's so moody; he ain't gettin' enough."

Ty couldn't worry about Gil's deprived libido at the moment. He was drawing near the huge, blue Victorian house at Jefferson and Eighth where he and his father lived. Well, behind which they lived. In the apartment over the three-car garage. Still, as his father was quick to point out, their dwelling was on the right side—that is, the Presidential side—of town.

As he approached the house, keeping to the shade of the handsome maple trees that graced Jefferson Avenue, Ty looked to see if his landlady, Miss Millicent, sat in any of the Victorian's many windows. Miss Millicent was 101 years old but still spry enough to live alone, and always full of good humor. Her favorite form of entertainment was looking out her windows. She had a rocking chair in front of almost every pane of glass in the house. Her favorite joke was that she might be a crazy old lady but she was never off her rocker.

Miss Millicent's observations took her from window to window, but Ty had never been able to discern a pattern to her movements. Her rhythms were unfathomable to him. So he had to be careful. He didn't want to be spotted, because Miss Millicent doted on him. If she saw him, he'd have to stop in and visit. Not that Ty minded; she was a sweet old thing. But he didn't want to be around when his father came home. So, as on a few other occasions, he'd have to slip past Miss Millicent.

Fortunately, that proved easy today, as she was looking the other way. From the cover of the shade trees, Ty spotted Miss Millicent looking out a window on the opposite side of the house from the driveway that led to the lodgings of Daulton and Son. The boy quickly stole up the street, darted to the garage, climbed the outside staircase, and entered his home.

He stepped into his bedroom and doffed Gil's clothes for his own underwear, socks, jeans, and sweatshirt. Then he lay flat on the floor and reached under his bed. In the far corner, up against the wall, was a small metal box. It lay there undisturbed in the world's most obvious hiding place. Which was precisely why Wesley Daulton would never suspect his brilliant son of using it. Ty pulled it out.

He sat on his bed and opened the box. In it was all the money he'd squirreled away for the last five years: $213.59. He'd considered the possibility of running away from his father since he was ten. He stuffed the money into his pockets and went into his father's bedroom.

On Wesley Daulton's desk, site of many a ghostwritten term paper, the boy found a nearly empty bottle of Old Crow. Doubtless, there was a full one in one of the desk drawers. The boy wondered if his father even bothered pouring his poison into a glass these days.

Ty saw the message light on his father's phone machine blinking. He hit the play button and listened to the message from Oak Crest Academy about his unexcused absence from school that day. He saved the message so his father could listen to it. That bourbon bottle was going to be emptied very quickly when Wesley got home. Especially after he read Ty's letter to him.

Ty told his father he was taking leave of hearth and home, at least temporarily. He told him about being chased through the woods of Oak Crest by a pack of thugs who had set upon him as a result of Wesley's term paper machinations. He told his father that it was only by great good fortune—on which he didn't elaborate—that he had escaped a beating or worse. He said there was not the slightest possibility he would ever return to Oak Crest Academy.

So, he told his father, either arrange for him to be transferred back to Elk River High School or accept that he had raised a runaway and a . . . *dropout!*

He knew that, with all of Wesley's academic pretensions, his father would rather see him engage in necrophilia than leave school unlettered. It might take another bottle or two for Wesley to see that he had no choice, but in the end he would call Oak Crest Academy and make the arrangements.

Ty finished by saying that he'd check back in a week or so to see that his wishes had been respected.

And if for some perverse reason they hadn't, well, he had his new friends, and he had his life savings with him.

By prior arrangement, Ty met Darien twenty minutes later at the Blast from the Past Diner at Lincoln and Seventh. It had been Darien's idea. He said even an old tunnel rat like him had to go and look at the sky once in a while—and eat something besides MREs. Darien dressed in black for his public appearance: moccasins, jeans, and turtleneck sweater. The two newfound comrades ate their burgers and drank their shakes in the back booth.

That late in the afternoon the lunchtime crowd was long gone, and there was no one nearby to inhibit their conversation. The boy listened to the man tell his stories of war and tunnels, and asked questions as they came to mind. Darien told Ty of moments of terror and rage and anguish. It became a biography that would linger in the boy's memory for a lifetime.

Later, the day became all the more memorable when Ty stepped out of the diner and almost bumped into Frank Murtaw and his goon squad from the rugby team. The same assholes who'd chased him through the woods the day before.

They grinned at Ty like hyenas. Ty started to shrink away, but Darien was right behind him. With a hand on his back.

"Hold your ground, bro," he said softly.

Frank said with a laugh, "Look who we found, guys. Our runaway bunny. We want to have a little talk with you, Tyler."

Darien stepped in front of Ty. Frank looked Darien up and down. He was three inches shorter than Darien, but sixty pounds heavier. And he had four friends with him.

"You with precious here?" Frank asked Darien. "You the exclamation point when he goes 'Eek!'?"

The put-down drew a raucous burst of teenage laughter.

Until Darien's right hand flashed out—and Frank's head jerked back and forth, keeping time to two jolting slaps.

Nobody was laughing now.

"You got anything else to say?" Darien asked.

Frank's eyes blazed with hatred.

"You nig—"

Darien's hand shot out again. This time, however, it locked onto Frank's throat.

"Unh-uh," Darien said evenly. "See, the only right answer to my question was 'No, sir. I be on my way right now.'"

Frank was turning bright red. He was too afraid to try to pull Darien's hand away. There was no telling how much of his throat might come with it. Behind him, Frank's buddies were unsure what to do. Then Mark Winters, second in the pecking order, tried to rally the others.

"Come on," Winters said. "He can't take us all."

"He don't have to," a voice replied.

Gil was pulling up to the curb on the stolen Harley. The motorcycle had been stripped down to its essentials.

"*Another* midget," Mark sneered.

Gil's eyes flared like the gates of hell swinging open. Reaching inside his jacket, he pulled out a Browning automatic and swung off the cycle. Everyone froze. Except for Gil. He walked over to Mark Winters and pressed the barrel of the gun between his eyes.

"On your knees, motherfucker," Gil said.

"Puh-please," Mark sobbed, "please . . . don't."

"Drop or I'll drop ya," Gil said coldly.

The boy sank to his knees. Gil kept the gun pressed against his head.

Ty looked at Darien imploringly. Darien released Frank. The tall, black vet kept his eyes on Gil.

"Your call, bro," Gil told Darien. "They were fuckin' with you."

"Waste one, you gotta waste 'em all," Darien said. "Noise might attract other folks, have to waste them, too." He shrugged. "Just ain't worth it."

Gil seemed disappointed with Darien's choice. He looked down at the boy on his knees in front of him . . . and for one breathless moment everyone thought he might render his own judgment. Then he stroked the boy's cheek with his gun.

"Your lucky day, sonny. It won't happen twice."

He stepped back, let the gun fall to his side. Sobbing with relief, Mark Winters scrambled to his feet. Then he and the rest of the Oak Crest boys ran for all they were worth.

Gil got back on his cycle. "I'm gonna be gone for a little while," he said to Darien. He cranked the Harley and rode off.

Darien watched him go, and then he told Ty, "We was just throwin' a scare into 'em. Ol' Gil's a pretty good actor, huh?"

Ty just looked at his friend, motionless, mute, and disbelieving.

Darien didn't try to bullshit the boy anymore. They both knew the truth. If Darien had given the word, Gil would have killed them all.

25

The Dream Warriors gang hadn't been able to extort protection money from Tran Chi Thanh. They hadn't been able to rob his store. They hadn't even been able to *inconvenience* the owner of Convenient Liquors.

On the contrary, their continuing efforts had cost them the lives of an additional half dozen members.

Now, people were daring to make jokes against the gang. Even within the gang, doubts crept in; cohesion and discipline were starting to suffer. It was only a matter of time before the Dream Warriors would be openly challenged by other merchants in the Little Saigon section of Westminster, California, and then they would be finished.

In desperation, the gang hit upon a tactic that worked. Since they couldn't strike at Tran directly, they beat and threatened to kill anyone they caught shopping at Convenient Liquors. Word spread swiftly through the neighborhood. Within a week the store had no customers.

The gang jokes stopped abruptly.

Tran closed his doors. Which was just what the gang wanted: a lesson for the others to take to heart. Even if they hadn't gotten their man, they'd killed his business.

Their satisfaction was short-lived, however. Because the day after Tran closed the store a huge sign appeared in his front window.

THIS TOO SHALL PASS, the sign said.

The Dream Warriors were outraged. But their fury was not easily vented. With Tran's store closed, and his whereabouts unknown, they had no way to strike back. And because the store windows were bulletproof plastic, they couldn't simply break in and tear down the sign. Then one Dream Warrior hit upon a solution.

Spray-paint the window and cover the sign.

That night, four gang members arrived at Convenient Liquors. Two to do the painting, two armed with automatic weapons to stand guard. None of them saw Tran lying on the rooftop across the street with an M-16.

The Dream Warriors were sitting ducks.

It was a classic example of guerrilla doctrine: When opposed by a superior enemy, fight him on your own terms; strike from concealment and disappear.

Tran was sure the ignorant young gangsters of the Dream Warriors had yet to learn the first lesson of war, and now these four never would.

The next day, a new sign appeared in Tran's window.

WATCH FOR OUR GRAND RE-OPENING SALE.

26 That evening, John called Jill's room on the house phone at the Mill House Inn. When she answered, he said, "This is John. I'm in the lobby. I tried to catch you at the union office, but you'd already gone. I'd like to offer you a room at my house."

There was a momentary silence on the line.

"Why?" she asked.

"I think you'd be safer there."

"Is something going on?"

"I just have a feeling."

"I'll meet you in five minutes."

"My car's out front," he told her.

When they stepped through the front door, Jill set down her bag, looked around, and turned to John.

"You do have a room for me? Apart from your own."

She felt awkward asking the question. Still, she'd known him for barely two days, and before she spent a night under his roof, she wanted to be clear on exactly where things stood.

"Sure," he replied, unembarrassed. "It was my grandmother's. It's at the opposite end of the hallway from mine."

"Oh," she said.

"I have a couple friends who stay here, too. Gil and another guy you'll meet. But I'm sure they'll respect your privacy. Besides, they're usually out a lot."

"I see. Well, that'll be fine then."

John hefted Jill's bag and took her upstairs to show her to her room.

Opening the door to Jill's room and setting down her bag, he added, "You also have your own bathroom."

Jill sat on the bed and gave it a little bounce.

"Just right," she said with a smile.

"Good. Well, I'll let you get settled."

The fact that John had been *such* a perfect gentleman almost annoyed Jill. Could he look at her sitting on a bed and keep even a stray improper thought from crossing his mind and off his face?

"I feel like we've known each other a long time already," she said softly.

"I've felt that way from the first time I met you."

"That's empathy," John said. "We have compatible scars."

He said he was going downstairs to put something on the stove, and if she was hungry she could follow the smell of food burning.

"Believe it or not, I can cook," she said with a smile. "Just give me a minute to get changed."

Jill wore jeans, sneakers, and a University of Chicago sweatshirt as she fried bacon for BLTs. John found himself staring at her as she cooked, watching the deft way she moved at the stove, the way her hair tapered at her neck—and, frankly, checking out how nicely she filled her tight, faded jeans. His thoughts surprised him.

It had been a long time since he'd considered a woman as either a friend or a lover, and longer still since one had cooked for him.

Jill said, "I called Marty McCreery to tell him about Tommy. As secretary-treasurer of the local, he's now the head man. But by the time I reached him, he already knew."

"It's a small town," John said.

Darien came in with Ty. John made the introductions. Darien was shocked when John told him about Tommy. He offered his condolences, then he asked if it was all right if he set up a cot in his room for Ty. John said it was fine. Darien said they'd stopped in for dinner but maybe they'd just go back out for a pizza.

Before he and Ty left, Darien whispered to John that they should have a private talk real soon.

Jill said good-bye to her new acquaintances, then picked up where she'd left off. "What McCreery hadn't heard about was Kushner trying to muscle the international back in."

"How'd he take that?"

"He said they should fuck off."

"Did you tell him you bloodied Kushner's face?" he asked.

She shook her head. "I didn't see any point in it."

"It might make him think you're the tough-as-nails attorney the local needs."

"Actually, that subject did come up. Not that McCreery came right out and said he wanted to replace me. That would have been disrespectful to Tommy's memory. But he certainly hinted that I might be in over my head here."

"And . . ." John wondered.

"And I did something I hate to do: I invoked my father's name."

"Did that do it?"

She snorted. "No. Oh, McCreery thinks my dad was great, no problem there. He just doubts I'm cut from the same cloth."

"That's why I thought the 'Our lawyer can beat up your lawyer' story might have helped," John said.

"I didn't want to stoop to that," Jill replied. Then she smiled bleakly. "So I stooped to something else. I told McCreery that I've already cashed the retainer check Tommy gave me and he can't afford another lawyer."

John laughed.

"Well, that should appeal to the treasurer in him," he said.

"Yeah," Jill said. Then she shook her head. "I want to help these people. I think I can help them. Why should it have to be so hard?"

"Because Marty McCreery is scared," John said. "Everybody in the union is scared. They think their futures are on the line, and they're right. Tommy told me that he had to lead the membership out on strike, practically drag them out, and now that he's gone . . ."

"They're really terrified," Jill said. Then she added, "Especially if they think Hunt is behind Tommy's murder."

John said, "So what Marty McCreery wants now is someone he sees as just as tough as Tommy, someone who can fill his shoes."

Jill leaned forward and looked John right in the eye.

"He may not know it yet, but that's me."

John nodded, honestly believing her and hoping with all his heart she wouldn't meet the same fate Tommy, and so many others he'd loved, had.

27

Johnny Fortune kept finding holes.

Doolan claimed this area of operation had more holes than a golf course with gophers. And John's incredible instinct continued to pick up hot spider holes. These were small, murderous, VC sniper posts. They connected to the main tunnel systems, so the VC had a built-in getaway route.

To John's surprise, Doolan was getting pretty good at sensing enemy presence. For the most part, John was able to chalk up Doolan's awareness to experience and his keen vision and hearing. But every once in a while, Doolan seemed to just know things, too.

But even Doolan didn't compare himself to John. Johnny Fortune was the one with the gift. The second sight.

The problem was, his fame had spread to the other side. The VC knew him by name and had added him to their Ten Most Wanted list. They'd put a bounty on his head. That was the word from the unit's Kit Carson Scout, a former VC himself.

A bounty. Just what the fuck he needed.

One Sunday evening, Doolan slid into the foxhole he and John would share for the night. It was still light enough for him to see John bent over a sheet of paper, drawing some kind of chart.

"What's that?" Doolan whispered.

"Charlie's tunnels. What we've found of them so far and how much else I guess there is."

To Doolan, it looked like a map of the New York subway system. He was stunned by how extensive Johnny Fortune imagined the enemy's tunnels to be.

"That fucking much?" he asked.

John said, "I'm trying to be conservative. But if you're Charlie and you're facing us—with all our firepower—you got only one choice. Dig, dig, dig."

"Jesus," Doolan said.

For the first time, John thought he saw despair in his friend's eyes.

Doolan took the first watch and let John sleep. He couldn't have slept anyway. He wasn't the type who got spooked, but seeing Johnny's chart of the tunnels had completely unnerved him. The damn thing had seized his heart with cold, bony fingers and refused to let go.

Doolan looked at his sleeping friend and whispered, "Johnny, they're gonna get us."

When Doolan woke John for his turn to stand guard, he told him he didn't want to go down any more tunnels.

"Okay, Jamie," John said.

"I don't want you to go down, either."

John said, "Look, man, I feel safer down there. I'm in my element."

"I don't give a shit about your element."

"Then look at it like this, Platoon Sergeant. The more we know about those tunnels, the safer we all are."

As much as Doolan hated it, the military logic was compelling.

What he hated even more was that his friendship with Johnny Fortune, his sense of responsibility as platoon sergeant, made Doolan follow him down the next hole.

John crawled point. The first part of the trip was uneventful. No Charlie. No booby traps. No POW grunts. No big deal. Just a long crawl through a cold, stinking hole. Until they came to the water trap.

Velez had told them about these bastards. Charlie would dig a U-shape bend in a tunnel and fill it with water. That way if the grunts tried to gas the dinks out of their tunnels, the gas would hit the water and go no farther.

The problem for a GI facing a water trap was you never knew how deep or how long it might be. If you dove in, you had to take it on faith that you could get to the other side in one breath.

And wouldn't get stuck in the middle.

John told Doolan what he'd found. Doolan said fuck it, they should get out. John was tempted to agree, but this was his first water trap. It presented a challenge.

Maybe it was a moat protecting some military treasure.

He uncoiled the rope they each carried and tied it around his ankle. He whispered his plan to Doolan. He'd enter the water. If he got stuck or was about to run out of breath, he'd give the rope a tug and Doolan would haul his ass out. If he got to the other side and there was no problem, Doolan could follow.

"You're fuckin' crazy," Doolan hissed.

"It'll only take a minute," John said.

"We're backin' out now, and that's an order."

John said nothing, waiting for Doolan to come to his senses. Doolan knew better. The first thing Velez had told them was that in a tunnel there was no rank.

In the darkness, Doolan's hand found John's arm.

"Look, Johnny," he said, "let's get outta here. I got this real bad feelin'. I'm about to shit my britches."

John had never heard Doolan admit to fear. It stunned him. But the pull of his curiosity, the desire to beat the water trap, was too strong.

He said, "I'll be right back, and then we'll di-di."

John slipped into the trap before Doolan could reply. The water was cold and foul. But he had enough clearance to make it without getting stuck. Still, he felt a wave of relief when he was able to turn upward, toward the far surface of the water trap . . .

Until he saw the light.

He came up in a chamber lighted by a portable generator, the biggest chamber he'd ever seen in a tunnel system. It had to be big. A crew of dinks was working on two 105mm howitzers. Fucking field artillery inside a tunnel. It boggled his mind.

The VC were as surprised to see John as he'd been to see the weapons. Their amazement was the only thing that saved him. They were still reaching for their weapons when he was already back in the water. He made the return trip in nothing flat, but when he surfaced again he was more scared than ever.

Doolan was gone.

.   .   .

It was pitch-black on this side, of course, but John knew immediately that his friend was no longer there. He didn't believe for a second that Doolan would have just split on him. Something had happened.

John retraced the path he and Doolan had taken, crawling as fast as he could. There were no branches to this tunnel, no trapdoors up or down to other levels. There had been no booby traps to worry about on the way in, so he could go flat out now. He heard his hands slap the tunnel floor and felt his heart in his throat.

As he hurried, Doolan cried out to him in the distance. "Aaaaargh, Johnny, help m—"

Then there was only silence.

John pulled his revolver and crawled at a furious pace. Even with all the racket he was making, he still heard the sound. Metal on rock-hard clay. A grenade was rolling toward him.

He took a deep breath, covered his head with his arms, drew his legs up to his chest, and pressed himself against the left-hand wall of the tunnel.

There was a flash of light and then nothing.

The next thing he knew, he was above ground looking up at Gil Velez.

"Don't worry, man," Velez said, "the dust-off's on its way."

He tried to speak.

Gil grinned. "Whaddya want to know? How come you're not dead? Medic's been pickin' fragments outta ya. Dinks used one a their homemade grenades. The kind they make outta our old C-rat tins. Mustn'a had too much of a load. It'd been one a ours, bro, you'd be ground round."

John managed to croak out one word. "Doolan?"

Velez sighed. He squatted down next to John.

"They told us he went down with you, man. . . . Problem is, we couldn't find him."

Nobody ever found Doolan.

28 On Wednesday morning, Jill Baxter, John Fortunato, and Marty McCreery, secretary-treasurer of Local 274, sat with the three other members of the local's executive committee—Pete Banks, Sid Tomlinson, and Harry Waller—at a table in a basement meeting room of the Church of the Resurrection. Jill had made a point of taking the chair at the head of the table. Everybody wore black, and the mood was appropriately grim.

Tommy Boyle's funeral service would start upstairs in fifteen minutes. The church was full. The organ in the choir loft could be heard, faintly, playing Mozart's *Requiem*.

Jill looked at McCreery, on her immediate left. She took a sheet of paper from the sleek, black attaché case she'd brought with her and slid it over to the secretary-treasurer.

"This document releases me from any responsibility for representing Local 274, Brotherhood of Manufacturing Workers, in its labor actions against Pentronics Systems," she said bluntly. "It voids my agreement with Tommy Boyle to assume those responsibilities. I'll need at least three of your signatures on it."

Marty shifted the piece of paper to his left, and the four union men craned their necks to examine the document.

Jill continued, "It also holds me harmless for your decision to terminate my services."

Marty and the others looked at Jill for an explanation. Her face was as still as granite, and as hard.

"You sign that paper," she said, "you can't come back later crying to a court that what happened to you—say, your strike failing—was my fault."

Marty McCreery angrily said, "We can take care of ourselves."

He grabbed the document, pulled a pen out of his coat, and signed it. Then he pushed the piece of paper over to Sid Tomlinson. Sid, a more careful sort, decided to give the document a thorough reading before adding his name to it.

While they waited, Jill said, "Let me ask you something, Mr. McCreery. Were you appointed or elected to your present position?"

"Elected," Marty said emphatically. "Unanimously."

"Unanimously, my, my. And did Tommy Boyle happen to endorse you?"

Sid looked up from reading the agreement. "Tommy *slated* him."

"Marty ran unopposed," said Harry Waller, the man on the far end, "and with Tommy's backing, no reason why he shouldn't have gotten everybody's vote."

"I still did the job, and a helluva job, too," Marty said vehemently.

"And we know him," added Pete Banks, an obvious friend of Mc-Creery's. "We've known Marty a lotta years. You, lady, who the hell are you?"

Jill said, "I'm the woman Tommy thought was man enough to take on Tony Hunt."

Implying none of them was. Even so, Sid and Harry didn't seem to take offense. In fact, the dig brought a little gleam to their eyes.

"You gonna take all day with that, Sid?" Banks asked Tomlinson. Grabbing the agreement, he signed his name to it without giving it a second glance. "Now, you all know where I stand. I'm going upstairs."

He slammed down the pen and left.

Marty McCreery spoke in a flat voice, "Sid . . . Harry? You gonna sign so we can get upstairs, too?"

"You want to be the new president of the local real bad, don't you, Marty?" asked Harry Waller. "You ever think maybe somebody else'd like that job, too?"

Harry reached out and sent the pen skittering back across the table. Marty had to catch it before it fell to the floor. Then Harry left without signing.

Marty didn't need him . . . but he did need one more signature to avoid a deadlock of the executive committee; Tommy's death had left them with an even number.

"Sid?" he said.

"I'm thinkin'," the heavyset man replied.

Sid Tomlinson took out a handkerchief and dabbed at his brow. He looked at Marty and he looked at Jill. He looked at her and he pressed his lips together and he wiped his brow again.

"Goddamnit, Sid, we've got to get upstairs. Whose side are you going to take here?" Marty demanded.

Sid didn't respond to his union brother. He continued examining the woman lawyer. Finally, he found his tongue and asked her, "Tommy hired you on the square, right?"

"What do you mean?" she asked evenly.

"I mean, he coulda gone to anyone . . . any lawyer . . . a man. He coulda done that, but he picked you because you're good."

"For a fight like yours, I'm the best."

Marty McCreery sneered.

"Then you didn't get the job because . . . Lord, I just can't say it."

"No, Sid," she said. "I didn't get the job because I was sleeping with Tommy. I never did more than shake the man's hand. I'd never heard of him before he called me."

"God Almighty!" Marty McCreery exploded. "That's what you're worried about? Who's fucking who. What's wrong with you? You want to take a crack at this broad yourself, is that it?"

Sid's fat hand shot out with the speed of an adder, fastened around Marty's tie, and yanked him close.

"I'm a good Christian man, Marty McCreery, and you know that. I've been married thirty years and never even thought of another woman but my wife. Now, I don't hold with violence, but you make another remark like that, I just might forget my Bible lessons."

He shoved Marty back into his seat, hard.

Then he turned to Jill. "These other fellas might have their own reasons for wantin' you to stay or go, but I don't mind telling you, I'm scared. I don't know what's going to happen to the union or the company or this town. I wish with all my heart that we still had Tommy here to lead us; I'm sure most of us do . . . but if you're the one he picked for our lawyer, then I'm with you." He heaved himself to his feet and added, "I'll pray for Tommy's soul, John."

"Thank you."

And as his better nature overcame his anger, Sid even patted Marty on the shoulder before he left. Marty was not comforted.

"We're stuck with each other, Mr. McCreery," Jill said. "If it means anything to you, Tommy really did choose me on merit. I will do my absolute best for Local 274, and I'll remain completely neutral as to who should be Tommy's successor."

Marty got to his feet. He scooped up the agreement, folded it, and stuck it in an inner pocket of his suitcoat. "I only need one more signature."

John looked out over the crowd from the pulpit of the Church of the Resurrection. Jill sat in the front row with the members of the executive committee. In the pew behind them were Darien and Ty.

He wondered briefly where Gil was. Ceremony was an important part of life to him. Especially something as solemn as the funeral of a fellow vet. And Gil and Tommy had been simpatico, spending many a night drinking and carousing together.

He studied all the other faces staring up at him. He saw that their emotions were finely balanced between heartbreak and anger. They looked for words of comfort from the man who only now realized how deeply Tommy's death had wounded his soul. They waited patiently as he groped for a way to put his pain into words, to find meaning in the death of someone who'd been so important to them all.

John sought inspiration from the wonderful structure his grandfather had built. He'd bought the church after Bill Deeley, who'd been the last pastor, left the priesthood to marry the woman he loved. The Catholic church had had no one to replace Bill, and the Church of the Resurrection had lain vacant for six months until John stepped forward to purchase it.

John had never considered closing the church to the public. He'd asked the now-married Bill Deeley back to be Church of the Resurrection's pastor once more, if no longer its priest. The services held here were ecumenical and interactive; faith was maintained by a daily dialogue of the congregants, not by adhering to a rigid catechism written by a distant hierarchy.

John used the church as a place to be close to his family, a place where he might honor their memories. And Doolan's. But he'd never anticipated having to use it to bury Tommy.

"Tommy Boyle was my brother," he began. As tears formed in his eyes, John added, "He was your brother, too. He was the brother of every man and woman here who worked with him, whose job he made more secure, whose standard of living he fought for, whose day he brightened with his smile. We've lost Tommy now . . . but I want all of you to know that our loss is his gain. Tommy has gone to a better place. I *know* he has."

Jill Baxter felt a tremor pass through her. Until now, she'd had her doubts about Tommy's visitation. But looking up into John's eyes, she believed. She said a silent prayer that her father had also found that better place.

Amid all the tearful faces in the congregation at that moment, two jumped out at John.

Standing at the back of the church, Sheriff Orville Leen kept his face a blank mask. His stoicism was tested by the silent but palpable hostility of everyone around him.

And just a few rows from the front sat Bobbi Sharpes. Her features were so taut with rage John could imagine granite being ground to powder between her teeth. For an instant, her blazing eyes locked onto his. Then she turned her head away and covered her face with her hand.

John continued, "From the day I was born, Tommy fought for me. As I grew older, he fought *with* me for the right to continue to be my protector. As a man, I knew I had to face my own challenges, but in the back of my mind was the comforting certainty that if I ever needed him, my brother would come on the run to help me.

"For the past twelve years, Tommy has helped all of you in the union. He led you at a time when the working men and women of this country have been under constant assault. He fought hard, and, for all I know, maybe he even fought dirty. Believe me, nobody knows better than I do that Tommy was far from perfect."

Jill looked up and wondered just how much John knew.

"But, whatever his faults, Tommy made sure you all had jobs that would let you hold your heads up high. He did that, and then he died fighting for you once more. I don't see how we could live with ourselves if we let him down . . . if we don't push this strike to victory for him."

John closed by asking everyone present to join him in the churchyard, where Tommy would be buried—and where Tommy's labor lawyer would address them.

Tommy Boyle was laid to rest next to John's parents and grandparents, in the adjacent churchyard. John threw the first shovelful of dirt into the grave.

Then Jill stood on a folding chair that had been brought from the church. She looked out at a sea of unfamiliar faces and watched their sorrow turn to curiosity and anxiety as they wondered just who she was and what she had to say about their futures.

John had gathered these people together for her, but Jill knew that if she hoped to gain their trust she would have to address them alone.

"My name is Jill Baxter," she began in a strong, clear voice. "I barely knew Tommy Boyle . . . but I've heard of him all my life. I've kept a picture of him in my heart since I was a little girl. It's the picture of a man whose strength of character was so great that he could never be content to fight only his own battles. He was compelled to fight for the rights of the people he worked with, the people he lived with. He fought for his family, his friends, and his neighbors . . . and ultimately he died for them. For *us*.

"The reason I know all this is because my father was that same sort of man. He labored and he fought so that men and women of ordinary circumstances might work in dignity. So that they could house and feed and clothe their families by earning a fair wage. So that they could face the sorrows of family illness without the additional worry that medical expenses would leave them destitute. So that when they reached old age they would know a time of rest and security, not privation and despair. These were the things my father, Grady Baxter, worked for, and, like Tommy Boyle . . . he was killed for his troubles."

Tears started to stream from Jill's eyes. She accepted the handkerchief a woman in the crowd extended to her; the woman wiped away her own tears on the back of her sleeve.

"I've always treasured the memory of my father," Jill continued. "But there are times, too, when I resent him. He worked so hard to help so many people, most of whom he didn't know personally, but when I needed him, he was gone. I yearn for my father more times and more deeply than I can tell you, so I have a pretty good idea of how you must be missing Tommy Boyle right now. But maybe, as I sometimes resent my father, you might start resenting Tommy. Resenting the fact that, like my father, he wasn't smart enough or tough enough or ruthless enough to get the bastards before they got him."

Jill delivered the last line with a rage that had simmered a lifetime, and it resonated with the crowd. She'd given voice to their anger, and now it showed on their faces.

"This is what led me to follow in my father's footsteps: the conviction that the bastards of the world aren't going to get me—I'm going to get them!"

The crowd roared its approval. A thousand fists shot into the air.

"Tommy hired me to represent your local, to represent you against Anthony Tiburon Hunt—"

The mention of the enemy's name drew jeers and catcalls. Jill let the anger play out.

"But now, with Tommy's passing, I must tell you frankly that your leadership is divided over whether I should stay. I must also tell you that while I'll gladly fight my enemies, I will not fight people who would likely be my friends. So, now, you must tell me whether I should stay or I should go. . . ."

Marty McCreery opened his mouth, but as Jill's final words reached the throng, he hesitated. After that, it was too late.

"Stay!" yelled the woman who'd given her handkerchief to Jill. "Stay!" yelled a hundred, then a thousand more. "Stay, stay, stay!" roared the crowd.

Jill bowed her head. Then she looked up and raised her arms for silence.

"When Tommy Boyle stood up to Anthony Hunt at the plant gate three nights ago, he told Hunt that he'd never win by using scabs."

"Goddamn right, he won't!" a man yelled, and drew a cheer.

"Tommy told Hunt that there would be no place in Elk River for scabs. Nobody will sell them a meal, a drink, a loaf of bread, a carton of milk. Not a Coke or a candy bar. Not a newspaper or a stick of gum. We will not be violent, but we will deny the scabs . . . and management—"

The inclusion of the privileged class of Oak Crest brought another shout of approval.

"We will deny management and their scabs," Jill continued, "any and all sense of community with us. We will not talk to them. We will not listen to them. We will not look at them—except with contempt."

Jill held up her hands for silence as another roar crested.

"And we will *not* give the sheriff's department the least excuse to arrest any of us ever again."

That thought immediately sobered the crowd; it brought back vividly how they'd lost Tommy Boyle in the first place.

"We can win this battle," Jill said.

"We *will* win," she promised them. "If we stick together."

At the fringe of the crowd, standing next to Sheriff Leen, Deputy Billy Shelton belched his contempt. The rude sound drew hostile looks. Billy glared back defiantly.

Leen led him over to their cruiser before things got out of hand. He was wondering what the hell to do with the idiot when Billy himself provided an answer.

"Lookit that prick over there," he said.

Leen followed Billy's gaze and saw a big hulk with a block-shaped head. The sheriff had never laid eyes on the man, but he knew immediately who he was. Tony Hunt's hired goon, Krieger. He was sitting on the roof of a black sedan parked down the street. The ugly sonofabitch even smiled and waved to them.

Which gave the sheriff an idea.

"Billy, just to show you I'm keeping an open mind about who shot Tommy Boyle, why don't you keep a real close eye on Hunt's boy down there the next couple of days?"

Billy couldn't believe his luck. "You're lettin' me off the leash?"

"I'm giving you a little room to run," Leen said.

Billy took it and bolted.

Watching him, the sheriff wasn't entirely sure he'd done the right thing. But at least it was something. Might even work out for the best. Just look at Billy getting in old Krieger's Halloween mask of a face. Sonofabitch wasn't smiling now. But Leen was smiling when Krieger hopped down off the car and landed on Billy's toes.

Yes, the sheriff decided, come what may, Billy Shelton and Krieger deserved each other.

Bill Deeley, the pastor of the Church of the Resurrection, helped Jill down from the chair. Then he stepped up onto it himself. He spoke in a firm but kind voice that was used to carrying to the far reaches of large gatherings.

"I'd like to add just a few words before we all leave here today. I know there's no need to remind anyone of how difficult the days ahead will be for all of us. And I fear they may be made more so by a division of loyalty between old friends and neighbors who seem to think that their interests are diverging. I ask you, please, remember that these times will be trying for *everyone* in Elk River. And I beg of you—do not lose sight of charity and compassion for those who may come to disagree with you.

"May God bless us all," Bill Deeley concluded.

When Krieger entered Tony Hunt's office, he was still steamed from his encounter with Billy Shelton. The last thing he needed was Hunt laying his power trip number on him. But there he was sitting behind his desk giving Krieger the old stone face.

In fact, Hunt was in a foul mood of his own. He'd spent much of the day fencing with his investment banker, Carter Powell. Powell was sniveling again that his superiors would soon find out that Hunt's collateral was worthless, which would put Powell's head squarely on the chopping block.

The pitch of Powell's whine told Hunt the banker was about to buckle and confess everything. So Hunt had resorted to the only available strategy: He'd sucked Powell in even deeper.

He'd reassured the twerp that all was well, that wealth beyond imagining would soon be his, and most important, he'd convinced Powell to commit more money to him. Hunt would like to see the banker explain *that* if he decided to cop a plea.

He'd also spent time replaying in his mind the night of the riot at the plant. Originally, he'd assumed that he'd merely been grazed by a bullet meant for Tommy Boyle, a hypothesis that seemed especially sound after Boyle had been killed. But today . . . today he considered the possibility that the bullet might have been meant for him. He had plenty of enemies, too. He could have been the one getting buried today.

It was all very well to own your own town, Hunt thought, but until he brought the natives firmly under control, he'd have to be very careful.

But the thing that was *really* bothering him was John Fortunato. The way that cocksucker slammed him back into that chair—in front of that goddamn sheriff. What really strained his self-control, though, was that Irish Jackie's parting advice had come back to him, creeping into his mind after all these years like a vile malediction from the little bastard's grave: *Don't try to overstep yourself, lad.*

Hunt took a deep, cleansing breath and returned his focus to Krieger. "I met the man who took your picture."

"Fortunato."

Krieger was amused. Hunt frowned. "How did you know?"

Krieger smiled. "I just bought his three books."

"What books?"

"Fortunato's picture books. You haven't seen them?"

Krieger had a hard time not laughing: the Harvard hotshot didn't know his stuff.

Insolence, Hunt thought. Yet another problem. Well, it would soon be time to clean house. Krieger—whom he'd hired because he thought it would be amusing to have a thug like his own father working for him—would have to go. But first . . . "I want Fortunato dead."

"Me, too," Krieger said. "But after seeing his stuff, I might ask him for his autograph first."

"You think this is funny?" Hunt asked coldly.

"In a way, yeah," Krieger said, indifferent to Hunt's darkening mood. "What I'd really like is for him to autograph that picture where I'm trying to ice him."

"I want him dead," Hunt repeated.

That picture would go great on the cover of his life story, Krieger thought. He'd have it written someday.

"I want *you* to kill him," Hunt added.

"Tell you what," Krieger replied cockily. "You kill Fortunato, I'll kill the sheriff." Krieger knew who'd sicced Billy Shelton on him. "I'll even throw in a certain dipshit deputy for free. That should solve all of our problems."

Krieger knew he was pushing Hunt here. But he no longer gave a fuck. Doing Hunt's heavy lifting was losing its appeal. Other notions were forming in Krieger's head.

Hunt inspected his lackey as if he were an exotic bug that he'd just noticed. "Are you saying you won't do it?"

"Remember our deal? I do your dirty work, and you teach me to be a bigshot businessman. So I can steal whole companies instead of spare change from convenience stores. Well, lately I've been haulin' plenty of your shit, but I ain't been learnin' diddly."

"Then you haven't been paying attention," Hunt said.

Krieger shook his head. "I'll tell you something right now. You want Fortunato dead not for business reasons but because, one way or another, that guy twisted your dick."

Hunt gave no sign of taking offense. On the contrary, he smiled. Had Krieger been older, more experienced, or even less certain of his own vast brutality, he might have taken the smile for the warning sign it was, but he went on heedlessly.

"I'll tell you something else. You're too scared to do it yourself."

Hunt took a second to examine the accusation. *Was* he afraid of Fortunato? No. He'd stood fast against Tommy Boyle and his mob . . . but Krieger hadn't seen that. Which was just as well. Always best to have the element of surprise on your side.

Krieger, still having his fun, said, "Of course, I could be wrong. Tell you what. I'll set Fortunato up just right . . . and *you* pull the trigger."

It was only when his boss replied that Krieger first got the idea he might not have the situation sized up exactly right.

"Go ahead," Tony Hunt said. "Set it up."

29 That day, the arson at the Traveler's Delight Motel became a homicide.

Two investigators from the county fire marshal's office found a hand. It poked up through a jumble of collapsed beams and other rubble. The flesh and musculature had been burned away, and the bones were scorched. The hand's middle phalange was extended in postmortem disapproval.

The senior investigator nodded. "This *is* fucked."

When they found just what accelerant had been used to start the fire, the investigators decided it was double-fucked.

Orville Leen put down his phone.

The arson investigators had just informed him of another goddamn murder. With the three men killed in the plant riot, Tommy Boyle gunned down on the street, and now this body turning up at the scene of an arson fire, he'd had more killings on his books in the past three days than in the previous five years.

For the first time, in any serious way, Orville Leen felt a strong impulse to retire. But not before he locked up whatever sonofabitch was responsible for all this mayhem and returned some measure of sanity to his once-peaceful county.

John knocked on the door three times. He had to wait five minutes before Bobbi Sharpes appeared.

"You as miserable as me, Johnny?" Bobbi had a soft Tennessee accent.

Even in grief, she was one of the most striking women he'd ever seen. Glossy black hair framed a face that Rodin might have sculpted on his best day. The forehead was smooth, the browline strong, the cheeks high, the nose straight, and the lips full.

The centerpiece of Bobbi's face was a set of blue-violet eyes that normally sparkled with intelligence, challenge, and a mocking sense of humor. Normally, but not today.

"I miss him very much," John said.

"Come on in, Johnny. I'm sorry it took me so long to come to the door. Billy came by the other night. I wanted to make sure he wasn't back to try his luck again."

John stepped inside.

"Let's go to the kitchen and find a bottle," Bobbi told him. "We'll drink to the dearly departed."

Bobbi toasted Tommy's memory, and John downed the shot she'd given him. She didn't drink hers. She merely looked at her glass before setting it down on the kitchen table. Then she wrapped both arms around herself, warding off a chill that wasn't in the air.

"I think you're the only man I'd let in here right now," Bobbi said. "The only one I'd trust not to try and *console* me." The anger still burning in her eyes warned him not to try anything to prove her wrong.

"I'm here because I saw how upset you were in church this morning. I wondered if you wanted to talk."

Bobbi bit her lip; she remained silent.

"I want to find out who killed Tommy," John continued.

She looked at her drink as if she wanted it badly. Then she lifted her glass and poured the whiskey very carefully back into the bottle. "You think I did it, Johnny?"

"I think it's possible you could kill someone."

Bobbi smiled bleakly. "You're right about that. I sure gave it my best shot with Billy the last time I saw him."

"You were mad at Tommy, too."

Her smile filled with sorrow. "How much did he tell you about us?" she asked.

"He told me he wanted you to divorce Billy and marry him. Why didn't you?"

Bobbi capped the bottle and got up to put it away. She looked at him a long time before answering.

"I don't have the best of judgment, Johnny. Look who the last man I married was, and the one before Billy was worse. I have better luck with boyfriends."

"Tommy's leaving made you mad, though, didn't it?"

"Sad," Bobbi corrected.

"And seeing him with other women?"

Bobbi started to shiver. She laughed bitterly. "No, you surely didn't come to comfort me. Yeah, it made me *very* mad to see Tommy with other women."

"Did you kill him?" John asked quietly.

"I loved him more than my own life, Johnny."

John believed her . . . but he hadn't heard an answer to his question. "Did you kill him, Bobbi?"

"No," she answered. "I wanted him to be our baby's daddy."

30 Darien was sitting out front when John returned to his house on Via Michelangelo. And Darien didn't like to sit *anywhere* that would make him an easy target.

"I been waitin' for you," he told John.

"You want to go inside?"

Darien did, it was obvious, but he shook his head. He was controlling his fear. "Let's just sit here and talk quiet."

"Okay."

John sat on the step next to him and waited.

"We gotta get Gil to go see Dr. Risom," Darien finally said.

John had referred Darien to the psychiatrist when the former POW had first gotten in touch with John after coming home. Darien had spent two years in therapy. John had also given the therapist's name to Gil, but he had refused to see her. Gil had said he'd *liked* the war.

"Why?" John asked Darien.

Darien told him about the incident with the five Oak Crest teenagers.

"I tried to tell Ty it was all an act, you know. That Gil was just throwin' a scare into those punk kids. But it was no act. Gil was one breath away from killin' them all."

"Sounds like he was provoked."

Darien gave John a look.

"John, if I killed everyone who called me nigger, I'd need the Pentagon to keep the body count."

Darien told him about Gil's stealing the police Harley, too.

"What the hell is that all about?" John wondered aloud.

Darien could only shrug.

"You remember what Dr. Risom said?" he asked. "It's okay to get pissed off, you just gotta keep your responses *appropriate.*"

John nodded.

"Well, our boy Gil ain't close to appropriate lately."

John said, "I'll talk to him first chance I get."

Darien sighed and said, "Good."

"How's our new recruit?" John asked.

Darien's demeanor did a complete turnaround.

"He's somethin'," Darien said with a grin. "Someday, that boy'll make us all proud."

After Darien had gone inside, John stayed seated on the front steps. He mulled Darien's point about appropriate responses. Maybe Gil hadn't been so off base. Where was the loss if a pack of rich punks picked the wrong guy to torment? Or, in Darien's case, who'd care if a bumper crop of mean-spirited, foulmouthed bigots bought the farm?

Come to that, if he actually found Tommy's killer, should he turn him in and hope for justice, or simply ding the fucker himself?

Just as that thought entered his head, a black sedan eased up to the curb. The same car used in the kidnapping. He knew it from his photographs.

Krieger—that's what Tommy had said his name was—got out from behind the wheel. There was no forgetting that face. Krieger smiled at John and started up the walk. He had a book in his hand.

Krieger looked at him, and then he looked the house over, studying it, like he was a tourist. Or a burglar. John remained seated but held up his hand when Krieger got to within ten feet of him.

"Close enough," he said calmly.

Krieger stopped, but he kept smiling. He held up John's book, *Moments of Truth.* "This sonofabitch really knocked me out. These pictures are fucking amazing."

The guy sounded like an old-time radio announcer. One given to profanity. The velvet-smooth voice was soothing when you heard it. Surreal when you saw its source.

"You buy that book or steal it?" John asked.

Krieger laughed. That sounded good, too.

"Bought it," he replied. "Bought all three of 'em. You're something else, man."

"Funny world, isn't it? One night you're trying to kill somebody, a few days later you're a fan."

Krieger's smile turned wicked. "That's just what I said it was. Funny. So I figured we should meet before we got back to business."

He opened the book to an aerial shot of Mount Kilauea, looking almost straight down into the cone. An erupting geyser of luminous red-hot magma shot up toward the viewer like a fountain from hell.

"I gotta know," he said, "how'd you get this one?"

"Helicopter. An army friend did the flying."

"What, you were all strapped in?"

"No. I was just sitting in the bay."

Krieger tried to tell if he was bullshitting. Then decided he wasn't. A liar would have made more of it.

"My favorite's still this bastard on the cover, this lion," Krieger said. Then he asked abruptly, "You got my picture the other night, didn't you?"

"Yeah."

"It's great, isn't it?"

"It's dramatic. Your face, the gun, the bullet just leaving the barrel. You'd like it."

The bullet leaving the barrel? How the fuck could you top that? Krieger wondered. "I'll give you ten grand for it."

John shook his head.

"Twenty."

"It isn't for sale," John told him.

"Come on, man. Takin' that picture to the law ain't gonna do jackshit for you, if that's all you got."

"I've got this," John said.

He took his .38 out of the pocket of his windbreaker. He'd started carrying the weapon after Tommy got shot.

"See," he said, "life gets funnier all the time. This time, I've got the gun. And you don't."

The humor was lost on Krieger, who took a half step backward.

"Did you kill Tommy?" John asked.

Krieger knew that in most cases if a guy pulled a gun but kept on talking he wasn't going to use it. But he didn't feel most cases applied to this particular guy.

"Why ask? If I say no, you won't believe me."

John felt maybe it would be appropriate to shoot this goof regardless; even if he hadn't killed Tommy, he'd certainly tried to kill John himself. He couldn't decide.

"I think you'd better go now," John said with a growing awareness of the trigger under his finger.

But Krieger had one more request. He held John's book up, off to the side, careful to keep his hands away from his body.

"If I can't have my picture, will you autograph your book for me?"

"Sure," John said.

He put a round through the lion's head.

31 "I wasn't suicidal," John said. "I never tried to take my life. I was just indifferent to death."

He and Jill were sitting in his living room. They had a fire going and she was looking through a copy of *Moments of Truth* as John recounted his day for her. She'd asked him if he'd wanted to die when he'd been doing the book.

Then she asked, "Did your shrink ever see this?"

"We talked on the phone right after it came out. I told her just what I told you."

"What did she say to that?"

"She said I needed someone to live for."

Jill laid the book on the coffee table. Her next question came hesitantly.

"Hasn't there ever been anyone?"

John nodded. "The editor of my books. Her name is Tess. We came close, but she had to stay in New York for her job, and . . . and I had work to do here."

"It's too late for Tess?"

"She married a very nice guy. They have two beautiful kids. What about you?" he asked. "Who do you live for?"

"My one beautiful kid."

"You have a child?"

"Yeah, I live for her and my mom."

"You got a picture?"

She rose to get her wallet. There was an easy, athletic grace to her step. She kept herself in very good shape, and again he was surprised at his physical attraction to her. That kind of thing hadn't happened to him for a very long time . . . not since Tess.

She sat down next to him, close, and showed him two snapshots encased in plastic: a handsome woman in her early sixties and a little girl with chestnut hair and green eyes.

"My mom and Carlie. She got her daddy's coloring."

He'd already noticed that Jill didn't wear a wedding ring. That made questions about Daddy—and how Jill had parted with him—unnecessary.

"She got your looks, though."

"Is that a compliment?"

"Depends how you feel about yourself," he replied.

"Pretty good, that's how I feel."

"Me, too," he said.

He moved to kiss her, but she stopped him. The flickering firelight accented the mischief in her eyes.

"I have to warn you, Fortunato," she murmured. "From someone who autographs a book the way you do, I'm going to expect something pretty special."

"Your editor should have quit her job," Jill said.

They'd moved from the rug by the fire for the first time to the comfort of John's bed for the second.

"I like your pictures very much," she said. "Even the ones that aren't shocking have an element of surprise to them. It's like you open your eyes wider than the rest of us and notice things we all miss."

"Comes from spending a lot of time in the dark."

His breath felt warm against her neck, and for several moments they lay snugly silent. Just as she sensed that he was falling asleep, Jill asked, "What are you going to do next about Tommy?"

"Seek professional help," John whispered.

32 Thursday morning, John drove to the hospital to see Tommy's private investigator, Phil Henry. He thought the injured PI might let him in on some smoother moves than just asking people, "Hey, did you kill Tommy?"

Henry communicated in writing, holding a pen between the index and middle fingers of one casted hand. John told him about Tommy's murder and Henry expressed his condolences.

"Funny," he wrote, "I can do this for some people but not others."

John showed him the picture of Krieger he'd taken.

"That's the sonofabitch."

"Do you think he shot Tommy?"

Henry thought for a minute. "Don't know. Tommy p.o.'d a lot of people."

John asked the investigator if he had any suggestions about how he might start looking for who shot Tommy.

"One," Henry wrote. "Check Tommy's place."

John grimaced, dismayed that he hadn't thought of something so elementary.

"Don't be hard on yourself," Henry wrote. "You lose someone, things aren't normal, you don't track right."

"Yeah," John said with a sigh. "I suppose."

"Two," Henry wrote. "Find a cop you can trust. One who'll tip you if the sheriff is covering up."

"How am I supposed to do that?"

"Look for a cop from a union family."

Henry frowned and wrote some more.

"Don't know how to get at Hunt. Trying—and fucking up—was what landed me here. Would love to look at his private files, though."

Henry flipped the page of his writing pad to a clean sheet.

"Been thinking. Riot—arrests—unforeseeable. So who knew Tommy was still in jail?"

"The cops," John said.

"And others busted. Plant guards. Hunt's men."

"But only the cops knew when Tommy would be released."

"Maybe killer just patient. Gets call. Waits and sees. What's to lose?"

Henry instructed John to get hold of the phone records for the sheriff's station and see what numbers had been called the night of the riot. And to check the union people who'd been busted that night to see if anyone remembered hearing any peculiar conversations.

Then he wrote that he was being picked up by a friend that afternoon to go to a hospital in another town. He didn't say where. But he left a phone number.

The last thing he wrote was: "Destroy these notes."

Jill Baxter went to Local 274 Thursday morning. Marty McCreery had already moved into Tommy's office by the time she'd arrived. His supporter on the executive committee, Pete Banks, was plunked down in Tommy's guest chair. The door was closed.

Sid Tomlinson and Harry Waller, the opposing faction, were discussing matters in soft voices, so as not to aggravate the situation in front of the local's receptionist-secretary, Sharon Waddell.

Sharon was the woman who'd given Jill her handkerchief at the graveyard, and she was more than pleased to see the labor lawyer that morning. Sharon also knew, despite all the whispering, exactly what was going on. So along with Sid and Harry, she got Jill situated. Harry had the bright idea of putting Jill at Marty McCreery's desk; teach him to go poaching other people's places.

Jill wouldn't have chosen to antagonize Marty McCreery, but like the others she was put out that he had usurped Tommy's office—and she wasn't going to alienate her allies.

Besides, Marty's desk had a phone, and that was all she needed. She spent the morning organizing Elk River. Out of the one hundred and twenty merchants she called, only two didn't quickly fall in line with the boycott of the scabs and plant management.

A gas station and a coin-and-stamp shop were the only holdouts. The station owner said he was closing up and going fishing in Arkansas until things were settled. The other dissenter swore he'd sell to anybody he damn well pleased.

Numismatists and philatelists aside, Tommy Boyle's plan was in effect. Anyone who crossed the Local 274 picket line at Pentronics Systems would not be able to buy a thing in Elk River. Scabs would be pariahs.

It was already a source of great humor that the scabs who'd been burned out of the Traveler's Delight Motel had to be put up in the main dining room of the Oak Crest Country Club.

The joke was that working for Hunt didn't pay much but you got to rub elbows with the upper crust . . . eat their leftovers, too.

Marty McCreery and Pete Banks came charging out of Tommy Boyle's office when they saw Jill start to rummage through Marty's desk.

"Hey, what the hell do you think you're doing?" Marty demanded.

Jill regarded McCreery and Banks calmly.

"Looking for some figures I need."

Marty slammed shut the drawer Jill had opened.

"You stay out of my desk."

"I'm sorry," Jill said, unruffled. "I thought you'd moved into Mr. Boyle's office."

By now, Sid and Harry had come over. Sharon Waddell and a number of strikers who'd come in to get their picketing assignments were watching.

"Yeah, Marty," Harry said, "we've been meaning to ask you about that. As in, what majority of the executive committee gave you Tommy's office?"

Jill did not want the onlooking membership to get distracted by petty bickering among its leaders. They had to have faith in these people for the strike to succeed; they had to think that the welfare of the membership came before its leaders' personal ambitions.

"Gentlemen," she said sharply, cutting off Pete Banks before he put in his two cents. "The figures I need are really quite important. I'm sure you know the ones I mean, Mr. McCreery." She gave her nemesis a penetrating look. "Why don't we all step into Mr. Boyle's office and discuss them?"

It was very close quarters indeed for five people in the tiny office. Sid, the largest, pressed himself against the door, effectively blocking off its pane of glass. Marty sat behind Tommy's desk; Pete stood next to him. Jill was sandwiched between Sid and Harry. The executive committee was convened.

"You shouldn't be talking about this," Marty told Jill grimly.

"What?" Harry asked.

"Yeah, what?" Pete seconded.

"This is information your colleagues should have, Mr. McCreery," Jill said. "I'd be remiss not to share it with them."

She told them about Tommy's not sending in their union dues for the past two years and that the local wouldn't be receiving strike pay from the international. Harry, Sid, and Pete were as stunned as Jill had been.

"You didn't think we should know this?" Harry asked Marty.

"I'm your friend, Marty," Pete said. "How could you not tell me?"

Sid didn't say a thing. He just took in every word.

Marty was groping for answers when Jill relieved him of that burden.

"Listen to me," she told the men harshly. "You work out your seating plans and all the rest of your petty political bullshit later, when the membership isn't around. In case you've forgotten, Tony Hunt is the enemy here. He's the sonofabitch we have to beat, and right now he'd be laughing himself sick if he could see this sad-sack performance."

She stared daggers at Marty, Pete, and Harry. The resentment of men who weren't used to being publicly scolded by a woman clouded their faces—still, not one of them uttered a syllable of objection.

Jill took a breath. "Mr. McCreery, what I want to know is, how much money have you put aside for strike pay? How long can our membership last on the picket line?"

Marty looked like he'd sooner give blood than part with that information.

"A month," he said finally. "At half pay. But I can't tell you how many people have called already and asked for their strike pay in a lump sum."

"Don't give it to them that way," Jill said.

"No kidding," Marty answered snidely.

"Make sure everyone shows up at picketing assignments," she continued, ignoring his tone. "Dock anyone who doesn't."

"You take the heat for that one, lady," Pete Banks said.

"That's why I'm here," Jill replied evenly.

Sid spoke up for the first time.

"The ones we'll have to watch are the merchants. I know they said they'll play along, but it really goes against the grain of those Chamber of Commerce types to do anything that makes the cash register stop ringing. Most of them are Presidentials, too, and, deep down, you know how they feel about us Hardwoods."

Jill asked to have the distinction explained to her, and learned about the historical stratification of the town and the resentment engendered among the merchants when their erstwhile underlings found the opportunity to better themselves by working at the plant.

Understanding the significance, she said coldly, "We'll picket every major store, too. Any of the owners waver, we'll tell them: You sell to scabs, you won't sell to us."

All of them nodded, impressed—even Marty.

"In this fight, everybody takes a side . . . but, goddamnit, if we fight among ourselves, we do it privately. Do you all understand?"

A quartet of tight nods answered her.

33

Orville Leen rode alone.

Behind the wheel of a patrol unit, thinking of himself as a cowboy lawman, Leen snorted. Those loose cannon heroes were a crock of shit. Your everyday cop filled out reports for everything except picking his nose.

In any decent department, the cowboys never made it through the academy, and if one or two slipped through they usually had their badges yanked before they finished their probationary period. Real cops just couldn't get away with crazy crap.

With one possible exception. A sheriff.

When you were the chief law enforcement official of a small county you answered to no one except the voters and the state's attorney. And if the next election was over two years away and the state's attorney was your old fishing buddy, you really answered to no one at all.

Orville Leen had never thought in such terms before. He'd never had the need. Now, he found such thinking both liberating and comforting.

Was this the real reason he'd sicced Billy Shelton on Krieger? To free himself up? He had to admit it felt good to do his own driving again. It might be interesting, too, if he actually had to draw his weapon for the first time in years.

He drove through the business district observing the union pickets marching along in front of the stores. They were orderly. Some were even shooting the breeze with the deputies who were assigned to keep them in line.

He'd posted his people to picket-watching duty after that lady lawyer had called to tell him what the union planned to do. Leen thought it was a pretty interesting idea. Discriminating on the basis of where people stood in a labor dispute.

Damned if he knew of a law against it.

With everything quiet in town, the sheriff headed out toward the plant. It was time to find out who shot Tony Hunt.

The guard captain sensed that the sheriff was in no mood to be messed with. When Leen asked him to open the plant's main gate, he complied immediately.

A crew of union pickets watched with silent interest.

The sheriff asked the picketers if any of them had seen where Tommy Boyle and Tony Hunt had been standing the night of the riot, at the moment the shot was fired. Three of them had. Leen called two deputies over to act as stand-ins.

He stepped out into the street and thought: In order for Hunt to have been hit the way he was, the shot would have had to come from . . .

The municipal storage facility across the street? The land over there sloped upward. Unless the gunman had been able to hover above the mob like a hummingbird, that was where the shot must have been fired.

The sheriff crossed the street and rousted a city payroller from his nap to open the storage yard for him. He strode to the back of the storage yard, past earthmoving equipment, snowplow blades, and a broken-down garbage truck, to where the slope of the land was the highest. There, he turned.

Several of the strikers had stepped out into the street to watch him. From his vantage point, Leen could see the heads and shoulders of his Hunt and Boyle stand-ins. The rest of their bodies were hidden by the strikers who stood in between.

At that moment, his "Tommy Boyle" turned sideways to look around at the sheriff; the people in the street shifted, too, leaving his "Tony Hunt" a lot more exposed. Suddenly, Leen had a whole new fix on things. He tried to envision the scene as it had happened the night of the riot. . . .

Boyle and Hunt were facing off over there. A mob of strikers filled the street. The shooter tried to draw a bead, but bodies were shifting every-where. Then the shooter locked in on his target . . . Tommy Boyle. Not

Tony Hunt. But Boyle moved at just the wrong time for the shooter, and the round wound up nicking Hunt.

Thinking about Boyle as the target made sense, Leen realized, if you considered that after missing him with a difficult shot, the killer was persistent, came back later when Boyle was alone, and then made a shot that was a piece of cake.

Leen looked around, hoping that he'd be lucky enough to find some shred of physical evidence. He crisscrossed the yard, keeping his eyes on the ground. He found nothing. But when he looked up again he noticed the sun reflecting off something metallic stuck in the rear tire of a backhoe.

He walked over and carefully dug a piece of metal out of the tire tread with his pocketknife. It was a shell casing. He dropped it into his shirt pocket.

He was about to go back to his car when he felt someone watching him. He looked up and saw Hunt in his top-floor window. Didn't a busy man like Hunt have something better to do than look out his window? And he thought again about Hunt's barging into his office. Trying to push him around. It brought a mangled scrap of Shakespeare to mind: *That guy up there did protest too much.*

Why?

Because he had something to hide, and he was worried.

Sweat, you bastard, the sheriff thought, and gave Tony Hunt a cheery wave.

34

Hunt was still looking out his window as the sheriff drove away. Seeing that hick lawman over there brought back the idea that someone had been shooting at *him*, not Boyle. It couldn't have been Krieger himself, because he'd been at the motel evicting its occupants . . . but he might have had somebody else do it for him. One of the thugs he'd used in that botched kidnapping of Boyle's PI?

He turned from the window. He kept his face a perfect blank. "You may have a point," Hunt said, "about getting rid of the sheriff."

"Don't forget Fortunato," Krieger said gleefully, propping his feet on Hunt's desk. "He's yours."

Hunt didn't respond. He turned back to the window.

The guy was really a disappointment, Krieger thought. Not at all the cutthroat captain of industry he had hoped for.

Krieger's entire criminal career had made an abrupt turn when he'd shared a cell at Stateville with a forger named Bernie who'd copped to a murder-two plea after he did in his partner with a fountain pen. Krieger was up for a manslaughter rap, having hanged his stepfather with the same belt the prick had used to beat Krieger before he got his growth.

It was Bernie who told Krieger the inspirational story of Michael

Milken. Milken had come up with *the* scam of all time—junk bonds—and when he'd got put away all he did was twenty-two months at a Club Fed, suffering nothing worse than the loss of his frigging wig. And when he walked out he still had a billion bucks to his name.

Hearing that, Krieger decided business was the name for crime that really paid. So when he got out of the joint, he sent out a mailing. Not of his résumé, which was nonexistent, but of his rap sheet, which was encyclopedic.

With each copy, he'd sent a simple cover letter: "Egon Krieger offers his heavy lifting and planting services to the busy chief executive on the go."

Krieger reasoned that guys who stole billions, even legally, were sharks. Which meant they'd have work for a leg breaker. Or they'd like to have one around to support their image. Either way, he could trade his talents for a reasonable salary and a chance to learn the big-time stealing business from the best.

Out of twenty solicitations, Krieger had received eight job offers. He'd accepted Hunt's when he'd learned that the guy's middle name actually meant "shark" in Spanish.

What a dipshit mistake.

Then again, it probably didn't matter. In the last twenty-four hours, Krieger had undergone a change of heart. Now he wanted to be a photographer. Those pictures of Fortunato's had been just too cool. And with what Krieger knew—of creeps and crooks and nightcrawlers, all the things they did—*he* could get some pictures that'd pop your fucking eyes out. Too bad Fortunato wouldn't be around to teach him the finer points.

Still, he had Fortunato's books—including the one the SOB had drilled yesterday—for inspiration. Once Krieger had gotten over being pissed for having been scared away, he'd had to admire the guy's style.

And, damaged or not, he knew that book would be worth a fortune someday. All he'd have to do would be to put a little label on it: "Bullet hole compliments of author." Fucking thing had to be unique. And always would be—once the guy was dead.

"Fortunato's mine," Hunt said, interrupting Krieger's reverie. "Have you set it up?"

"Tomorrow night," Krieger answered.

35

Teddy Stinson and Felton Markus left the plant twenty minutes after the sheriff. They'd just come out of their chip fabrication class, and each of them had a hundred-dollar signing bonus check in his pocket.

Teddy and Felton were scabs.

Teddy'd been a steelworker. Felton had been on the line at a GM plant. Now, both were learning to assemble microprocessors.

Felton, tall, white, and bulky, was complaining about how little high-tech paid compared to steel and wheels. Teddy, short, black, and wiry, put the matter into perspective.

"Fuck it," he told Felton. "These days a guy with any kind of a job is a hero. Means he ain't a bum who quit tryin'."

The two men fell silent as they crossed the picket line outside the gate.

"Shit-eating scabs," one striker hissed.

"Cocksuckers," said another.

The two cops on hand made a point of stepping between the strikers and the scabs. They didn't seem to mind the picketers' trash-talking, though. Which led Teddy to think, What's sauce for the goose . . .

So, he said to the strikers, "Pardon us, boys, we gotta go cash our paychecks."

The cops looked at each other. One said to Teddy, "Get the fuck outta here before we turn these guys loose on you."

Felton hurried off. Teddy followed slowly, never looking back but listening closely.

"Nigger!" a shrill voice yelled.

Teddy smiled. What he heard was a cry of futility, some redneck just sticking his tongue out. He and Felton were safe for the time being.

Felton saw it differently. When Teddy caught up he said, "Are you crazy? You want them to kill us?"

Teddy shrugged. "A man can take just so much, an' I took all mine."

Felton stared at his short companion. "Sounds like a good philosophy to back up with a gun. You got one?"

"Ain't got a gun," Teddy replied. "But I got me a .357 Magnum imagination."

The two men were able to cash their paychecks at Riverman Savings because the checks were drawn on an account there, but the service wasn't exactly cordial. They were each given a hundred-dollar bill and told, no, they couldn't have tens and twenties. No smaller bills were available.

A bank that couldn't break a hundred.

In short order, the pair found a lot of other places where they weren't welcome. They couldn't buy a cassette player, a tape, or even batteries. They couldn't buy cigarettes, candy, or a newspaper. Nobody in Elk River would sell them a goddamn thing. And everywhere they went, pickets were watching them.

"This sucks," Felton muttered. "Let's go back to the country club."

Teddy said, "In a minute. I've worked up an appetite."

Directly ahead was a large supermarket. With another picket line out front.

"They ain't gonna sell us anything, either," Felton complained.

"Oh, I believe they will," Teddy replied.

The two men crossed the picket line and went inside the food store. The manager was a woman with peach-colored hair sprayed as hard as shredded wheat. The way she made them, it was like they wore name tags: HI, I'M A SCAB. MY NAME IS . . .

Teddy picked up a blue carrier basket. He smiled as they went past the manager's elevated cubicle and said, "Pleasant afternoon."

The woman scooped up her telephone. Teddy and Felton stopped at the back of the produce aisle.

"You hungry for anything in particular?" Teddy asked.

"They *ain't* gonna sell us anything," Felton insisted.

"C'mon, man, play along."

"Okay, I'd like a steak."

"Think of something ready-to-eat. My treat."

Teddy tossed a Golden Delicious apple to Felton and picked out a McIntosh for himself. He took a big bite.

Catching on, Felton grinned and did the same.

"Let's see what they won't sell us now," Teddy said.

They accumulated bags of apples, pears, and plums; two half gallons of milk; three pints of ice cream; a bottle of chocolate syrup; a package of cookies; a tub of soft cheese; two loaves of bread; and a pound of spiced ham before the manager and two boxboys caught up with them.

"You're not welcome here," the woman told them.

Teddy replied, "That's okay, we don't like you, either. We're just here to shop."

"We won't sell to you," she said. The boxboys tried to look mean.

"We got a little problem then. See, we been nibblin' at everything in this here basket. You don't sell it to us, you're out, what, twenty, thirty bucks."

The woman said, "Jergen, go get me a deputy."

"That's fine," Teddy said. "We'll just pick up a few more things while we're waitin'."

Felton asked, "Do we have too much stuff for the express lane?"

Teddy was eating from a box of Ritz Crackers and Felton was shooting Reddi Whip into his mouth straight from the can when the deputy found them at a checkout stand. Each had his hundred-dollar bill in hand.

Try as he might, the cop couldn't think of a charge to bring against two men who were willing to pay for the food they'd eaten.

By divvying up their purchases, Teddy and Felton each broke his C-note. But they did have to bag for themselves.

When they stepped outside with their groceries, all the pickets were bunched up behind a good-looking blond woman. It looked like she was the only thing holding them back.

The woman said, "Score one for you, boys. But you want to be careful. I can't be everywhere, and neither can the deputies."

Felton didn't say a word, and for once Teddy's mood turned somber. The small black man straightened up and held his head defiantly high.

"You think we're your enemies?" he asked. "Well, my man here had fifteen years in with the UAW; I had eighteen with the United Steel Workers. We been on strike, we carried picket signs . . . and look where it got us." Teddy shook his head.

"We aren't your enemies. We're your future."

36 Tommy had given John a key to his town house on the day he'd moved in, but this was the first time John had ever used the key, the first time he'd ever been there alone. As he opened the door, he half expected to find the place trashed. But everything was in its place. Even the silence had yet to be disturbed.

John closed the door behind him and locked it.

He looked around. There was a framed photo of Tommy on the wall in the living room. Not one of John's, but he'd have been proud if it was. Tommy was at a lectern with a sheet of paper in one hand, a fist in the air, and a wide smile on his face. All around him, the membership of Local 274 was on its feet cheering, laughing, and weeping with joy as their president announced the terms of the new agreement with Pentronics Systems.

That had been only three years ago. Now the union was on the run and its leader was dead. John felt a terrible loss.

"Talk to me, Tommy. Tell me what happened. I need to understand."

The phone machine was blinking. It sat next to the phone on a pass-through counter to the kitchen. The call counter indicated one message.

John hit the play button. The message that emerged was just one word: "Shit."

And that was indistinct, fading as though it had been said while the caller's phone was being hung up. John turned up the machine's volume and replayed the message. This time he could tell that the voice was female. And angry, not just disappointed.

The voice sounded familiar, too. Bobbi Sharpes? John pressed the save button so the "Shit" wouldn't be erased.

He looked around and wondered what to do next. The place was as neat as a pin, but something didn't seem right. What?

He went into the kitchen and poked around. He turned the dial of the refrigerator to a colder setting to preserve the food inside, knowing he'd be the one to come back and clean out the fridge.

He looked next at the nook off the living room that Tommy'd used as his home office. There was an appointment book on the desk. He flipped through the pages. Only one entry stood out.

It was a referral for a labor lawyer and a comment on her qualifications: "Jill Baxter/kicks ass/takes no prisoners."

John smiled. He looked through Tommy's files. To his untutored eye, all seemed to contain routine union business. He'd have to bring the kick-ass lawyer back for an expert opinion. He tucked the appointment book in his jacket pocket. The one that didn't hold his .38.

He headed for the stairs leading up to Tommy's bedroom. That's when it hit him: cigarette smoke. The odor was stronger here, it'd stayed in the carpet and the drapes. But Tommy hadn't smoked.

He entered Tommy's bedroom, a place he'd never been before, and a new scent was added. Perfume. The fragrance seemed vaguely familiar. Just the way the voice on the machine had. Bobbi Sharpes again? Or one of the sweeties who'd come after her?

The ashtray on the nightstand next to Tommy's bed had been wiped clean, but there were five books of matches in it. Four were from local bars and lounges; one was from the Traveler's Delight Motel.

John scooped up the matchbooks and put them in the pocket with the appointment book. He was about to look through Tommy's dresser when the door downstairs rattled.

Someone was trying to get in.

When the door swung open, John jammed his gun into the face of the man trying to enter. Sheriff Orville Leen let out a howl as his nose, already battered from the riot, once again gushed blood.

The sheriff got a handkerchief into place before another uniform was ruined. He managed this without dropping the lock picks he'd used to open the door. John kicked the door closed and led him to a bathroom.

While the sheriff applied a washcloth to his nose, John went to the kitchen to get him some ice. He dropped some cubes into a plastic bag and wrapped a wet dish towel around the bag. He waited for the sheriff to come out of the bathroom.

Leen was not happy.

"I think you broke my goddamn nose."

"Could've been a lot worse," John said without remorse. He sat down in Tommy's easy chair. Leen glared over the ice bag at him.

"You got a permit for that weapon?" the sheriff asked, clearly hoping John didn't.

"Yes, I do. I also have a key to the front door, and a right to be here. How about you? You have a warrant? Or are you just doing a little breaking and entering?"

Which is exactly what Leen had been doing. Not that he'd expected to be caught and questioned about it. But the way things had been going lately, he probably should have. He slumped down on the sofa.

"Me being here like this looks like shit, doesn't it?" Leen sighed.

John nodded.

"And every time I see you I seem to be stepping in another pile." The sheriff readjusted the ice bag. "You think I killed Tommy Boyle?"

"No," John said.

"But I might be in on it in some way, right?"

John didn't answer.

"I came here looking for evidence," the sheriff said. "Why are you here?"

"I'm Tommy's executor. I have to secure his belongings."

"Concealing evidence of a crime is a crime."

"If I find anything, it'll get to the right people."

"Shit," the sheriff said.

He got up and took the ice bag away from his face. The bleeding had stopped, but his nose was bent, and the discolored skin under his eyes was getting darker again.

But he looked John straight in the eye.

"I don't know how just yet, but I'm gonna prove to you that you can trust me, Fortunato. When I do, if you know something, I'll want you to tell me."

John stood up, too.

"That's better than asking me to take you on faith."

John opened the door for the sheriff, and Leen gave him back the ice bag. The sheriff gingerly put his fingers to his face.

"This poor nose," he said.

John stepped into his church, genuflected in front of the altar out of habit, and made his way to the bank of candles set against the wall.

He put twenty dollars into the poor box, picked up a taper, and lit four candles. Two each for Doolan and Tommy. He'd forgotten them last night. Going to bed with Jill had distracted him. It had been the first time he'd forgotten to light Doolan's candle since the last night he'd spent with Tess, when she'd told him that she was marrying someone else.

John apologized to both Doolan and Tommy. Then he lit two more candles in case he didn't make it that night, either.

Ron Narder dragged home after another exhausting day. Coordinating all the personnel needed to keep peace at the profusion of picket lines around town, maintaining some semblance of a normal patrol function, and doing both without racking up so much overtime he busted the department's budget were enough to give a man a migraine. He wanted nothing more than a kiss from his wife, a bite to eat, and, please God, at least six straight hours of sleep.

But when he stepped through his front door, he saw that Clare and his seven-year-old son, Danny, had waited dinner for him. Clare had even set the table in the dining room, as if his arrival were a holiday or some other special occasion. Narder was moved almost to tears. They sat down as a family and, holding hands, gave thanks for all their blessings.

The chief deputy was blessed enough to make it all the way through dessert before his father stormed into the house.

"Clare, Danny," the old man said, "I'm sorry to be interrupting your dinner." Then he turned to his son. "Ron, you hear what happened at Food Giant this afternoon? Milt was on the line there, and he told me."

"I heard, Dad. Give me a minute here while—"

"I don't have a minute. This is too damn important!"

Ron Narder's forbearance snapped. He stood up so abruptly his chair tipped over. He thrust his face at his father and said in a low, ominous tone, "This is *my* house. I make the decisions here. And right now I'm going to thank my son for waiting for me to come home before he had his dinner. Then I'm going to kiss him good-night. Then he's going upstairs. *Then* we can talk. Are we clear on all that?"

Any criminal suspect hearing the menace in the chief deputy's voice would have banished all thought of resistance. Deke Narder, though, looked every bit as furious as his son, and was unwilling to yield an inch.

"I'll be on the front porch," the old man said, and added with sarcasm, "If you can spare a minute." He stormed out.

Danny and Clare both looked shaken by the confrontation. Ron dropped to one knee and opened his arms to his son. Without hesitation, the boy ran into his arms, and Narder hugged him tightly.

"Grandpa's upset about the strike," he explained in a calm tone. "I guess I am, too. We're gonna see if we can work it out now. You go have your bath, and get a good night's sleep. I love you." He kissed his son on a downy cheek.

Ron whispered to Clare to run Danny's bath good and loud and close the bathroom door tight. When he stepped onto his front porch, the chief deputy's mood was far from conciliatory.

"What?" he asked bluntly of his father. What the hell did he want? What did he think gave him the right to barge into another man's house, ruin his evening, and upset his family?

"That's just what I want to know from you," Deke said. "What are you going to do about these goddamn scabs, pulling their stunts like they did today at Food Giant? Verna told them she wasn't going to sell to them, and they went ahead and ate a bunch of food anyway. And that damn deputy down there, Floyd Peters, didn't even arrest them!"

The chief deputy rubbed the bridge of his nose, then looked at his father. This was the man who'd taught him right from wrong. And now he seemed to have forgotten every last lesson he'd passed along.

"Floyd Peters didn't arrest anyone because he *couldn't* arrest anyone."

"Why the hell not? Those scabs disobeyed the store manager."

"Listen to yourself! You're a union man, bleeding in your guts because of this strike, and you want my deputies to arrest people because they didn't obey a supermarket manager? How'd you like it if I had to arrest strikers because they didn't listen to their managers? Those scabs weren't arrested today because they hadn't done anything *illegal*. They've got the same rights as anyone else. Which includes the right to shop."

Deke Narder's face grew grim in the yellow light of the front porch. "You know where I was today?"

"No." Now that he thought of it, he was surprised that he hadn't heard from his father before this.

"You remember Steve and Cookie Hiller?"

"The guy who replaced you in Quality Assurance?"

"Yeah. Him and his wife. I'm godfather to their little girl. I took all of them over to St. John's in Springfield today. Doctor over there wanted to see them. Got some test results back. . . ." Deke Narder seemed to choke on what he had to say next. "That little baby—just twenty-two months old—has leukemia."

"Oh, Jesus."

"You got that exactly right. Because the cost of the only treatment that might save her, a bone marrow transplant, is enough to make Jesus weep."

Ron couldn't find a word to say.

"Of course, Steve and Cookie don't have insurance anymore . . . just their tough luck their baby got sick while Daddy is on strike . . . their tough luck vile pigs like Tony Hunt don't want to pay their workers a living wage or provide health benefits."

Deke Narder shook his head in sorrow and disgust. "But it's worse than tough luck that you deputies let those goddamn scabs get away with anything they want. Between them and Hunt, they're killing that little girl . . . and the rest of us won't be far behind."

Ron turned away from his father and started down the steps toward his patrol unit.

"Where are you going?"

The chief deputy stopped and looked back. "I'm going to take up a collection for the Hiller girl. From every deputy in the department."

His father stared at him as if he hadn't heard a word he'd said.

"In the car coming back," Deke told Ron, "nobody said anything the whole way home. Steve and Cookie just sat in the back seat, rocked their baby, and cried. And I couldn't help but think: What would I have done if this had happened to my child, and someone like Tommy Boyle hadn't made sure I had health insurance? And I wondered what you and Clare would do if it was Danny got sick, and you didn't have a job or any benefits."

The chief deputy didn't know how to answer his father.

"Ronnie," the old man said, "you're just breaking my heart."

Bill Deeley stopped by John's house that night. The pastor was calling on John to ask his permission to make a change in the Church of the Resurrection. The very idea of a change in the church jolted John, and what Bill Deeley had in mind would have Michelangelo Fortunato spinning in his grave.

But when John heard Bill's reasoning, he said, "If you're right, if it comes to that, go ahead and do it."

37   Friday morning, Tony Hunt picked up his phone and made a call.

One of the first steps Hunt had taken when he'd decided to break the union was to acquire a spy within its ranks. Someone near Tommy Boyle who could be a source of worthwhile information. Someone who could be pressured or someone who could be bought. A discreet background check by a firm of high-tech snoops out of St. Louis quickly found his man . . . Pete Banks.

Banks had the gambling bug. Unlike so many of his kind, he didn't labor under a ruinous debt; he simply faced a credit ban at every gambling boat in the Midwest, his preferred venues for throwing away his money. Banks was described to Hunt as a guy who craved to play high-stakes Twenty-one but rarely mustered the cash to do more than pump the quarter slots—and look longingly over to where the real action took place.

Corrupting him with a few thousand dollars and the promise of more had been child's play for Hunt and had already paid high dividends. Pete Banks had been the one to tell Hunt that Tommy Boyle had a private dick snooping on him.

And just minutes ago Banks had delivered another nugget: Local 274 was almost broke. Hunt found the irony delicious.

The secretary of the man Hunt was calling answered. He heard her gasp when he announced himself. He knew it would be a minute before he was put through; there'd be a hurried discussion on the other end as to what Hunt was doing.

The delay gave him time for reflection. He'd never actually killed anyone before . . . and now he was planning to murder Fortunato for his insolence. Hunt eyed the handgun on his desk. It was suitably small and easy to conceal but had a reassuring heft. He grabbed the weapon and extended it at arm's length, trying to imagine Fortunato staring down his barrel right now.

At that moment, the secretary came back on the line. Politely, she asked why Hunt was calling. Tony Hunt lowered his gun. Back to business as it was really practiced.

He said, "Please tell Harold Noyes I'd like the Brotherhood of Manufacturing Workers to organize my new workforce."

"Sure, he made a call, I saw him myself."

"Tommy Boyle made a phone call from this station the night he was arrested?" Orville Leen asked Ron Narder.

"Absolutely. Per your orders. Everybody got read his rights, and everybody got one phone call. And . . ." Narder yawned. "And I gave Boyle his. He seemed grateful, too."

Leen said, "To you personally, because you let him have the phone call?"

"Well, yeah." Narder tried hard not to sound defensive.

"You did the right thing, Ronnie."

"I sure as hell try to," the deputy said, rubbing his eyes.

"You remember what time you let Boyle have his call?"

"I logged it. But I remember, too. It was right about two A.M."

"Did you hear who he called?"

"No, he was talking real quiet. And I didn't want to crowd him too close."

The chief deputy's manners were actually something Leen often wished more of his people had. So he wasn't about to chastise the man for them now. Except he'd just fallen asleep.

"Ron? Ronnie!" That got his eyes open. "You didn't hear anything at all? What Boyle was saying?" the sheriff asked.

"Not words."

"Well, what else was there?"

"Tone," Narder replied drowsily. "He was whispering, like I said, but it was real intense."

"An argument?"

"Not on Boyle's part. I could see his face. He wasn't angry or nothin'. It was just like he'd made some big decision and was saying that was the way it was gonna be."

"Anything else? That you noticed, I mean."

"Well, I can't swear to it, but I thought he was talking to a woman . . . and when he put down the phone he sorta nodded to himself like he'd just done the right thing."

Orville Leen didn't know if it mattered whether Boyle'd called a woman, but at least he had one more lead to pursue in a homicide that had damn few of them.

He said, "Ron, get on over to the phone company. Be real nice so they cooperate without needing a warrant, but I want that phone number Boyle called. I want to know who he was whispering to."

The deputy said, "Sure thing, Sheriff."

"After that, Ronnie, go home and get to bed. Come back in when you can stay awake."

Narder smiled, saluted, and headed for the door—where he stopped and squinted back at the sheriff. Probably wasn't a good idea to bring up the subject when the man had been nice enough to give him the day off—after he'd been out half the night collecting for that poor Hiller kid—but the question had been eating at him since he'd walked into the room and seen that Leen had his sunglasses on once more.

"Sheriff, you bang your nose again?"

38 Ty and Darien were having dinner Friday evening in EE, the chamber below the baseball diamond at Eleventh and Elm. They'd just finished playing a game of Charlie 'n' Joe, and Ty was asking questions about how the tunnels had been dug.

"Where'd you put all the dirt?" he wanted to know.

Darien smiled at him. "You got all the brains. You tell me: If you take dirt outta one hole, where's the best place to put it?"

"Another hole."

"Right."

"But what kind of hole is big enough?"

"Yeah, what kind?"

Darien enjoyed Ty's company immensely. The boy was so smart it was a pleasure just to sit and watch him think.

"A quarry? No. You dump tons of dirt right out in the open, people will notice. It's gotta be a hole that's hid—" His face lit up. "A mine . . . an *abandoned* mine."

" 'Played out,' is how they put it, I believe. Lots of old coal mines like that around here."

"That's great." Ty was delighted. "It's perfect. Nobody will ever know."

Darien nodded. "Me 'n' ol' Gil got the notion when we bought our excavatin' equipment from a minin' company in Pennsylvania that went toes-up."

The dialogue continued.

How come they didn't have to support their tunnels with timber to keep them from caving in?

Well, was the soil soft or hard?

Damn hard, like cement.

Clay, Darien told him. A subsurface horizon of clay. That was like the Nam, too. Except there it had been red and here it was brown-gray.

Were there problems for them digging in America that Charlie didn't have in Vietnam?

Well, what about the weather?

It gets a lot colder in Illinois. . . . The ground freezes.

Down to four feet sometimes, Darien said. That limited digging in winter to areas below the frost line.

"How come the tunnels don't fill with water when the town's right on a river?" Darien asked the boy, hoping to stump him.

That one took Ty about ten seconds to answer.

"Because the land runs uphill, and water always seeks its own level."

"Right. We dug, but we stayed above the water table."

"What about floods?" Ty asked.

"What about 'em?"

"Well, most rivers flood at one time or another. Did you check the historical records on the Elk River? If it flooded bad, it might overcome the slope of the land."

The idea sent chills down Darien's spine. All those years of planning and digging, thinking they had everything covered . . . and they could be drowned like rats?

"I'm sure John thought a that," Darien said.

But he'd never heard John mention it. Or Gil. *He'd* never thought of it. But a fifteen-year-old kid with less than a week of tunnel experience had.

Made a man humble. Or want to kick himself.

Ty asked, "Why did John start digging in the first place?"

To take his mind off the terrifying image of flooded tunnels, Darien told Ty the story of Doolan.

"This guy just disappeared?" Ty asked. "That's crazy. People don't just vanish."

"You don't know shit about war," Darien snapped, his mood shifting dramatically. "Guys disappeared. You get under an artillery round or a five-hundred-pound bomb, ain't gonna be nothin' left but smoke and regrets. Lotsa other shit can happen, too."

Ty kept quiet. He knew it was no time to argue.

To Ty, the tunnels had been a miraculous avenue of escape from the bullies at school, the way he'd met a new friend, an underground world of games and adventure. For the first time, however, he understood that they meant a lot more to the three men who had dug them.

"I'm sorry," he said.

Darien nodded, but his thoughts were a million miles away.

That was when Ty made himself a promise. He was going to solve the mystery. He was going to find out what had happened to Doolan.

39 "Sometimes I think I should be a football coach," Jill said, staring into the steam rising from her cup of coffee, "with all the pep talks I have to give."

Looking at her, John realized that another night of romance was not in the offing. She'd just told him of her efforts to maintain union morale after yesterday's debacle at the supermarket.

"You get your people turned around?" he asked.

"I tried, but that guy's parting shot took the heart right out of them: 'We aren't your enemies. We're your future.' Shit."

"You believe he's right?"

"He will be if we don't fight harder than Hunt."

"When I talked to Tommy's private investigator, he said he'd love to get a look into Hunt's private files. Maybe there's some way you can snoop on him through legal means. Maybe find he's vulnerable somewhere."

Jill nodded, but without enthusiasm. John grabbed his jacket off the back of a chair.

"Come on, I want to take you out for a drink."

"What?"

"At the bar where our local cops drink," he said. "Tommy's PI gave me another suggestion."

The Tin Star, owned by Burt Kozak, a former Elk River deputy, catered to department personnel. It was a place where off-duty deputies could drink, share shop talk at the back of the joint, and know that Burt would keep any civilians out of their hair at the tables up front. The place didn't go silent when John and Jill entered, but the volume control on casual conversation definitely went down a notch. The half dozen deputies gathered at the rear were following their basic cop instinct and watching them.

On the drive over, John had told Jill about Phil Henry's suggestion: Find a cop with union connections. John didn't know many deputies, but he knew the chief deputy, having been introduced by Tommy, who had said Narder came from a good union family. He was their man. And right now he was standing at the back of the bar holding an institutional-size mayonnaise jar filled with cash.

Jill took a seat at a table while John walked over to the gathering of deputies. She sized up the chief deputy. Tall, dark, and solid. Burt started to say something to John, but Narder waved him off. He listened to John for a moment, put down the jar, and followed John back to where Jill sat. John made the introductions.

"Yeah, I remember you from the other night," Narder told her. "You gave the sheriff a real hard time."

"Not hard enough to keep my client alive."

The chief deputy ignored the taunt and turned to John.

"I'm genuinely sorry about Tommy."

John nodded. But Jill didn't let him off that easy.

"Tommy Boyle did a lot of good things for your family, didn't he?" she asked. "Got them a living wage, and health benefits that kept up with costs. Saw to it that they were treated like human beings."

Anger flared in Narder's eyes. He sat down opposite Jill and gave her a hard stare.

"Maybe you deputies ought to think things through," Jill continued, meeting Narder's stare. "You reduce the earning power of the workforce at the plant, you reduce the town's tax base. That happens, even you cops will feel the pinch. Maybe they'll starting laying you guys off, or cutting your pay and benefits."

In the now-silent bar, Jill's voice carried the length of the room. She was beginning to draw hostile glances from the other deputies.

"Lady," Narder said, placing his hands flat on the table, "I get the same story at home. I know all about the union and what it does." There was more than rage in his eyes; there was a heavy measure of heartache, too. "I grew up in a union house, and I liked it. I had a good life. I wish things now could be the way they were then, but they aren't. And fuck me if I know what to do about that!" He slammed a fist on the table so hard he cracked the Formica. When he got control of his emotions again, he continued, "So I do what I can. Just about every spare penny of my pay is going to family or friends or whoever is on the picket line and having a hard time. But to earn that pay, I have to do my job. And my job doesn't let me take sides. I go by the book, and if that's not good enough for you or anybody else, it's just too damn bad."

Jill had more to say, but John cut her off.

"What about the sheriff, Ron?"

"What about him?" the deputy asked flatly.

"Is Leen taking sides?"

The cold, hard stares of every cop in the place pressed against them. Jill could feel a physical chill, and imagined their bodies being carried out the back door, never to be seen again.

John either didn't notice or didn't care.

"Why would he do that?" Narder asked with quiet menace.

"Why was he having a little heart-to-heart in his office with Hunt right after Tommy died?" John replied. "I walked in on them and I asked, but I never got an answer."

Narder lost a little of the starch in his neck when he heard that.

"And yesterday, while I was at Tommy's place cleaning up, why did the sheriff let himself in without a key or a warrant?"

Now a look of genuine uncertainty crossed the chief deputy's face.

John continued, "See, if I find out a thing or two about Tommy's murder, I'd feel better knowing there was someone with a badge I could trust. Someone I could give evidence to who wouldn't just bury it." He leaned closer to Narder. "So tell me, Ron, you gonna go by the book no matter what? No matter where the evidence leads?"

Ron Narder didn't hesitate.

"No matter what, no matter where," he said.

When they stepped out onto the street, a shudder passed through Jill.

She said, "Those last few minutes in there reminded me of your book."

"*Discord?*"

"*Moments of Truth.*"

· · ·

John's house was dark when they entered. He felt Jill moving toward him, but her kiss came as a surprise.

"I didn't think you'd be interested tonight," he said.

"Me either. But after the scene at that bar . . . I want you to remember you have something to live for."

She kissed him again.

"You want to light a fire?" she asked.

"Just what I had in mind."

She cuffed him on the shoulder.

"We better use my bedroom," John said. "There's company in the house tonight."

He felt her go tense in his arms.

"It's okay," he said. "It's just Darien and Ty."

She relaxed, but leaned back against his embrace, trying to see his eyes. It was too dark. "You can really tell who's here?" she asked softly.

"Yeah," he said, but remembering how she could distract him, he added, "for the moment."

John knocked softly on the bedroom door.

"Come in," came a whispered voice.

The lights were out in the room, but John had no trouble stepping past Ty, asleep on a cot, and crossing to Darien's bed.

"Everything okay?" he asked. It'd been a long time since Darien had slept in the house.

"You ever think about the tunnels flooding, man?" Darien asked quietly.

"Doesn't look like rain," John said.

"I'm serious."

John squatted down next to where his friend lay.

"It could happen," he replied, "under the right conditions. But the soil will let a fair amount of water filter right through it; that was why we had to line the water traps with plastic sheeting."

"You sayin' we all right for floods?"

John told him a story he'd heard. Back in '67, the First Battalion of the 277th Infantry decided that the way to destroy a tunnel complex they'd found was to divert the nearby Saigon River into it.

"And?" Darien asked.

"They pumped eight hundred gallons a minute into those tunnels for thirty-eight hours. The water drained right through the soil."

"Man," Darien said, his mood brightening, "you just can't beat a tunnel."

"Yeah, well, don't bet Mother Nature can't go army engineers one better. . . . And don't forget what the B-52s did."

The strategic bombers had collapsed a number of tunnel complexes in the Iron Triangle late in the war, and left John wondering if Doolan had been held prisoner in one of them during a raid.

But Darien didn't have to worry about B-52s, and learning that John *had* thought about flooding eased his mind greatly. In the dark, he reached out to his friend.

"I'll say a little prayer for Doolan tonight."

John exchanged a brief dap—the grunt's soul handshake—with Darien and left the room thinking of friends past and present.

Which made him wonder again where Gil had gone and what the hell he was doing.

40 Ty sneaked out of the house the next morning before Darien woke up. He thought he'd gotten away clean, but when he reached the sidewalk and looked back, there was John Fortunato in a first-floor window looking out at him.

The boy didn't have any doubt that John had followed him right down the stairs without his knowing it. He made a mental note not to challenge John to play Charlie 'n' Joe anytime soon.

John waved to him. Ty waved back.

Ty turned off Fifth Street onto Lincoln Avenue. In the block ahead, a knot of strikers leaned against a car parked in front of Dorner's Department Store. They were drinking coffee from paper cups. A stack of picket signs stuck out of the car's open trunk.

Suddenly, one of the men pushed himself off the car and pointed down the street. An old yellow school bus was coming up Lincoln toward him.

But this was Saturday morning.

The strikers grabbed their picket signs and poured into the street, yelling at the bus. The old crate tried to pick up speed. It barely wheezed past before the strikers could block it. The narrow escape didn't stop one man from hurling a metal thermos bottle through the bus's back window.

His friends gave him a cheer. The congratulations were cut short when the Sheriff's Department car that had been following the bus pulled over and two deputies grabbed the man.

Ty watched the bus roll past. A woman in the back clasped her hands to her forehead. Blood flowed through her fingers. The man seated next to her, desperately trying to come to her aid, had murder in his eyes.

Ty could tell because, as he passed, the man focused all his rage on him. The boy wanted to yell that *he* hadn't done anything. But the bus was gone before he could find his voice. And what would be the point? That woman hadn't done anything, either.

Ty sat on a bench waiting for the Elk River Library to open. He had a small pad of paper on his lap. On the top sheet he'd drawn a pattern of dots.

He was trying to free his mind from an inferred constraint in reasoning. The circumstances of Doolan's disappearance—all those years ago—just didn't make sense. Regardless of what Darien had to say about the mysteries of war.

Stripped down to essentials, Doolan was last seen—or, more accurately, heard from—between Point A, where he and John had entered the tunnel, and where a squad of soldiers waited, and Point B, where John was wounded.

John swore he had passed no intersecting tunnel or trapdoor between the two points. And from what Ty had seen of John's abilities, he didn't doubt John had it right.

Yet Doolan went somewhere—Ty refused to admit the man had just disappeared. It was a given that he didn't pass Point A, where the squad of soldiers waited. It was possible that Doolan had been forced to crawl over John at Point B while he lay unconscious, but Ty rejected that assumption.

If that had been the case, why hadn't the VC taken John prisoner, too? Or at least made sure he was dead?

So, back to the problem: Doolan went somewhere between Point A and Point B without there being anywhere to go. Somewhere in that construction was an inferred flaw. The fact that there had to be a flaw was obvious; the nature of it was not.

Ty studied his pattern of dots. Three rows of three dots formed a square:

• • •

• • •

• • •

The problem was to connect all nine dots using only four straight lines without picking up his pen.

He'd been given the problem in freshman math and had solved it easily. What had surprised him was how difficult it had been for his classmates to unravel. Not because they were dumb—well, not all of them—but because their reasoning was falsely constrained. To solve the problem, you only had to go beyond an inferred limit.

Ty was sure that to solve the Doolan problem he had to do basically the same thing, though perhaps on a more subtle level. As a meditation, he kept drawing dots and connecting them with lines.

After several minutes, he heard the door to the library being unlocked. Ty put his pen behind his ear, his pad in a pocket, and went inside. Listening to all of Darien's stories, he realized how ignorant he'd been about the Vietnam War. The conflict had ended little more than twenty years ago, but it was already ancient history to his generation. In fact, he knew more about the wars between Rome and Carthage than he did about the one in which over fifty thousand Americans had lost their lives.

But then, the history of the Vietnam War wasn't taught in U.S. high school curricula, at least not any he'd been offered. Ty felt some independent research into the subject would help him understand what his new friends had been through. Might give him a foundation from which he could make an intuitive jump toward the solution of the Doolan mystery.

He was well versed in how to use a library, but he asked the head librarian for her recommendations on the subject. She pulled out: *The 13th Valley; No Bugles, No Drums;* and *Johnny's Song—Poetry of a Vietnam Veteran.* She said when he was done with those, she could suggest several more books. And Ty could see that for a small-town library the shelves held a surprisingly large number of titles on Vietnam.

The librarian guessed what he was thinking and explained, "My son served there."

She left without saying if he'd ever come back.

Ty had already learned the war was a sensitive subject with certain people. Which was why he intended to keep his research to himself.

• • •

Ty read the volume of poetry and sampled each of the novels. His head was spinning with the images and emotions of war as he left the library. He was so lost in thought he almost bumped into the small man and the large boy on the sidewalk in front of him.

"Well, well, well, the wayward son. The *dropout*," Wesley Daulton added acidly.

Ty looked up. He saw his father and Frank Murtaw. The interesting thing was that Ty had no strong reaction to seeing either of them. His father's sarcasm didn't bother him, and Frank no longer scared him.

All he felt was annoyed. Somewhere in the maelstrom of his thoughts, he felt there had been the first glimmer of inspiration, and now it had vanished.

"What do you want?" Ty asked his father.

"An apology would be an appropriate beginning. For coercing your father's complicity in your academic degradation."

Ty said tonelessly, "You'd know all about degradation, wouldn't you?"

Wesley's normal flush deepened to carmine. He slapped his son's face. His son kicked him sharply on the shin.

"You vicious brat," Wesley hissed. "I'm disowning you."

"I'm cut out of your will?" Ty asked in mock horror. Then he added, "Guess you'll have to write Lumpy here's papers all by yourself. If you can manage."

The remark cut deeply. But it was Frank Murtaw who responded to the insult.

"Hey, you little prick, you think you're so tough now you don't need your psycho friends to protect you?"

Ty put his hand in his pocket and said, "Eat shit, Lumpy."

Frank took a step forward, and Ty drew the butt of a gun out of his pocket—stopping the larger boy cold.

"Maybe I'm a psycho, too, these days," Ty said. "You want to try me? Maybe I'll shoot you, Lumpy, because you're too stupid to live. It wouldn't be murder; it'd be natural selection."

Ty pulled the gun all the way out. Frank ran, and Ty's father was hard on his heels before the boy had the weapon clear.

Somebody else noticed, though. A pair of hands sounded sardonic applause. Gil was lounging on his Harley at the curb again like some malevolent guardian angel.

"That was great, kid. Faked 'em out of their fuckin' socks. With a starter's pistol yet."

He crossed to Ty and took the gun from him. It was the one Ty used to play Charlie 'n' Joe. "I bet even *you* forgot it was a phony," Gil added.

Ty had.

"See," Gil told him, "what *really* scared 'em was your hate. That was the genuine article, and hate's a powerful thing."

Ty's notebook had fallen out of his pocket. Gil picked it up, handed it to him, and said, "You're all right, kid. You want a ride home?"

41 "What can I do for you, Ms. Baxter?" Sheriff Leen asked. The woman looked just as angry as the last time she'd barged through his door.

"I've come to see Dexter Carlisle, Sheriff."

He'd been right. Dex Carlisle was the moron who'd damn near blinded the woman on the bus that morning.

"You looking to bail him out?"

"No, Sheriff. Just to talk to him. I also want to apologize on behalf of Local 274 to you and to the deputies who arrested Mr. Carlisle."

The sheriff stared at her. He had to be dreaming. Tommy Boyle's lawyer was saying she was sorry?

"Apologize?"

"Mr. Carlisle's behavior was disgraceful—"

"Not to mention felonious."

"That, too," Jill readily conceded.

Maybe this was all a trick, Leen thought.

"How is the woman who was injured?" Jill asked.

"She's at the hospital. They've been plucking glass out of her eyes over there, and she'll probably need plastic surgery. Her husband wants Carlisle's head."

"I don't blame him," Jill said. "I'll inform the hospital to forward all the bills to the union office."

Now, Leen thought, he understood. "In return for the charges' being dropped?"

"Without condition," Jill replied.

So he was back to square one. If she hadn't come to post bail or work a deal, why was she here at all? He didn't believe it was just to pass a moment's polite conversation with the prisoner.

Jill saw the unspoken question on Leen's face. "Sheriff, I won't pretend I have any love for scab labor. We're in a desperate fight here. If we lose, we lose everything. But I *despise* thugs and bullies."

Leen did, too. That was why he'd become a cop. Still, it made him uneasy to know he and this female lawyer had something in common.

"Follow me, Ms. Baxter," he said. "I'll take you to see Carlisle."

He took her to his lockup, and what she had to say was anything but polite. She reamed old Dexter a second bunghole. Not only wasn't she bailing him out, she was taking his strike pay and applying it to the injured woman's medical bills. Not that his money would be enough, she said. So what the dumb bastard had done was to take money away from his co-workers and their families . . . he'd given the whole local a black eye . . . he'd acted like a mindless hoodlum . . .

By the time she was done, Dex Carlisle had retreated to the corner of his cell and wrapped his arms around his head. Jill Baxter thanked the sheriff for his cooperation and stomped out, madder than ever.

Leen watched her go, and he thought it was getting too damn hard to know who his enemies were.

Marty McCreery sat at Tommy Boyle's desk and felt distinctly uncomfortable. Marty could hold his own with anybody in the local, but with John Fortunato looking at him, he couldn't help but feel that he didn't belong in Tommy's chair.

Which was the big reason he was glad he could help John with the favor he asked. John wanted to know if anybody in Local 274 knew somebody at the phone company who could get him some phone records. It was Marty's good luck that he did. His cousin's ex-wife, Patsy Haliburton, was a supervisor in directory assistance for the phone company. If John wanted some numbers, who could be better than Patsy?

"She can get a list of the calls made from the sheriff's station the night of the riot?" John asked.

"Patsy could tell you who the president calls from the phone in his potty."

Would she be willing to help?

"Yeah, I helped her pick up the pieces after my no-good cousin ran off with the Avon lady."

"Good. And ask her for a reverse directory and a list of numbers called from Tommy's home phone in the past month, too."

"No problem," Marty said, hoping John would leave before he started squirming.

Tony Hunt got a call from Pete Banks, his spy at Local 274, that morning and was given information for which he paid a thousand dollars. Forty-five minutes later, Harold Noyes, the international president of the Brotherhood of Manufacturing Workers, got back to him.

The bastard had been cunning enough yesterday to have his secretary tell Hunt that he would have to get back to him tomorrow. Yes, he'd been told, Mr. Noyes would call even though it would be Saturday.

Hunt wanted to use Noyes to supplant Local 274, to cut it off and have it wither and die. At the same time, Hunt would give himself political cover and inoculate himself against a union that would represent the workers' interests instead of his.

Overnight, Noyes had determined that Hunt must need him worse than he needed Hunt. Now, Noyes was trying to hold him up before he'd agree to organize the plant's new workers. Not for the workers' benefit. Token wage increases had been agreed to in the first five minutes. No, what they were discussing was Noyes's "cooperation fee."

Hunt had, of course, expected Noyes to be greedy . . . but Banks's call had given him a tool to sharply limit that greed.

Noyes told Hunt, "I think, in light of your current situation, wanting to get your plant back in operation quickly, that certain special considerations would be in order for me to help you. After all, it will put me in a delicate situation as the president of the international union. Why, my political opponents might even accuse me of selling out a loyal local shop. I'd need some . . . emoluments, shall we say, to make them see it my way."

Why don't you just say *spread the graft*, asshole? Hunt thought.

"How much?" he asked bluntly.

"I was thinking that the most persuasive argument that I could bring back to my colleagues would be to say we'll have a percentage of your annual profits."

Hunt gave Noyes points for gall, thinking he could actually become Hunt's partner.

"I have to confide something to you, Mr. Noyes," Hunt said.

"Yes, what's that?"

"I've learned that your relationship with Local 274 was, shall we say, unfriendly? That Tommy Boyle hadn't paid his local's dues for the past two years. That—"

"Lies! A pack of goddamn lies!" Noyes erupted.

"Then is it also a lie that Boyle suspected you of looting union funds?"

Hunt listened to Noyes sputter for several seconds before cutting him off.

"Here's the deal, Noyes. I'll pay you a fee for your cooperation, all right, but it will be a flat one million dollars per year. You buy as many of your pals as you need to with that. You go along, or *I* might be the one to whisper in the appropriate ear that your stewardship of the BMW should be investigated. And what with your stormy relationship with Tommy Boyle and the unfortunate circumstances of his death, who knows if you might not be stuck with a murder rap, too?"

Noyes's sputtering increased in volume and duration, but before Hunt hung up he had the deal done on his terms.

He smiled to himself, gleeful at the thought that he'd been able to use dirt that Tommy Boyle had dug up. For which he'd pay only a thousand dollars to Banks. *A thousand dollars!* Who said you can't find a bargain nowadays?

Hunt felt so expansive, he even hoped the cards would be kind to that little weasel Banks the next time he sat down at a gaming table.

42

Gil's stolen Harley was parked in the driveway when John returned home. He decided that it was time the two of them had their heart-to-heart. He stepped through the back door and saw he had a full house. Jill, Darien, and Gil were seated at the kitchen table eating, Ty was at the counter pouring chocolate syrup into a glass of milk.

"Hey, buddy"—Gil waved to John with a hand that held a can of beer—"long time."

"New bike?" John asked.

"Yeah." Gil nodded. "Got a real deal on it."

John got a beer out of the fridge and joined the group at the table.

"Where've you been?" he asked.

Gil was chewing, so he took a slug of beer to clear his throat.

"Friend died. Had this problem, you know, but the end . . . it's always a goddamn surprise." A faraway look entered Gil's eyes, a real sense of loss. Then he shrugged.

"I rode down to Texas to visit the family."

Texas was Gil's home state. The friend could've been another Lone Star vet or someone going back even further. That would explain his recent moodiness and his absence, John thought. If not his sudden penchant for grand theft.

"Anyway," Gil said, "I decided it was time to come back home. You know, make sure we didn't have any dinks comin' through the wire."

Gil glanced idly at Jill as he made the last remark. From her lack of a response he knew that John hadn't told her about the tunnels; the three of them and the kid were still the only ones who knew.

Darien said, "I'm gonna make another sandwich, John. You want one?"

As he passed behind Gil, Darien flashed John a look: *You think he's okay now?*

"Yeah, I guess," John said, answering both of Darien's questions.

"Ham or beef?" Darien asked.

"Ham on rye," John replied. He turned to Jill. "How's your day going?"

She told him how. About the attack on the bus, confronting Dexter Carlisle at the lockup, and that she was going to inform the local's executive committee that she'd resign if they supported Carlisle.

"Wait a minute," Gil said, "you're the union lawyer, but you don't want to fight scabs? What am I missin' here?"

Jill said, "I'll fight *anybody*." *Including you,* her look added. "What I won't do is start a fight."

Gil returned Jill's stare. "Then you better remember you didn't start this one. And you ain't gonna win it unless you get your head right."

"Meaning what?"

"Meanin' you back your people one hundred percent, lady. You don't expect them to fight with one arm tied behind their backs, the way the goddamn politicians did with us. You think those scabs don't know they're stealin' somebody else's job? They know. And you can bet they'd rather see your ass starve than theirs."

Gil pushed back from the table.

"You get into a fight, you go all out or you get killed. Don't ever forget that."

He left the room. Darien and Ty excused themselves a minute later.

"You agree with him?" Jill asked John.

"About Vietnam, yeah."

"And here?"

"We're not at war here. Yet."

Jill sought the privacy of her own room. John gave her an hour alone before he knocked on her open door.

"You want to talk, or should I go away?"

Stretched out on the bed, she inclined her head for him to come in. He closed the door behind him and sat in his grandmother's rocker. Jill stayed on the bed.

She said, "You know what really bothers me?"

"I can guess. The attack on that bus worked."

"Yes, it did. I just got off the phone with my dear friend Marty. He told me there are scabs walking out of town on Highway 98, and others have shown up at the bus depot wearing signs that say 'Leaving town.' "

"And the union people think that's great?" John asked.

"They did until I reminded them that they can't muscle Hunt into giving them their jobs, salaries, and benefits back. And if they keep up the violence, they'll force the sheriff into Hunt's camp."

"How'd they react to that?"

Jill smiled grimly. "Let's just say they were receptive when I said we all needed a couple of days to reassess our relationship. McCreery had a hard time not laughing out loud."

John knew there was more to come, and he didn't have to wait long.

"I'm going to Chicago tomorrow."

"Coming back?"

"Yes. If I quit, I always do it in person. And if they fire me, I'm sure they'll want the pleasure of telling me to my face."

"Want some company up in the big city?" he asked.

She shook her head. "I'll be busy. I'm going to take your suggestion and see if I can dig something up on Hunt."

John said, "That's rule number one: Know your enemy."

"No," she replied. "Rule number one is always remember your reasons for living."

She extended her hand to him and he joined her on the bed.

They lay beneath the covers, looking up at the ceiling, Jill snugged in close under John's arm. For several minutes, they were content in their silence. Then Jill said, "Tell me how you got started on your photography career."

John felt the heat of her skin against his, and the pleasant hollow ache in his loins. It was a fair enough request, he thought. And anticipating the pleasure of another kind of intimate sharing, he told her . . .

"You remember this picture, son?" Al Fortunato asked John.

It was John's second morning home after getting out of the Hines VA Hospital, near Chicago. He sat down on the sofa next to his father and took the snapshot from him. There was a small diagonal cut in the upper right corner, in the white border around the image. The mark—one of several tactile cues in the family photo album—was how John's sightless father *looked* at pictures these days.

"It's Mom," John said evenly, not sure if he was ready for whatever his father had in mind. "It's the first picture I ever took."

"With that Kodak Brownie she gave you for your fifth birthday. You remember *why* she gave it to you?"

"Because I got angry I couldn't draw Grandpa Michelangelo's church. I thought it was unfair that he could build something so beautiful and I couldn't even draw it."

"Right. So your mother gave you the camera to take a picture of the church . . . and you were so happy you said you were going to become the best photographer in the world. You started by taking your mother's picture. It was so beautiful it always broke my heart to see it. Tell me, Johnny: Is it still beautiful?"

As portraiture, it was exactly what you'd expect from a five-year-old: it was fuzzy, his mother's face was tilted to the right, and the top of her head was out of frame. For all that, there was a sense of life and love in his mother's eyes and a smile that wounded John every time he looked at the photo.

He had to clear his throat. "Yeah, Dad. It's still beautiful."

His father nodded as if there could be no other answer. "John, there's somebody I'd like you to meet."

His name was Arthur Cargill. He was a World War II veteran and a Vietnam War protester. His group, GIs for Peace, took the position that no young American should ever be asked to fight unless—as had been the case with his generation—U.S. territory had been attacked and the government was willing to use nuclear weapons to bring the conflict to a swift conclusion.

Of course, that likely meant the United States would never fight another war, but that was what Cargill had in mind. He'd been a combat photographer. He'd recorded the war in Europe in all its bloody detail from the D day invasion of Omaha Beach through the Battle of the Bulge to the fall of Berlin. When he left the service he put his camera down and vowed never to touch it again. Rather, he used his horrifying photographs to illustrate why the country's youth should not be asked to sacrifice themselves for anything short of national survival.

Al Fortunato had heard him speak against the war at the University of Illinois. He talked with Cargill afterward, said that he agreed with him and that he didn't need to see his pictures because he'd fought in Europe, too. While John was in rehabilitation, Al had contacted Cargill and asked him if he could help his son, teach him photography as a way to forget his war.

At that time, Cargill was a watercolorist who specialized in nature scenes, but he agreed to do it—without ever picking up a camera himself. He met John at a bar in Champaign, Illinois, bought him a beer, and asked, "So why do you want to learn photography?"

"I want to see if I can do it as well as I did when I was five."

Cargill grinned, intrigued. "Okay, but you'll have to tell me when we get there."

The next day, Cargill outfitted John with a Nikon camera body and an assortment of lenses. He took John to places like the Shawnee National Forest, Starved Rock State Park, and the Indiana Dunes, where they'd drink beer and talk and Cargill would paint landscapes. At night, he'd teach his student about the properties of different types of film and how various lenses gathered light. The following morning, John had to go out and shoot a photo that would capture not just the image but the feeling of Cargill's painting of the day before. Upon returning from their trips, Cargill showed him how to process and print his film.

When both men agreed a year later that John certainly was as competent as any kindergartner in the land, Cargill put one final question to his student: "What's the most important thing to remember about any picture you take?"

John, who was sharing a six-pack with his mentor at the time, said, "Always remove the lens cap."

Cargill choked on his beer. Then he laughed. "Okay, we'll skip the Socratic BS. But remember this: When you take a picture, make it your own. Do something that comes from inside of you, something nobody else could ever do."

"Because of my wounds," John told Jill, "I'd been retired from the army instead of discharged. That gave me travel benefits. I could fly free in military transports anywhere in the world on a space-available basis. We called it Space-A."

"Sounds great."

"They owed us a lot more, but you took what you could get. Anyway, I wanted to photograph more than just the Midwest. I started traveling around the world. And I found there were some shots I wanted to get that . . . required a certain amount of risk. I also found I didn't mind taking those risks.

"I was in Australia when I bumped into Gil again. Way the heck out in Perth. He was seeing the sights on Uncle Sam, too."

"Had he been hurt and retired, too?"

"Yeah. Gil has a prosthetic right foot. He lost his real one in a tunnel."

"I never noticed."

"Not surprising. He's real good with it. That time in Perth, he was learning to surf—just to show up the army doctors who said he'd never walk too well again." John laughed and shook his head.

"What?"

"I was just thinking. That guy doesn't take crap from anybody. Not only did he surf, he did it with a forty-five strapped to his waist. Said any great whites that came after him, he'd scatter their shit for them big-time. The Aussies loved it. Except for the cops. They didn't want a fad to start. Anyway, we exchanged addresses and promised to keep in touch.

"When I came home my Grandpa Devlin saw my pictures and said they ought to be published. He started calling people he knew and eventually I found my publisher."

John sighed softly and his eyes lost focus. "So, really, it all started with a snapshot of my mother."

Jill rolled on top of him, looked down, and brought his attention back to her. Then she kissed him.

"You just love me for my stories," he said.

"I love you for who you are," she answered.

43 Jill woke up just in time to see John fire his first shot through the window that overlooked the backyard. The sharp crack of the gunshot was followed by an explosion, and a fireball painted a spiked blossom of orange, yellow, and red against the black of the sky.

She was on her feet when, from the bedroom down the hall, she heard Gil's voice yell, "Incoming!"

Moments later a second gun sounded from the house, and then a third. A second explosion boomed, this one close enough to illuminate John's face with demonic light.

Through the gunfire, Jill heard a window shatter downstairs. She was wearing the pajamas that she'd put on when she'd gotten up to go to the bathroom. She yanked the bedroom door open and ran out to the top of the stairway. The house was on fire.

The curtains at the sides of a shattered window were aflame, and the rug below was catching fire. The shriek of a smoke detector became a sound track for destruction.

As she watched, a second Molotov cocktail smashed through another window. A gout of fire sprang across the hardwood floor. It pounced on a love seat, devouring it.

The heat was already intense, but the light was diminishing as thick smoke filled the air. Jill saw Ty come out into the hallway. She yelled to him, "Tell Darien and Gil that we've got to get out *now!*"

She ran back into her bedroom. But when she delivered the same message to John. He didn't seem to hear her. He wasn't shooting any longer; he just stood looking out at the trees that ran from his yard to the boundary line of the property.

"John," she yelled desperately, "we've got to get out."

Still, he didn't respond. Thinking he must have been wounded somehow, she was about to grab him when he suddenly raised his gun and fired a single shot.

Then he turned and said, "Got the fucker."

He crossed to Jill, picking up his clothes from the floor where he'd dropped them. Until that moment, she hadn't realized that he was still naked.

Tony Hunt hid behind a cottonwood tree across the street from the front of the Fortunato house. He was dressed in black from head to toe. His face was covered with pancake makeup so it wouldn't reflect light. Krieger had told him if he got caught with black clothes and camouflage paint on his kisser there'd be no explaining it to a cop. Get caught in black threads and makeup, hey, you were just trendy.

Krieger had equipped Hunt with a pump-action shotgun. Hunt felt clumsy with the weapon, but Krieger had assured him that, within its range, it was much more of a sure bet than a handgun.

The plan had been simplicity itself. Krieger would lob firebombs into the rear of the house. The fire would wake Fortunato, drive him out the front door and right into Hunt's gunsight. Hunt would finish him off.

As easy as it sounded, Hunt couldn't help but feel he'd made a horrible mistake. Not in wanting to kill Fortunato but in letting Krieger devise the plan. Hunt had always prided himself in being the master of his own fate; he'd always conceived his own strategies. Far more often than not, they'd worked brilliantly. True, he'd suffered a serious setback last year, but he'd still left himself situated to make a fortune beyond imagining with Micro-Cosmic. Whatever else he did, Hunt always left himself wiggle room for his next turn at the game.

That was what had him so uneasy now. Krieger's plan should drive the quarry into his sights . . . but would there be time to get away? Had the dullard thought of that?

And now the whole place was burning down, but the damn front door hadn't budged. So where the hell was Fortunato? The fire department and the cops would be arriving any minute.

"Come on, goddamnit," Hunt muttered. "I don't have all night."

The five residents of the burning house crouched near the entrance to the basement with wet towels over their faces. They looked at the front door.

"Ambush?" Darien asked.

"Yeah," John said.

"How many?" Gil asked.

"One."

Gil said, "You want me to take him out?"

"How you gonna do that?" Darien wanted to know.

Gil pulled a fragmentation grenade out of his pocket.

"Now if I'd been thinkin' ahead," he said, "I'd'a had, maybe, a light anti-tank weapon with me."

John wanted to take one last look at the house where his family had lived for three generations. He couldn't. The smoke was too thick. And they were wasting time recklessly. Jill, who didn't know they had a way out, was trembling with fear.

"Do it," John said.

Gil pulled the pin and threw the grenade through a front-room window. John led them all down into the basement.

Hunt peered around the tree. He was getting very jumpy. Maybe he should just fire a blast into the door. That would keep Fortunato inside.

He couldn't wait much longer. He heard sirens, and they were close. Any moment now, he'd have to get out of there.

That was when something came crashing through a window *out* of the house at *him*.

Krieger regained consciousness. He lay in the woods behind the Fortunato house feeling like an elephant had tap-danced on his chest. He'd been shot.

He couldn't believe he'd actually been hit while he was dodging back and forth behind all those trees. In the middle of the fucking night. But then he hadn't believed it when he saw his first Molotov get blasted out of the air like it was just a real interesting kind of skeet shoot they had going on. And then the whole fucking house had seemed to open up on him.

But Krieger had come prepared, he'd persisted. He'd brought enough firebombs to burn down Chicago again. He'd also brought a Kevlar vest, which was the only thing that had saved him.

If he had been saved. Right now he felt like he'd never get up from this spot again. He was in too goddamn much pain.

Still, he could see that the house was going up like a torch. That made him feel better. It was just too bad that great picture Fortunato had taken of him was turning to toast, too.

Of course, if Fortunato had somehow gotten out and managed to get Hunt instead of the other way 'round—and Krieger wouldn't bet against it—maybe he'd ask him to take another one.

Tony Hunt didn't know what was flying through the air at him, but he knew what to do. He flung himself behind the thick trunk of the cottonwood.

The grenade went off a second later. Red-hot fragments of metal sheared bark off the tree and imbedded themselves deeply into it.

Hunt wasn't hit, but he no longer heard the sirens. He no longer heard anything except the furious ringing in his ears. He climbed shakily to his feet, one hand against the tree trunk, trying to keep his balance.

He staggered off down the street, shotgun still in hand, just hoping to get away.

There was no doubt about it now. This had been a serious mistake.

Jill, who thought all of them would die horribly any moment now, watched in amazement as Darien lifted a section of the floor at the back of John's basement darkroom. He stepped aside and Ty slid easily into the opening and disappeared. Darien followed. In an instant, he, too, had vanished.

Gil turned to Jill and said grimly, "You better be tight with a secret, lady."

Then he jumped through the opening in the floor and was gone.

Jill felt dizzy and started to sway. She half expected the White Rabbit to pop up out of the hole, call her Alice, and ask what was keeping her.

John put his hands on her shoulders and steadied her. "Come on, we've got to get out of here." He led her to the opening. She took one stomach-churning look over the edge and firmly dug in her heels.

"I can't . . . I can't go down there!"

The house above them was fully engaged in flames and about to collapse on their heads, and Jill still refused to go down the hole. Tears glittered in her eyes.

"I . . . I used to think about my father dying so miners would have better pay," she sobbed. "It always made me crazy because no amount of money in the world would ever get me down a coal mine."

John realized that she might actually allow herself to die rather than go into the tunnel. He was considering a sucker punch when he remembered the only leverage that might work.

"Your daughter," he said. "Carlie. Your reason for living. Rule number one is remember your reason for living. Are you going to let thugs take you away from your daughter the way they took your father away from you?"

The question stunned her.

"The only way you're ever going to see your little girl again is by going down that hole," John told her.

Then the whole house groaned. A cataract of fire poured into the basement as a section of the first floor collapsed.

"Move, goddamnit!" John roared. "I'll be right behind you."

Trembling, Jill got down on her hands and knees and slithered feetfirst into the tunnel. John was right behind her, but before he closed the trapdoor he took a final look at the house his grandfather had built, the only home he'd ever known, now just fuel for the inferno.

There were tears in his eyes, too. He wanted to rage at what had been done to him. He wanted to swear a vow of vengeance. But he couldn't do either. He felt he didn't have the right. During the war, he'd seen too many innocent people burned out of their homes. People who never had a hope of either justice or retribution. Now, it had happened to him. Which just showed he was nobody special.

Like all the other refugees, he'd simply have to flee for his life.

Be grateful he had a way out.

John let the trapdoor fall.

44

Orville Leen stared at the pictures of the charred ruins. He could almost smell the smoke. That beautiful old Fortunato house, built by God's local handyman, was gone.

He looked across his desk to Ron Narder. "Did anyone get out?"

"We don't think so."

"How many bodies?"

"None, so far."

"*None?*" Leen's eyes went wide. "Well, Jesus Christ, how do we know anybody died then?"

Narder pulled a picture from the stack he'd handed the sheriff. It showed a burned-out vehicle. "That was a Ford Explorer parked in the driveway. Got the VIN off the engine block. It was John Fortunato's car."

"Just because a man's car is home doesn't mean he's there, too. Didn't Fortunato have some people living with him?"

"Two army buddies."

"Couldn't he have been out with one of them?"

"Could have been," Narder conceded. "But neither of them owns a car that's registered with the state."

The sheriff knew people still walked places, of course, but that left an obvious question: If everybody in the house had all of a sudden gone out for a lifesaving stroll, where the hell were they?

Leen looked at the photo of the ruins again and sighed. Cremated, that's where they were. Their ashes scattered by the wind across half the state by now. A few days of digging at the scene might turn up some leg bones or skulls, but likely not much more.

"So the probable death toll's three?"

"Most likely four. I think that lawyer woman was with them, too."

Narder explained that Jill Baxter had checked out of the Mill House Inn the previous Tuesday evening in John Fortunato's company. Leen closed his eyes and pinched the bridge of his battered nose.

"What do we know about the fire?" the sheriff asked.

"Definitely arson. Fire investigators found three incendiary devices in the trees behind the property."

"Incendiary devices?"

"Gasoline bombs," Narder explained.

"Jesus Christ," Leen said, opening his eyes in anger. "This shit has got to *stop.*"

"There's more."

"What?"

"Shrapnel."

The sheriff's mouth went slack with disbelief.

"We found bits of metal in a tree across from the front of the house. The pieces came from a fragmentation grenade."

"Who made that identification?"

"I did," Narder answered. "It was the same kind of frag we used in the Corps. There were also some gouges in the grass next to the tree. Like somebody had been lying in wait there and the toes of their shoes dug up the turf when they got up."

"The fire started in back, and someone was waiting to ambush anybody who came out the front door?"

Narder nodded.

"And somebody inside the house figured that out and decided to fight back with a goddamn hand grenade?" The sheriff shook his head, looking suddenly much older. "Ronnie is it me or is this whole world going crazy?"

The chief deputy didn't offer his opinion.

"Any signs of who might've lobbed the Molotov cocktails?" Leen asked.

"No prints on the ones that were left behind. But the first fire crew on the scene did report a man on a motorcycle riding away hell-bent-for-leather just as they were arriving."

"Did they give a useful description?"

The chief deputy shook his head. "It was dark, he was gone in a heartbeat, and they had a fire to fight. No luck on the man or the bike. There is one thing, though."

"What?" the sheriff asked.

Narder laid a slip of paper on Leen's desk.

Leen flicked his eyes at it warily. "What's that?"

"The phone number Tommy Boyle called the night we locked him up."

Now Leen studied the number. "Whose is it?" he asked.

"The Traveler's Delight Motel," Narder said laconically.

"Sonofabitch, that's the last place that got burned down."

Bobbi Sharpes was walking up Beech Street that Sunday morning, on her way home from a service at the Church of the Resurrection, when Billy pulled up alongside her in his personal car. He let it idle along to keep pace with her. There was no one else in sight. Billy smiled at his wife and got right down to business.

"I killed him," he said. "I killed your precious Tommy Boyle, and I just wanted you to know it."

The only sign that Bobbi was even aware of Billy was a sudden tightening of her jaw.

"It's what any good husband would do, don't you think?" Billy persisted. "Protect the sanctity of his marriage."

Bobbi continued to ignore him.

"See, I had to tell you because otherwise you'd never know who did it. What happened to the murder weapon was, oops, it sorta got away from me as I was crossin' the Mississippi. Shame to lose an expensive weapon like that, but a man's gotta make sacrifices upon occasion."

Bobbi kept walking. She opened her purse as if she were rummaging for house keys.

"I'm prepared to go right on sacrificin', too. I may not be able to make you love me anymore, but I'm gonna play pure hell on any other boyfriend you find."

Finally, Bobbi stopped and faced him. Billy pulled over to the curb, grinning.

"Why don't you just try and kill *me?*" she asked. "Oh, I forgot. Any time you've raised a hand to me, it just didn't work out, did it? Last time I had that bottle of booze handy, and I split your skull for you. The time before that I laid a steam iron on your arm, and you had to tell everybody you burned it on an exhaust pipe. The truth is, Billy, I'm meaner than you . . . and you're afraid of me."

Billy reddened, the grin on his face changed to a rictus.

"So if I ever want a boyfriend, or even just feel like makin' you mad, I'll sit in my living room window and show the world what you've seen the last of."

"You bitch," Billy hissed.

"But I'm not going to do that. You know why?"

Billy didn't. So Bobbi told him.

"Because I'm carrying Tommy Boyle's baby, and someday when he grows up he's going to come kill you."

Billy slammed his gearshift into Park. He had one leg out of the car when Bobbi sprang. She threw her weight against the car door, pinning his leg to the frame. Billy howled. Bobbi's hand came out of her purse and sunlight flashed against silver. She drove a pair of nail scissors an inch deep into her husband's shoulder.

She'd been aiming for his neck.

Billy shrieked. He frantically yanked the shifter back into Drive and hit the gas. The car shot off down the street. The acceleration spun Bobbi around, but she somehow kept her feet. Half a block away, Billy stopped, pulled his leg into the car, and discarded the scissors that had impaled him. The door slammed and the car squealed around the corner.

Bobbie Sharpes stood in the street, breathing hard, her face white with fury.

"Don't you think you got away from me, you bastard," she said in a steel whisper.

Tony Hunt sat in the office of his Oak Crest home. Seven hours after the grenade had gone off his ears still rang, but his hearing was coming back. He couldn't remember the last time he'd felt so grateful just to be alive.

On the way home last night, he'd dumped Krieger's shotgun into one of the creeks that ran through town. There'd be no way to trace the weapon back to him.

The whole disastrous affair made him conclude that Krieger not only had to go, he had to die. And soon. Before the monster could place him in mortal jeopardy again.

In the meantime, Sunday or not, Hunt had business to conduct. The first thing he intended to do was to buy Riverman Savings, the town bank.

45

A dead man's apartment seemed the perfect place for John and Jill to hide out. John suggested they might be better off if the world were to think—at least for a while—that they had died. But Jill felt obliged to let Local 274 know she was still alive. Without her, she said, Marty McCreery would take over, Hunt would eat him alive, and that would be that for the strike and the union.

John conceded the point. And had to admit it would be easier for him to keep looking for Tommy's killer if he didn't have to be sneaky about it; he was having a hard enough time as it was. So they wouldn't pretend to be dead . . . but they wouldn't let it be known how they'd saved their skins, either.

Darien and Ty, however, chose to remain below in the tunnels; if they had to reach John and Jill, they'd emerge long enough to make a call to Tommy's place and leave a message on his machine.

Gil hadn't stayed in the tunnels thirty seconds after their escape. He was out the trapdoor that opened among the trees of John's backyard, telling Darien, on the run, that he had to get the stolen police Harley out of there before the cops came and found it. So, once again, nobody knew where Gil was.

The first thing Jill did upon arriving at Tommy's was head into the bathroom, muttering, "Never, never again. Not for anyone, or any reason."

Her crawl through the tunnels had been hard on her. They'd had to go several blocks to get to the exit nearest Tommy's town house. The worst part had been the mole. The small furry burrower had popped out of its own excavation and met Jill, crawling along the tunnel floor, face-to-face.

The memory of her shriek still echoed in John's head. He'd told her that it was harmless. She wasn't comforted. He didn't tell her about the rats, snakes, and bugs that routinely found their ways into the tunnels.

While Jill showered, John browsed through Tommy's closet, looking for something to wear. A trip through the tunnels always left your clothes filthy.

He was surprised when he found feminine clothing hanging at the far end of the rack. It looked like several pieces of a new spring wardrobe. He took out a white cotton sweater and a pair of pale green slacks.

He laid the clothes out on the bed. They looked like they'd be just the right size for Jill. So whose were they? He looked at the labels. Foley's. The store wasn't local. Had Tommy been seeing someone from out of town?

Jill entered the bedroom wrapped in a towel and saw the sweater and slacks on the bed. "Well, Tommy told me he wasn't hurting for ladies. Guess this proves it."

John nodded, thinking there was something important here, something about these clothes that might point him toward Tommy's killer. But he wasn't able to put his finger on it. He told Jill there were more clothes in the closet, then went to take his own shower.

He dressed in some of Tommy's old sweats. They were oversized for him, and he felt an unexpected pang of regret, like he was a kid pretending that someday, with a little luck, he'd grow up to be just like his big brother. The heartache made him aware that should he find Tommy's killer, he'd have nothing left to distract him from facing his loss head-on.

Jill was on the phone in the kitchen talking to her daughter when he came downstairs. She wore the outfit he'd laid out for her, and looked good in it. Trying not to eavesdrop, at least conspicuously, he went to the refrigerator and opened the freezer compartment.

He took out a can of concentrate and made orange juice. He poured two glasses, then put Jill's glass on the counter next to the phone and started to leave the room. She caught his wrist and nodded for him to stay. He did.

The conversation drifted from Carlie's bravura performance at a Suzuki piano recital, to school, to making sure that she listened to Grandma, to always saying her prayers.

When Jill hung up there were tears in her eyes.

"So happy I could cry. Pretty silly, huh?"

She tugged a paper towel from a roll hanging on a wall rack. She dried her eyes and took a deep breath. Then she walked over to where John sat and kissed him.

She said, "Thank you for getting me out of the house last night, and through those tunnels today."

John nodded. "She must be a terrific kid."

"She is."

"No one could blame you for going home now."

"I wouldn't care if they did," she said.

Up until that point, John had known her as a lawyer and a lover. Now he saw her as a mother, and with this change came a beauty unique to that role. It sparked a longing in his heart for yet another person he'd lost.

Jill saw the faraway look in his eye.

"Are you all right?" she asked.

John hid the truth with a smile. "Sure. Just thinking how good you look in found clothing."

Jill smiled, too, and extended her arms.

"Not a bad fit, either. I even found some racy lingerie. The panties fit, but the bras . . ." She pulled the front of the sweater outward. "Whoever they belong to puts on more of a show than I do."

For a quicksilver instant, the image of Jill holding the sweater out suggested someone to John. But she let the sweater go, and the image slipped away.

"What?" she smirked. "You like 'em real big?"

"I like *you*, top to bottom."

She waggled her eyebrows. "Well, my bottom ain't bad."

He laughed. "So I've noticed."

"You want to notice again?"

On the way to the bedroom, a question occurred to John.

"You know where Foley's is?"

"The department store?" she asked. "It's in Texas."

It was just after midnight when John leaned over the bed and softly kissed Jill. He'd thought she was asleep, but she opened her eyes.

"Where are you going?"

"Church."

"Why?"

"To light some candles for Doolan and Tommy."

She thought for a second, then said, "Do me a favor?"

"What?"

"Light one for my dad, will you?"

"Sure," he promised.

46 The clerk at the Sheriff's Department impound yard almost fell off her stool when she saw John the next morning. He'd come to claim Tommy's car, having lost his own.

The clerk didn't come right out and ask him why he hadn't died in the fire that had the whole town talking, but she wanted to, and John knew that word of his survival would swiftly get back to Leen. The sheriff would be looking to question him immediately thereafter.

John would have preferred to talk to Leen later rather than sooner, but he needed a car, and he wanted to see if there was any useful scrap of information he might find in Tommy's.

Jill walked to the storefront offices of Local 274. She wanted time alone to give her second thoughts a once-over. Yesterday, she'd told John that she believed the strike would fail without her help. And while she hadn't changed that assessment, right now she was leaning in the direction of resigning as the local's lawyer.

The firebombing of John's house, the subterranean horrors of the tunnels, and, most of all, the thought of losing her daughter had been just about enough for her to ask John for the number of that shrink of his. She liked to think she was tough, and she'd never considered herself a quitter . . . but what the hell was the point of risking her ass when guys like McCreery and Banks just wanted to boot it out of town? Hell, she could hang Tony Hunt out to dry for them and they'd still resent her— probably more than ever.

So she walked into Local 274 having decided to quit. Five minutes later she got the phone call that changed her mind.

Marty McCreery was the first to see her. He was sitting on the corner of Pete Banks's desk and dropped his coffee into his lap.

"Jesus!" he shouted, jumping up as much from shock as the scalding.

Then Sharon Waddell, the receptionist, shrieked and ran to embrace her. Other office staff and strikers clustered around her, overjoyed to learn that she had somehow survived. Finally, Sid Tomlinson, the born-again gentle giant of the executive committee, had the sensitivity to give her a little elbow room by using his bulk as a buffer zone. The warm reception was making it harder for Jill to tell them she was leaving.

Marty, bless him, steered her back the other way.

"We thought you were dead," he said, unable to keep all the disappointment from his voice. "We thought you died at John Fortunato's house."

"I'm alive," she replied. "John is, too."

"Wasn't anyone home when . . ." a woman striker began.

Jill said, "We were there."

"Was it really arson?" a man asked.

"Gasoline bombs."

A chorus of exclamations and curses came from the group. Then came the inevitable question.

"How in God's name did the two of you get out?" Marty asked. "I drove by the place—hell, everyone did once the word spread—and I can't see how *anyone* could've got out."

A woman shook her head. "You don't even look mussed."

Jill was clean and groomed. She had on a floral print dress and a pair of shoes she'd found in Tommy's closet. Today, she felt uneasy about wearing the borrowed clothes. It would be embarrassing to be confronted by their rightful owner.

"We were there," she repeated. "Getting out wasn't easy. But for right now that's all I can say."

Jill turned the discussion to the strike. She was pleased that the boycott was holding but unhappy to hear that several members had bailed out Dex Carlisle.

"Don't you understand how that makes the union look?" Jill asked Marty.

"It wasn't me," he said defensively. "It was individuals acting on their own."

More than a few of those present supported Carlisle's act: A scab got blinded, that was her tough luck. The welcome for Jill noticeably cooled. The room was silent, and Jill was about to tell them they could run their strike any damn way they pleased—and without her help—when the phone rang.

Marty picked up. "Local 274."

He listened and frowned. His face went red, and he shouted, "You sonofabitch! You can't do that! We'll take you to court. . . . We'll . . ."

Marty's eyes settled on Jill, and he was confronted with a terrible dilemma. He'd just threatened to take someone to court, to file a suit. Presumably with great urgency. To do that, he had to have a lawyer—immediately. There was no way for him to deny it: He *needed* Jill. He swallowed enough pride to leave a bitter taste in his mouth for the rest of his life.

He told Jill, "This guy says he's the business agent for the international, and they've decertified us as a BMW local. On top of that, the international has signed an agreement with Hunt to organize his scabs, and any of our membership who want to join, as a new local."

This bombshell produced an uproar among the strikers. Marty shouted for quiet. He extended the phone to Jill. Between tightly compressed lips, he managed to squeeze out a single word of entreaty. "Please."

Jill was reluctant, but Marty McCreery wasn't the only one in that room to consider. Many people there had supported Jill and were counting on her. Finally, she took the phone.

"This is Jill Baxter," she said. "Who am I talking to?"

"To someone a lot tougher than Vic Kushner," a deep voice replied.

"Am I supposed to be afraid?" Jill asked.

"No, from what I hear, you're supposed to be a charcoal briquette."

With that one flip line, the guy pressed the hottest button Jill had. Another goddamn bully. If she walked away from this fight now, she'd better plan to use her law license for nothing more daunting than house closings and zoning appeals.

She said, "Keep thinking that way, buddy, and watch how fast I stop all your bullshit with an injunction."

"You're next, lady," the voice said, obscenely intimate. "Take it as gospel . . . from the guy who did Tommy Boyle."

The caller broke the connection.

.   .   .

Hunt was in his office. His effort to buy Riverman Savings had gotten off to a good start. His new, tame union was shaping up nicely. He was regaining control, feeling strong again.

Krieger was still missing, but that was just as well.

Hunt was sitting at his desk devising a plan to deal with Sheriff Orville Leen when there was a knock at his door. The door opened and a black face peeked in.

"Mr. Hunt?"

"Who are you?"

The man stepped into his office. He was short, but lean and fit. His twill shirt and pants were old, but they were also clean and sharply creased.

"My name's Teddy Stinson. I work for you. I woulda asked to come in, but your secretary ain't here."

Hunt's secretary wasn't due for thirty minutes; he'd arrived early.

"What do you want?" Hunt demanded.

The man kept his eyes on Hunt as he crossed the plush carpet of the office. He didn't seem intimidated by either Hunt or the rich surroundings.

"I have something to tell you."

"Which is?"

"Which is, half the people you got working for you are about to take a walk—even after the announcement this mornin' about the new union and the pay raise. I know, because I heard 'em say so. And it won't do no good to bring any more in."

Hunt had always scoffed at the idea of information bubbling up from the bottom to the top, but some instinct warned him to take this little man seriously.

"You're concerned for my welfare, Mr. Stinson?"

"No, sir. For mine."

Teddy Stinson kept looking Hunt straight in the eye.

"A few years back, I wouldn'a taken a leak on the job I'm doin' for you. But right now it's the only job I got, so I wanta keep it."

"Such honesty," Hunt said with an icy smile. "What's the problem, Mr. Stinson? Working conditions?"

"Unh-uh, living conditions."

"Perhaps you could be a little more specific."

"Let's just say country club life ain't for everyone. I go into the men's room out there at the Oak Crest CC, the regulars act like I should be handin' them a towel. Either that or they better be careful droppin' their pants, 'cause all us brothers been in prison and you know what happens when we see a white backside." The small man snorted. "I believe I could cause a heart attack, I ever dived into the swimming pool out there. If that ain't enough, you finally make some honest money, you can't even spend it because nobody in this town'll sell you nothin'. A friend of mine named Felton had enough and left this morning, and a whole lotta other folks are about a half step behind."

Hunt hadn't taken Tommy Boyle's boycott idea seriously. But this man was telling him that ostracism was an effective weapon, a real threat to his plans.

"I'm working on new employee housing right now, Mr. Stinson. You can tell your co-workers that. And I'll come up with a plan to deal with the local merchants' boycott."

"I already got a plan," Teddy Stinson said.

Hunt smiled wolfishly. He gestured to a chair.

"Please sit down, Mr. Stinson," he said. "I'm always happy to hear a good idea from the shop floor."

47 A cursory search of Tommy's car turned up only a Juicy Fruit chewing gum wrapper in the ashtray, a clue beyond John's powers of divination.

He drove to Local 274. In light of the international's threat, the union office was a beehive of frantic activity. Jill had no time to give him more than a smile and a wave. After a number of handshakes and pats on the back, John was able to get a moment with Marty McCreery.

Marty's contact at the phone company had come through. He handed John the lists of phone numbers he'd asked for.

Bobbi Sharpes was stunned when she saw John. No sooner had she opened her front door than her hand flew to her mouth. It wasn't enough of a barrier to muffle the sob that escaped her.

"You all right, Bobbi?" John asked.

By way of an answer, she threw her arms around him and kissed him. It was the most intense platonic kiss he had ever received: full on the lips, with warmth and softness and pressure. Despite all that, John felt as if she were trying to resuscitate him, not arouse him.

She'd thought he was dead, too. He put his arms around her to reassure her. After a moment, she pulled back to look at him.

"It's okay, Bobbi," he said, "they didn't get me this time."

She smiled shakily, took his hand, and pulled him inside. They sat in Bobbi's living room and she told him what had happened with Billy.

"And two minutes after I get home," she added, "my phone rings and it's Alice Wills. You know, she's the one who found Tommy? She tells me your house had burned down and nobody got out. I thought she was trying to be kind—you know, having the news come from her—but the more I studied on it the more I felt there had to be some sneaky meanness in a woman who'd make two such calls."

She pushed her glossy black hair back from her face and smiled ruefully.

"I'm a fine one to talk, as mean as I am. I'm probably just taking out all the hurt and hate I was feeling on poor Alice." She took John's hand and held it between both of hers. "I can't tell you how glad I am to see you again, Johnny."

He knew exactly what she was feeling, even if she hadn't worked it out for herself yet. If a seeming miracle could restore him to life, why not Tommy?

Denial and resurrection were ideas to which John had addressed himself countless times. But he didn't want to go down that road right now with Bobbi. He gently pulled his hand free.

"Bobbi, do you believe what Billy told you? About killing Tommy?"

She shrugged in uncertainty. "That's the real pisser, ain't it? Just by saying he did it, he's done enough to drive us crazy. I can see him doing it, but I can see him *claiming* to do it, too, just to hurt me. How are we ever gonna know?"

"You think you could get him to repeat his confession? Get it down on tape?"

Bobbi shook her head. "Billy's not smart, but he's real close to sly. I don't think he'd ever repeat it. Not unless it was over one of our graves."

Then John asked her the question that had brought him to her house that day. "After you and Tommy broke up, was he seeing anyone special?"

She laughed mirthlessly. "He was out hustlin' the ladies. But as big as Tommy was, his new girlfriends never felt real safe if I walked into a place. They'd duck and hide behind him. All I saw was a lot of hairdos and backless dresses."

John thought of the woman's clothes in Tommy's closet. "If Tommy had been seeing someone special, someone afraid of you, they might have met somewhere private."

"Might've been screwing in his bed, the same place we made our baby."

She wiped a tear from her eye. "People sure know how to mess up their lives, don't they, Johnny?"

The question required no answer.

Certainly not from him.

Stepping out of Bobbi's house, John was stunned to see someone *he'd* thought was dead. Krieger. The SOB was driving along the street in his black sedan. Without conscious impulse, John got into Tommy's car and followed him.

He was certain he'd shot Krieger in the woods behind his house two nights before. Certain that Krieger had been the one throwing the gasoline bombs. It had to have been him. When John wouldn't sell him the photo he'd taken, Krieger had come to destroy it. What other reason could there have been to attack his home?

John experienced a dizzying moment of self-doubt. He had to white-knuckle the steering wheel to keep himself in place. Had he shot somebody else? Or was he losing the ability to tell when he'd eliminated a threat to his life?

He couldn't believe that. As soon as he'd pulled the trigger he'd *known*. The feeling was too certain, too familiar; the flood of mortal relief had been too real.

Krieger *had* gone down.

So why was he still alive?

John was determined to find out, but then he heard a siren coming up fast from behind. Krieger must have heard it, too, because the black sedan suddenly shot forward.

John pulled to the curb. He'd have to deal with Krieger later.

He expected the Sheriff's Department patrol car to roar past, but the driver caught sight of him and came to a screeching stop. Billy Shelton was behind the wheel. For a breathless moment, he and John stared at each other.

John searched Billy's eyes to see if Tommy's killer lived behind them. Billy tried to determine if John was really alive after all.

Billy's question was more easily answered. The deputy tore his eyes off John and resumed his chase. But Krieger's sedan was out of sight by then.

Darien and Ty were sitting in HQ eating MREs of roast turkey breast and cranberry sauce for lunch when Gil entered the chamber. A long look passed between the two vets.

"Everything cool with your bike?" Darien asked.

"Yeah. I got away just ahead of the fire brigade. Felt so good flyin' along on that hog I just kept goin' a few hundred miles. Thought maybe I should ride right up to Alaska. Maybe circle the North Pole a time or two and see what looked good from there."

Ty looked up at Gil. He didn't seem drunk or stoned, but he sounded just like Ty's dad when he went off on a ramble about something he'd never get around to doing. The boy didn't know what was bothering Gil, but he felt sure the little vet was as trapped as any alkie who lived inside a bottle.

Gil spotted Ty looking at him, even seemed to know what the boy was thinking, but he didn't take offense. Instead, he grinned devilishly.

"Hey, kid. You did all right back there at John's house. Didn't have a chance to return any fire, but you maintained. Kept your head real good. But you know what I think you need? A training exercise."

"What?" Darien and Ty said simultaneously.

"Yeah, man." Gil replied, and he walked over to Darien, led him to the far side of the chamber, and the two had a whispered conversation for a full minute.

Ty wasn't sure he liked this. And when he heard what the two vets had decided, he definitely didn't like it.

They gave Ty a flashlight, a commando knife, and a .38 with five live rounds. Then they showed him a tunnel map and told him the objective he had to reach. They told him he was Joe—and that both of them were Charlie.

He got a five-minute head start.

If they caught him, they'd kill him.

"You're kidding, right?" Ty asked.

"Four minutes and fifty-five seconds," said Gil.

Ty crawled off as fast as he could—certain that this was just some kind of mean game. At least he hoped it was.

It seemed well short of five minutes when Ty first thought he heard something behind him, approaching from a great distance. But who was it? Darien would never kill him, he knew that. But Gil . . . he wouldn't swear to it.

Gil was most likely a little crazy.

Then the thought occurred to Ty that the army—the real one—did make recruits crawl under live machine gun fire when they went through training. He'd read that somewhere. Maybe that's what Darien and Gil were doing to him now. Teaching him to keep his head down. Because if he stuck it up . . .

Oh, God! He crawled faster, thinking he had to be the one who was crazy for getting himself into this mess. The sound behind him kept getting closer. Whoever it was seemed to be moving at a speed that was more than human. Ty crawled as fast as he could, but it wasn't fast enough to keep his heart from climbing into his throat.

The sound—it had a harsh scratchy quality—was overtaking him relentlessly.

Ty stopped and turned. He curled himself into a ball against the right-hand wall of the tunnel and took out his .38. With the live ammunition. He held his flashlight in his left hand. Darien and Gil were both right-handed. They'd have to shoot across their bodies to hit him; they'd have to see past the flashlight beam he'd snap on and fervently hoped would blind them.

He couldn't believe that he was about to die—or to kill someone.

How could he shoot Darien? How could he even shoot Gil?

The sound was rushing upon him now. He had no more time to agonize, no time to wonder why the sound was so uncharacteristically scratchy. Ty flicked on his flashlight . . .

. . . and the biggest rat he'd ever seen in his life came to a quivering stop not five feet from him. Ty screamed—and fired. He emptied the revolver, blowing the rat to bits. His ears rang like a fire alarm. He stared at the scattered remains of the giant rodent and had a hard time not losing his lunch. Shortly, though, he came to an inescapable, infuriating conclusion.

He'd been tricked.

When he reached his objective, EE, the chamber below Eleventh and Elm, Darien and Gil were already there. Gil was drinking a beer; Darien had a bottle of water. They both wore Cheshire grins.

"You kill poor ol' Lucy, our pet rat?" Gil asked.

"Hope he used all five on her," Darien said.

Ty trembled with rage. "You *motherfuckers*."

Gil laughed. But Darien sighed and opened his hands in a gesture of peace.

He said, "Gil had the idea you ought to know what it meant to be really afraid down here—"

"And have the experience of firing live ammo," Gil added.

"So you could see how you'd respond. How you *should* respond to save your own life. I thought that was a lesson worth learnin'."

"Yeah, but we didn't want you shooting at our asses, so we volunteered Lucy."

Darien tossed a Coke to Ty.

"We're proud a you," he said.

Gil gave him a thumbs-up. "Yeah, by today's standards, you're not a cherry anymore."

Ty didn't want to pout in front of the two men—or admit that they had a point—so he just took his soft drink and sipped it silently in the far corner of the chamber.

John and Jill were eating a dinner of carry-out Chinese in Tommy's dining nook when the phone rang. The sheriff's voice came over the answering machine speaker.

"Fortunato, you there? This is Orville Leen."

The sheriff waited for a response.

"Well, if you aren't, you probably will be. And if I can figure out where you'll go, so can whoever burned down your house. I highly recommend that you come see me ASAP. We can talk, and I'll put you somewhere safe. . . . Oh, and I'm glad you're alive, too, Ms. Baxter." The sheriff snorted. "Never thought I'd be saying that."

He hung up.

John said, "You have a new admirer."

"Probably a good thing," Jill replied.

She told him about her conversation with the "business agent" from the international.

John frowned. "This guy told you he killed Tommy?"

"He said he *did* Tommy and I was next. I took *did* and *killed* to be synonymous. Don't you?"

John nodded and told her the story of Bobbi Sharpes and Billy Shelton. It was Jill's turn to frown.

"The deputy confessed, too?"

Then John told her about seeing Krieger. He explained why he thought Krieger had to be behind the firebombing.

Jill made the logical inference.

"Krieger is Hunt's agent. If Hunt wanted us dead, it had to be to stop my union efforts or your investigation."

"Or both. He could've had Krieger murder Tommy."

"Or, after their confrontation at the plant, maybe Hunt did it himself. . . . But Hunt got shot that night, too. He wouldn't have arranged that."

"Yeah, I've thought about that," John said. "I could come up with only one answer."

"What?"

"Tommy had a lot of people mad at him."

Jill just nodded.

"I think," John said, "he had more than one killer after him at the same time."

It was indeed a horrible possibility to consider, but from what Jill had learned about Tommy Boyle in little more than a week's time, she didn't find it far-fetched. The late union leader had seemed to pick up enemies faster than a stray dog gathered fleas.

"I think you're right. So we have to sort out who actually killed him."

"And who knows if somebody else won't pop up and take credit?" John asked bleakly.

48

Krieger interrupted Hunt's dictation.

He'd driven straight to the plant to get away from that dick-licking deputy—a glare at whatever numbnuts was on duty at the front gate was all he ever needed to gain admittance—but he'd waited until all the white-collar staff had gone home before he entered Hunt's office. Now, the bastard was putting down his microrecorder and sizing up his chances.

As far as Krieger was concerned, he didn't have any.

"You ran, you sonofabitch." Krieger loomed over Hunt like the due bill of a misspent life.

For the bulk of humanity, having Krieger breathing implicit threats down their neck would inspire terror, if not actual heart failure. But Hunt had considered it inevitable. Had prepared for it.

"And how did you arrive at that conclusion?" he asked evenly.

Krieger dropped into a chair. "You know how I know you ran? The guy you were supposed to kill, he isn't dead. Fortunato got outta his house. I saw him today. He was just about riding my bumper." Krieger leaned forward. "You chickened out."

Krieger saw Hunt's eyes narrow. Mr. Bigshot didn't like the news about Fortunato's being alive. But Krieger was proud of the way he was handling things. Cool. Smart. Just like . . . Fortunato. What a hoot, he thought, the fucking guy was becoming his hero.

Hunt misinterpreted the grin on Krieger's brutal face for derision.

"I stayed until he threw a grenade at me," he said.

Krieger laughed out loud—then stopped abruptly. With anyone else, Hunt's excuse would have been a joke. But with Fortunato . . .

"You know what? I believe you," Krieger said, getting to his feet. "You did have a good reason for running. Just like I do now. Come on, get up. We're going out to your house, and I'm going to help myself to whatever I can find as severance pay."

Hunt rose and casually slipped his hand into his coat pocket.

"You're leaving my employ?" he asked.

Krieger laughed once more. "Let's just say I'm going to pursue other career opportunities . . . and with Fortunato around, you oughta give that some strong thought yourself. Now, get your ass in gear."

But Hunt didn't move.

"You don't think I could shoot someone under any circumstances, do you?"

Krieger looked at Hunt, still grinning, and shook his head.

"You talk tough, but deep down . . . you don't have the stones."

Hunt took out his gun and shot Krieger in the chest five times.

"Guess I do," said Hunt.

49 Ty was in the tunnels looking for Doolan. Darien was sleeping in HQ. And Gil had gone topside to roam around on his Harley again. Ty hadn't been able to sleep after what had happened with the rat. So he went into the system to work on the mystery.

He went in the dark. The way John did it. The only time he turned on his flashlight was when he estimated he was back to the spot where he'd killed the rat. He didn't want to crawl through that mess. He didn't have to; the mess was gone.

Something had eaten the splattered rat.

Ty reached the segment of tunnel that had been dug specifically to resemble the stretch where Doolan had disappeared twenty-seven years ago. He stopped and sat and thought. On paper, the problem seemed susceptible to intellectual solution. But down here in pitch blackness with the rank, musty smell of the earth all around him, he wasn't so sure. After a few moments, Ty realized he was not alone.

"So did you find him?"

John!

Ty had never heard him, or smelled him, and certainly hadn't seen him. He'd just *felt* someone present.

But John had located him first.

"Find who?"

"Doolan. You're looking for him, aren't you?"

Ty was glad that John couldn't see him blush.

"Doolan?" he bluffed.

"It's okay, you don't have to lie."

"You don't mind what I'm doing?"

"All I want is an answer. Peace of mind."

"I'll get it for you." Ty hardened his resolve.

There was a moment of silence, then John spoke.

"I've got something to do. You want to help?"

"Absolutely," Ty said.

During the war, one of the most effective tactics the army used against the Vietcong tunnel forces was PSYOPS, psychological warfare operations.

Thousand-watt speakers were mounted on gunships that flew at night. Broadcasts boomed out to the enemy hiding beneath the earth. Recordings of small children cried for their fathers. Wives begged their husbands to come home. A wandering soul wailed in torment because he'd been buried in an unmarked grave, and then he warned of an imminent bombing raid. Charlie was urged to give up while he still could.

One of the first demands the North Vietnamese made at the Paris peace talks was for an end to all PSYOPS. John was about to launch a PSYOP against Tony Hunt.

He had just the tool he needed because he kept all his important photo negatives and prints in airtight storage in HQ. It was a long-standing precaution, so they wouldn't be lost to theft. Or fire.

It had been Gil's idea to tunnel under the Pentronics plant. Ever the military thinker, he'd said they couldn't let a target like that go unexploited; Charlie never would have. John had gone along. Still doing penance, at that time, for Doolan's disappearance, he'd had enough guilt to tunnel to China. Now he was glad he had access to Hunt's base of operations.

John and Ty slithered out of the tunnels through an exit among the weeds at the rear of a storage building at the newly renamed MicroCosmic, Inc. They crawled to a corner of the building and peered toward the plant's front gate, half a mile away. With the plant still largely shut down by the strike, large areas of the complex had been left unlighted that night. Here and there, exterior lights mounted on various buildings provided islands of illumination in a sea of blackness.

Outside the front gate, union members marched with the grim persistence of an engine stuck in neutral but not yet out of gas. Several members of plant security kept their eyes on the picketers, but there wasn't a guard to be seen anywhere else on the grounds. The two infiltrators couldn't have asked for a better setup.

John handed Ty a .38 and whispered instructions to fire it into the dirt as a distraction only if he judged that John absolutely needed help getting away.

John had a clear path to the office building where Hunt worked. His idea had been simply to leave his calling card at Hunt's front door, a little taunt Hunt would find impossible to ignore. But much closer than that, at the back of the fabricating building, a single car was parked under a light. A big silver Lexus. The license plate read: CEO. Hunt's wheels. A gift from God.

John moved toward the car at a purposeful pace. He was dressed in commando black and effectively invisible as he kept to the inky shadows . . . but something brought him up short, stopped him while he was still twenty feet away from the car. He extended his consciousness. He couldn't see anyone in the car, nor could he *feel* anyone inside. But something made him very uneasy about that gleaming luxury vehicle. Then he saw it. Something broke the contour of the rear seat back; the corner of a large bulky object stuck up. It couldn't have been a person, or John would have felt the presence of a living being.

Standing motionless for several more seconds, John let the past catch up to the present, and the memory clicked into place: body bag. Hunt had a corpse in his car.

He crept forward and peered through the window. The body was wrapped in black plastic. The driver's door was unlocked.

He took a quick look around. Nobody. Anywhere. Just like an army firebase, he thought, the plant expected any confrontation to come from conventional forces and conventional quarters; the last thing they would guard against was a guerrilla raid from below. Even so, there was no telling when someone might come for the car, even Hunt himself. John quickly opened the door, leaned over the back of the front seat, and moving the plastic aside, he saw—

Krieger!

He recoiled, barely catching himself before he leaned against the horn.

He looked again. The man he'd thought he'd killed but hadn't was now dead. Had *Hunt* done it? Why was the body in Hunt's car? Was somebody else running a PSYOP on the man? John didn't know, but fate had given him the perfect place to leave his calling card.

As he exited the car, John thought that the army would have awarded him a medal for the way he would mess up his enemy's head with this one.

Within seconds, he and Ty were back inside the tunnel system. John wished that he could see the look on Hunt's face when he opened his car door.

The thing that had surprised Hunt was the absence of blood. Where was the blood?

He stepped around his desk, cautiously, gun still in hand. Could Krieger possibly be faking? Should he shoot him in the head? No. That would make a mess beyond cleaning.

Then Hunt saw the stain on the carpet. Not blood, but urine. Not only had Krieger's bladder vented but, Christ, so had his bowels. The sonofabitch.

Hunt tried to ignore the stink and bent over the body. Krieger's shirt had been shredded by the hail of gunfire. Beneath the tatters, he wore a bulletproof vest; the slugs were all embedded in it.

That explained the lack of blood, but now Hunt wondered *why* Krieger was dead. He pulled the vest away. The bastard's chest was a crimson web of broken blood vessels with a dense purple puddle at the breastbone. Krieger had died of a broken heart.

Hunt laughed.

He dug the slugs out of the vest and put them in his pocket. No one had seen him shoot Krieger. His office was soundproofed, so no one had heard him, either. The only piece of physical evidence was the pee stain on his carpet, and he'd scrub that out in the morning.

Krieger had entered his office after his secretary had gone home for the night—and who was going to miss the sonofabitch anyway—so Hunt didn't have to worry about being the last person seen with him. All in all, this was shaping up as the perfect crime.

Hunt then called down to the guard captain. He told the man that he'd had a warning the union might try something desperate tonight. He wanted all personnel watching the main gate.

Next, he moved his car from its slot closest to the executive office building to the back of the fabricating plant. He left the car unlocked. He didn't want to be fumbling for his keys when he came back with the corpse. He also looked into his trunk to be sure there was room for Krieger. There wasn't. He had enough room for half a dozen suitcases and a set of golf clubs, but not for a six-foot-six body double for Frankenstein's monster. Not unless he chainsawed the sonofabitch in two. It'd be easier dumping Krieger off the dolly into the back seat, anyway.

From his car, Hunt went to Maintenance and found a large dolly, a roll of black plastic sheeting, some electrician's tape, and a utility knife. He brought these items back to his office and plastic-wrapped Krieger. He laid the dolly on the floor and rolled Krieger's shrouded form onto it. Next, he taped him in place. Hunt paused to pour himself a stiff drink from his office bar. He looked at what he'd achieved and tried to think if he'd overlooked anything. After several reviews, and the decision to forgo a second drink, he decided he hadn't.

Within the hour, he would drop this sack of shit into the Mississippi and no one would be the wiser.

Tony Hunt squatted and firmly seized both of the dolly's handles. "Here we go, you prick," he said harshly.

He raised the dolly with surprising ease, pleased that he was still more than man enough to lift over 250 pounds of dead weight.

He rolled Krieger's body all the way to the Lexus without a hitch. He opened the back door, sliced through the tape that held the corpse to the dolly, and Krieger had the decency to fall almost perfectly across the back seat. When Hunt shoved Krieger's legs inside the car it forced one of the corpse's shoulders to ride up above the seat back. He'd fix that later. Push him down completely below the window level.

But right now he had to return the dolly, tape, and utility knife to Maintenance. It wouldn't do to leave them where they had no reason to be. That was just the kind of overlooked detail that got people caught. Hunt closed the door on Krieger.

He wouldn't be gone long, so he left the car unlocked.

When he got back he was sure everything was perfect. He opened the driver's door and slid inside. He closed the door behind him and switched on the dome light. He turned to the back seat to jam the body down and—

He saw Krieger's face! Twisted in a snarl. He was firing a gun. The bullet was just leaving the barrel. It was coming straight at him!

Tony Hunt almost screamed. But then his brain told him he was looking at a photograph. Just a photograph.

"Sonofabitch," he said. "Fortunato."

50 It was a morning of firsts for Teddy Stinson. The first time he'd ever ridden in the back of a limo. The first time he'd ever been paid to go shopping. The first time he would ever threaten anybody with anything other than physical harm.

He thought he could get used to the high life.

To Teddy's right was Grayson DeVoe III, attorney-at-law. DeVoe was as black as Teddy. On the jump seats across from them sat Carmen Torrez and Marvella Wood, two fellow replacement workers and people of color.

The women were nervous, but the chance to spend five hundred dollars of the boss's money on themselves had persuaded them to accompany Teddy.

Trailing the limo was a Dodge Caravan containing four of DeVoe's "law clerks." Two blacks, a Mexican, and a Samoan. They could've lined up on either side of the ball for any team in the NFL. Teddy thought the Samoan was a nice touch; you didn't see many people playing the South Seas angle.

Grayson DeVoe III and the four clerks escorted the new plant workers across the picket line in front of the Food Giant supermarket Teddy and

Felton had visited five days earlier. They marched directly to the manager's station, towing a deputy sheriff along as an observer.

"Good morning, madam," DeVoe said politely. "I'm an attorney representing these three people."

He extended his card to the manager. She didn't take it.

"Representing them for what?"

"They wish to shop here and have retained me to safeguard their civil rights."

"There's nothing says we have to sell to them. Isn't that right, Fred?" the store manager asked the deputy.

The deputy knew his duty.

"I'm gonna use your phone to call the sheriff, okay, Verna?"

"Damn right," she said.

The union people had entered the store by now and were watching the scene unfold. The four clerks kept their eyes on the picketers.

"I'm afraid you do have to sell to them," DeVoe told the manager. "You see, it's the law."

"No, it ain't. I know what you're up to; you're tryin' to say we don't like coloreds. Well, how about this, Mr. Smarty-pants—you and your glee club over there can shop all you want. That'll show color ain't the problem here."

DeVoe smiled thinly. "That's very good of you, madam, but I'm afraid you can't choose which members of the minority community you'll serve and which you won't."

Teddy took a candy bar off a display rack.

"Hey, you, stop that. You can't get away with that again."

Teddy tore the wrapper off. A picketer tried to snatch the candy bar from him, but the Samoan blocked the way and shook his head sternly.

Verna was livid. "Fred, I'm filing a shoplifting complaint against that man."

The deputy spoke more urgently into the phone.

Teddy took a bite out of the candy bar. Then he passed it to Carmen and Marvella. Emboldened by their escorts, the two women took defiant bites, too, and the candy bar was gone.

"Teddy," DeVoe said.

Teddy put a dollar on the manager's counter to pay for his purchase.

"I won't take his money," the manager declared.

"Then, madam, I will sue you and the owners of this store for more money than you've ever dreamed of. And I assure you that when I'm finished, all of you will be shown to be the bigots you are. On national television."

A hothead from the line yelled, "Fuck you, Ace!"

As in ace of spades. DeVoe shrugged, his point made.

"Fred, arrest these people," Verna commanded. "All of them. Get them the hell out of my store!"

The deputy hung up the phone. He looked at DeVoe, his four piano movers, the scabs, the union people, the store staff. He unholstered his gun without pointing it at anybody.

DeVoe started to speak.

"Shut up," Fred warned. The deputy had been given his orders, and now he acted with confidence. "This is the way the sheriff wants it, and this is the way it's gonna be."

The strikers were ordered out of the store. DeVoe's party was escorted to the stockroom—where they wouldn't be the target of a metal thermos or any more lethal missile. Verna was told to get on the phone with the people who signed her paycheck. And rubbernecking shoppers were told to get the hell on with their shopping.

The matter was resolved fifteen minutes after Leen arrived. The scabs were allowed to shop. Verna got the word from her employers. Jill arrived in time to see Teddy and friends pushing their shopping carts up and down the aisles. Teddy smiled when he saw her.

"Looks like we won this round, too," he said.

Jill spoke urgently with the supermarket employees. Verna, four checkers, three stockboys, and the janitor all walked out. Every one of them had family on strike from the plant. They agreed that they'd be goddamned before they served scabs.

A college kid saving for the fall term's tuition and a single mother stayed. They rang up and bagged the scabs' purchases. They also drew dozens of hate-filled stares through the store's windows. Leen left a deputy behind to look after them.

The Stinson shopping caravan had just begun. Several of the stores they visited were closed in the middle of normal business hours. But others refused to follow Jill's desperate improvisation on Tommy Boyle's strategy. They remained open, and the scabs shopped at clothing stores, drugstores, and discount stores. Carmen bought a pound of fudge at the Sweet Tooth.

Those merchants who had gone along with the boycott most grudgingly caved in most willingly to the threat of being sued. For many of the Presidentials, it was all the excuse they needed. They were hard put not to show their glee that the damn Hardwoods were getting their long-overdue comeuppance.

The fragmentation of Elk River had begun.

. . .

That Tuesday, after the news spread that the boycott had been broken, Bill Deeley stopped traffic, pedestrian and vehicular, along Riverfront Drive dead in its tracks.

He leaned a long ladder against the front of the Church of the Resurrection and climbed it with a bucket and a brush in his hand. Reaching the arch over the main entrance, he dipped the brush in the bucket and began to paint—to deface—the most beautiful building in town, the landmark that symbolized Elk River for all who lived there.

It was outrageous! Why, Elk River had never even had the least bit of a graffiti problem, and here, in broad daylight, was the church pastor marring the building that more than a few people believed was the town's gift from God.

An elderly man shouted at Bill, "You stop that, you stop that this instant! Come down from there!"

But Bill didn't. Not until he finished covering one of Michelangelo Fortunato's beautifully cut, glowing pieces of limestone with penitentiary-gray paint. Then he hauled the ladder and paint back to the church basement.

He didn't have a word to say to the indignant onlookers.

The Brotherhood of Manufacturing Workers, International, set up shop that same day. They opened their new office directly across First Street from Local 274. An insurance broker had been at the address only the night before.

By noon, the union name and logo had been painted on the window. A large cardboard sign was placed beneath these hallmarks. It said: 1,100 JOBS AVAILABLE. UNION PAY AND BENEFITS. UNION MEMBERSHIP REQUIRED. INQUIRE WITHIN.

The half dozen stalwarts of labor who manned the new office looked as if they fed at a steroid trough and picked their teeth with broken femurs.

But they didn't scare Marty McCreery. When he saw the jobs sign go up, the secretary-treasurer and would-be president of Local 274 snapped. He grabbed his bowling trophy from its shelf and raced out into the middle of the street. He flung the symbol of the highest athletic honor of his life through the new union's window.

Only the timely, tire-screeching arrival of Chief Deputy Ron Narder, riot gun in hand, prevented bloodshed. He arrested Marty McCreery.

But he couldn't save Marty's trophy. The biggest of the international's goons snapped the little golden figure of the bowler off the base of the trophy with his bare hands.

That afternoon, another Help Wanted sign was posted at the entrance of Tony Hunt's plant. It stopped the pickets dead in their tracks. Twelve jobs were available. The positions were in plant security. Guards.

The jobs offered, to the penny, the same wages and benefits workers had received before going on strike. Compared to what Hunt was currently willing to pay plant workers, or what they could get anywhere else, it seemed like a king's ransom.

Twelve jobs. Eight men and four women on the picket line. Nobody had any trouble with the arithmetic. All of them heard the thirty pieces of silver being dropped at their feet.

Six of the men and three of the women bolted to embrace betrayal. They were welcomed through a Judas gate.

51   Tony Hunt sat in his office that morning more determined than ever to see John Fortunato dead. A single question pounded against his brain like a hammer on an anvil: *How?*

How had Fortunato gotten out of his burning house alive? How had he gotten into Hunt's plant and out again without anybody seeing him? And most of all, how was Hunt going to kill Fortunato now?

Hunt had a million things to do, but he couldn't rid his mind of Fortunato. This maniac made Tommy Boyle seem like a piece of cake. After seeing that horrific photograph of Krieger last night—and he had no doubt that Fortunato had both taken it and left it for him to find—Hunt had remembered the one detail he'd previously overlooked.

Last night, he had gone back to his office and reloaded his gun.

Then he returned to his Lexus and called Security on his car phone. He told them to open the front gate; he'd be leaving in a hurry. He rocketed past the stunned guards and turned onto Riverfront Drive, where he quickly dropped down to the legal limit. This wouldn't be the time to get stopped for a traffic violation.

He headed straight to the Mississippi, watching his rearview mirror for any sign of Fortunato. Once he reached the dark, empty highway, Hunt almost wished that the bastard would show himself. He had his gun. He'd shown that he could use it. And the Big Muddy could accommodate two stiffs as easily as one. But Fortunato did not appear.

Hunt found a spot along the eastern bank of the Mississippi where he could pull his car off the road. When he was sure there was no one around to see him, he dragged Krieger out by his heels.

He grabbed the photo of Krieger off the body, and by the dome light of the car took another look at it. He had to admit the image was unique. With an inward laugh, Hunt almost wished he had one of himself just like it. He shredded the picture and threw it into the water.

Then he kicked Krieger's body into the river, bidding it good riddance. But Krieger wasn't done causing Hunt trouble. The body hit with a splash but didn't sink, because Hunt had never thought to weigh it down. Then the current tugged the plastic sheeting off the body, and Krieger's corpse rolled over onto its back, staring up through dead eyes into the light of a crescent moon. Krieger's mouth seemed to twist into a wicked smile.

Hunt later told himself he hadn't left the scene with any undue haste.

That morning, he called in his chief of security and reamed the fool for allowing a trespasser to enter and exit the plant at will. The security chief knew of no trespasser. He asked Hunt what he was talking about and what the intruder had done.

Hunt had no way to respond. He couldn't confess to Krieger's murder, and he didn't know how Fortunato had gotten in. Deprived of an answer, he simply stewed.

The security chief thought he saw an opportunity. He said that while he and his men did their best, the plant was a big place, and adding more men would be a great help.

Hunt looked out his window at that moment and his malicious imagination immediately came up with an idea that dovetailed nicely with his security chief's empire building. There were pickets outside his gate, as usual. He counted them. Twelve.

"All right," Hunt said, "here's what you'll do. . . ."

He laughed out loud when he saw the pickets change sides, throwing their signs back over the gate. His laughter died, however, when he happened to look across the street at the city's storage facility.

He'd seen something or someone over there on the night of the riot, the night he'd been shot. At first, he'd thought Boyle had been the target and he the innocent—well, the bystander, anyway. Then he'd considered that he himself might well have been the target. And now . . . now . . .

The epiphany hit Hunt like a thunderbolt.

Maybe *Fortunato* had been the one who'd shot him. Why not? He was Tommy Boyle's blood relative. He could have done it. And where else could that shot have come from? It *had* to be the storage yard. Sure, that was why he'd seen the sheriff poking around over there. Even that hick lawman had figured it out and . . . and maybe there was a way from over there to over here. But how?

His security chief had assured him that the plant's fence hadn't been breached. And Fortunato certainly hadn't parachuted in. So if the intruder hadn't come through, and he hadn't come over, he'd had to come . . .

. . . under?

Frank Murtaw stole his father's Glock semiautomatic pistol that morning. He cut school and went into the Oak Crest woods to find Ty Daulton. He was going to kill the microscopic sonofabitch.

Him and his freak friends.

Burn them all with the same clip. It was too bad Frank couldn't lay his hands on an Uzi. That'd be just the thing to whip out against Ty's dinky little peashooter. The size of Ty's gun was one of the things that had bothered Frank most. He'd run from a gun so tiny he'd come to ask himself if it'd been real. Or if it could have hurt him even if it had been.

He'd shamed himself by running away. First from that psycho on the motorcycle, then from the pipsqueak himself.

As a result, he was getting his ass handed to him every time he stepped onto the rugby field. All the other guys sensed his weakness. They plowed right over him.

Well, no goddamn more, Frank thought.

He stopped in the woods at the point where he last remembered seeing Ty. He looked around. He didn't know shit about tracking; he didn't know oaks from oats. But that didn't matter.

He was going to search every square inch, every bush, every tree, until he found out how that little bastard got away. Then he'd sit tight and wait for him to come back.

52　　John went to Local 274 to pick up the reverse telephone directory that Marty McCreery had obtained at his request. When he arrived, he learned of Marty's arrest and saw the international's goons in their new office across First Street for himself.

Despite Marty's antagonistic relationship with Jill, John fronted the 10 percent of his five-thousand-dollar bond. He didn't think it would help the strikers' morale to have their highest elected official languishing in jail. Together with several of Marty's union brothers, John took him home to his wife. Marty was no longer outraged, he was despondent. And his mood quickly spread among the friends who'd brought him home.

So much for the morale boost.

John returned to Tommy's place and sat in the living room with the reverse directory, matching names to the phone numbers that had been called from the sheriff's station on the night of the riot. The list was hundreds of numbers long. Checking each one had all the appeal of root canal work.

He started at the beginning and worked steadily for hours. All the calls except three had been made to the homes of union members. Get-me-outta-here calls. To post a fifty-dollar bond, you called your wife, not a lawyer. The exceptions had been made to the homes of deputies. Home-late-Honey calls.

John had hoped to find some sign that Tommy had tried to call some-one. To find some trail that would lead somewhere. But maybe Leen hadn't allowed Tommy a call.

There were a few numbers left from the wee hours of the morning. 555–2828 . . . the Traveler's Delight Motel.

Tommy?

Who else would call a motel from jail?

Especially one that had been used for scabs and later been burned down. Had Tommy somehow found out Hunt's plan to use the motel for his strikebreakers? Had he ordered the arson? From jail?

A hundred other questions whirled through John's mind. He was reaching for the list of numbers Tommy had called from his home phone during the past month when there was a knock at the door. A voice called out.

"You in there, Fortunato?" Sheriff Leen asked. "Somebody's got the light on. Don't you think it's about time we talked?"

John stashed the phone records and opened the door.

John and the sheriff regarded each other at little more than arm's length.

"You want to tell me how you got out of your house?"

"No," John said.

"You see who the bad guys were?"

"No."

"You want to tell me, at least, did *anyone* die in that fire?"

"Nobody died."

"Which explains why we never found so much as a charred bone. But it wasn't because people didn't try to kill you."

John bided his silence.

"We found firebombs and grenade fragments," Leen continued. "Now, you show up like Lazarus in a fireproof suit, only you don't have anything to say."

"You find Tommy's killer yet?" John asked.

Leen looked like he'd just swallowed a cow pie. "No. I'm trying, but I've been a little busy lately. How about you?"

"I've heard of two confessions," John said.

"What?" the sheriff asked sharply.

John told him what he'd heard from Jill and Bobbi Sharpes.

"Billy confessed, that sonofabitch? And some union slimebag, too?"

"Let's not forget the death threat Jill Baxter received."

"I won't. I got enough problems without lawyers getting killed." Leen smiled grimly. "Especially when they know people who grow their own hand grenades."

John was glad the sheriff had understood him.

"You might want to keep a real close eye on Billy, too," he said. "I think Bobbi might kill him."

"Maybe I should let her. If I can't make a case against him, we'll chalk it up as justifiable homicide."

"Aren't there laws against that?"

Leen shook his head. "The only law that stands a chance around here is gravity. And I wouldn't even bet on that one." The sheriff tried one more time. "You gonna tell me how you got out?"

"No."

"Then I guess we're done."

John said, "There's one more thing."

"What?"

"You know Hunt's personal thug?"

Leen nodded. "That guy who looks like Karloff and sounds like Crosby."

"Yeah, him. He's dead."

"You kill him?" the sheriff asked.

"No. I think Hunt did."

"You know where the body is?"

"No."

"You want to tell me how you found out about this murder?"

"No."

"Shit," Leen said, "I can't even think of a good way to threaten you. Throw you in jail, you might pull some goddamn Houdini disappearing stunt on *me*."

John smiled. "Talk to Hunt," he said. "See what he has to say about it."

Tony Hunt closed the deal on buying Riverman Savings that afternoon. The first thing he did was review the mortgage portfolio. He segregated all the loans made to members of Local 274 and issued instructions to begin eviction proceedings immediately on anyone more than one payment behind. He intended to solve the problem of where to house the scabs in short order.

He also looked into the accounts of Sheriff Orville Leen.

53 Jill looked physically exhausted and emotionally drained when she returned to Tommy's town house that night. John had cooked pork chops, but neither of them had taken the first bite.

"I don't know if we're dead yet," Jill told him, "but we're on the critical list. I got a preliminary injunction against the international to keep them from organizing the scabs, but that was from a friendly, neighborhood judge. They'll be in court in Chicago tomorrow appealing it."

"The judge went along because of community interest?"

"No, I had to give him some cover. I told him about that accusation Tommy had made about the international settling strikes because they were looting strike funds. Now I have to substantiate that allegation. I've checked Tommy's files and I didn't find anything. Maybe Tommy's investigator has evidence, but I can't find him, either."

She looked defeated.

"I know how to reach him," John said.

"You do?"

He told her the number to call.

"Tell whoever answers I gave you the number. I don't know if Phil Henry has what you want, but you can ask."

She gave him a weary smile. "Any more rabbits you can pull out of your hat?"

He gave her a dollar instead of a rabbit.

"This makes me your client, right? Privileged conversation and all that?"

She nodded. "You commit a crime or something?"

He told her about going to Hunt's plant, finding Krieger's remains, and how he'd passed the information along to Leen.

Jill brightened immediately. She said, "If the sheriff can make an arrest and Hunt gets indicted, it'll change everything."

"Funny world, isn't it, where murder is good news?"

"It's a goddamn cruel world," Jill replied, "but sometimes things even out. And if they do, you don't question your luck."

"Don't count on getting too lucky. I couldn't give the sheriff enough information to go roaring off to make an arrest. The reason I told you at all is I think Hunt's got his problems, too. And maybe I can help him along a little in that department."

"And while I'm in Chicago for the appeal I'll do that research on him we talked about."

John said, "I thought maybe I'd make the trip with you, just so you get up there safely."

"Ride shotgun?"

"I thought I'd bring a few grenades."

"Grenades," Jill said. "Sure. They're just the thing to discourage tailgaters."

Jill packed her wardrobe of found clothes in a borrowed suitcase, John took the illicitly obtained phone records and two grenades, and they set off for Chicago in a dead man's car. Be a helluva situation to explain if a cop stopped them, John thought.

They left after midnight with Jill driving. No one tried to shoot them or run them off the road. Still, they were watchful, and neither of them spoke until they could see the lights of Chicago just ahead.

Then Jill said, "If it turns out I need some time . . . if a delay of some sort might put Hunt in a box . . . could you arrange that?"

"Are we conspiring here?"

She gave him a look. "We're having a privileged conversation."

"Well, if you're hinting at, say, sabotage at the plant, the situation would have to be extreme, because that could mean revealing the tunnels."

"The situation's already extreme. If I ask for help, it'll be life or death."

John thought about it. "Okay. Especially if it's your life or mine."

He kissed Jill before she got out at the Palmer House, and then drove over to Holy Name Cathedral. It was locked at that hour. He woke a priest at the rectory, gave him a hundred dollars, and asked him to light a dozen candles.

John thought that should cover everyone.

Then he drove home. Bone tired, he went down into the tunnels to sleep in HQ. Leen had been right. Someone else might find him at Tommy's place, and John didn't have a secret avenue of escape there.

As he drifted off, John thought this must be how it had been for the VC: never knowing when—or if—you'd live above ground again.

54 Tony Hunt searched the municipal storage yard across from his main gate that night. He'd bribed his way in. It hadn't cost much. What could he do, steal a snowplow?

The union hadn't replaced its defectors, so there was no picket line outside the plant that night. The only people watching Hunt were his own guards. They had no idea what the hell he was doing, walking around over there with a flashlight, and they knew better than to ask.

Hunt tried to remember where he'd seen the flicker of movement from his office window. He'd had the impression that it was toward the rear of the property. He saw that the ground back there sloped upward to a cinder block wall. A stand of waist-high weeds ran along the wall's base.

He walked to the rear of the yard. He looked at the wall. It had to be ten feet high. The guy who'd shot him would have needed a ladder to get up there. Besides, the movement he'd seen from his office had come from somewhere lower than that. . . . He couldn't get the idea out of his head that Fortunato had entered his plant from below. But how in God's name could he do that? Then a thought occurred to him: Maybe there was an old sewer line around. Or an obsolete steam tunnel. Something that was no longer in use but was known to a local like Fortunato.

Hunt swept an arc of weeds aside with his foot, looking for a metal access cover. The undergrowth was too thick for him to see through from a standing position. He got down on his hands and knees and pushed the weeds aside. He found everything from empty wine bottles to used condoms to dog shit.

He was about to give up when he found a small scrap of a photograph: a tiny image of a large breast. He picked it up. The fragment had been part of a photo that had been torn apart. Curious, Hunt looked for other pieces of the picture, and bit by bit, limb by limb, he searched them out. Joining them together in the dirt nearby, he assembled a wallet-size snapshot of a voluptuous nude.

Only the model's head was missing.

He finally found it, the shred of photo showing the head of a saucy bottle blonde, sticking up in the crack of . . . it wasn't a sewer cover . . . it was rectangular . . . a wooden lid of some sort. Using the weeds as a handle, he yanked upward.

A trapdoor opened. The hinged side was flush with the base of the storage yard wall. Hunt shone his flashlight down into the opening. At first, he couldn't understand what he was looking at. The construction was dirt, not concrete, so it wasn't a sewer. The smell made him think more of a grave than a toilet, and it was pretty damn small.

He couldn't have fit into it.

As he pondered, something with an endless number of legs scuttled out of the hole and across his shoe. Hunt jumped back, shaking the creature off him and biting back a curse. The trapdoor fell back into place. It fit snugly and was invisible.

That's when it hit him. The thing was a goddamn tunnel. *Fortunato's* tunnel. For some lunatic reason Fortunato had tunneled into his plant.

A second insight jarred him.

How had Fortunato gotten out of his burning house alive? Through *another* tunnel. Jesus Christ, Hunt wondered, how many holes had Fortunato dug? Whatever the number, the guy had to be as crazy as a bedbug. And now the SOB was after him.

This was serious. Tony Hunt knew he had to do something fast. But what? Put out a contract with the Orkin man?

When Ron Narder got up in the middle of the night to use the john, he saw his wife sitting in her reading chair staring out the bedroom window. She turned toward him when she heard the bed creak. Neither of them seemed to know what to say, so Ron just shuffled off to the bathroom.

But when he got back to bed he knew he'd never fall asleep without

Clare next to him. He set his feet on the floor and said in a tired voice, "It's about Marty McCreery, isn't it? The fact that I arrested him. Dad came by, or called, and gave you an earful."

Clare shook her head. "I haven't heard from your father all day."

"But somebody told you."

She nodded.

"Clare, not only was it the right thing to do, I probably saved Marty from getting busted up real good. Those goons they've got at the new union are bruisers, and you can bet they haven't been told to turn the other cheek."

"That's not . . ." she started. "Well, that's only part of it. I know you do your job the right way, Ronnie. I'd never fault you for that." Clare Narder moved to the bed, sat next to her husband, and took his hand. "I'm just so sad that it's come to all this. Did you hear what happened to the picket line out at the plant?"

Narder hadn't, so she told him.

"I know those women," Clare said, meaning the ones who'd gone over to the company. "I called all three to ask why they did it. Two of them cried and said their pride just wouldn't let them accept food stamps and welfare for their families, and that was what it would come to real soon. The other one got angry with me, said I had a husband whose job wasn't threatened and it was her goddamn right to come out on the winning side, too."

Clare Narder hung her head in sorrow. Ron put his arm around her.

"I imagine it's pretty much the same for the men who crossed, too," she said. "But right now all of their friends and neighbors from the union just think they're traitors."

Then she asked him if he'd seen what Bill Deeley had done to the Church of the Resurrection. The question gave the chief deputy a jolt, first because he hated to think of anything bad happening to that church, and second because it scared him that he seemed to be losing track of what was happening in town.

"What'd he do?" Ron asked uneasily.

She told him about the defacing. He understood intuitively what the pastor's purpose was. "It's a mark of shame," he said. "Bill's using the church to show us our souls."

"And they're in a pretty sorry state, aren't they?"

Ron and Clare held each other through the night, but neither of them slept.

·   ·   ·

Neither did Tony Hunt, and finally, in the wee hours, he thought of someone who might possibly help him with Fortunato and his tunnels. He called the most-reviled man of the most-disgraced presidential administration in American history. The dirtiest trickster of them all was an old friend of Tony Hunt's; they'd done business together and had always admired each other's ruthlessness. More important, Hunt had provided untraceable funds for some of the most underhanded maneuvers the political operative had ever conceived. Now a right-wing radio raver, the man was not only awake at that ungodly hour, he was happy to take Tony Hunt's call.

He listened to Hunt's story about tunnels without interruption. Then the trickster said calmly, "I've got just the guy you want."

Better yet, he didn't ask Hunt for a dime. Said this one was for old time's sake—but let him know if it turned out to be anything he could use on the air.

On the Mississippi, forty-five miles north of St. Louis, the *Delta Darling* riverboat casino was heading home after a profitable night on the water. On deck, a couple fondled passionately beneath the light of the moon. Pete Banks, gambler and Tony Hunt's stoolie inside Local 274, hadn't let a few lousy little labor problems interfere with his favorite pastime. In fact, after pointing out to Hunt the union members who'd be most vulnerable to the plant owner's eviction strategy, Banks had the best gambling night of his life, a run of twelve straight passes at the craps table. The redhead he was with had played a hunch and piggybacked her bets to his. So it looked liked Pete was about to have the best night of his life, period.

Their hands were full of hundred-dollar bills and each other. They were tucking Franklins into progressively more intimate areas of each other's clothing. It was a risky game. The money was new. A paper cut might send either or both of them overboard.

But the flush of excitement from their score, the moonlight on the river, and the cool night breeze all made it too delicious to stop. She took his zipper down. He tensed, but she was deft. Wrapped him like a smoky link. All he felt was the kiss of crisp currency and the caress of lacquered nails. His turn. He reached under her skirt and . . . her shrill scream in his ear made his heart skip a beat. Christ, he hadn't even done anything yet.

So why couldn't he get his breath back?

Then he heard the redhead babble and saw her point at something out in the water. It was a . . . a guy? Hung up on a root or something?

The forward motion of the boat soon made up for Banks's myopia. Now he saw what had caused his new girlfriend's commotion. Krieger! Tony Hunt's hatchet man. Sticking out of the Mississippi like he'd been crucified there. . . after he'd had his eyes plucked out.

Pete Banks's stomach clenched and his throat constricted. He couldn't get any air. The boat drew close to Krieger's ghastly cadaver. The dead man seemed to be staring up at Banks with those empty sockets. Then something long, dark, and slimy oozed out of the corpse's mouth, dropped into the water, and swam away.

Pete Banks wondered in horror, Was this what you got when you worked for Tony Hunt?

As if in answer, a giant unseen hand gave Pete Banks's heart an agonizing squeeze, crushing it like a rotten tomato. He felt himself falling backward over the boat's railing. In his last moment of mortal consciousness, he saw the redhead reaching out . . . for him, he thought.

Until she plucked the roll of hundreds neatly from his hand.

55 Frank Murtaw had stayed out all night. He'd thought maybe that little shit Ty had gone nocturnal on him. So he'd waited in the woods, ready for him, eating all the candy bars he'd brought with him.

As the night gave way to the first shadings of Wednesday's dawn, Frank was hungry, cold, and tired. He'd also been eaten alive by mosquitoes. He'd bet he looked like some movie ghoul by now—all lumpy, bumpy, and swollen up. Ready for a hockey mask.

He smelled, too. And he had to take a leak. Bad.

Man, what he was going to do to Ty when he caught him. . . .

Frank looked for a private place to relieve himself. Considering his general appearance, he didn't want to aggravate matters by whipping it out and having some granny come along on her nature walk.

He saw a place where a bush butted up against a rise, urgently scuttled over there, and unzipped. Damn, he thought, letting go was one of life's great pleasures.

Niagara—fucking—Falls.

Frank looked down to make sure he wasn't splashing his shoes. No problem. He scanned the dirt he was irrigating, looking for some bugs to drown. Pay 'em back for the misery their kind had inflicted on him all night long. But no luck. *Nada.*

The funny thing was, though, his piss wasn't even pooling. It was disappearing right into the ground. How the hell did you explain that? When he finally finished and tucked back in, Frank bent down to take a closer look.

His forceful stream had washed a layer of dirt off the ground and left . . . what? Wood? Frank tore a big handful of leaves off the bush and brushed away more dirt. In little more than a minute, he had the trapdoor open and was looking into a hole.

That's where his piss had gone. . . .

And that little prick Ty, too.

The hole was way too tiny for Frank to fit into, but that didn't matter. Now he knew Ty's secret. Sooner or later, the little shit would be back. He was closing in on him.

Billy Shelton knew he was in deep shit the minute he stepped into the sheriff's office.

"You're fired," Leen said.

"What for?" the deputy demanded.

Leen's tone was as hard as the look on his face. "According to information I've received, you're a confessed murderer."

"That bitch."

Billy had never figured that Bobbi would go to the sheriff. He thought she'd keep things between them. Inside their marriage. He surely hadn't told anyone she'd stabbed him.

Then Leen informed him that Bobbi hadn't opened up. He'd heard the story from John Fortunato. Bobbi had just corroborated it when the sheriff had talked to her.

"You also threatened to kill any man Ms. Sharpes took up with."

"She's my wife, goddamnit!"

"She's filing for divorce today," Leen said. "She told me she doesn't want any doubt that her baby isn't yours."

Billy's face went purple.

Leen continued, "Do you wish to repeat your confession to me at this time?"

"Fuck you," Billy said.

"Billy, I don't know if it's dumber to kill a man or pretend that you did, but either way you're too goddamn stupid to be a cop. Give me your badge and your weapon."

For a second, Billy looked like he was going to *use* his weapon on the sheriff. He reconsidered when he saw Leen look past him. Chief Deputy Narder stood in the doorway with his gun on Billy. When Billy looked back at the sheriff, he had his gun on him, too.

The sheriff said, "I don't care if you did throw the murder weapon in the Mississippi. If you killed Tommy Boyle, I bet I'll catch you anyway. And if I had more than hearsay to go on, I'd lock your sad ass up this minute."

Billy dropped his badge and gun on the sheriff's desk and left.

Orville Leen passed word that he wasn't to be disturbed for any situation that didn't involve the loss of life. He had to catch up on his reading.

Lab reports connected with the murder of Tommy Boyle had been piling up on his desk, but with all the sundry insanity he hadn't had time to read them.

Now he learned that the shell casing he'd found at the storage yard was from a .223-millimeter cartridge. This was the standard load for either an AR-15 or an M-16 rifle. Hunt had been shot with a military-style assault rifle.

He moved on to the arson report on the fire at the Traveler's Delight Motel. Two facts jumped out at Leen: the accelerant used to spread the fire was C-4 plastic explosive, and the human remains found at the site had been identified as female.

The coincidences were starting to stack up, and Leen hated coincidences as much as any other cop in the world.

Tommy Boyle got arrested. He called the Traveler's Delight Motel from jail. The chief deputy thought Boyle had been talking to a woman. Boyle was shot dead after being released. The motel burned down shortly after that, killing one female. Two dead people and one phone call; the connection was undeniable in the sheriff's mind.

But who was the woman? Somebody Boyle had been screwing? How many women had the man needed? After all, Boyle had been seeing Bobbi Sharpes, had gotten her pregnant.

Maybe the dead woman had been keeping an eye on the scabs at the motel for Boyle. He'd had a female lawyer, why not another private investigator—to go along with that Phil Henry fella—this one a woman?

Then there was the C-4. It took a certain background to know that stuff burned as well as blew up. When you added in the .223 shell casing, it summed up to somebody who was familiar with a lot of military firepower.

On the other hand, Boyle had been killed with your run-of-the-mill nine-millimeter weapon, available to anybody. That didn't fit the military pattern.

The arson at the Fortunato house had involved gasoline bombs, also a garden-variety weapon . . . but *somebody* inside had thrown a hand grenade. Back to the military theme.

Leen decided that it was time he and Fortunato came clean with each other. Maybe they could get somewhere. He picked up his phone and called Tommy Boyle's apartment.

The goddamn phone machine picked up. Tommy Boyle's voice spoke to him. The sheriff hated that.

"This is Leen," he growled. "Are you there, Fortunato?"

His patience lasted ten seconds.

"Well, shit. Come see me as soon as you can, all right? It's time we got this fucker settled."

At forty-three homes across Elk River that morning, men and women about to leave for picket duty found sheets of paper had been tacked to their front doors while they slept. Each sheet bore an identical declaration: NOTICE OF INTENT TO EVICT.

The homeowners were informed that they had missed two or more mortgage payments. Unless their loans were brought up to date by close of business that day, legal proceedings to repossess the dwellings and evict their occupants would be initiated the next day.

The notice was signed by the bank's new president, Anthony Tiburon Hunt. Clipped to each notice was a business card from the president of the new BMW local.

A note on each card read: "Need a job? See me."

Sheriff Leen had just decided to go out and look for John Fortunato when his phone rang. His first thought was to check whether his instructions had been followed.

He picked up the phone and asked, "Is this a matter of life and death?"

"In a manner of speakin'," a deep voice drawled. "Leastwise, there's a corpse involved. An' your office asked mine to be on the lookout for any loose bodies."

The voice belonged to Sheriff Don Corliss of Calhoun County, one of Leen's longtime friends in law enforcement. Calhoun County was forty miles south of Leen's bailiwick in Fox County.

"What'd you find, Don?" Leen asked.

"A floater." Calhoun County was on the Mississippi. "Well, actually, he was hung up to dry by the time we got 'im, but he'd been in the river, all right."

"Big guy?"

"Super *de*-luxe."

"White?"

"As a Klan picnic."

"Looks like he stepped out of some Hollywood horror movie?" Leen asked.

"Prob'ly wasn't real pretty before he went in the water, and you know how a stint as fish bait does a body."

"Just looking at him, who's he remind you of?"

"Other than my wife on a good day . . . I'd have to say Mrs. Stein's little boy, Frankie."

So Fortunato's tip had been legitimate, Leen thought.

"Can you send him right along, Don?"

"I'll FedEx him, you want to pay the freight."

56 The Dream Warriors gang of Westminster, California, was no more. It had been decimated by the guerrilla tactics of Tran Chi Thanh, merchant. Then factions fell to quarreling. Internecine shootouts finished the gang.

Survivors hung out at local video arcades and collected public assistance. One or two of the more ambitious went back to school.

Tran was an unspoken hero in his community.

Walter Desmond was a former CIA spook. At the midpoint of an otherwise undistinguished career, he'd had a bright idea and, with official blessing, had taken it private. Desmond called his idea "the Talent Pool."

Simply put, his plan called for extending visas and resident alien status to foreign nationals possessing unusual talents who in the normal course of events would have been shot down over the ocean had they tried to enter the United States.

These immigrants were led to believe that only bungling bureaucrats and good luck were responsible for their admission to the country. The first half of the equation was what made the idea such an easy sell.

Once these shady characters were in place and well on their way to becoming affluent Americans, they were susceptible to threats of blackmail—that is, deportation—unless they put their talents to use as directed.

Tony Hunt's old friend from Washington, D.C., had called Walter Desmond about the plant owner's tunnel problem. Leave it to him, Desmond had said.

The next day, Desmond and an associate walked into Convenient Liquors and patiently negotiated its maze in the company of Jimmy Giap, erstwhile Dream Warrior. None of them was smiling.

Jimmy fingered Tran. "That's him. He's the bastard you want."

There was a gleam of satisfaction in the boy's eyes, that of a wounded snake managing one last venomous bite.

"Mr. Tran Chi Thanh?" Desmond asked the store owner.

Tran took his eyes off the boy and looked impassively at the Yankee. He nodded slightly.

Now, the American smiled.

"Greetings from the United States government," Desmond said. He showed Tran a fake INS credential. "Let's go into your back room and talk."

Tran walked into his storage room with the Yankee. The other American waited out front with Jimmy Giap. The Yankee took a seat and waited for Tran to sit behind the desk where he did the paperwork for his store.

"Mr. Tran," he said, "you lied about your past political affiliations to get into this country."

"You are mistaken," Tran said flatly.

The Yankee shook his head, a small gesture ironclad with certainty. "You were a Communist, Mr. Tran. Worse than that, you bore arms for the National Liberation Front, the Vietcong." The Yankee leaned forward. "You killed Americans."

Tran said nothing, and the Yankee sat back.

"We let just about anybody in this country these days, Mr. Tran, but fortunately we do draw a few lines. Communists who spent years killing Americans, them we can still kick out."

The Yankee smiled again. "How would you feel about a return to your homeland, Mr. Tran?"

Tran wanted to bolt . . . to disappear . . . to kill this vile Yankee. He could do it, but where would he and his family run? They knew nothing of America other than this small part of Southern California.

But Tran knew a great deal about human nature, and he was sure this Yankee wanted something from him. The threat of deportation was his leverage.

"What do you want?" Tran asked flatly.

"There's a gentleman in the Midwest who's having a problem with some sonofabitch who dug himself a bunch of tunnels. We want you to take care of him."

Tran was staggered by the very idea. An *American* tunnel system? And this madman wanted him to fight in someone else's earth? That would be suicide.

The Yankee read his thoughts.

"Not an easy chore, I know. But it's either that or 'Hello, Ho Chi Minh City.' Maybe you could take a few bottles of your stock along with you, sell them off the back of a bicycle."

The very threat foreclosed any option Tran had. He'd sooner die now than return . . . and take his family back? Never. But he did have one question.

"Jimmy Giap helped you find me?"

"We knew you were in the Westminster area. Jimmy and a bunch of his friends down at the local game parlor were happy to tell us where. Jimmy, he wanted to see the look on your face."

Tran knew he'd been a fool not to kill all the Dream Warriors. But as long as some were still alive . . .

He said, "I will need help."

Desmond smiled thinly.

"Sure, you will. And I bet we can persuade Jimmy and a few of his pals to join you for a little fun, travel, and adventure."

57 Jill Baxter had been the first girl to crack the Little League gender barrier in the town of Charlottesville, Virginia, where she'd grown up, so there were times when she thought in terms of baseball metaphors.

She struck out when she tried to reach Tommy's investigator at the number John had given her. She'd been told that the man had gone "somewhere warm to heal up." He'd call her when he got back.

She whiffed again in appeals court. The judge lifted the injunction. The Brotherhood of Manufacturing Workers, International, was free to organize the workforce at MicroCosmic, Inc.

After she returned to her hotel room, though, Jill started hitting line drives off the outfield wall. The old girls network came through for her.

She called a former classmate at the University of Chicago Law School who now worked for the Commodity Futures Trading Commission in Chicago. That friend called a friend with the Securities Exchange Commission in New York. She, in turn, called a friend at an investment banking firm.

That friend was the freshly dumped mistress of Carter Powell, Tony Hunt's investment banker, who was trying hard to tidy up his life. That bitter young woman, who feared she'd lose her job next, was only too happy to tell Jill everything she needed to know about Tony Hunt, his finances, and his new business, a wealth of information that Powell had passed along as pillow talk.

Among the nuggets Jill gleaned was the fact that Toshiro Yoshihara, the inventor of the microprocessor on which Hunt's new business was based, was stashed at the Miyako Hotel, right there in Chicago, under the name of Stanley Rice.

Jill called Yoshihara immediately and urgently asked for an appointment. The man was initially reluctant even to admit his real identity, but Carter Powell's former sweetie had given Jill a whole bandolier of ammunition to work with. She asked Mr. Yoshihara if, by any chance, Anthony Tiburon Hunt had been tardy in providing payments that he contractually owed the inventor. She heard the pseudonymous Stanley Rice take a deep breath. Right then, she knew she had him.

And when he hesitantly asked if they might dine together while they talked, Jill guessed the man was also lonely. Not that she would offer him anything more than polite company and a very strong argument about why he should make a radical change in his plans.

Still, Yoshihara was the key. Jill was sure of that. She was stepping up to the plate with the bases loaded and two out in the bottom of the ninth.

58 John was about to check Tommy's home phone records when Ty poked his head into HQ. The boy entered the chamber and straightened.

"Can I ask you a question?" he said.

"Sure, what is it?"

Ty hesitated.

"Is it about Doolan?" John asked.

"Well, yeah, indirectly. But more about you."

"It's okay, Ty, but what is it? I've got some things to take care of."

"Oh, sorry. I'll leave."

John was losing his patience. "Ty."

"Well, I know how good you are in the dark and all, but I was wondering . . . what's your biggest weakness?"

The question surprised John. He'd never really thought about it. Which was pretty arrogant. Pretty damn dumb, too. After serious consideration, he said, "I'd say my hearing. It's not bad, more like average. Doolan, on the other hand, had incredible hearing. He . . ."

John stopped when he noticed the blank look that had come over Ty's face.

"You okay?" he asked.

"Huh?"

"You just spaced out."

"Oh." He grinned. "I'm onto something."

"You want to tell me what?"

"I can't. I don't know yet. It all starts at a subconscious level . . . it's, well, ineffable. But if you push it, you smush it. You gotta let it cook."

Gotta let the ineffable cook, John thought. Darien said the kid was a genius; John was beginning to believe it.

"Let me know when dinner's on the table," he said.

Ty didn't move.

"Something else I can do for you?" John asked.

"Well . . . I'm out of ammunition."

Ty showed him the .38 he'd used to shoot the rat.

John wondered if it was smart to let a boy genius loose with a loaded weapon. But Ty had shown restraint, followed orders, when John had taken him to the plant.

"You understand the responsibility that comes with carrying a firearm?" John asked.

Ty nodded gravely.

"And you think you're good enough down here not to shoot Darien or Gil or me by mistake?"

A question Ty could answer more easily now. "Yes."

"And you have no intention whatsoever of taking your weapon above ground?"

"No."

John trusted the boy. He nodded to a footlocker.

"Help yourself."

A minute later he was alone again checking Tommy's phone records.

Harlan Welch had been born union and he was going to die union. Real union. Not that phony bunch of thugs handing out nickel-and-dime jobs for that shitheel Tony Hunt. And if being union meant Harlan couldn't have his house, then nobody else was going to have it, either.

He loaded his family into their car. Their possessions went into a U-Haul truck. Then Harlan went inside the home on Hickory Street that he'd made payments on for sixteen years and dumped gasoline all over the floors. He stood at the front door and lit a cigarette.

He touched the glowing ash to the rolled-up copy of his eviction notice. It caught nicely. Harlan dropped it in a puddle of gas and jumped back.

Harlan waved farewell to his neighbors on either side. One called the fire department on his portable phone. Both had their garden hoses already going.

As the Welch family left town, there was smoke in their rearview mirror and tears in their eyes.

John came out of the tunnels to use Tommy's phone.

As he walked to Tommy's place, he heard the clamor of sirens. In the sky, not far to the west, a dense column of black smoke rose over a neighborhood of small, well-tended houses. Someone else's home was turning to ash and rubble.

A tension grew in John that he'd first felt more than two decades ago and ten thousand miles away. He'd already exchanged his camera for the small revolver in his pocket, but now he wished he had his M-16 in his hands. He wished he had Doolan walking his slack.

His hometown had become a ville. Hootches were being torched. Sides had been taken. Blood had been spilled, and there would be more to come.

He'd found that Tommy's home phone bill listed three calls to the Traveler's Delight Motel in the hours preceding the riot at the plant. It also noted four calls to Austin, Texas, during the prior two weeks.

John didn't recognize the Texas number, but the listing helped to crystallize a number of things for him: who'd been smoking in Tommy's apartment, who'd been wearing perfume there, who'd left the clothes Jill was now wearing. It all led him to one very unpleasant conclusion as to who'd killed Tommy. He'd know for sure when he called the Austin number.

He hoped to God he was wrong.

When he stepped into Tommy's place the message light on the answering machine was blinking. The counter indicated three messages. He hit the play button.

Leen's voice told John to come see him so they could get things settled.

Jill asked him to arrange a small delay—say, two weeks—per their earlier discussion.

The last message had come in minutes before he'd stepped through Tommy's door. It was from Gil: "Our cover's been blown, man. Hunt knows about the tunnels. We just took our first POW!"

59 Chief Deputy Ron Narder brought Tony Hunt to the morgue as instructed. His orders had been concise. Fetch him or arrest him. Hunt had chosen to be fetched.

Not that he liked it.

He looked down at the body on the metal platform as the attendant drew back the sheet from its face. Hunt didn't flinch. His self-control was more than a match for the situation. He was on top of his game. Besides, once the deputy had told him he had no choice but to come along with him, he'd half suspected that sonofabitch Krieger would be causing him further trouble.

"That's Krieger," Hunt said. "Or what's left of him."

Leen addressed Narder and the attendant.

"Will you gentlemen excuse us, please?"

When they were alone, Leen looked directly at Hunt.

"I have information you killed this man, Mr. Hunt. Would you care to comment on that?"

Hunt's smile was as cold as the morgue's meat locker temperature.

"I've been meaning to have a little chat with you, Sheriff," he said.

The sheriff had expected the businessman to be rattled when he saw the body and was accused of murder. Instead, Hunt acted like a cat cornering a canary.

"Does that mean you're ready to confess?"

Hunt laughed. Then he casually covered Krieger's remains with the sheet and slid the body back into its compartment, as if to shut the door on both the corpse and the subject.

"No, Sheriff. I want to talk to you as your new banker."

Billy Shelton was waiting at the curb, leaning against his personal car, when Tony Hunt stepped out of the hospital.

"Offer you a ride, Mr. Hunt?" he asked.

Hunt thought he recognized the tall, rawboned geek grinning at him. "You're a cop, aren't you?"

"I was," Billy said. "I'm not now."

Hunt didn't want to hear about it.

"I was fired," Billy said.

"I called for my car," Hunt said. "It'll be along shortly."

"The sheriff thinks I killed Tommy Boyle."

That got Hunt's attention. He looked at Billy through narrowed eyes. "Did you?"

"Let's just say I'm a handy fella to have around. I was out to the plant hopin' to talk to you when I saw that suck-up Narder drive off with you in the back of his unit. I followed you over here, and I checked with a couple people I know. They tell me that big bastard you had workin' for you went toes-up."

"You have a point in there somewhere?" Hunt asked coolly.

"My point is, I'm better'n your friend in the morgue. You need some special help, I'm your man."

Hunt was about to say no when his wicked imagination sprang another idea on him. He asked Billy, "How do you feel about the sheriff?"

Billy looked around to make sure no one could hear him.

"I'd be happy to kill the sonofabitch," he whispered.

Hunt's car pulled up.

"I'd be happy about that, too," Hunt said.

Then Hunt got in his car and left. He imagined the geek standing there, trying to work it out. What should he do? Commit a murder on spec in the hope of getting a job? From the looks of him, he might be dumb enough to think so.

Hunt felt pleased about the way he'd handled the encounter. He'd learned a lesson from dealing with Krieger. Some people you put on your payroll, some people you didn't. You just let the geeks kid themselves that there might be a pot of gold at the end of the rainbow.

Chief Deputy Ron Narder was bitterly disappointed. He didn't know what the hell was going on anymore. He'd figured the sheriff was going to bust Hunt for murder. Otherwise, why brace him at the morgue with a stiff for company?

Narder had been overjoyed about bringing Hunt in. He was a law officer first, but if he could help the union within the course of his duty, he'd do it in a heartbeat. And if he went home with the story of how he'd been the one to collar Hunt, his father probably would have kissed him, and his wife certainly would have.

But fifteen minutes after he'd left the bastard with the sheriff, out Hunt walked, as free as a bird. He spent a few minutes talking to that shitheel Billy Shelton and then drove off in his damn luxury car, Billy leaving right after with a grin on his face that Narder hadn't liked at all. The sheriff came out a few minutes later, and the look in Leen's eyes told the chief deputy not to say a word.

So he hadn't.

It didn't keep him from thinking, though; it didn't keep him from remembering what that lawyer woman had asked about whose side the sheriff was on. Narder's mind went straight at the question: How had Hunt talked his way out of a murder bust?

Or had he *bought* his way out?

And what the hell was this latest errand he was doing for the sheriff all about? When they got back to the station, Leen had given him a sealed nine-by-twelve Sheriff's Department envelope. He was to take it to Tommy Boyle's town house. Put it in a dead man's mailbox and ring his doorbell once.

Narder decided that Orville Leen was losing it. But he followed his instructions to the letter. Then he went home and told Clare what had happened so she wouldn't have to hear it from somebody else.

After that, he called a half dozen of his best friends on the force. They had to be prepared in case the sheriff . . . well, the chief deputy didn't want to even complete that thought.

The town was still buzzing about what Bill Deeley had done to the Church of the Resurrection when, late that Wednesday afternoon, he did it again. This time he covered two more of Michelangelo Fortunato's limestones, one on either side of the original, with drab gray paint. If he kept up, the entire arch over the main entrance would be wreathed in shame.

As before, pedestrians and motorists stopped to watch—but this time nobody uttered a word of protest.

60   At twilight, Darien and Ty sat in the woods across the river from Tony Hunt's plant.

"You okay?" Darien asked softly.

"Yeah," Ty said. But occasionally his body was still racked by a tremor.

They could see a half dozen security guards standing around the entrance to the tunnel system that came up at the rear of the MicroCosmic storage building, the hole John and Ty had used to stage the PSYOP against Hunt. As Darien and Ty watched, a car pulled up and Hunt got out. He looked at the hole in the ground and then at his watch. He spoke to the captain of the guards and left. The security men maintained their vigil.

"They wonderin' what the hell happened to that little brother we caught. What's his name again?"

"Teddy Stinson," Ty said. "And we didn't catch him, you did. I fucked up."

Ty had been moving through the system shortly after leaving John in HQ that morning. He'd been thinking some more about the Doolan problem, factoring in what John had said about his hearing. It was at that precise moment when Ty heard someone coming through the tunnel straight at him. Someone who crawled too loudly, smelled wrong, and held his flashlight directly in front of himself—the "Hey, here I am, shoot me" position Darien had warned him never to use.

All of which added up to one thing in Ty's mind: intruder!

The guy caught a glimpse of Ty in his beam.

"Hey!" he yelled. Definitely not Darien, Gil, or John. Ty quickly backed around a bend in the tunnel. He heard the intruder hurry to catch up with him.

There was a trapdoor in the ceiling ten meters back. Ty scuttled to it and climbed up to the next level. He silently shut the door behind him. His heart was in his throat.

He heard a voice below him mutter, "Motherfucker."

Ty wasn't sure just what to do. The guy had a flashlight; all he had to do was point it up and he'd see the trapdoor. Ty could fire a round from his .38 down his level of the tunnel and the guy would hear it, maybe think he was being shot at, not be in such a hurry to open the trapdoor. Ty could get away and raise a warning.

Except who knew where the guy would be in the system by that time? He might even go back up to the surface and tell everybody what he'd found. Ty didn't want to let that happen. He'd just considered the possibility that this was a fight there'd be no backing away from when the trapdoor slammed open in front of him, a light in his eyes blinded him, and somebody grabbed the front of his shirt.

The next thing he knew he'd been yanked down to the lower level by the intruder and he was wrestling for his life. Ty reached for his .38 and got his hand on it, but his opponent seized his wrist before he could bring the gun to bear. He rolled Ty beneath him and, by the beam of the fallen flashlight, the boy saw the knife in the man's hand.

The man was far stronger than Ty, and against his weakening resistance, the intruder pressed his knife toward Ty's throat. Ty felt the cold breath of death wash over him.

Then, without warning, the intruder grunted and collapsed on him, the knife knicking Ty's left ear. Darien had bashed the man on the head from behind. Ty's friend had been in the right place at the right time to save his life.

Darien dragged the intruder to EE, tied him up, and blindfolded him. By the time the prisoner regained consciousness, Gil had appeared in the chamber, his nose for any scene of conflict as infallible as ever.

The captured man said his name was Teddy Stinson. He had a stash of hundred-dollar bills packed into a money belt, made from an old T-shirt, tied around his waist. He told them Hunt had found a tunnel entrance on his plant's property and had paid Teddy ten thousand dollars to go down the hole. Hunt wanted Teddy to come back and report what he'd found, but since Teddy already had Hunt's money, all he intended to do was split.

He said he wouldn't have pulled the knife on the boy if the boy hadn't gone for his gun.

Gil wanted to kill Teddy Stinson then and there, and might have if Teddy hadn't had the wit to understand who he was dealing with and identify himself as a fellow Vietnam vet. He made his appeal to the two men he was sure were former comrades-in-arms. He said he hadn't told Hunt squat and he wasn't about to.

Teddy presented his case in cool, even tones. He wanted to live, but he wasn't about to beg. That, as much as his military service, bought him some time. Then Darien said John had to be in on any decision they made.

So they left their prisoner bound and blindfolded while Gil went to call John, and Darien and Ty went to spy on Hunt's plant.

As they sat in the woods, Darien told Ty, "What you shoulda done was shoot right through the trapdoor."

"Kill him?"

"He tried to kill you. You remember that."

Ty would never forget it.

Darien added, "Gil always says there ain't no second chances in a tunnel. But you got one. So you best figure your luck's all used up."

Ty nodded dispiritedly.

"Don't fuck up no more, okay?"

"Okay."

"I'd miss you," Darien said.

After a while, Darien asked, "You remember our talk about people disappearin'?"

The sun was low by now and Darien's face was in shadow; Ty couldn't see his expression.

"Yeah," he replied carefully.

"Reason I got so upset was I disappeared once myself."

"What do you mean?" Ty asked.

Darien's voice took on the quiet tones of reminiscence. "My unit was out humpin' your basic search-'n'-destroy mission one day, workin' our way through elephant grass so high 'n' thick you couldn't see two feet in front a you. We were all boo-coo nervous 'cause Charlie was real active right then. The platoon had taken three KIA the day before."

Ty wanted to offer words of understanding and support, but he didn't know what to say. He kept quiet.

"I was walkin' point," Darien continued, "and all of a sudden, *whump*, Charlie's mortarin' us. Maybe it was just one round for all I know, but that one sends me flyin'. I get the feelin' like I'm Superman or somethin'. Except I remember thinkin' he didn't fly backwards.

"Next thing I know, I wake up inside a tunnel with two broken shoulder bones. Dinks had to do that so they could fold me up 'n' get me down the hole. I useta weigh two-twenty."

"You're kidding," Ty said.

"Nope. Don't know why they didn't just ding me. Guess they wanted prisoners to interrogate. They said they was gonna send me up north. Problem was, I was busted up, and they just couldn't manage pushin' my big black ass *uphill*."

"What happened?"

"Two things. They put me on the VC diet plan so they'd be able to get me outta there by 'n' by. And me bein' a brother who was gonna be around a while anyway, they decided to sell me on the revolution."

"Make you a Communist?"

"Don't laugh. Some grunts *did* switch sides. Anyway, I figured it was in my interest to learn everything I could. So I pretended to play along. Them boys thought they had a real prize in me. Told me all about their tunnels 'n' how they used 'em. Told me all sorts a shit. Got real friendly with me.

"It was all real helpful when I got healthy 'n' skinny enough to bust out. But the one thing they didn't tell me was how to find my way home. I had some real-life games a Charlie 'n' Joe with them dinks like you wouldn'a believed."

Darien lapsed into silence as he replayed those memories to himself. He wasn't ready to tell Ty about his collection of enemy ears.

"Anyway," he concluded, "I mighta stayed disappeared if I hadn't a bumped into ol' John 'n' Doolan. Sure as hell, nobody in my unit knew what'd happened to me."

"Why're you telling me all this now?" Ty asked.

"I was just thinkin' . . . in a way, you done disappeared, too. From your daddy's life."

"He's a drunk and a sonofabitch," Ty countered bitterly. "He saw me the other day, he wasn't glad to see me; he was toadying around with the guy who chased me into your tunnels in the first place. Fuck him."

The two of them were quiet as a symphony of cicadas struck the first notes of their nocturne.

"I was a drunk, too," Darien said finally. "Down in our tunnels is where I hide from my thirst. . . . Maybe your daddy ain't got nowhere to hide."

Ty didn't respond. Darien knew all about how a body had to step lightly around someone else's touchy subjects, but he wasn't about to back off.

He said softly, "When I thought about missin' you, I thought about missin' *my* boy. I only see him twice a year. Then I thought about how your daddy must feel, that's all."

"He doesn't miss me," Ty said coldly.

"If he don't, he will. If you don't—"

The sound of an approaching helicopter cut Darien off. The man and the boy craned their necks looking for it. Within seconds, they saw the aircraft pass overhead. It had civilian markings, but the contours of the machine sent a chill through Darien.

"Looks like a goddamn Huey," he muttered.

"A what?" Ty asked.

"What we used in the Nam. A troop carrier."

Darien picked up the binoculars they'd brought with them. He focused on the helicopter as it came in for a landing at the plant. Then he sucked in his breath sharply.

"An' *goddamn*, lookit there."

He handed the binoculars to Ty and pointed at the six figures jumping from the helicopter. With the field glasses, in the dying light, Ty could see they were small men with Asian faces.

"Fuckin' Charlie's come to town," Darien said.

61 John had put off the phone call as long as he could. Then the doorbell rang, and that let him put it off a little while longer. He picked up his gun and asked himself who the hell would ring Tommy's doorbell.

He went to the window and nudged the curtain aside. He saw Ron Narder get in a patrol car and drive away. He also noticed an oversized envelope sticking out of Tommy's mailbox.

He waited until he was sure Narder was gone and then retrieved the envelope. He sat on the sofa and opened it. Inside, there was a stack of papers held together with a bulldog clip.

On top was a note from Leen: "Carry on."

The first page John read was a ballistics report on a shell casing from an AR-15 or M-16 rifle. The casing was believed to have come from the shot that hit Tony Hunt on the night of the riot at the plant. John knew immediately which type of rifle had fired the shot, and it was enough to prompt him to make the call he'd been putting off.

He picked up the phone and dialed. A machine answered. A recording of a woman's voice said hello and gave her name.

"Sorry I can't come to the phone . . ."

The voice was husky and full of sexual challenge. The same voice that had said "Shit" on Tommy's phone machine. Now that John heard more of it, he could tell. It belonged to the woman who'd left all the little signs of her presence in Tommy's apartment.

"Leave your number," the recording said. *"If you sound as sexy as I do, I'll get back to you."*

Always the tease. The perfect style to go with the bottle-blond hair, the bright eyes, the big bouncing boobs. John didn't know why he hadn't thought of her before. Maybe because she wasn't his style at all.

But she had been Tommy's.

And Tommy's killer's.

The phone machine beeped its readiness to accept a message.

"I hope you're happy," John said.

Part Three

Payback is a motherfucker.

—USMC proverb

62

That night, John went to the church his grandfather had built, lit candles for Doolan, Tommy, and Jill's father, and mulled the subject of murder. The ones that had been committed, the one he was thinking of committing.

He sat in the front pew, alone in the darkened church, and asked for a sign. It didn't have to come from God. His mother, father, or grandparents would do. Even Tommy, whose salvation was as suspect as John's own, would be okay.

Tell me, Tommy, he thought, do you want to be avenged?

Is that what you deserve?

Does your killer deserve to die?

It gets so complicated.

John felt that it would be far more cruel to let the killer live. He now knew—after reading through the reports Leen had left for him—that after shooting Tommy, the killer had struck again. And *that* murder would eat at him every day of his life.

Was that punishment enough?

John sat in his church and asked for guidance. Please, he prayed, somebody tell me what to do.

. . .

Bill Deeley gently jostled John's shoulder. John opened his eyes and squinted at the sunlight coming through his grandfather's stained-glass windows.

"You okay?" Bill asked.

John smiled, because he was okay. He knew now what he had to do.

"You know, Bill, spending a night in this place is enough to restore your faith."

"You've seen what I've done?" Bill asked.

John nodded. "Let's just hope it works."

The night in his grandfather's church had worked for John. The answer had come to him while he slept, and it was forgiveness. If the killer would just say he was sorry for Tommy's death, John would let him live.

Leaving the church, John fervently hoped that he could get just those two simple words from the man: I'm sorry.

But he knew it wouldn't be easy.

Ty spotted John in Riverfront Park. A patchy morning mist from the river still covered the park. The boy knew instinctively that John was heading for a tunnel entrance, and he also knew he had to stop him. Gil had been setting out booby traps all night long.

Ty considered shouting, but that didn't seem the way someone—a soldier—bearing secret information should do it. He ran after John as quickly and quietly as he could.

John disappeared into a thicket of trees and the fog. Ty slowed down. He knew how tense everyone was lately. He didn't want John to take his head off by mistake. He had to be smart about this.

He came to a stop in a hollow where the fog had condensed to pea soup. He couldn't see a thing. He bent down and found a long twig with his hand. He snapped it three times. Then he waited.

He gave himself ten seconds, and then he'd have to take the chance of calling out John's name. As he counted, an eddy of wind tore a gap in the fog and gave him a clear view of the river. The breeze died and the fog quickly patched the hole.

Ty went out of the moment. He stopped counting because something more urgent percolated toward his consciousness, something very close to the surface. He was sure that if he stood still for just a few more seconds . . .

A hand reached out of the murk and clamped itself around his mouth, cutting off any chance for Ty to scream.

John whispered in the boy's ear, "I got your message with the twig. You okay to be let go now?"

Ty bobbed his head, and John released him.

"What's up?" John asked.

Ty told him about the booby traps.

"Why would Gil do that?" Ty could hear the frown in John's voice.

"Hunt's brought in the VC," Ty said.

"What?"

Ty told him what he and Darien had seen at Hunt's plant, and how they'd been out all night looking for John to warn him about Gil's booby traps.

"What happened to the POW?" John asked.

"We got rid of him."

"*Killed* him?"

"No. Let him go, told him not to go to Hunt, to get out of town."

"The guy agreed?"

"In his own words, he was 'happy to *di-di*.'"

John snorted. "I wish we could all *di-di*."

But this time *he* couldn't rotate home because he *was* home. Elk River was where he belonged. He and the boy went to another entrance, the one Gil had said would be the last to be booby-trapped.

Ty followed John, struggling to recapture the thought that had been on the verge of crystallizing. He couldn't quite do it, and knew it would be counterproductive to push.

But it was definitely something to do with Doolan.

63

Marty McCreery rose from bed early that morning in the iron grip of despair and fatalism. The strike was lost. It was only a matter of time now. Hunt was going to win. No two ways about it.

It was obvious to Marty that Hunt and Harold Noyes, president of the BMW, International, had made their devil's compact to grind the life out of Local 274 between them. There would be an inevitable flow of workers—probably scabs at first, but then a stampede of Marty's own people desperate to save their jobs—to the new union, and that would be it. Local 274 would be left to organize the buggy whip industry.

Not even Tommy Boyle could have saved them now.

Marty's depression deepened when he thought of Tommy. Why hadn't he involved Marty more in his planning? In this private moment, Marty could admit to himself that Tommy had handpicked him to be the local's number-two man, and without Tommy's support he'd never have become the secretary-treasurer. But he must have seen something in Marty to choose him over the others. So, why hadn't Tommy trusted him more?

Why hadn't he involved him in whatever was going on with that private investigator he'd hired? Why hadn't he asked Marty's opinion about who he should have hired for the local's attorney? That way Marty could have gotten behind the lawyer, even if it had been that damn know-it-all Jill Baxter. Most of all, Marty wondered, why hadn't Tommy made it plain that Marty would take over if something happened to him?

Probably because Tommy Boyle couldn't imagine anything bad happening to him—and, to be honest, nobody else had imagined it, either. Now, Tommy lay dead . . . and death really didn't seem so daunting to Marty McCreery right then.

Which was why he'd decided to go goon hunting.

He'd made his choice as he lay in bed next to his wife of thirty-two years. Harriet still slept deeply. After he'd spent all last night filling her heart with his rage, fear, and despair, she'd suggested that they each take a sleeping pill so they could rest; maybe in the morning they'd think of some way they could start over.

The sedative had worked for her. For Marty, it might as well have been a sugar pill. At dawn, he got to his feet and dressed. He went downstairs, where he wrote a note in the soft glow of the day's first light. He took a last look around the place he'd called home for thirty years.

It gave him bitter satisfaction to know that nobody, not even that cocksucker Hunt, would foreclose on him. He *owned* his house, and it would pass to his wife.

Marty went back to his bedroom and put the note on his pillow. He kissed his wife's brow, careful not to let a tear spill onto her. With his heart breaking, he left her. He walked out of his house armed with a handgun and a tube of superglue.

His note said: "This is the only way."

Marty banged hard three times on the door to the scabs' union. Then he took shelter behind his car, which he'd parked out front. A moment later the door opened. The goon who'd torn Marty's trophy in two stepped out, yawning.

As he looked around, rubbing his eyes to see who'd awakened him, he tripped over something sticking up from the sidewalk.

Which was exactly what Marty had wanted.

"What the fuck?" the goon said.

He looked down to see what had caused him to stumble. He blinked several times and even bent over. When he was sure that someone had put the figurine of the bowler back on its base and stuck the trophy to the sidewalk, he jerked upright and looked around.

Marty shot him three times.

His fourth shot brought the entire storefront window down. Marty ran screaming like a banshee toward the open door, bounded over the dead man, and fired wildly as he reached the threshold.

A shotgun boomed from inside the office, and Marty was flung back out onto the sidewalk. He was dead before he landed next to the little gold trophy that noted his name and his 198-pin average.

The death toll at the scabs' union climbed to five when the paramedics were unable to save the man they'd found inside with the shotgun in his hands. Marty McCreery, at the cost of his own life, had made it a clean sweep of the four thugs who'd spent the night in the storefront.

The two remaining bruisers from the union's organizing staff drove up while the crime scene investigation was in progress. They told the sheriff they'd spent the night in a social club in East St. Louis. After seeing their fallen colleagues and the hostile crowd gathered across the street in front of Local 274, they decided to leave town.

Leen detailed a car to escort them out of the county. Then the sheriff stepped over to where Marty lay with a gaping hole in his chest. He squatted over the body.

"Well, you poor, sad sonofabitch, you did it," he told Marty. "Closed them down for now. Probably made yourself a local legend, too. They'll be drinking to you tonight, but I doubt any of it will be of comfort to your wife."

"Sheriff," Ron Narder said. "Can I have a minute?"

Leen looked up to see his chief deputy. He straightened.

"Did you send anyone to let Mrs. McCreery know and to keep her the hell away from here?" the sheriff asked.

"Yes, sir."

"Okay then, Ronnie, let's go over to my car."

The two men stepped through the crowd, which parted for them silently. Once they were inside Leen's car, Narder came straight to the point.

"Sheriff, we need help. I think you ought to call the state police."

Leen looked squarely at his subordinate. "I already did that. They weren't inclined to lend a hand."

"I think they would now."

"You lost faith in me, Ron?"

Narder kept quiet, but held Leen's stare.

Leen said harshly, "Let's have it, Chief Deputy. You got something to say, now's your chance."

"Sheriff, you've been runnin' hot and cold ever since the strike started.

And once Tommy Boyle got killed, you've been even harder to figure out. You have me bring Hunt in so you can arrest him. We both know that. Only Hunt has a private little chat with you and suddenly he's a free man. You tell me what *that* looks like."

The sheriff knew exactly what it looked like, and he felt a bitterness he could taste. Narder reached for his badge. Leen grabbed his wrist and stopped him.

"I'll tell you when I want that."

Narder pulled his arm free. "You don't have to."

Leen tried to calm himself before he had an aneurysm.

"Ron, I promise you this: I am *not* in the bag to Hunt. Things may look bad, and you might even wind up arresting me one day soon, but I *never* took a payoff."

Narder slumped back in his seat. "This goddamn strike is killing our town, Sheriff. I've met with a number of deputies, and if Hunt brings in more goons, and they try to break heads, we're going to leave our badges at home. We'll fight on the same side as our families."

"I can't approve of that, Ron," the sheriff said. "But I do see where that point of view is getting real popular."

The sheriff looked through his windshield to where the mortal remains of Marty McCreery were being zipped into a body bag.

Bill Deeley heard about the shooting, and he had his ladder and paint out again that morning. When he reached the top rung, he found a surprise. Someone had tried to scrub one of the stones clean. He repainted it, and covered four more.

It was only when he finished that he heard the sobbing. He looked across Riverfront Drive and saw the elderly couple. An old man was comforting his crying wife. Bill didn't see that they had a ladder with them, but the old man's hands did have gray paint on them.

64 Tran sat on his haunches next to the small hole in the ground at the MicroCosmic, Inc. plant. His nose wrinkled at the scents of the alien soil. He was displeased that the color of the earth here was a gray-brown instead of the familiar red of home. For the first time, he appreciated the bravery of the Americans who'd crawled into the tunnels of the NLF.

Tran had no doubt he was dealing with the same men here. He remembered their name: tunnel rats. Tran and his comrades had feared the tunnel rats far more than other Yankees.

Now, these same American soldiers had their own tunnels. Going into them would be suicidal. But returning with his family to Vietnam would be worse than death. Tran's dismal thoughts were disturbed by the whining of those who had betrayed him. The five former Dream Warriors stood ten meters to his rear: Jimmy Giap, Vinnie Vinh, Stevie Tho, Bucktooth Lu, and Eddie Ky.

With them was the American overlord, Hunt, and his armed henchmen.

"Man, don't it blow your mind the way old gooks can just sit on their heels like that?" Jimmy Giap asked.

"Yeah, and what's he sniffin' for?" Vinny Vinh wanted to know. "I can tell from here, my shit smells better than that goddamn hole."

None of the young criminals was proud of the way they'd caved in to the ex-CIA spook, Walt Desmond. Desmond had simply collared Jimmy Giap at Tran's request, rounded up four of Jimmy's former gang-banging brethren and told them he had a number of murders in his files for which he could frame them so beautifully they'd be sure to get the gas chamber . . . unless they decided to lend a hand. The erstwhile Dream Warriors understood extortion; they got on the plane for a distant land. Now, they were wondering if they'd made the right choice.

At the hole, Tran sniffed one final time. No enemy soldier waited patiently below to ambush them. Patience had never been a Yankee virtue, and the odor of Americans was distinctive.

Still, he was sure this entrance had been booby-trapped. Tran rose with the ease of helium. The gang-bangers fell silent at his approach.

"How long has man you sent down hole been gone?" Tran asked Hunt.

It was eight A.M. Teddy Stinson had gone down the hole at ten the previous morning.

"Twenty-two hours," Hunt said.

"You have found no . . ." Tran struggled for the proper word. "Pieces?"

"Pieces of what?" Hunt asked.

"Of man. Ear, head, genitals."

"Oh, fuck me," Jimmy Giap moaned. He fell silent immediately when Tran turned his pitiless gaze on him.

"No," Hunt said, "nothing like that."

Tran shrugged. "No matter. He will not be back."

Tran strode to one of the crates of weapons Desmond had provided. He opened the lid and took out a hand grenade. He showed it to the Dream Warriors, explained how it worked, and then he grabbed Jimmy Giap's forearm.

"The hole," he said simply.

"What about it?" Jimmy asked.

Tran pulled the pin with his teeth and slapped the live grenade into Jimmy Giap's hand.

The gang-banger reacted like he'd been shot out of a cannon. He reached the tunnel entrance in nothing flat. He flung the grenade down the hole, then dove for cover. An instant later the ground shook with *two* explosions, the second—the booby trap—was far larger than the first.

When the smoke cleared, the entrance to the tunnel was blackened but undamaged. This soil may have been alien to him, but Tran saw that it was every bit as hard as that which he had known at home. Anyone who had labored to dig through such earth would not be displaced easily. If at all.

Jimmy Giap stood up on wobbly legs and staggered back to his group. All of them were shaken.

Tran said to his conscripts, "If you want to live, you will follow all orders. If you don't, the Americans will kill you, the tunnels will kill you, or I will kill you."

Then Tran gave each of them a flashlight and made them enter the hole.

When Tony Hunt got the news about the slaughter at the union office, he was furious. Not at the loss of life but at the loss of momentum. He was certain that within another week the trickle of workers deserting Local 274 would have turned into a flood and the strike would have been broken.

Now, he'd have to phone Harold Noyes and tell him that he needed more help. And that would mean more aggravation. An increase in Noyes's payoff.

Hunt fumed. How could one crazy bastard cause him all this trouble? Where were the goddamn cops? Why hadn't they stopped this madman?

Before he phoned Noyes, Hunt called the sheriff. It was time to crack the whip. The call had to be patched through to the sheriff's car, but the sheriff took it.

He goddamn well better.

Hunt told Leen that the union office would be repaired today. A new staff would be on the job tomorrow. He demanded that police protection for the office be provided around the clock as of this minute and until further notice.

Further, the sheriff would start evicting delinquent homeowners today, and to hell with waiting for any goddamn court orders. Those union bastards had better be out by sundown. His workers would be moving in tomorrow morning, and they'd better have police protection, too.

Leen acquiesced to each demand without a murmur.

When he put down the phone, Hunt realized how much circumstances were pressing on him—far more than he'd let himself admit. That call to Leen's car just now had gone out over the air, on the police frequency. Which meant every cop in the county with his radio on had heard it.

Discussing private business in public was hardly Tony Hunt's style . . . but now that he thought of it, maybe it wasn't such a bad way to undermine the sheriff with his men. Let them hear who was really the boss around here.

But just as Krieger had earlier missed the warning implicit in Hunt's deadly smile, Hunt overlooked the red flag of Sheriff Leen's seemingly servile complicity.

In any event, it was done, and now it was the time for Hunt to make his next move.

He had another sign put up on the plant gate: NEW HIRES GET $500 BONUS +++ SIX MONTHS FREE RENT.

Within an hour, he had his first takers.

65 Billy Shelton went out cruising, hoping he'd come up with some kind of bright idea. He couldn't kill the sheriff. As an ex-cop, he knew how hard it was to get away with killing a cop. A plain old flatfoot cop. And killing the sheriff of an entire county? Forget about it.

The problem was, killing Leen was just what Hunt had hinted that he wanted. So, what else could Billy do for Hunt that'd be just as impressive, something that'd let Billy reap a rich reward from the bastard?

It was a real pisser.

Still, Billy was determined to do *something*. He'd get next to Hunt and have some of the bastard's money rub off on him. Then he'd see how Bobbi felt about him; she'd beg him to take her back. He turned onto Highway 98 and stomped on the gas just for the adrenaline rush.

While entertaining pleasant thoughts of Bobbi groveling in front of him, Billy saw opportunity approach in the oncoming lane. It was that lawyer lady, Baxter, heading into town. Even zipping right past her, he could see the gleam in her eye and the hard smile on her face. Looked like she wanted to shout for joy but was saving it till she had company.

Now what would make a union lawyer so happy? Billy wondered. Hell, the question answered itself. She'd found some way to put Hunt's dick in the wringer.

And wouldn't the bastard be grateful if Billy stopped her?

Billy threw his car into a smoking, bootlegger's turn. He flipped on the switch for the siren he was no longer supposed to have and put the pedal to the floor. Of course, he had no powers of arrest anymore, but *she* didn't know that. And he did have handcuffs. And a gun.

Billy grinned when she pulled right over like a good little law-abiding lawyer. He nosed in behind her and got out of his car.

Well, here we go, he thought. He was taking a big risk here. But compared to killing a sheriff, kidnapping a lawyer was peanuts.

John and Ty found Darien in EE, the chamber below Eleventh and Elm. The space was crowded with food, medical supplies, and weapons. Sweat ran down Darien's face, and he looked dead tired, but he smiled at the new arrivals.

"Good to see you two," he said. "Ol' Ty catch up with you, John?"

"Yeah," he said. "Where's Gil?"

"Out scopin' Charlie. Once he was done settin' out the traps, he couldn't wait to go see 'em."

"You moved all this stuff from CR?" John asked. CR—under the Church of the Resurrection—was the chamber closest to Hunt's plant.

"Didn't want Charlie to get it," Darien answered. "You know, with enough C-4, we could just seal off the section near the plant. That way, Charlie can't go too far unless he feels like diggin'."

John asked him, "How would you feel about that?"

"Got mixed feelings," Darien admitted. "When I saw them little bastards I thought, Do I haveta go through all that shit *again*? On the other hand, I got a real urge to show 'em what happens when they fuck around in *our* backyard."

John nodded. He heard the passion in Darien's voice and was surprised how deeply it resonated within him.

Fate was offering them a chance to get back at the VC. Or a reasonable facsimile. It was almost like being given an opportunity to get even for Doolan. Too good to pass up. Almost made John forget *he* could get killed.

"What about Gil?"

Darien smiled. "He's chompin' at the bit, man."

John smiled, too. Grimly. "Yeah, he always was a bloodthirsty little sucker."

Ty watched the two men. They seemed to be working themselves into a gleeful frenzy. The boy wondered if he was the only one who was afraid.

Then a thought struck *him* that was shocking . . . irresistible . . . repellent. He turned to Darien for help. "I just got this crazy feeling I should go see my father. You know, just in case. But that *is* nuts, because I still hate the bastard, and he wouldn't give a damn if I died anyway."

John and Darien's mood turned sober and they regarded the boy in silence for a long moment. Then Darien stepped forward, gently put his hands on Ty's shoulders, and looked into his eyes.

"You say you hate the man, and maybe you do. But ain't a child been born who don't want his daddy to love him. You're thinkin' you could get killed, so maybe what you feel is the man should have one last chance at lovin' you. But you're afraid he'll just turn his back on you again. Thing is, unless you try, you'll never know."

Before Ty could respond, John added softly, "This outfit's easy on giving honorable discharges. You can have one any time you want."

The boy stiffened and stepped clear of Darien.

"No!" he told John flatly. "I'm one of you. I'll be back."

Then Ty turned and disappeared into the tunnels.

An epidemic of blue flu hit the sheriff's department as soon as Orville Leen gave the orders to start evicting delinquent homeowners. Twenty-four members of the forty-five-deputy department developed sudden and incapacitating illnesses. The remainder, with varying degrees of reluctance or indifference, did as they were told.

Ron Narder absolutely refused to evict people who hadn't been given due process. Only Leen's comment that Narder might one day arrest *him* kept the chief deputy from quitting altogether. Now, Narder wanted that day to come so badly he could taste it.

As soon as word of the evictions got out, a large crowd of union demonstrators appeared at the sheriff's station. Curses were hurled, the sidewalk was spat upon, and two windows were smashed. Signs appeared among the mob: DO IT MARTY'S WAY.

Deputies stood guard over their station with riot guns ready to fire.

Elsewhere in the town, five two-man teams of deputies set about the work of enforcing the eviction notices. Some residents had to be dragged out kicking and screaming and throwing punches. Others went with fatalistic numbness, as if they half expected a bullet in the back of the head.

Before the end of the day, twelve homes had been forcibly vacated. Half of those displaced found shelter with relatives and friends. The rest took sanctuary in the basement of the Church of the Resurrection.

.　.　.

Ty didn't find Wesley Daulton at home. He'd expected that his father would still be sleeping off his morning drunk. But neither man nor bottle was to be found.

Miss Millicent told him his father had gone on an errand to Oak Crest. That would be a long walk for Ty, but he felt a compulsion approaching dread to see his father. Did he *really* think he was going to die? Or that his father would care if he did? He didn't know.

And how would he feel if his father *did* turn his back on him again? Or, worse, if he mocked what Ty was feeling?

He didn't know that, either. But a sense of uneasiness welled up in him when he realized that, in his haste, he'd forgotten to leave his loaded .38 in the tunnels.

After all, he thought, he'd pulled a gun on his father once before.

Ty knew why his father had gone to Oak Crest: he'd resumed writing term papers for the pinheads at the academy. That meant the best place to find him would be one of the drops his father used near the school—places where ghostwritten schoolwork could surreptitiously be exchanged for the pocket change of the lazy affluent.

As Ty entered the exclusive enclave, memories of the humiliations he'd suffered from the likes of Frank Murtaw flared into malignant life. He took a deep, steadying breath to repress his anger. He didn't care about those jerks anymore. He had new friends, a new life, and . . . sweat popped out on his brow as he remembered that he'd just committed himself to those new friends and a fight that might end his new life.

This time the realization hit hard—he might actually die soon. It filled his mouth with a cold, metallic fear that almost made him gag. He wondered if this was anything like what Darien or John or even Gil had felt going to Vietnam when they weren't much older than he was now. No, he decided, it had to be much worse for them. They'd been drafted, taken from their homes and forced to fight in a strange country on the other side of the world. Oddly enough, the insight that his friends had known worse and not succumbed comforted him.

If they could make it through there, he could make it through here.

He looked at the houses he was passing. They got larger and grander as he went uphill. Material success was directly proportional to elevation above Elk River and its peasants. He'd always resented this before; now he didn't care.

He had firsthand knowledge that the grandest house in the world burned just as easily and brightly as the most humble cottage.

There were no cars on the street, and Oak Crest had no sidewalks to invite casual pedestrian traffic. Ty walked at the side of the road. As he neared the top of the hill he came upon a scene that made him duck behind a tree. At first, he wasn't sure what he was seeing. Then his mind focused and told him: At the entrance to an ornate house, the deputy who'd come to school last semester to give the annual scare lecture against drugs was lifting a person out of the trunk of his car.

A woman in a skirt. Wearing handcuffs. Her arms pinned behind her.

Ty looked around to see if there was any other witness to this bizarre event. But because of the large wooded lots in Oak Crest there was only one other home from which anyone could have seen, and that house looked empty.

When Ty looked back, his heart turned to ice.

The woman was Jill Baxter. Now Ty saw that she was also gagged, and the deputy—Shelton, that was his name—held a gun against her back. He marched her up to the huge house and pushed her inside.

Ty's mind reeled. Was the deputy going to shoot Jill? The boy had taken the first step in a mad dash toward the house when his intellect asserted itself and stopped him cold. He knew unquestionably that the house didn't belong to any deputy. It was a rich man's house, belonging to someone who could buy and sell Deputy Shelton seven days a week . . . someone who could pay to have Jill kidnapped.

The process of elimination was immediate. Tony Hunt.

Ty didn't know what Hunt's plans for her were, but Jill was definitely in danger. Going for help might take too long; Shelton might move Jill. A new thought chilled him: Shelton was a *cop*. What if kidnapping Jill was part of some police conspiracy? He couldn't go to the sheriff for help then. He'd have to act on his own.

He had his brain. And a gun. And . . .

Ty heard someone walking up the road behind him. He quickly stepped back behind the tree. As he peeked out from behind it, he saw Frank Murtaw come around the curve in the road. The big bastard was so filthy and disheveled he looked like he'd been run over by a mulching mower, and his head hung down as if it weighed a ton. He never saw Ty. He just trudged on by and into the house with the view of Hunt's place.

A wonderful idea occurred to Ty.

He'd drop in on his old friend Frank.

Tony Hunt's phone was pissing him off no end.

It began with a call from Harold Noyes. Noyes started to ream him good for *letting* four of his best men get killed by that lunatic Marty

McCreery. Delivering abuse was far more to Hunt's taste than receiving it. He cut off Noyes with the promise of another million dollars . . . which the president of the BMW, International, could either distribute among the families of the deceased or put into his own pocket, whichever he pleased. That shut the bastard up.

Then Hunt told Noyes he wanted the new local's office restaffed and reopened forthwith . . . because there was still the little matter of allegations of Noyes and his cronies looting union funds that could be brought to the attention of the authorities.

Hunt's next call came from Carter Powell, his banker. That sonofabitch knew about the killings at the new local, too. To have heard so fast meant he had a spy at the plant. Powell told Hunt he was very worried. About himself. His position was at risk if the strike turned into a debacle. He knew MicroCosmic, Inc. was situated in the hinterlands, but the way things were going, it could be located in North Dakota and the national media was bound to notice soon.

Accordingly, he was convening a meeting of the loan committee to consider the viability of continuing Hunt's financing. Powell told Hunt to put his house in order before the committee met. He had four days.

Hunt thought of mentioning to Powell that he should consider the viability of continuing his own existence, but decided to save that card for another forty-eight hours. The passage of time would lend credibility to the idea that Hunt had set up a contract on Powell. To wit: The day you withdraw my financing is the last day of your life.

That ought to hold the little weasel in line, but if Powell were actually able to tap some unsuspected reserve of character and withdraw Hunt's financing, Hunt would have him killed—he might even do it himself. But right now he had neither the time nor the funds to arrange a murder.

Hunt had barely hung up on his banker when a thought occurred to him that froze his marrow. Had Powell's spy found out about the tunnels Fortunato had dug under the plant? Had the spy passed that information to the banker? No, he couldn't have, Hunt realized. That bit of news— that a madman planned underground warfare against the banker's investment—would have unhinged Powell. He would have confessed to his superiors immediately, or shot himself.

Hunt had to keep Fortunato's tunnels a tightly held secret at any cost.

He was concentrating on a way to do that when another call was put through. Mr. Stanley Rice, his secretary said. Yoshihara! The foundation on which everything rested. Whatever he wanted, coming at a time like this, couldn't be good.

It wasn't. The inventor wanted to renegotiate his deal. He wanted a larger equity position and a ten-million-dollar advance as a token of good faith. He hoped it wouldn't inconvenience Hunt to make the funds available to him by Monday next.

"After all, old boy," he concluded, "I am the sine qua non."

A goddamn Jap with a Brit accent threatening him in Latin was more than Tony Hunt could take. He wanted to kill someone. Now.

At that precise moment, his private line rang.

Hunt looked at it, stupefied. The line existed for use by only one person—and Krieger was dead.

Goddamnit, he'd seen him in the morgue!

He picked the receiver up slowly and held it several inches from his ear. If he heard that incredible voice . . .

"Mr. Hunt, you there?" Thank God. The voice was as flat and Midwestern as a cornfield.

"Who is this?" Hunt demanded.

"Billy Shelton. We talked the other day."

The idiot deputy.

"How did you get this number?"

"Found it in your house."

"You're in my home?" Hunt was so enraged his voice trembled.

"Yes, sir, but don't get angry. I brought you a little present."

66

Tran did his best to choke down the cheeseburger.

During the war he'd had to subsist on rancid rice balls. Other times, he'd eaten rats he'd caught in the tunnels. Still other times, he'd simply gone hungry. But never had his stomach revolted so strenuously as with this capitalist abomination.

In the fading light of dusk, he looked over at his conscripts. They devoured their cheeseburgers the way a thirsty man drank water. In great gulps. Tran found it hard to believe that he shared a common ancestry with them.

A nauseating dinner was far from his only problem. The American overlord had ordered a black plastic screen to be erected around the area of the tunnel entrance. A portable toilet had been brought in for their use. They had been told to stay inside the screened area.

Tran knew the enclosure would make a wonderful target for a Yankee mortar crew sitting in the woods across the river. That he was forced to sit inside such a target was intolerable. More and more, he came to sympathize with the plight of the Americans who'd fought the NLF.

Their sense of vulnerability must have been terrible. As to their sense of purpose, Tran wondered if they had been any less bewildered then than he was now. And like them, all he wanted to do was to flee the madness and make his way home to his family.

Which was just what he was planning to do.

After he'd forced each of the erstwhile Dream Warriors into the tunnel and shown them the earth wouldn't crush them or steal the air from their lungs, Tran had set out alone for a longer exploration of these Yankee tunnels. The exercise had given him intensely mixed feelings. He'd felt foreboding; any doubt that the masters of these tunnels would be formidable foes had disappeared. At the same time, there had been a sense of comfort to be moving through such familiar spaces.

True, he had suffered many hardships in the tunnels, but he had enjoyed the most glorious victories of his life in them, too. In a strange way, being back in a tunnel now made him feel very young and fiercely strong again.

Tran found a booby trap, one that was obviously placed and easy to disarm. He saw it for what it was: an invitation to false confidence and a far more deadly ambush somewhere ahead. He refused to take the bait, but that was when he first conceived his idea for escape.

The idea grew as he contorted his small, wiry body to turn around and retreat to the entrance. He knew with certainty that the underground system through which he moved must have several openings. If he made his way to one and escaped directly, the American overlord would merely send his agent, Desmond, after Tran again. He would face the threat of deportation—or worse—once more.

But what if the overlord had every reason to believe he had died beneath the earth? Then Tran would be safe.

Tran had emerged from the tunnel just after dinner had been delivered. Now, he watched his conscripts, their guts bloated, their flatulence already beginning, settle down for the night. They whispered and snickered quietly among themselves, doubtless at his expense.

The fact that they would have to die to make his plan work pleased Tran greatly. Of course, he might have to do some real fighting, too. But he'd always been good at killing Americans. And he had no objection to killing more.

John sat alone in the woods across the river from the plant as the sun went down. He saw that some sort of barrier had been put up around the tunnel entrance. That bothered him. He wanted to see these new enemies with his own eyes.

After Ty had departed, John had asked Darien for a detailed description of the men who'd landed at the plant.

"Dinks, man, six of 'em. VC. Victor—fuckin'—Charlie."

Darien was still keyed up about it.

"What were they wearing?"

The question was simple enough, but it threw Darien. Like John had been talking a foreign language. What the hell did their clothes have to do with anything? Which was just what Darien asked him.

"You said these guys were dinks, VC," John told Darien. "So what I want to know is, were they dressed for the part? Did they wear fatigues, black pajamas, coolie hats, what?"

Darien thought a moment. "Seems like four, no, five of 'em had on high-tops, baggy pants, 'n' satin jackets."

John asked, "That sound like any VC you ever saw?"

"No," Darien conceded. "But no question they was dinks. And number six, he was right in fashion. All in black. Not pajamas, but shirt, pants, 'n' shoes."

"How many of them looked to be around our age?" John bet he knew the answer.

"Number six," Darien said, looking into his memory. "The rest was kids."

"Who'd be too young ever to have been VC."

Darien considered. "Yeah, but plenty old enough to shoot a gun, and number six, he's Coca-Cola, bro. The real thing."

John said, "In that case, maybe we'd better call him Number One."

Then John had gone to see the enemy for himself. He thought maybe he'd find Gil in the woods, watching the plant, too. But Gil was gone.

John decided that there was nothing to be gained by staring at the barrier. But with the arrival of darkness he took out the flare gun he'd brought along for the purpose of running another little PSYOP.

He fired a round over the enclosure. Just a message to Number One that his arrival had been officially noted. Now he'd wonder if the next projectile would contain high explosives.

Which should keep him and his troops from getting a good night's sleep.

John waited until the illumination from the flare had died. Then he went to look for the apology he was still seeking.

67

To Bobbi Sharpes's way of thinking, it was too late for Billy Shelton to say, "Sorry, just kidding."

Bobbi believed that he'd meant every word he'd said. Billy was going to do everything he could to make her life miserable, and once he was served with the divorce papers, who knew what that fool might do?

She'd already asked herself a million times whether the creep *really* had shot Tommy. Since she had no way of ever knowing for sure, she decided to take his word on that score, too. He'd done it.

Now she had to make good on her own word: Billy wasn't going to get away with it. She was going to settle matters as soon as she could. Now.

She'd be damned if her baby was going to have Billy Shelton hovering over his life like some toxic black cloud. She put the .22-caliber revolver, which she'd bought the day after Billy had made his boast, into her purse.

The clerk at the gun store had told her, "It don't look like much, but it's the favorite of your Chicago Mafia hit man." That was good enough for Bobbi.

She drove over to Billy's apartment. She could imagine him swinging the door wide, seeing it was her, thinking she'd come to beg him to leave her alone. Or, even better, that she'd come back to him. He'd start to smile, and then quick as a wink she'd put two in his head.

But the sonofabitch didn't answer when she rang.

He wasn't home.

Bobbi was seriously disappointed, but her fury didn't lose any traction. She returned her gun to her purse and dug out a pen and a Post-it note.

She wrote: "Come see me."

She stuck the note on the door. Unsigned. He'd know who it was from, and he'd come running.

As she got back into her car, she realized that this way was even better. Now, she could say she'd invited Billy to come see her and work out a reasonable agreement, but he'd turned violent. Tried to have his way with her.

What choice did she have but to defend herself?

John couldn't find Tommy's killer anywhere. Feeling frustrated, he decided to see if Jill had left a message for him on Tommy's answering machine. He was mildly surprised, and disappointed, that she hadn't.

He became uneasy when he called her hotel in Chicago and was told she'd checked out. Using a bit of persistence and the lie that he was Jill's husband, he got the concierge to tell him that Jill had left that morning in a rental car he'd hired for her.

John's heart turned to ice when he called the state police to check on the possibility of an accident and heard that Jill's rental car had been found abandoned ten miles outside of Elk River on Highway 98.

The state trooper said he'd appreciate hearing from John if he found her before they did.

Tony Hunt walked into his living room and found Tommy Boyle's lawyer tied to a Chippendale chair that had been set in front of the fireplace. The cretin who'd kidnapped her sat on a sofa trying to decipher that day's *Wall Street Journal*. He grinned at Hunt as he entered, but didn't bother to stand.

Billy said, "Mr. Hunt, you don't like this little gift I brought you, I'll take her back to the shop and see if I can't do better next time."

Hunt was not amused.

"If you ever break into my house again, you won't have a next time."

Billy had hoped Hunt would overlook that little fart at the dinner table.

Just like he was going to overlook Hunt's ridiculous threat to kill him. Even if it made him want to pistol-whip the dumb bastard.

Restraint was possible because Billy could see he'd caught the brass ring: Hunt *was* glad to have the little lady in his grasp. His eyes gave him away.

But since the man had his little soap opera going here, Billy would play his part. He stood up, stepped over to Jill, and bent to untie her.

For the first time, Billy saw a spark of life in the woman's eyes. She hadn't even blinked when Hunt came in. It was like she'd gone into a trance or something when Billy had tied her up.

"Sorry I put you to all this trouble, lady," he muttered. "Guess I just shoulda sent flowers."

"Wait a minute," Hunt snapped.

Billy straightened up.

"What?"

"You're going to let her go?"

"Well, you don't seem to want her, and I like a woman who's a little taller myself, so what the hell else am I gonna do with her?"

"She'll accuse you of kidnapping." Alarm flickered in Hunt's eyes. "She might even say *I* had something to do with it."

Billy smiled. The man just couldn't say, Thanks, buddy. Here's a nice piece of change for your bother. He had to invent reasons to keep the poor woman. Well, he'd just offered Billy a chance to show him just how valuable he could be.

"That's okay," the ex-deputy said. "She can accuse all she wants. It's what she can *prove* that counts. See, nobody saw me grab her, nobody saw me bring her in here, nobody's gonna see me let her go. Believe me, after twenty-odd years as a cop, I know what'll get your ass grassed better than some *labor* lawyer. *I'm* the expert."

Billy hoped that spelled out his credentials plain enough for the sonofabitch.

But Hunt had a question.

"Why haven't you gagged her?"

"I did when she was in the trunk of my car. In here, you don't want to push it too far. Take the risk of asphyxiation. Curtains are drawn, and she ain't gonna make a peep."

"How do you know?"

Billy pulled a small bottle of Tabasco sauce out of his shirt pocket. The fiery sauce had come from Hunt's pantry.

"Painful, but not harmful," he commented. "Cayenne pepper's good, too. An open mouth's a mighty hot mouth. You give them water only when they promise to be good. Wasn't even necessary with her; someone raised her right."

More than just life flashed in Jill's eyes, but Billy missed it this time. Despite his initial misgivings, Hunt was impressed.

He said, "I'll keep her."

Jill's face became impassive again. Billy knew when to be graciously quiet. He just let himself look pleased.

Hunt added, "And I think you should be rewarded for your initiative." He did a quick calculation of what he could afford to pay this jerkwater opportunist, then cut it in half. "Does twenty-five hundred dollars sound fair?"

Billy kept his smile and nodded.

"Sure. That's a fair day's wage."

The Murtaw home had a burglar alarm system, but Frank had left the back door unlocked. Ty stepped inside. He kept his hand on the doorknob, ready to run if he saw Frank's parents. Or if the family had a dog. He wasn't going to shoot everything in sight like some helter-skelter maniac.

With his heart in his throat, he gave a low whistle, just loud enough to bring a dog running. There was no canine response.

Ty moved away from the rear door. He quickly went through the kitchen drawers until he found the one that every house had, the junk drawer. He took out a roll of electrical tape and stuck it in his pocket.

He eased into the dining room. Soon, he was certain that Frank was home alone. Starting up the stairs to the second floor, he heard a shower running and Frank singing—mangling—a Green Day song.

"Basket Case."

Just what Ty felt like, creeping around the Murtaw house.

Frank Murtaw's only gift as a singer was volume. It would be no problem to catch him off guard, as well as off-key. Gun in hand, Ty popped the shower stall door open just as Frank went retro and launched into "Foxy Lady."

Ty pulled back the hammer of the revolver, just in case Frank was even dumber than he figured. But Frank just stood there with soap in his eyes, his mouth open, and no desire to put up a fuss at all.

"Turn off the water and get out of there," Ty said quietly. "I've got work to do."

Ty directed Frank to a room at the front of the second floor of the house. As he'd hoped, it was a bedroom with a phone. He had Frank strip the top sheet off the bed and roll himself up in it as tight as a mummy. Then Ty sealed Frank in with the tape he'd brought from the kitchen.

"Tell me where your credit cards are," Ty said, "and when your parents are coming home."

Perversely, being rendered helpless finally brought out Frank's anger. He snarled, "Fuck you."

Ty considered putting his gun in Frank's left ear and threatening his life . . . but he thought he'd already done pretty well bluffing Frank into bondage. He didn't know how much farther he could successfully push the hard guy act.

It took him only five minutes to find Frank's credit cards anyhow.

68 The demonstrators outside the sheriff's station had gone home and the broken windows had been covered with plywood, but two deputies with shotguns remained on guard out front. When John Fortunato arrived, they demanded to know his business before admitting him.

He found Leen in his office staring at a picture on the wall of his graduating class from the police academy.

John knew the look. It was the same way he stared at pictures of his old army unit. A photo of clear-eyed, unlined young faces was the perfect lens for examining all the character defects, bad choices, and hard luck that had carried you so far from innocence and promise to your present sorry state. And every such picture seemed to come with a laugh track of personal demons that erupted at each self-recrimination.

"Do you know about Jill Baxter?" John asked bluntly.

Leen turned his eyes to his visitor. "State police called about her car."

"Nobody's found a body, have they?"

"No."

John breathed a small sigh of relief. "You looking for her?"

"As much as I can," the sheriff said.

That was no comfort, but John was sure Leen didn't have any comfort to give. He turned to go.

"You get the little package I sent?" the sheriff asked.

John turned back. "Yeah."

"Was it any help?"

John didn't reply, but Leen could read his face.

"You figured it out," he said. "You know who killed Tommy Boyle."

John remained silent.

The sheriff gave a small shake of his head and resumed looking at the picture of long-ago better days.

"It's okay, you don't have to tell me. You take care of it any way you see fit. That's the way things are around here right now. Every last man for himself."

"You understand what I told you now?" Billy asked.

"Yes, I understand," Hunt said.

"Those little tricks should open her right up without bruisin' anything but her pride. You find out what you want, and it still ain't a bit of skin off anybody's ass to let her go."

Hunt nodded.

"You get carried away, though," Billy warned, "it gets tricky, danger-ous . . . and a whole lot more expensive."

"I understand," Hunt said more sharply.

Billy grinned and opened the door.

"Just so you do." He gave Hunt a little salute. "A pleasure doin' busi-ness with you."

Billy left Hunt alone with Jill.

From Frank Murtaw's bedroom window, Ty saw Billy Shelton leave the house across the road, just as earlier he'd seen Tony Hunt arrive.

He'd been pleased to see that his conjecture about who was behind Jill's kidnapping had proven out. It also gave him a thrill that he'd be pitting himself against the most powerful man in town. He waited until Billy drove off, and then he stepped over to Frank.

"Open up," Ty said.

"Hey, you said we—" Frank didn't bother to finish. He just clamped his mouth shut. What a dolt, Ty thought.

He pinched Frank's nose shut until he had to open his mouth for air. When he did, Ty stuck a sock in it. He couldn't have Frank yelling for help while he used the phone. From his post at the upstairs window, Ty called for pizza and beer. He directed that each be sent to Tony Hunt's address. He paid for the purchases with Frank's gold card.

When he got off the phone, he removed the gag. Frank spit to clear the awful taste from his mouth. Ty considered giving Frank a sip of water. The impulse died as soon as he remembered who he was dealing with.

He wondered if he should do *anything* for Frank. The big jerk had told Ty—after Ty had melted a couple of Frank's favorite CDs—that his parents would be in New York for two more days. Ty paused to think if any considerations for his prisoner were warranted.

He decided no, not immediately.

"I've got to go out," he told Frank. Then he warned, "Don't do anything that might start a fire."

The very idea made Frank's eyes pop. That was just what Ty wanted: to bind him psychologically as well as physically.

Pleased, Ty hurried downstairs to put the finishing touch on his plan for Tony Hunt.

When he got home, Billy had twenty-five hundred dollars cash money in his pocket, a bounce in his step, and a song in his heart.

He was sure that Hunt would call him back to drop the lady lawyer off when he was done with her, and he'd do it for free. He felt confident the slimy bastard would have plenty of paying jobs for him now.

If only he didn't fuck up and kill the woman.

Billy was feeling too good to let that possibility worry him for more than a second. He got a real jolt of juice when he saw the note on his front door.

Would you look at that, he thought: "Come see me."

Billy riffled the thick roll of bills in his pocket.

See her? Hell, he'd give her a tour of the mint.

John checked the Mill House Inn and Local 274, but Jill wasn't to be found at either location. He began to cruise the streets.

He couldn't get the international's death threat against Jill out of his mind. As the day ended and darkness fell, it kept him fixated like water torture, each drop splashing into an acid pool of fear. He didn't know which goddamn way to turn.

Without making a conscious choice, he found himself driving past the Church of the Resurrection. The lights were on. It was too late for any normal service. He pulled into the lot and parked.

He noted how the wreath of gray paint over the entrance seemed to grow every time he passed by. It struck him as a depressingly accurate measure of what was happening to Elk River.

He walked through the open front door and saw that there were easily a hundred people inside. Some knelt with their hands clasped and their heads bowed, some said the rosary, others just looked at the altar. More than a few cradled the heads of sleeping children on their laps.

Bill Deeley came over. He told John about taking in the homeless families and sheltering them in the church basement. He hoped John didn't mind.

"Do everything you can," John told Bill. Then he went to the side of the church and lit all the usual candles. And one for Jill, with the fervent prayer that she was still alive.

He didn't know if he could take losing anyone else.

69

Tony Hunt slapped Jill Baxter hard enough to leave his handprint on her cheek. Her head jerked to the side from the force of the brutal blow. Even so, she didn't cry out, didn't say a word.

Billy had told Hunt not to hit her . . . but the bitch just kept on ignoring him. Acting like he wasn't in the room. Or it didn't matter if he was. Hunt wasn't buying this out-in-the-ozone act of hers. She was just trying to show him she could tough it out. He had to show her she couldn't.

So fuck Billy and his Dick Tracy suggestions: Stick her fingers in water so she'd pee herself. Turn the heat up so she'd get tired and thirsty. Shine bright lights in her eyes to give her a headache. Kid's tricks.

Hunt sat opposite his prisoner and tried to stare her down. He couldn't do it. He couldn't find any hint of awareness behind her eyes. They were as flat and opaque as painted glass. Maybe this zombie routine of hers was more than an act, he thought. Maybe she'd really found a way to go somewhere inside her head and be safe. If she could do that—hide and emerge at will—she would be a formidable opponent.

He was surprised that as he continued to examine her he was getting hard. Offhand, Tony Hunt couldn't remember the last time he'd had sex.

The average woman held no more sexual attraction for him than an inflatable doll; both were empty vessels in his view. But this woman, this one was clearly made of sterner stuff. And, he thought, his handprint on her face added character to her otherwise routine blond good looks.

He wondered if she could maintain her splendid detachment if he forced himself on her. Perhaps he'd find out later. Right now, though, there were more important matters to pursue.

"Let's start again," Hunt said evenly. "How did you get to Yoshihara?"

It had to be her doing that Yoshihara was extorting him. Between the bastard's Japanese heritage and his English education, he was far too well-mannered to have changed their agreement on his own. Hunt had discovered the Nip and enticed him away from his father's firm. Taken him to the mountaintop and shown him the kingdoms of the world. . . . Then this bitch had come along and pulled the same stunt on good old Mr. Rice.

"You slept with him, didn't you?" Hunt inquired calmly. "You screwed the little yellow bastard round-eyed."

He might as well have been Nixon talking to the White House paintings. She remained as impassive as ever. Remembering one of Billy's suggestions, and reconsidering its merit, he thought he might turn up the heat in the house . . . just to see if she'd sweat.

Hunt continued in an unruffled tone. "Well, how you seduced Yoshihara really isn't important. But I'm afraid I do have to know how you found out about him. And how you knew where to reach him."

He delivered the last line with a tone of almost parental wheedling—and when she remained stone-faced, he delivered another stunning blow, this time to the other side of her face.

Then Hunt sat back and watched. Her head straightened more slowly than it had the first time, and blood ran from her nose, but still she hadn't uttered a sound. When her head came to a rest, her chin was held at precisely the same angle as before, pointed up.

Defiance.

Fascinated, Hunt couldn't help but nod his approval. "You're good. You're very, very good. Even so, this can't be much fun for you."

But it was for Hunt. He couldn't remember the last time he'd been so excited with a woman. It was no longer a question of if he would take her, only when.

"Do you know who's spying on me for my banker, my dear?"

When he got no response, he slapped her viciously again.

"Have you, perhaps, had a look at my balance sheet? The real one?"

The ghost of a smile flitted across Jill's battered lips, and Hunt realized that he'd received his first answer. But that didn't matter, nor did it bother him that she knew he was vulnerable. The point was, she was far more vulnerable than he . . . and they'd established their pattern by now. He asked a question, she said nothing, and then he lashed out. As he did now.

Hunt licked his lips as her head once again righted itself like some impossibly well-made mechanical doll. He could stand the pressure in his loins no longer; he would take her here, he would take her n—

But before he could take anything at all, the doorbell rang.

Hunt stared at the door, dumbfounded that the outside world would intrude at such a moment.

Because he was looking the other way, he missed the one instant of hope that passed through Jill's eyes. Hunt fiercely glared at the door, challenging the bell to defy his will and ring again.

It did. Insistently.

Hunt showed Jill a gun. He said he'd shoot whoever was at the door and then her if she called for help. He received no more reaction to his threat than he had to his questions. Jill sat there mute, unseeing, bleeding from her nose and the corners of her mouth.

Hunt shook himself, took a deep breath, and forced a mask of civilization onto his face. He returned the gun to his coat pocket and went to the door. He switched on the exterior lights, opened the door, and stepped outside, expecting anything but . . .

"Pizza."

There was a middle-aged fool in need of a shave handing him a large, flat cardboard carton with grease stains on it. Incredulous, Hunt took it.

The delivery man stood in front of him as if waiting for something.

"What is this?" Hunt demanded quietly.

"This is your double-supreme pizza, as ordered."

Hunt groped for a hidden, sinister meaning.

Before he could discern one, however, another deliveryman pulled up to Hunt's house; this one brought him a six-pack of beer. Domestic. The plebeian brand conferred on him a flash of insight. This was the work of someone with unsophisticated taste and a small budget; this was an adolescent prank. Somewhere, probably not too far away, youthful miscreants were enjoying a great laugh at his expense.

That such a moronic interruption had come at such a singular moment was almost too much for Tony Hunt to handle . . . but handle it he did. There was nothing to be gained from taking out his anger on the two fools in front of him. Quite the contrary, restraint was called for here.

Hunt explained to the deliverymen that he and they were all the victims of a practical joker. Since the pizza and beer were already paid for, the delivery guys were happy when Hunt let them keep their wares for themselves, and they were delighted with the tips he gave them for their troubles. They left smiling.

Hunt waved them farewell, a guy who could take a joke and even be gracious about it. That's what they'd remember, if anyone asked them. His demeanor had hardly been that of someone in the midst of committing a heinous crime.

Then Hunt went inside and closed the door.

He had someone waiting for him.

From across the road, where he lay hidden in the underbrush, Ty watched the deliverymen depart. He had paid close attention.

The first thing he'd noticed was that the arrival of unfamiliar vehicles and drivers had aroused no perceptible attention from a dog, either inside the house or outside.

Neither had he seen anyone peeking out a window while Hunt was out front.

There was a margin for error of unguessable size, but Ty would bet that Hunt was alone in the house with Jill. Whatever was going on in there, he felt sure it was something Hunt didn't want anyone else to see.

Ty counted to thirty-Mississippi after Hunt closed his door. Then he picked up the large box lying next to him and made his move.

Tony Hunt took his seat and observed Jill Baxter. He looked for any sign that she had changed in any way while he'd been gone. The only things he noted were that her bleeding had stopped and her bruises were ripening. He remained as fascinated as ever by her preternatural stoicism.

He debated taking her just as she was, but in the end decided to wash the caked blood off her face and see if he could find a condom lying around somewhere. With an inward smile, he thought if he couldn't find any, he'd have a pack delivered. After all, unusual circumstances or not, practicing safe sex was still in his own self-interest. He'd just risen to attend to these matters when the doorbell rang again.

Hunt ground his teeth. There were limits to his patience, even in a delicate situation such as this. He was sure a giggling, acne-scarred pack of cretins was plaguing him with these interruptions, and he vowed to find and castrate every last one of them.

He waited to regain full self-control before he answered the door . . . and he realized that several seconds had gone by and the bell had yet to ring again.

Hunt found this ominous.

The joke was turning serious.

Or perhaps it wasn't a joke at all.

He took the gun out of his pocket and stepped silently to the door. He discreetly eased aside the curtain. He'd forgotten to turn off the outside lights, so he had no trouble seeing: A package sat on his walkway, perhaps fifteen feet away.

A large, gift-wrapped package tied with a ribbon and a bow.

Hunt realized that a malicious intelligence of a high order was at work here. As was a wicked sense of humor. This went far beyond the level of any teenage prank. He could ignore the package, of course, but if he did, he felt sure he wouldn't like the consequences.

What he couldn't do was summon the police to remove it. Not with dear Ms. Baxter there. Even the hold he had on the sheriff was not enough to make Leen look the other way on a kidnapping.

Seeing no one outside his door, Tony Hunt carefully opened it. He stepped out with his gun held at the ready, but no target presented itself. Only the package. He was tempted to just shoot the damn thing.

Cautiously, he moved forward, fixated on the package. On the wrapping paper, a pattern of party hats and noisemakers surrounded wishes for a happy birthday. The ribbon was red and inexpertly tied. Still, the damn thing captivated him. So much so that he didn't notice the small figure that silently slipped around the corner of his house. Hunt continued to inch closer to the box.

He was within five feet of it when he first heard the sound: Ticking!

The damn thing was a bomb! And as big as it was, it would make that hand grenade that had been thrown at him seem like a firecracker. He had to get away!

Hunt turned to run, determined to put the entire bulk of his house between him and the explosion—but there was a kid in his way, bringing him up short. The kid looked like he was a prepubescent altar boy, but he had assassin's eyes. And he smashed Tony Hunt squarely across the face with the barrel of the gun he held in his hand.

Ty put his gun in his pocket and stuck the unconscious Hunt's weapon in his belt. Then he grabbed Hunt's collar with both hands, dragged him inside, and closed the door. When he turned around, Ty saw Hunt's battered captive.

"Jill!" he yelled.

He ran to her, horrified by the terrible damage done to her discolored and swollen face. There was dried blood everywhere; a vessel in her right eye had burst. And she looked as if she were in shock. Ty had to get a bread knife from Hunt's kitchen to saw through the panty hose Billy had used to bind her arms and legs.

Then, gently, Ty helped Jill to her feet. She leaned heavily on him, but the focus came back into her eyes. After a moment, she recognized him and put her arms around Ty and brushed his cheek with disfigured lips.

She saw Hunt lying in a pool of his own blood on the floor, and noticed the gun stuck into Ty's pants.

"Did you shoot him?" she croaked.

Ty shook his head.

"Too bad. . . . If I could . . . hold a gun, I would."

70

Bobbi Sharpes didn't shoot Billy Shelton the moment he came through her door because the sonofabitch sneaked in through her bedroom window. He waited until she had the lights out and was almost asleep. Then he dropped a flurry of paper on her, just about gave her a heart attack.

Reflex action brought Bobbi bolt upright in bed. Moonlight showed her that Billy was standing not twelve inches away. Her gun was under her pillow. She knew that making a lunge for it would be the wrong move.

For the moment.

Billy whispered, his voice all intimacy and honey: "What you just felt was twenty-five hundred dollars, cash. There'll be a lot more where that came from, too. Why don't you keep it, and we'll kiss and make up. I'll just slip in alongside you there, and pretty soon, why, we'll be mister and missus again."

Billy had his shirt unbuttoned, and he opened his pants. He was smiling, damn near drooling, at what he thought he was about to get.

He didn't even take his pants off, just pushed them down over his hips. Then he pushed the straps of her nightie down and slid it past her breasts.

"Been a long time, baby. Way too long."

Billy lay down *on* her, not next to her.

Bobbi could feel the gun under her head, but her arms were pinned at her sides and she had no way to reach it. She fought back her loathing for the man atop her. She made herself relax, hoping that Billy would, too.

She had to deceive him, make him believe she wanted him. She would try to be subtle, not say anything, but shift her weight, move her shoulders, give him the idea that she wanted to be on top, ride him for all he was worth. Billy had always liked that.

But for that to happen, he'd have to play along and roll off her. If he did, that's when she'd go for her gun.

Ty's plan had worked. Jill was free, and he had her. He picked up the gift-wrapped box so the Murtaws' kitchen clock wouldn't be found in front of Hunt's house, and led Jill out to the street. Uncharacteristically, though, he hadn't thought far enough ahead. Now, that he had Jill, what did he do with her?

Given her condition, there was only one place he could think to take her: Frank's house. He'd get her over there, take a good look at her, and see if he should call 911.

He helped her upstairs to Frank's room. Ty's nemesis lay where he'd left him. Jill glanced at Frank, all wrapped up on the floor, but didn't seem to comprehend what she was seeing. Ty helped her to lie down on Frank's bed.

Frank was agog. He started to say something.

Ty told him to shut up, he didn't need distractions. He'd only brought Jill upstairs so he could keep an eye on both of his problems.

He took off Jill's shoes, got a washcloth, and gently blotted the blood off her face. She looked bad, but after seeing that a deputy had been involved in the kidnapping, Ty was leery about involving any authority that would notify the sheriff's department. He covered her with a blanket. Then he went into the adjoining bathroom and found an ice bag. He didn't want to leave her, but he took the chance of dashing downstairs to the kitchen to get some cubes to fill the bag.

While he was there, he heard two things, a heavy thump and Frank's shout. When he raced back to the bedroom he saw that Jill had rolled off the bed. She lay sprawled on the floor, her face white as a sheet.

John was asleep when Jill came to him. He saw her smile and felt a comforting warmth. She reached out a hand to caress him—just the way his grandfather had so many years ago. The hand never reached him. It was jerked back suddenly, and he was left cold and alone.

He awoke gasping, unsure of where he was. Then he saw the soft glow of incandescent light on stained-glass. Jesus crushed the serpent under his heel. He was in his church. Alone now.

Uncertain whether he'd just had a nightmare or Jill had died.

Billy lay atop Bobbi, nuzzling her throat, nibbling her ear. His breathing was heated and audible. It was all Bobbi could do to keep from screaming in disgust, but she forced herself to stay calm and be ready. Her moment would come.

He whispered, "Baby, you don't know how many times I thought about this, how hard it was to wait."

He stuck his tongue in her ear, and Bobbi's body spasmed from head to toe. Billy grinned, misinterpreting revulsion for ecstasy.

"Liked that, huh? Well, sweetheart, maybe ol' Billy's learned a trick or two since the last time you had the pleasure of his company. Gonna make you forget all about that shitheel Tommy Boyle."

The words were no sooner out of his mouth than Billy pulled his head back; he stopped squirming against her breasts.

Bobbi saw that something was going through his head. Something he'd just said—hearing it out loud—had stopped him cold. What? He looked down at her, then pinned her hands with his. His eyes were hard and mean.

"But we got Boyle's little bastard with us right now, don't we? You're carrying it in your belly."

The smile that formed on Billy's lips was as vicious as the look in his eyes.

"Well, maybe once we get goin' real good, I'll bang its little brains out. If not, we'll go down to the clinic tomorrow and finish the job."

That was it.

Bobbi had heard all she needed. It didn't matter now that her gun was out of reach, because she'd forgotten all about it. As Billy forced her legs open and brought his head forward to kiss her, she struck.

Bobbi opened her mouth and pulled back her lips. A quicksilver shiver of gallows humor flashed through her: The fool thought she was rising to meet his lips. But when Bobbi turned her head, her target wasn't Billy's mouth. It was his nose.

At the last possible instant, Billy's eyes calculated her true destination and sent the horrifying message to his brain. He tried to pull back, but momentum, gravity, and fate worked against him. He was too late.

Bobbi's teeth snapped shut on Billy's nose with all the strength in her jaws. She tasted rank flesh and hot blood on her tongue. It made her growl as she cut and tore her way through skin and cartilage.

Billy tried to pull back and force Bobbi's jaws open at the same time. Finally, he lurched free, not from his own exertions but because half of his nose was gone.

He wailed when he saw Bobbi spit it out. Unable to help himself, Billy's hand went to his face, and he seemed to shrink physically when it touched the raw, open wound.

For a moment, they stared at each other, stunned by the sheer savagery of it all. Then Billy realized that something else was exposed, dangling and vulnerable. He struggled with his free hand to pull up his pants.

Bobbi finally remembered the gun. She dove for the pillow, fumbling to get the safety off before Billy could pounce on her. Within seconds, she had the gun in hand and cocked.

She turned, expecting to blow Billy out of the air like a clay pigeon . . . but he was gone. He'd cut and run.

Bobbi got up, made sure that he was out of the house, and locked all the doors and windows. Then she flushed Billy's nose down the toilet, gargled and showered. She collected the money and stacked it on her dresser; she'd decide what to do with it later.

When she got back in bed, she put her hands on her abdomen and told her baby she was pretty sure they'd seen the last of Billy Shelton.

Ty pulled his mouth off of Jill's and listened for a heartbeat. He heard one, and another. He saw her chest rise and fall. Color seeped back into her cheeks.

The boy's face was sheened with sweat. He was amazed that he'd been able to bring her back with CPR. He didn't know how long he'd been working on her, or how long she'd been out when he found her, or . . .

He didn't know *anything*. And he damn well needed to get help from someone who did, and fast. He saw that Frank lay looking at him, amazed.

Ty said, "I'm calling 911, just don't say anything, okay?"

Frank didn't say a word. As soon as Ty was off the phone, he stepped over to Frank.

"When I let you go, you should be too stiff and weak to do anything dumb, but just in case you're not, remember that I've still got a gun."

Frank was skeptical. "You're really going to let me go?"

"Yeah."

Ty started to rip the tape away. He stopped just long enough to look Frank in the eye.

"Now you know how it feels to be humiliated," he said. He freed Frank from the sheet. As predicted, the larger boy could barely move. Ty told him, "I won't say a word about this to anyone, if you won't."

Lying there nude and exposed, Frank was too ashamed to respond. He covered his crotch so Jill wouldn't see him if she opened her eyes.

A siren wailed in the distance. Ty couldn't worry any longer about Frank's delicate sensibilities. He didn't have much time to get Jill out-side—to say he'd found her at the side of the road.

Exerting every ounce of strength he had, Ty picked her up in his arms. If she were strong enough to go on breathing, he was strong enough to get her down the stairs and out the door.

71

The sun had just come up when John left the Church of the Resurrection. He saw Ty climbing the front steps toward him. The boy looked haggard and had bloodstains on his shirt, but he was grinning ear to ear.

"Jill sent me," Ty said. "She's going to be okay."

For a moment, John felt so disburdened of fear it was hard to keep his feet. "Tell me what happened," he said.

Ty did. He finished by saying he'd spent the night at the hospital with Jill and she'd sent him to tell John she was all right. Somehow she'd known he'd be at the church.

"She gave me a kiss," Ty added with a grin and a blush.

"I feel like kissing you myself," John said.

John laughed when Ty stepped back. He told Ty to get some sleep. The boy agreed wholeheartedly.

"I'll be down in HQ doing just that," he said.

Tran kicked his sleeping conscripts awake. They got to their feet grumbling, but formed up into a respectably straight rank. He glared at them until he was sure he had their attention.

"Today," Tran said, "we will kill Americans."

The Dream Warriors risked sidelong glances at one another and wondered what this crazy gook was talking about. *They* were Americans. They'd been born in this country like anybody else, had grown up listening to rock 'n' roll and going to the beach in Southern California. You couldn't get any more American than that.

Tran let them have their moment. Then he continued, "You will be frightened, but you will overcome your fear. You will do this for one very simple reason . . . it is the only way you will live to see your homes again."

He hated the words even as they left his mouth. In war, pragmatism was rice paper; idealism was forged steel. But he could conjure no ideal for which to fight, with which to inspire, and vermin such as these would only laugh at ideals anyway.

But their fear was real, so he played on that. He told them once again that disobedience would mean death.

He gave them their objectives, a flashlight, a knife, and a revolver. Bucktooth Lu, the smallest, got shoved to the front of the line. Jimmy Giap managed to weasel his way to the end. But Tran didn't care. One-by-one, he sent them down into the hole.

He did not expect any of them to survive the day.

Earlier that morning, Tran had been summoned to the overlord's office. The Yankee seemed more demon than human to Tran. An adhesive bandage ran diagonally across his face from brow to cheek. His eyes burned like napalm. His flesh was as pallid as a corpse.

He asked Tran a simple question: "What is the surest way to win a war?"

Tran's answer was doctrinaire: "Kill the leaders, subvert the people." Unbidden, he elaborated on the Communist catechism. Subversion, Tran said, may be achieved by an appeal to a new ideal, by providing material benefits, or by terror. Usually some combination of the three was necessary.

The overlord nodded as if he agreed completely.

Hunt had regained consciousness that morning shortly before dawn. He'd awakened with a terrible sense of foreboding, unable to move a single muscle. For several minutes, he feared he'd been paralyzed, but little by little physical control returned. This was small comfort, however, as even the slightest movement detonated a pain in his head that nearly sent him reeling back into blackness.

So he lay still and did his best to gather his wits.

The first thing he noticed was that he rested inside his house, not outside of it—the last place he remembered being.

And since he was home, not in a hospital or at the sheriff's station, that meant the cops hadn't been called. Which meant that kid had to be the one who'd dragged him inside. No act of kindness, Hunt knew, the kid had only wanted to make sure Hunt wasn't discovered before he could get well away . . .

. . . with the woman Hunt's every molecule had been screaming for.

He had to admire the kid's intelligence and grit, but that didn't lessen for a second the hate he felt for him, or his determination to find the kid and rip him limb from limb. Where had the kid come from, he asked himself, and why had he taken the risk of getting involved? And where the hell did a milquetoast like that get a gun?

Hunt had no answer for the first question. For the second, he considered it more likely than not that the woman meant something to him personally. He knew her. And since she was the union's lawyer . . . God, the kid had to know Fortunato, too. At least, Hunt had to assume so, if the kid knew the lawyer. And it wouldn't be a reach to think a maniac like Fortunato would have any qualms about giving a kid a gun.

So where did that leave him?

With more enemies than he'd imagined . . . and a new and immediate problem to solve. Beating a kidnapping rap. He forced himself to stay in control, and recent words of wisdom came back to comfort him: It doesn't matter what you've done, it only matters what can be proved.

Hunt struggled to his hands and knees. He crawled to the window next to the front door and looked out. The gift-wrapped package was gone. The kid had taken it, of course, but it was one less thing for him to worry about.

Moving slowly and with great care, Hunt made it to his bathroom, cleaned himself, bandaged the laceration on his face, and got dressed. After a thirty-minute rest to recover from these exertions, he drove to the plant.

And now, after hearing the advice of his Asian mercenary, he felt up to solving the first of his problems. Eliminating the only person who could *prove* he'd been involved in the kidnapping and battery of Jill Baxter.

Billy Shelton.

Hunt took out a local phone book. In any big city, with serious crime and vengeful criminals, cops, as a rule, went unpublished in the phone book. But this was Elk River . . . and right there was the listing for the former-and-soon-to-be-late deputy.

72

Billy Shelton woke up utterly amazed that he'd been able to fall asleep. But his eyes were no sooner open than they filled with tears again. He still couldn't believe it.

He had no goddamn nose. He sounded like an asthmatic wheezing into a megaphone.

He touched the wound again. It was worse than before, swollen and inflamed. The slightest probing contact sent knives of pain slashing through his head. Some malevolent impulse told him that if he didn't want to die of an infection he'd better go look at it and clean it.

"No, no, no!" Billy moaned.

He couldn't *look* at it; he couldn't let anybody *see* it. How would he ever explain? My wife bit my nose off? People would laugh themselves to death.

Then you better swallow your gun, buddy, the merciless part of his mind told him.

He thought about that, and it brought him an odd kind of comfort. Sure, a head shot. *Bang, boom.* Gone. Wouldn't matter about a nose then. Half of his head would be gone.

It wasn't like he had a future. The sheriff had told him he was after his ass. Hunt would never use him again now that he was a goddamn freak. And what woman would ever look at him without cringing?

More to the point, how could he ever hope to get it up again? He'd had Bobbi right where he wanted her, where he'd dreamed of having her for so long, with just enough of a struggle to make it all worthwhile. And look what happened.

No, don't look! Don't *ever* look.

Billy got his Beretta, clicked off the safety, and put the gun in his mouth. Just as he was about to pull the trigger, Bobbi's image popped into his head. She was smiling gleefully.

She hadn't wanted a reconciliation last night. She'd set him up, and like a prize chump he'd fallen for it. And wouldn't she be tickled to hear he'd blown his brains out?

Then the idea hit him that maybe Bobbi would stop by and try to finish him off. Sure, that'd be just like her. But what if he got her first? The notion of a *murder*-suicide pleased Billy no end. Just the way the two of them should go out.

He was smiling around the gun in his mouth when the doorbell rang. Startling him. Making the thumb he had on the trigger twitch.

Blowing his brains out.

Standing outside Billy's door, finger still on the bell, Hunt thought the deputy was shooting at him. He dropped to the steps of the row house and pulled out his own gun.

To his credit, Hunt held his fire and waited to see what happened next. Nothing did. No shots, no voices, no footsteps. He heard a dog bark but didn't see anybody when he turned to check the street. It was still early, and he was the only one out.

He got to his feet and peeked in a front window.

Billy sat on the sofa, slumped forward, with his head between his knees and a gun dangling from his hand. The back of his head was a red swamp, half of which had been drained onto the wall and ceiling behind him. Hunt realized he was looking at a suicide.

The dimwit had saved Hunt the trouble of killing him.

But what possible reason could a moron like Shelton have had for killing himself? And did his suicide implicate Hunt in the kidnapping? He'd also intended to see if Shelton could give him a lead in finding that damn kid who'd clubbed him and taken Jill Baxter.

Now, the numbnuts would be of no use to him.

It was intolerably frustrating. Had he arrived a minute earlier, he could have asked the sonofabitch any question he'd wanted. But he had to ring the bell just as the gun had gone off.

Hunt could barely control his anger. Another asshole. First Krieger and then this one. He swore *never* to hire another thug. Somewhere down the street, the dog resumed barking. It was all Hunt could do not to search it out and shoot it.

"Sheriff, this has got to *stop*. Practically every time I take Albert for a walk these days, somebody's getting *shot*."

The complaint ringing in Leen's ears came from Alice Wills, schoolteacher, blabbermouth, and discoverer of Tommy Boyle's corpse. Albert was the Dalmatian pup darting anxiously about the sheriff's office looking for a spot to raise his leg.

"I hid behind a car, of course, when I heard the gun go off, but I had a terrible time holding Albert still and keeping him quiet."

It was testimony to the thinness of Leen's ranks that morning that Alice and Albert had been able to waltz right in on him. The men who'd been standing guard out front were now catching what sleep they could in empty cells, and the number of blue flu deputies who refused to carry out evictions without court approval had increased by four.

"If that man had seen us," Alice said, placing a hand over her fluttering heart, "we probably would have been *murdered*."

Would've been a shame about the pup, Leen thought. From force of habit more than actual concern, he picked up a pencil, opened a notebook, and responded.

"What man?" he asked.

Alice Wills smiled triumphantly. "Well, Mr. High-and-Mighty himself. Anthony Tiburon Hunt."

Leen snapped the point off his pencil. The gaze he leveled at the teacher made her shrink back in her chair.

"Let me get this straight. You saw Tony Hunt fire a shot at someone."

Alice corrected him. "No, I didn't say that. I *heard* a shot. Then I saw Mr. Hunt with a gun in his hand. He was standing at the front door of a row house."

"There was just the one shot?"

"That's all I heard."

Leen knew he was lucky that a busybody like Alice happened to be nearby, and that he'd put the fear of God into her recently. Otherwise a single shot—and that was all it had taken to do in Tommy Boyle—could easily have gone unreported. As short as tempers were these days, even the sheriff could understand people not getting involved in the plight of their neighbors.

"How'd you see Hunt?" Leen asked the teacher. "You said you were hiding behind a car."

"I peeked," Alice said.

"Where was this row house?"

She told him the address, and this time he snapped the pencil in two. He didn't know the addresses of all his people, but he sure knew where Billy Shelton lived.

The sheriff asked, "So you waited until Hunt left before you got up?"

Alice nodded.

"And you went over to the stoop where you'd seen Hunt standing, and you peeked into the window to see what happened, didn't you, Alice?"

She nodded again, looking ill from the memory.

"He was dead. His head was . . . *disgusting.*"

"Billy Shelton?"

"I couldn't tell. He was bent over, face down. But I saw his name next to the doorbell."

Of course, Alice might have told him right off who had bought the farm. But that would have spoiled the charm of her story; she'd hooked him with Hunt and paid him off with Billy. Still, Leen put both of his hands flat on his desk and spoke to her calmly.

"Alice, have you told anyone about this? Anyone at all?"

"No, I came right here. You're the very first person I've spoken to."

Leen smiled warmly. Alice reciprocated nervously.

The sheriff told Alice he was going to put her in protective custody for the time being. No, not in a cell. The county would put her up at the Mill House Inn. Yes, including room service. Yes, the sheriff would notify her school that she'd be missing work for a while, and he'd let her mother know she was all right.

But Leen was *not* going to have this woman run her mouth. She'd given him a great gift; he had every intention of taking advantage of it.

Leen asked her, "What were you doing out so early, anyway?"

Alice Wills sighed and said, "I'd rescheduled my dental appointment."

73

Gil Velez sat in the darkness of the tunnel system he'd spent years helping to dig, and he waited. He was patient but excited. There were dinks in the tunnels, little yellow people under the earth with him again.

He could feel them. Johnny Fortune wasn't the only one who could sense things in the dark. Hell, he was the one who'd taught John the right way to go down an enemy hole in the first place. *He* was the star. The pro.

Though Gil had never raised the subject, he'd always suspected that Doolan had disappeared because John had fucked up somehow, some way he never owned up to. That had to be what had eaten at him all these years.

Gil sat with his back to an earthen wall. Just to his left was the L-shaped intersection with the access corridor to Hunt's plant. He had his .38 in his hand, and he breathed silently through his mouth. At the right moment, he'd pop out, fire, and pop back around the corner. Then he'd hurry to the next ambush point.

But for the moment Gil waited in complete silence, so still Charlie wouldn't even hear his heart bump against his ribs, and his patience was rewarded. He heard the scrape of cloth moving clumsily over the hard soil.

The next thing he heard was hard to identify at first, a rhythmic clicking of hard surfaces. Then he knew what it was.

Teeth chattering. Some goddamn dink was scared out of his mind. Of course, maybe the guy crawling point was just a sacrificial lamb. He'd know soon enough.

The sound effects increased as the point man got closer. Gil could hear him breathing. The dink was gulping air. He'd even started to whisper something to somebody when he hit Gil's booby trap.

Then he screamed and started shooting.

Threaded through the gunfire was a hair-raising yowl—and frantic cries of "Get it off me, *get it off me!*"

Unlike the VC in Nam, Gil hadn't had the luxury of setting out a trap with something as deadly as a one-step viper. One bite, one step, *adios*. But the raccoon he'd captured seemed to be doing a respectable job.

A babble of voices joined the screamer, until one final shot rang out, and an older, authoritative voice ordered silence.

A serious sonofabitch.

Gil would bet he was the one who killed the coon. But the point man, who sounded seriously bitten and clawed, was still howling for all he was worth.

Gil knew he could get most of the dinks right now just by rolling a grenade around the corner. But where was the fun in that? This was the game of Charlie 'n' Joe he'd been waiting half his life for; he wanted it to last.

He'd take the dinks one at a time. Save that serious bastard for last. So he popped out around the corner, flicked on his light for just a second, and put the crybaby out of his misery with a single round.

He was gone before the return fire started.

74

Jill was spitting mad when John stepped into her hospital room. She had a doctor, a nurse, and now him for company. The nurse, getting ready to boot John's ass out of there, asked if he was a relative.

"Soul mate," he said.

The nurse frowned, but Jill laughed. Then she winced.

"You see," warned the doctor, "even the mild shaking incurred by laughter causes you pain, Ms. Baxter. There's no way I can allow you to leave this bed."

All signs of humor fled Jill's face. "There's no way you're going to keep me here."

The doctor turned to John. He looked as grim as his patient. "You're her soul mate? Well, if this woman insists on getting up and moving about, there's a good possibility she's placing her life in danger. So, if you know any way to keep her right where she is, now is the time to use it."

John thought he did, but Jill beat him to the punch.

She said, "If you mention a certain child's name, I'll never speak to you again."

Unable to discuss the welfare of Jill's daughter, John was helpless. He shrugged to the doctor.

"Sorry, I tried," he said.

"Tried what?" the doctor asked in exasperation. "This woman suffered head injuries only hours ago which caused her to lose consciousness and stop breathing. Now she wants to play Jimmy Hoffa."

John had heard about the blackout from Ty, but hearing it again from a doctor in a hospital room, and seeing the profusion of bruises on Jill's face, made things a lot scarier. He didn't say a word to her, but gave her a long, inquiring look.

Her rebuttal was immediate.

"The CAT scan didn't show any damage."

The comment was directed to John, but the doctor jumped right in.

"A CAT scan is not a divine seal of approval. Even the most advanced diagnostic tools are not one hundred percent accurate. And when it comes to head injuries that percentage falls off a cliff."

He paused to take a breath and give Jill his best medical stare.

"We don't know why you lost consciousness last night. Why you stopped breathing. Why you probably came close to dying. It would be best for you to remain right here—just in case we have to open the top of your skull."

John felt compelled to speak.

"I saw you last night," he said quietly. "Just like I saw Tommy."

Jill softened for a moment.

"I know. I saw you, too." Then her resolve firmed up again. "But I didn't die, did I?"

The doctor had no idea what these people were talking about, but he sensed he was about to lose the battle.

He shrugged. "Okay, just tell me one thing. How many fingers am I holding up?" The doctor raised his index finger.

Jill clenched her jaw and didn't say a word.

The doctor told her, "If you leave this bed, it will be against medical advice, with a signed waiver of liability, and you'll be a damn fool."

He stormed out. The nurse followed reluctantly.

"Help me up," Jill told John. "I'm getting out of here."

It hadn't been the reunion he'd anticipated.

"If you black out, I'm taking you right back to the hospital," John said. "I'll get you one of those beds where they can strap you in."

John had helped Jill get dressed. He'd supported her while she'd signed the release forms. Then he'd walked her out to the car and buckled her into her seat. Now, at her direction, they were heading to Local 274.

She looked at him, and he thought he was in for an argument, maybe even another threat of some kind, but what she said surprised him so much he asked her to repeat it.

"I said I love you, too."

He'd never said that to her. And now she'd told him twice.

"I'm sorry I haven't already told you so," John said. "For a time, I was afraid you'd never know."

Jill said, "I know. But you can say it anyway."

He said, "I love you."

"You're not one of those guys who's afraid to express his feelings, are you?"

"No, but I'm big on nonverbal expression. Real strong in the visual and tactile areas."

Jill grinned. "You're not so bad with words, either; I thought 'soul mate' was a nice turn of phrase."

"That just popped out."

"It's true, though," Jill said.

She put a hand on John's arm. "The thing I thought about, when I left my body, was how come I went to see you. Why not my dad? Or my mom or Carlie?"

John glanced at her. "Did you come up with an answer?"

Jill said, "I just told you why."

"You love the others, too."

Jill grinned once more. "Yeah, but just like Tommy, I knew *you* would get the job done for me somehow."

John laughed. "And what's the job now?"

"To hold out for just a little longer. Hunt's about to fold."

But when they got to Local 274, they saw that there was a line of people, most of them strikers, waiting to get into the scab's union across the street. Several new thugs kept order, admitting people into the office one at a time. Jill's eyes hardened when she saw what was happening.

A handful of grizzled union veterans stood in the doorway of Local 274. They watched the crowd across the street with a mixture of contempt and fear.

"What the hell is going on?" Jill asked, leaning on John's arm as he helped her out of the car.

"They think they won, those dumb bastards," a white-haired man snarled, and he spat on the sidewalk. "They think they beat Tony Hunt, and they're tellin' themselves they're happier than pigs in shit."

Jill was at a complete loss. "How could they have won? What happened?"

"Hunt agreed to give them all the conditions that Tommy demanded before the strike started. All they gotta do is sign up with the new union."

Jill was stunned. "Hunt has offered a contract with everything Tommy wanted in it?"

The old worker shook his head, and his lips formed a bitter smile.

"No, no *contract*. What Hunt's offered is his hand on the deal . . . and just look at all the fools who'll shake hands with the devil."

The man spat again.

At Jill's urgent request, Sid Tomlinson, the gentle Christian giant of the local's executive committee, found a bullhorn and gave it to her. Standing on the sidewalk in front of Local 274 with John holding her elbow for support, she came right to the point.

"Anthony Hunt is broke."

The people waiting in the line to sign up with the new local had studiously avoided looking across the street. They might have been trying to save their families and their homes, but they still felt like traitors. Even so, those first four words turned every head Jill's way.

"His bankers are about to withdraw his financing," she continued, her voice echoing down the street. "Any deal he makes today he won't be able to honor tomorrow."

That got the union goons going.

"Hey, fuck you, bitch, you're crazy!" one shouted.

"Shut up and let her talk," said a man in line.

Another goon yanked the man from the line and told him he was out, he could forget about getting a job.

Jill used the distraction to continue.

"You have a chance to buy the company right out from under Hunt, the chance to work for yourselves. All we have to do is hold out just twenty-four more hours and we'll *really* win. Please. Don't let Hunt trick you into giving up."

That was all she had strength to say, but the union goons didn't know that. Two of them started across the street toward her. They stopped when John took out his .38.

They'd been told what had happened to their predecessors. And a big heavyset guy who looked like he wasn't afraid of anything this side of the devil stepped up next to the guy with the gun . . . and there were the others bunching up behind them. Old coots mostly, but they looked like they'd fight to the death.

Then one of the goons was shoved from behind. It was the guy he'd pulled out of line, getting back at him. That little geek was ready to fight, too. It was all too goddamn strange. The goon and his partner quickly retreated to their side of the street.

They were jostled by several more people going the other way. The line for jobs with the new local wasn't nearly as long now. But others stayed behind, out of shame or disbelief. Jill counted noses, then she tugged at John's shoulder so she could whisper in his ear.

She said, "Remember that favor I asked? You think you could set off a small bomb or two?"

75

The second round of evictions began that day at eight A.M. It ended three minutes later when Barbara Duckworth, single mother of two, and third-shift circuit board assembler, told Deputy Clay Weltz she goddamn well wasn't getting out of her home.

"You show me a court order or you go to hell!" Barbara screamed through her barricaded door.

"I'm here on the *sheriff's* orders, lady," Deputy Weltz yelled back, "and one way or another I'm comin' in, and you're going out."

"Oh, yeah?" Barbara taunted. "Well, maybe you should just look behind you."

She prayed that the protection she'd been promised last night had shown up. Weltz prayed, too, as he whirled and pulled his weapon: Please, God, don't let me get shot.

He wasn't. Not yet, anyway. No crazed striker was lining him up in his sights, but Ron Narder and six other blue flu deputies were giving Weltz their best steely-eyed stares. All of them were dressed in civvies—but wearing their weapons right out on their hips.

Narder gave him a no-no-no shake of his head.

Weltz reholstered his weapon. He said, "I'm just following orders, goddamnit, Ron."

Narder replied, "No court orders, no evictions."

"But the sher—"

"Fuck the sheriff."

Weltz's partner was sitting in their patrol unit. He looked to him for support. That sonofabitch shook his head, too.

The deputy returned to his car, ignored his partner, and called the situation in to the sheriff. He was told to wait right where he was. But the sheriff didn't show up; two goons from the new union office did.

"Shows you who you're working for these days, doesn't it, Clay?" Narder asked.

The union gorillas had arrived with a new trick up their sleeves. They offered Barbara Duckworth a chance to jump the line of people signing up with the new local. She could be back on the job tomorrow, getting all the pay and benefits Tommy Boyle had demanded. She wouldn't have to worry about paying for her house or anything else.

Barbara had a question. "How long's the contract run?"

Indefinitely. It was a gentlemen's agreement between Harold Noyes and Tony Hunt.

Barbara told the two men to get the hell off her property.

Chief Deputy Narder and company made them comply.

Orville Leen went to see just how Billy Shelton had gone toes-up. He was surprised to find a reporter waiting for him. Up till then, a pestering pack of media jackals was the one plague he'd been spared.

Not that Elk River had enough media to form a pack. The town was served by WABE-AM, a radio station owned by the president of the Chamber of Commerce, and the *Elk River Record*, which drew most of its circulation with Sunday grocery coupons.

Stan Tacker from the *Record* sat on Billy's front stoop.

"They wouldn't let me in," he told the sheriff.

Leen knew the young reporter. Tacker was smart, had a nice way with words, and was cutting his teeth in the sticks before moving on to better papers in bigger markets.

"I'm ready to blow this pop stand," the reporter continued. "Been here eighteen months, making peanuts, putting together barely enough clips to get a job in Peoria." He stood and stretched.

Tacker was working his way up to something, and Leen waited him out.

"Strike sure livened things up, though. I've been covering it right along.

Watching all the main players. Keeping the body count." He riffled through his notebook. "Ought to make real interesting reading."

"Haven't seen any stories in the paper." Leen said it neutrally.

"You won't, either. Not with Norm 'Print-No-Evil' Nolan as our managing editor." Tacker grinned. "I heard Tony Hunt might buy the *Record*. Imagine what a propaganda organ it'd be then."

Leen chose not to react to that nugget of information, even though he found it interesting.

"Thing is," Tacker continued, "when you're a reporter with a good story, you can always find someone to publish it. I've been thinking I could go two ways. I could broker it to a big paper for a job . . . or I could do a book."

Tacker waited for Leen to react, but he didn't. So he explained the implications of his choices.

"I go to a big paper, show them what they're missing, I'll get a job, but they'll send a bunch of people to town. Then the TV stations will swoop down. After that, it won't be my story anymore. And you, Sheriff, you'll have more headaches than this burg's got aspirin."

Leen asked quietly, "You gonna tell me the book's a better deal for both of us?"

"Sure. I get the story all to myself. And you don't have anybody bothering you but me. And I've got good manners. I'd like to go inside. Please."

Leen smiled tightly. He nodded and put his arm around Tacker.

"Okay, I'm gonna let you take a look. I'll even let the M.E. say one word to you, homicide or suicide. I'm gonna do that, and you're not gonna breathe a word to anyone about anything until you get my permission. You know why?"

"Why?" Tacker asked suspiciously.

"Because I get the least hint you're breaking our deal, *I'll* call the big-town papers to come get the story. Then you won't have enough to trade for a book, a job, or a bus ticket to Peoria."

Leen had to give Tacker credit. He lasted long enough to see the body, hear the M.E. say suicide, and run back outside before he threw up.

The medical examiner, the evidence technician, and the deputy on the scene had left Billy just the way they'd found him. His ruined head was slumped between his knees, the stiffened fingers of his right hand still wrapped around his gun. Pathetic.

"A suicide," Leen muttered. "Who'd ever figure Billy Shelton for killing himself?"

"Not me," the M.E. said, "and just maybe he didn't. There's something bothers me I didn't mention with that snot-nose reporter kid around."

"What?" Leen wondered if nothing could be simple anymore.

"Well, look here, and tell me what's wrong with this picture."

The medical examiner took out a mirror. He held it under Billy so the sheriff could see the dead man's face. It was a mess, but it took him a second to understand why.

"His nose is missing," the sheriff said.

"And you don't shoot your nose off when you put your gun in your mouth. Now, look here." The M.E. used his pen to point to the reflection of several small red arcs in the tissue surrounding the area where Billy's nose should've been. "What do those look like to you?"

"Teeth marks?"

"Exactly."

"Somebody bit his nose off, and he shot himself?"

"Or somebody mauled him, he passed out from the pain, and the killer made it look like suicide."

"You find the nose?"

The M.E. shook his head. "For all I know, the madman who bit it off might've *eaten* it. This town has just come unhinged."

It was the damnedest thing Leen had ever heard of. Still, the medical examiner had just advanced the possibility that this death was a homicide. Which fit beautifully in the sheriff's mind with the fact that Alice Wills had seen Tony Hunt at Billy's door that very morning.

He turned to the evidence technician. "Did you check the doorbell and the doorknob for fingerprints before you entered?"

"Sure did, Sheriff," the man said. "Got a bunch of 'em."

Leen nodded his approval.

He was going to frame Tony Hunt for Billy's death. It was going to be beautiful. Airtight. Poetic justice. Hunt thought he'd built a box for Leen. Wait till the bastard saw the coffin the sheriff would manufacture for him.

Gil whistled the opening notes of "La Bamba" before entering HQ.

When he didn't get a response to his recognition signal, he started to worry, because he definitely heard someone breathing inside the chamber. He took out his gun. Darien would've whistled back right away if it'd been him in there. John, too. Even the kid had been told what to do.

The chamber was pitch dark, as was the tunnel where Gil crouched. He'd made the traverse from where he'd ambushed Charlie without a light. He could move in the dark because he knew these tunnels cold, knew things about them *nobody* else knew.

He also knew breathing patterns. Right now, he was listening to some-body sleep. It had to be the kid. Because it didn't smell like a dink, and no way would Darien or John be caught sleeping.

He put his gun away and crept into the chamber, crawled right up to the sleeper.

He flicked on his flashlight. It was the kid, all right. The boy's eyes popped open and immediately shut again.

Then the kid had a gun in his hand. It got there so fast Gil wasn't sure how it happened. He barely clamped his free hand around the kid's wrist before he could bring the weapon to bear on him.

"What the fuck are you doing? It's me! Gil!"

He felt the kid relax.

"You okay?" Gil demanded. "You straight we're on the same side?"

"Yeah, sorry."

"Goddam well oughta be."

Gil turned on the electric lantern and flicked off his flashlight. He told the kid that he'd whistled before he'd come in. If he'd scared Ty, that's what he got for not whistling back.

Ty apologized again. He explained why he'd been sleeping, and that Darien had said it would be okay because he and Gil would be out in the system and nobody would get past them.

When Gil heard Ty's story—about taking that lawyer broad away from Hunt—he was impressed. And the way the kid pulled his weapon on him like that—fast, no hesitation at all—that was gutsy, too. The little bastard was all right.

So Gil felt good about sharing his news with the kid.

"I got one," he said. "I dinged a dink."

"You killed him?"

"Dead as a fuckin' dodo." Gil told him the story in detail.

"How'd you have room to fit the raccoon into the tunnel ceiling?" Ty asked.

"I just dug a little space out of the tunnel ceiling for the cage I made," Gil replied. "Then I ran a nonreflective line from the door of the cage to the floor of the tunnel. Bump the line, the door flies open and you got a faceful of frantic 'coon."

The image was horrible . . . but that wasn't what Ty's mind had seized upon.

"You dug a new space for the trap?"

"Yeah, that's what I just said."

The idea that the tunnels could be altered, that they weren't *immutable*, was a revelation. Again, closer than before, a thought strained to break through to Ty's consciousness.

He asked Gil, "Did the Vietnamese ever complete their tunnels? Did they ever stop digging?"

"Are you kiddin' me?" Gil snorted. "You can bet those little fuckers are *still* digging."

Then he confided, "And so am I."

76 Tran made his conscripts drag the remains of both Buck-tooth Lu and the raccoon out of the tunnel. Once he'd disarmed the young hoodlums, he let them look upon their dead friend.

The animal had savaged Lu's face, and then the Yankee had shot the gangster in the head. The gang-bangers were struck dumb. The familiar violence of drive-by shootings and slain shopkeepers didn't faze them; raccoon booby traps and underground ambushes petrified them.

Tran looked at the animal. His shot had taken off the top of its skull. He wondered what other surprises the Yankees might have in store for them.

"You can fuckin' forget about me going back down there," Eddie Ky declared. "You can shoot me, I wouldn't care."

Tran shot the boy.

A summary execution was exactly what would have happened to him if he had voiced such disobedience to the NLF. Among guerrillas, discipline and self-sacrifice were all.

The point was not lost on Jimmy Giap, Stevie Tho, and Vinny Vinh. They looked at Tran with hatred, but the fear in their eyes was even greater than the loathing.

In a level voice, Tran addressed the secondary lesson of the day. He told his remaining subordinates the mistake that Lu had made in triggering the booby trap and how they could avoid such a fate themselves.

All three paid strict attention.

Tran nodded at the hole near his feet. "We will not use this entrance again. We will find another way into the American tunnels. A way they do not expect."

Tran had more to say, but the overlord had entered the enclosure. He looked at the two bodies on the ground, one of which lay in a pool of its own blood.

"A combat death, and a matter of military discipline," Tran said blandly. He gave the overlord credit—the Yankee didn't bat an eye.

Tran told the American that he and his men would have to find other entrances to the tunnels if they were to succeed. He asked for a map of the town indicating topographical features and points of local prominence.

He waited stoically to see if the overlord would lengthen his leash; he didn't show his pleasure when the American agreed to his plan.

Tran intended to leave the bodies of two more gangsters to be found above ground. Another he would leave in a tunnel, but accessible. His own body would presumably be buried in a section of tunnel he intended to collapse with explosives. These were the details of his get-away plan. All of them would be easier to accomplish now that he had freedom of movement.

The American asked Tran a question: Other than killing an enemy's leaders, what was the best way to bring him to his knees?

Tran replied immediately, "Find his center of life and destroy it."

The town of Elk River came to resemble an open-air insane asylum, with the inmates keeping one eye on each other and the other on the sky. Nature was abetting the tension that Friday with an afternoon that had grown oppressively hot and thick.

Exhaustion and her beating had finally forced Jill Baxter to take to a cot placed in Tommy Boyle's old office. She'd fallen asleep immediately. A crew of loyalists woke her hourly to make sure she hadn't slipped into a coma.

Local 274 suspended picketing for the day. Sid Tomlinson and Harry Waller, the two remaining members of the executive committee, decided it was pointless; the union didn't know how many members it could count on anymore. Even Pete Banks hadn't been seen for three days. The conventional wisdom was he'd skipped town. Strikers were told to go home, stay calm, and pray that Jill Baxter was right about Hunt's being in worse shape than they were.

But people felt too restless, too confined, and too hot to stay indoors. And the threat of imminent eviction had already dispossessed many of them of their sense of home, if not the actual roofs over their heads. A lot of angry people walked the streets.

The line at the scabs' union was gone, but a few quislings still found their way into the storefront. Some emerged doing their best to be invisible; others stuck their chins out defiantly. The goons protecting the premises sat outside looking sullen and mopping the sweat off their brows and necks.

Fistfights broke out at intersections where motorists argued over the right-of-way. A Presidential greengrocer who'd been a little too eager to break the boycott wrestled with a striker who'd kicked over an outdoor display of produce. Two women got into a clawing match at a Good Humor Ice Cream truck.

Trying to cope with it all was an undermanned, overworked shift of short-tempered deputies. They stopped fights and issued citations, but as long as both combatants were still upright they didn't make arrests. They'd be damned if they were going to do paperwork today.

The remaining replacement workers at the plant stayed at their stations, working continuous shifts or sleeping in place. They refused to leave the premises.

At the Church of the Resurrection, Bill Deeley brought out several buckets of gray paint and paintbrushes. He placed them to the right of a lawn chair he'd set up. Next, he brought out several buckets of hot, soapy water and scrub brushes and put them to the left. He leaned two ladders against the church. Then he stuck a sign in the grass: YOUR CHOICE.

Finally, he sat down with a glass of lemonade and waited.

When John entered the tunnels, he knew at once that someone had died in them. He could feel the decaying resonance of a final cry for life, an echo of mortality that would never fade completely. It chilled his soul.

A bitter irony filled him. He had labored beneath the earth through what should have been the best years of his life. All to solve the mystery of his friend's death. And do penance for it. He'd sought to re-create a world gone by down to the smallest detail. The one thing that had never crossed his mind was that his creation had to be baptized in blood.

It should have. Otherwise the tunnels were just a subterranean fun house, a flagellant's folly. Now, his oversight had been corrected for him, and the impact left him reeling.

Because, having found someone to live for, all Johnny Fortune wanted to do was get out alive again.

77

Bill Deeley didn't believe that God played favorites. Even though he'd been raised a Catholic and ordained a priest, Deeley never bought the idea that there was only one True Church. Nor did he accept that there were any chosen people. Nor could he give credence that the Koran was the sole passport to paradise.

He believed that God lived in and worked through every human soul.

But Bill Deeley had come to have a sneaking suspicion that, like anyone else, God did have his favorite places. And among them was the Church of the Resurrection in Elk River, Illinois. Whenever he looked at the church Michelangelo Fortunato had built without blueprints seventy years earlier, Deeley had no problem believing that its construction had been divinely inspired.

Every line pleased the eye, and the sum of those lines was so inevitable, so natural, it sometimes seemed this beautiful structure must have *grown* from the verdant earth on which it sat, that the river which ran past it must have changed its course for the joy of reflecting it.

These thoughts helped to inspire his self-doubt: How could he have marred such a masterpiece? Even with John Fortunato's permission, who was he to do such a thing? Deeley believed in the expiation of sin, and he was sure he would pay for what he'd done to the Church of the Resurrection.

He put down his lemonade and took out his rosary. Maybe the Blessed Mother would be able to comfort him. Lost in prayer, he was in the second decade of his beads when he felt a tap on his shoulder.

"Father Deeley."

It was the old man and his wife. The ones who'd tried to scrub off the paint. Many of the older congregants remembered him from when he was their priest and still addressed him that way.

"May we, Father?" the old lady asked, nodding toward the scrub buckets.

"Are you up to it?" Bill Deeley asked with concern. The couple had to be in their late seventies, maybe older.

"You just watch me," the old gent said. He pushed up his sleeves and firmly scooped up a bucket and a brush. He climbed the right-hand ladder while his wife steadied it.

That was how it began. People walking along Riverfront Drive saw the old man and his white-haired wife scrubbing away the paint. They came closer and saw Bill Deeley's sign.

The choice they were given was as simple as it was profound. A striker soon went up the other ladder, working opposite the old man. The two men didn't say a word; they just smiled at each other, then bent to their task.

Word spread. People who had been idly walking or riding around town now found a focus for their time and energy. They gathered at the church and pitched in with the cleaning, glad to have the opportunity to do something positive.

A tense moment flared when a Presidential merchant, an early boycott breaker, joined the effort. He was roughly jostled by more than one striker, but he held fast. "This is my church, too," he told them. "I'm as much to blame for what happened to it as any of you."

Bill Deeley handed the man a scrub brush.

"This is *God's* church," he said, "and with all our flaws, we are *all* His children."

After that, there was no denying anybody who wanted to help. And so many did that they brought their own ladders, buckets, and brushes. Hardwoods and Presidentials. Strikers and strikebreakers. Everybody labored.

Long after all the paint had been scrubbed away, and even as a yellow-white sky foretold an approaching storm, the people of Elk River scoured each stone of their church. They were overcome by their sense of common purpose and an awareness of their common plight.

Bill Deeley removed the buckets of paint. He saw the spirit of the place enter them. People were reconciling, finding the courage to admit their fears and the charity to understand the anxiety of their friends and neighbors.

When the first raindrops began to fall and lightning flashed on the horizon, Bill Deeley told everyone to take their belongings home. Then he invited all of them to return in an hour. There would be a service of thanksgiving—for all the blessings they still enjoyed.

Not a single soul declined his invitation.

"Daddy?" Jill Baxter asked.

She couldn't be sure it was him. She'd been very young when he was killed, and they were standing somewhere very dark. But the light on his miner's helmet cast its glow on a smile she somehow recognized.

"Come on, sweetheart, don't be afraid," he said. When he took her hand, she knew she had found her father.

He led her onto an open metal platform. It sank swiftly into a jet-black shaft. The tiny light on her father's helmet only made the darkness more crushing. She pressed in against her father and his arm went around her. Just as she was starting to feel safe they stopped descending.

Her father gently urged her forward, but she resisted. She didn't want to go. She knew she was in a coal mine and wanted no part of it. She saw other lights bobbing in the blackness above tired eyes and grime-covered faces. She heard the growls and bangs of the machines that the men operated to dig and load the coal. Terror chilled her; at any moment, she knew, their actions would bring the weight of the world crashing down upon them.

"Daddy," she cried, "why did you bring me here?"

"So you could face your fears, sweetheart. So you could face them down. You're strong enough. You can do it."

He squeezed her hand to reassure her.

Jill heard water dripping somewhere nearby. She was certain that something horrible was about to happen. Her heart twisted in her chest. She embraced her father and held on to him with all her strength.

She felt his hand stroke her hair. His breath was soft and warm on her cheek as he spoke to her. "Sugar, I can't tell you how proud I am of you, proud of everything you've done. Any trouble you have, you remember, I'm right there with you."

As comforting as his words were, Jill couldn't help but notice that the dripping sound was getting louder, more insistent and ominous. She tried to bury herself within her father, and just as his arms went around her the earth shook with a monstrous roar and she was torn away from him.

Jill awoke gasping. She was alone in Tommy's office. The storefront windows of Local 274 still rattled from a continuing clap of thunder. Outside, rain fell in sheets.

Jill's breathing returned to normal, and her fear soon left her. What remained was the comfort of her father's promise: He would always be there for her. Not even death could change that.

"Thank you, Daddy," Jill whispered.

John had two jobs left before the day was done. He had to sabotage Hunt's plant, and he had to confront Tommy's killer.

As he crawled through the pitch-black tunnel he became aware of how acutely focused his senses were. His fingers sensed the most minute cracks in the clay beneath them; he felt a murmur of air from a ventilation shaft; he detected a mosaic of odors from the musk of the soil to the reek of animal urine and the tang of his own perspiration; he heard scurrying rodent feet; and beneath it all he could feel in his bones the muted tectonic groan of an endlessly restless planet.

A trip that over the years had become as mindlessly routine as a stroll through a shopping mall was once again awash with stimulation. All because there were people down here who would kill him if they got the chance.

With every meter he moved forward, he crawled further and further back into memories of the past. He negotiated every ambush Gil had placed without difficulty. But as he went around each curve and through every trapdoor he became ever more irrationally anxious that he would hear Doolan call out to him again, beg him for help—and that once again he would fail his friend.

If that happened, he hoped the dinks had a better grenade to use on him this time.

There was nobody in HQ when John got there. He was glad. He didn't want to see anyone or tell them what he was doing. He turned on the electric lantern and got to work. From a storage locker, he took a map that was sealed in airtight, waterproof plastic.

The map showed the entire underground infrastructure of Elk River. All the utilities—gas, electric, water, sewage, phone, street lights, traffic signals, and cable television—were indicated. After several beers one night, Gil had told John that the town had better never get them mad at it or they could shut the whole damn place down.

Which was what John now intended to do to Hunt's plant.

He took a lump of C-4 explosive, no bigger than a Ping-Pong ball, and a detonator from the stockpile. He didn't have to nuke the electric grid, all he had to do was cut service to one customer.

He studied the utility map, then cross-checked it against the diagram of the one system the city didn't know about: his tunnels. He found the spot where he'd have to dig to gain access to the electrical grid, fixed it in his mind, put the maps back, and grabbed an entrenching tool.

He was about to leave the chamber when he decided to take some extra rounds for his .38. He didn't want to kill anybody, but he didn't want to die, either. He'd fight if need be.

John felt the presence of others in the tunnels as he crawled toward the plant. Not Charlie. The intruders hadn't gotten that far into the system. One time he detected—just felt—a human aura, a single presence; the other time he'd actually heard two sets of knees quietly scrape along a length of tunnel. The first encounter he took to be Gil, the second Darien and Ty. Both times, he avoided contact.

John stopped and waited when he got to the segment of the system that led to Hunt's plant. He waited at the same intersection where Gil had earlier lay in ambush. He sat perfectly still and cleared his mind. He opened himself to any telltale sign that these new VC were about.

He felt no living presence, but he was absolutely sure that this is where the killing had happened. Here, he could smell blood and vomit.

When he was certain there was no threat to him, he crawled into the corridor leading to the plant. In a rare departure from form, he took out a penlight and flicked it on for just a second. That was all he needed to see the blood, bone, and soft tissue splattered along the tunnel floor.

He crawled right through, stopped only a few meters beyond, and got on with the business of being a saboteur.

78 Tran studied the map he'd been given as he sat in the back seat of a large sedan the American overlord had provided. The three remaining Dream Warriors sat in the front seat, with Jimmy Giap behind the wheel awaiting instructions. Rain pelted the car.

As he examined the map, Tran thought of where he would dig tunnels under this town, what sites he would choose for entrances to the system. The overlord's factory was, of course, the most obvious choice. It was a target that any military man would want to exploit.

Where else? Tran asked himself.

The center of government, which also contained police headquarters, what the Yankees called City Hall. He would have an entrance near there. But even in this downpour Tran had no interest in risking exposure to American police by searching these areas.

Stretching along the river was a park. It began just outside the overlord's plant, ran past a church, and ended at a marina on the far side of the town. Tran was certain that there were entrances in the park. He was equally certain he could find them.

The problem was that their proximity to the factory meant the Americans were more likely to be expecting—and therefore prepared for—attacks from those quarters. And all this rain could soon cause the river to flood. Tran had no idea what precautions the Yankees had taken on this matter, but he was not going to risk his life on the possibility that they had miscalculated.

Tran stared out the window, surprised at himself. He was becoming involved in this matter as if it were a serious battle. It almost made him laugh.

There was no revolution to fight for; capitalism had triumphed everywhere. He had no country to fight for; he was an alien wherever he went. Despite everything, though, there was a matter of martial pride, the challenge of one soldier pitting himself against another.

The Americans would be far more worthy opponents than the brats sitting cowed in front of him. He would have to do them the honor of killing one or two before he fled.

He returned his gaze to the map. Reading it, he could tell that the area marked "Oak Crest" was on the rise above the town. This must be the wooded area with the large homes he'd glimpsed as they had flown in at twilight on the helicopter.

He knew from his time in California that wealthy Americans liked to look down on the poor in every possible way. Oak Crest, then, was where the town's rich would live. This area was also uphill from the possibility of flooding. And the wooded nature of the terrain would reduce the chance of discovery by the authorities and increase the opportunity to rid himself of his young hoodlums.

There was no question in his mind that there would be a tunnel entrance in this area. Concentrations of wealth were magnets for anyone with a gun. Or an army. Or a tunnel.

Tran gave Jimmy Giap the directions to Oak Crest.

From his rain-streaked window, Tony Hunt watched his slit-eyed runts drive through the plant gate. He felt no misgivings letting them wander around on their own. In fact, he liked the idea of turning them loose. He wanted to see what kind of hell they could raise, if they could bring him Fortunato's head.

He had no doubt that one bastard would have the stomach for it. Hell, the gook had shot his own man just to keep the others in line. Hunt admired the remorseless expediency of it. He only wished he could have seen it.

He turned to the four men who were waiting for him in his office. The international had sent them over.

"I want you to burn down a church," Hunt told them.

To a man, the thugs looked toward the window at the rain. It was coming down like a monsoon.

"You mean tonight?" one asked incredulously.

"Within the hour."

"How about if we blow it up instead?"

"That'll do."

"It'll take a while to get the explosives. They'll have to come from Chicago."

Hunt shook his head. More than enough explosives had been brought in for his tunnel fighters.

"I've got some you can use," he said.

With less than a skeleton staff on hand at the station, there was precious little to distract Orville Leen. He leaned back in his chair and closed his eyes. He listened to the thunder crash overhead and thought: Fire and ice. He took a grim joy in the simple, direct way nature resolved its conflicts.

His practiced ear told him that there was at least one more act to this storm, and maybe two.

Fitting accompaniment for when he killed Tony Hunt and resigned as sheriff.

Tony Hunt called his investment banker, Carter Powell, at home. Hunt grinned when he realized that he'd caught the sonofabitch in the thick of it with his wife.

"What do you want?" Powell asked coldly.

"I just wanted to let you know about a few new developments," Hunt said, "before the loan committee meets."

"We're fully informed."

Cocksure, Hunt thought. Rubbing his nose in it.

"Then you know about the tunnels?"

"Tunnels? What tunnels?"

Hunt had decided the moment was right to share his little secret. When he finished his story the banker sounded just the way Hunt had hoped he would.

"That's the craziest damned thing I've ever heard. You say some madman has tunneled under your plant . . ."

"Under the whole town, I think."

"Why in God's name would anyone do that?"

"In my case, sabotage."

"What!"

"My security people have found explosive devices at various locations around the plant."

They hadn't, but Powell didn't need to know that. And Hunt did have explosives handy. If he didn't get his financing, the game was over. Why not go out with a bang?

"You've notified the police?"

Hunt smiled. "I'm sure you've been *informed* about the situation with the local police."

"What about outside authorities?"

"Who knows how much time there is? I'm probably risking my life just sitting here talking to you."

"Isn't there anybody who can help?" the banker pleaded.

Hunt had him now. "As a matter of fact, there is. When I saw how crazy things were getting, I thought it might be useful to bring in a few people with special talents. One or two of them know about bombs."

"Well, put them to work, for God's sake."

"Don't you mean for *your* sake? If this place goes up in smoke, every penny you've invested goes with it. Of course, if I don't keep my financing, it doesn't matter to *me* what happens, does it?"

Which told the sonofabitch plainly enough that if Tony Hunt went down the tubes so did he.

"You won't help unless we back you?" Powell asked stiffly.

"I'm not known for altruism," Hunt replied. "If I don't have a fax here in my office in twenty minutes guaranteeing my financing, I'm walking out . . . and all you'll have to show for your money might very well be a hole in the ground."

The banker didn't even try to bargain; he caved.

Hunt broke the connection and laughed. He'd get the money he needed to keep going. His killer dink would take care of Fortunato. Destroying the church would break the back of the strike. It had been a near thing, but he'd done it. He'd won.

He sat in his office alone and couldn't stop laughing.

Until the lights went out.

John knew that as far as explosions went this was just a nickel-and-dime bang. But it sounded like the end of the world. His ears rang like crazy.

It was another indication of how much he'd forgotten about tunnel warfare. He should have been nowhere near that blast. He should have remembered how a tunnel magnified even the smallest explosion.

He pressed his hands against his ears, but he couldn't get them to stop ringing.

.   .   .

Orville Leen was on his way out of his office when his phone rang. It was an internal line.

"What is it?" he demanded.

"Sheriff, we just got word from the state police. They say storm surges and flooding are expected on the Mississippi and all its tributaries on account of this rain."

"They recommend the immediate evacuation of all low-lying areas. . . . Sheriff, I don't think we have the personnel to manage that."

Leen said, "You get on the phone to everybody who pins on a badge around here; you tell them to muster right now for emergency duty or they're fired."

"Yes, sir," the deputy responded.

The news was going to force the sheriff to change his plans some, so he amended his instructions.

"Don't bother calling Chief Deputy Narder. I'll talk to him personally."

Frank Murtaw was drenched, depressed, and thoroughly confused. His father's semiautomatic pistol was just a heavy lump in his jacket pocket. He couldn't have worked up the anger to shoot a paper target, much less Ty Daulton. So, he asked himself, what the fuck was he doing out in the woods in the middle of a thunderstorm?

The answer was that he *should have* wanted to shoot Ty. The little bastard had broken into his house, caught him in the shower, and rolled him up in that damn sheet. If all that wasn't reason enough to see red, he didn't know what was.

Problem was, Frank couldn't help but keep thinking how *cool* Ty had been. In fact, had Frank seen the same stuff happen in a movie, he'd have been *rooting* for the bastard.

He'd rescued a woman, for Chrissake! If you looked past all the bruises some asshole had laid on her, you could tell she was a babe, too. Then Ty did CPR on her when she stopped breathing. And carried her out to an ambulance.

Frank was sure that when she healed up she'd have to show Ty a little special gratitude for all that. Shit. Frank wished he'd been the one who had saved her.

But he knew he never would have. Because he knew who lived in the house across the road, where Ty'd had those deliveries sent. Tony fucking Hunt, owner of MicroCosmic, Inc. The guy who had the whole damn town on the run. The guy who Frank's father worked for and was so afraid of that he had pretended to be at the Mayo Clinic getting scoped out for some life-threatening disease when he was really in New York looking for a new job. No way would Frank have gone up against Hunt. Not for all the nookie in Hollywood.

But somehow Ty had used his pizza-and-beer scam to take that babe right away from Mr. Hot Shit. There wasn't much to that runt, Frank knew, but what there was had to be all brains and balls.

The other thing he couldn't get out of his mind was Ty's telling him that now *he* knew how it felt to be humiliated. He tried to deny it, but Ty's words made him realize just what an asshole he'd been. What right had he had to make Ty's life miserable? What had the little guy ever done to him?

Frank thought that the only bright spot for him was that when his old man got a new job, they'd move and he could start over at a new school. Maybe then he could try to act like he didn't have his head up his ass all the time.

He decided to bag this sitting in the rain shit before he drowned. But before he could get to his feet, he saw four dudes with flashlights coming down the trail.

They were all tiny guys, not any bigger than Ty, and even at a distance, with the rain pounding down, Frank could tell none of the four was from Elk River and for damn sure not from Oak Crest. He would have known about any flock of Munchkins.

As they got closer, Frank saw they were all Orientals. And they were looking for something. The one in front was checking all the bushes, pulling them this way and that. What the fuck was that all about? Frank stayed right where he was. Some instinct told him not to let these guys see him.

He was right, too. Because the little fucker at the head of the line found Ty's hole in the ground. Then he barked out something to the others, thrust a gun into each of their hands, and kicked their asses down the hole.

The head guy, who was a lot older than the others and looked as mean as he sounded, went down last. Before he closed the lid, he took a last look around. Frank wanted to run. But a stronger impulse told him to stay right where he was and keep his gun dry.

Maybe there would be a chance for him to be some kind of a hero after all.

79 Gil tracked down Darien and Ty in the tunnels and led them back to HQ. He wanted to discuss strategy.

"Those fuckers are up to something," he told them. "I think most of 'em are rum-dums, but at least one's an honest-to-God dink who knows his stuff. He's not gonna be dumb enough to come down the same hole twice."

Ty said, "Maybe the sneakiest thing he can do, then, is to come down the same hole twice."

Gil had come to respect the kid, so he gave the idea serious thought. But in the end he rejected it. "If we were dealin' with an American here, I'd say maybe. But dinks gotta be *sly*. Gotta put one over on you, come at you some way you'd never expect."

"You think ol' Charlie's lookin' for another hole to crawl through, then?" Darien asked.

"That's exactly what I think, and that's why we gotta split up, so we can be ready for them wherever they come in."

Darien didn't like the idea of letting Ty go off on his own. Gil knew his friend well enough to understand why his face had clouded over.

"The kid's gonna be all right," he said. "Shit, we'll give him an easy post. How about we put him on the Oak Crest line? Fuckin' people up there'd scream for the cops if they ever saw a dink that wasn't pushing a lawn mower."

Darien remembered what Gil had just said about Charlie's doing the unexpected.

"No," he said, "I'll take that position."

Gil shrugged. He didn't care. He was sure he knew the way the dink would come.

"Okay, I'll take the line from City Hall. You know Charlie's biggest thrill had to be stormin' our embassy in Saigon. I bet he comes in right under the flag again."

"I'll take the line from the plant." Ty still felt that was the sneakiest move.

Just before they dispersed, Darien asked, "You know where the hell John is?"

Gil's face was impassive. "I haven't seen him . . . but I got the feelin' he's down here somewhere."

Ron Narder was alone. Clare and Danny had gone to the Church of the Resurrection. Word of a reconciliation service that was in progress there had spread through the town with the efficiency of a jungle tom-tom.

But Narder had stayed home. He just didn't have any hope left that things could work out. When the phone rang, he picked it up, wondering who the hell could be calling.

"This is the sheriff, Chief Deputy. I have a job for you."

"Gee, that's a cryin' shame, Sheriff. I'm here in my sickbed, and now I *really* want to puke."

There was a moment of silence on the line. Then Leen said, "Ron, you got a right to feel the way you do, so all I can do is ask politely: Will you kindly get your ass into uniform, strap on your weapon, and go arrest that bastard Hunt for me?"

"What did you say?"

"Just do it, goddamnit," Leen ordered his stunned deputy. "I promise you'll like the results a whole lot better this time."

"For-tu-na-to!" The name was a curse coming off Tony Hunt's lips. He knew intuitively—instantly—who was responsible for his lights' going out, and he slammed his desk with both fists.

He quickly grabbed the phone to—

No dial tone. The phone was out, too. A growl began at the back of his throat as he groped his way to the stand where his fax machine sat. He snatched up the receiver.

His fax line was also dead.

A howl of animal fury burst past Hunt's bared teeth. He grabbed the fax machine in both hands, raised it over his head, and smashed it against the floor. His mind raged, asking what malignant fate could have allowed this to happen. He'd done everything necessary to win; he hadn't paid the least regard to ethics, morality, or law. Goddamnit, he *had* won!

Except now there was no way for him to accept the terms of surrender.

Which meant the game was over. When Powell was unable to transmit his fax to Hunt, the banker would know that something had gone seriously wrong. He'd understand that if Hunt wasn't waiting to rip the confirmation of his financing from his fax machine it was only because he couldn't. He'd think of Hunt's fairy tale–cum–prophecy of sabotage and pray that Hunt had been vaporized while the plant had been spared.

Regardless of specifics, he'd no more provide financing to Hunt now than a lion would spare a lame gazelle.

Hunt punched his office window so hard the glass shattered and fell to the pavement below. Rain whipped in and spattered against his face . . . and he noticed lights in the distance. The town hadn't lost power, only his plant had.

Fortunato had been able to target him selectively.

Down there in his tunnels, no doubt, he'd cut Hunt's power . . . and, doubtless, he was now on his way here to finish the job.

The thought of himself as prey, oddly, calmed Hunt. It dispelled his fury at what he'd lost, of what might have been, and allowed him to focus clearly on the moment. On survival. He found the gun in his desk drawer and thrust it into his pocket. He wouldn't wait for Fortunato, oh no. That maniac had made it clear there was no way to beat him in Elk River, the goddamned tunnel-riven pesthole.

So Hunt would retreat. Strategically.

He'd wait. Be patient. Recover. Plan from afar. And when the moment was exactly right . . . well, now that he thought of it, it might be fun, someday, to bury Fortunato alive.

Hunt left his MicroCosmic, Inc. office for the last time, having no need to turn the lights out behind him.

Rain battered the windows of Local 274. Jill Baxter awoke. Her face still ached, but her head felt like a working part of her body again, not some distant, hollow reporting center for fuzzy vision and muffled hearing.

The only other person in the local's office was a retired worker who'd come out to show solidarity with his union. He was snoring at the reception desk. Jill nudged Deke Narder's shoulder. The man jerked upright, embarrassed that she'd caught him napping.

"Where is everybody?" she asked.

"Church. Prayin' for miracles. That ain't my style, so I said I'd stay behind and keep an eye on you. You won't mention that I was resting my eyes here, will you?"

Jill shook her head. She looked out at the rain.

"Can you drop me off at the church?" she asked.

Deke said he would and left to get his car, saying he'd pull up to the door so she wouldn't drown.

Jill reached for her blazer. A slip of paper stuck slightly out of one pocket. She unfolded it. It was a note from John.

He'd written that he would knock out Hunt's plant for her, and then he was going to find Tommy's killer. He also told her who the murderer was.

He asked her to light a candle for him if he didn't come back.

80   Darien sat in the dark and waited. He'd been sober for over thirteen years. For all that time, the Elk River tunnels had been his refuge. Now, with these new goddamn dinks crawling around in the one place he'd felt safe, he knew he'd have to find another source of strength.

Maybe those people who relied on their Higher Power had the right idea. Not even Charlie could take Him away from you. Darien smiled as he remembered how you always wanted to be tight with God any time you might get your ass shot off.

Please, Lord, let it be that other cocksucker an' not me, but if it ain't, please, oh please, don't forget about me.

That was the grunt's prayer; he'd said it a million times in the Nam. Now he said it not just for himself but for his brothers John and Gil.

And he made a special plea for Ty.

Take me if you have to, Lord. Damn me if I'm no damn good. But spare that boy, please. He could grow up to be a fine man.

Darien hoped Ty would take his advice and make peace with his daddy. That thought led him to make a vow: If he got through this shit okay, he was going to make peace with *his* son, make things right between them.

Then Darien had no more time for prayer.

Dinks moving in the tunnel one level up. He could hear them. More than one of them, too. Damn, he'd been right. He'd had the feeling those sneaky little mothers'd come this way, and here they were. He gathered his legs beneath him in a crouch. Now, wouldn't ol' Charlie be surprised when he popped up through the trapdoor on them?

John didn't know yet whom he was creeping up on because he couldn't see in the pitch blackness, and with his ears still ringing from the explosion he'd set off, he certainly couldn't hear anything. But up ahead there was something that lived and breathed and gave off body heat, and that something was too big to be anything but a man.

As he edged silently closer, his sense of smell sifted through the array of odors in the tunnel and told him who was in front of him.

Some people might not like to think so, but John knew that different races produced different body odors. And within groups, an individual's scent was also distinct. You spent enough time underground in the dark and you became as much tunnel bloodhound as you did tunnel rat.

He was about to softly whistle a warning, the signature notes of "Under the Boardwalk," when instinct constricted his throat. He and Darien weren't alone.

Goddamn, it was the dinks.

Stevie Tho, the Dream Warrior crawling point, made squishing sounds as he moved. He couldn't help it, he'd gotten soaked. Clomping around in the mud had fucking ruined his Air Jordans.

Now what was he doing? Crawling through some hole in the ground that reeked worse than a skunk's butt. That, and just waiting for somebody to come along in the darkness and waste him. It was too goddamn much.

Well, he had a gun in his hand, and if he was going to die anyway, he didn't see why he shouldn't take down that crazy old gook who'd put him there. The whole thing would have been so simple, Stevie thought, if the bastard had just paid the protection money for his goddamn liquor store like a normal person.

Stevie knew that the gook would open up on him as soon as he turned around. He just hoped he could get off enough rounds to do him in, too, before he got it.

Of course, the other guys in between might get hit in the crossfire, and it'd be too bad if his friend Vinny Vinh got it, but it wouldn't bother

Stevie a bit if that chickenshit Jimmy Giap got drilled right between the eyes.

He saw in the beam of his flashlight that he was coming to the end of this tunnel. It dead-ended just ahead. There was some kind of trapdoor set in the floor, and he'd be fucked if he'd go through that.

Stevie turned on Tran, ready to die.

He did, but not from a gunshot. A big black hand shot up from the trapdoor, turned Stevie's neck in the direction it was going, and just kept turning until it snapped.

Tran was ready for the American. But not for the method of attack. He had expected the Yankee to pop up and shoot, giving Tran a head and a chest as easy targets. Deprived of those, he shot at the only thing he could, the hand that had wrung the hoodlum's neck as easily as if it had belonged to a chicken.

Tran hit the hand with a .38 slug from his Smith and Wesson, and he heard the American scream as the long, black arm swiftly disappeared into the lower level, like an eel retreating into coral.

The two living gangsters in front of Tran were as motionless as their fallen comrade. The tunnel veteran bristled with contempt. They didn't even have the instinct to pounce on a wounded enemy. Tran roughly squeezed past them to take up the pursuit.

Darien jumped up before John could do a thing, and in a seamless sequence there was a shot, a cry of pain, and he was right back down.

John covered the distance to the trapdoor in the blink of an eye. He pushed Darien aside, yanked the lid shut, and fired three rounds through it to give the dinks something to think about.

"*Di-di*, man," he hissed to Darien.

Darien was bleeding and had only three limbs to use, but he *di-died*. John gave him a ten-second head start, then backed down the tunnel, his gun out and ready to blast the next person who came through the trapdoor.

Above, Tran waited. He'd been out of position to shoot when the second American arm popped up. But he'd seen clearly that it had been white. Then the door had slammed shut and shots had been fired through it.

They had their intended effect. Knowing there were two Yankees below, one of whom was unwounded and deadly, Tran waited. Patience *was* one of his virtues.

Of the two gangsters who had been behind him with their guns, only one remained. Vinny Vinh had seen his chance to flee and had taken it. Jimmy Giap remained rooted to the earth.

Tran looked at him and said softly, "No one left to hide behind."

81

That fucker Hunt had given Narder the slip. By ten minutes. At least that was what the guard captain was telling him as they stood at the plant gate with the rain pounding down on them. Narder looked at the man and believed him.

The chief deputy asked the guard captain if the storm had knocked out the plant's power. The guard captain shrugged and replied that they'd lost power just before Mr. Hunt left. He'd had to open the main gate manually, Mr. Hunt had been in such a hurry. Got real mean when the captain had suggested that if he waited a while maybe the power would come back on.

Narder muttered under his breath that it was too damn bad they'd been able to open the gate at all. Shoulders hunched against the rain, he stomped back to his unit. He hated having to make this call.

As screwy as things were, nothing should have surprised Narder, but Leen's reaction did. When he heard the chief deputy's news, he seemed almost happy.

"You know why he's running, don't you, Ron?"

Narder didn't have a clue. And said so.

"Because he killed Billy Shelton."

"What?"

"A witness came forward this morning. She put Hunt at the scene, and the evidence technician lifted prints from Billy's doorknob. I called Hunt to come in so we could check them against his prints. I would've sent somebody to fetch him . . . but we had this manpower shortage, and now we got this weather threat tying everybody up."

The idea that his dereliction of duty had made it possible for Hunt to get away made Narder sick. "Jesus, Sheriff, we gotta put out an APB on this bastard."

"Chief Deputy, the flood threats are pretty much statewide. There aren't a lot of cops on doughnut patrol tonight. The only way we get this bastard is if you or I do it."

"Yes, sir," Narder said grimly. "We'll get him."

"One more thing, Ron."

"Sir?"

"Consider this cocksucker armed and dangerous. Take all appropriate precautions."

Ron Narder knew he'd just been Bonded—given his license to kill. But he thought how much better it'd be to drag Hunt in alive. Throw his ass in the slammer. Let him rot there in his own bile. Every day Tony Hunt spent behind bars, Ron Narder's life would be a little sweeter.

His sending Hunt to prison might even heal his father's broken heart.

Gil was getting impatient.

He refused to believe that he'd been wrong about where the dinks would show up next. It made too much sense to him that they'd hit where they could cause the most embarrassment. So where the hell were they, already?

"Come on, you miserable little fucks," he muttered.

Hearing his own voice shocked him, because he'd never broken silence discipline before. It made him aware that he was getting *recklessly* impatient.

Yet he remained convinced that he'd made the right choice; stupid Charlie just couldn't find the entrance. That left him no choice except to go above ground and get them.

He'd have preferred to fight it out in the tunnels, but he couldn't wait. He headed for the surface.

. . .

Half of the demolition crew Hunt had ordered to blow up the Church of the Resurrection bailed out when they saw the building. The two men weren't practicing Catholics, but they'd been raised in the faith, and once they laid eyes on the place, with those incredible stained-glass windows all lit up and Jesus looking straight down on them, well, no way they were going to bomb it.

It would be like trying to mug God. Not only was it wrong, it was a sure loser. They just took off into the rain.

A third pulled out when he got close enough to hear the singing coming from inside over the downpour. He figured there had to be a few hundred people in there, easy. Blowing up a building was one thing—mass murder was another.

But the last thug cared nothing for human life and believed there was no God for him to fear. He was a man who'd been paid to do a job, and he intended to do it.

As he huddled in the mud with the rain beating down on him, Frank couldn't help but wonder what was going on down that hole. Ty was probably down there somewhere. And all those tiny chinks, or whatever they were, were down there with their guns, too. Of course, Ty'd also had a gun the last time he'd seen him.

Over the rain, he strained to listen for the sounds of gunfire. All those guys with weapons in a small dark hole—it wasn't hard to think somebody might get nervous, pop off a few rounds. But all Frank could hear was the rain beating down on his head.

Finally, his curiosity got the better of him. He crept out of his place of concealment and headed for the hole. Maybe if he lifted the lid, he could hear something. Maybe he should take his own gun out, too. Just in case.

Frank was almost to his objective when Vinnie Vinh popped out of the hole with his flashlight on. Two teenage boys who had never met, who had no basis for either affection or animosity, regarded each other wide-eyed across a distance of ten feet. Each fastened onto the only detail that was immediately significant: the other guy also had a gun.

Vinny, having more experience in such matters, shot first.

But Frank, who was only grazed on his left shoulder, shot best. His bullet hit Vinnie in the middle of his forehead, killing him instantly. When Frank looked down into the dead kid's vacant eyes, he fell to his knees and threw up.

Then, stopping only to pick up the dead guy's flashlight, he ran back behind the bush where he'd concealed himself. Because all he wanted to do was hide.

He knew he had to have some help figuring out what to do next. Turn himself in? Run? Pretend like he'd been home the whole time? What?

Back at HQ, John turned on the lantern and looked at Darien's wound. The dink's round had gone straight through his right palm. The bleeding wasn't bad, but the slug had left a spiderweb of splintered metacarpals in its path.

"Congratulations, bro," John said. "You're out of the war."

Darien grimaced. "Jesus, it hurts."

They turned when they heard someone enter the chamber. Ty.

"You and Gil were right," the boy told Darien. "They aren't going to come from the plant again. So I came back here to see— What happened? You've been shot!"

Despite his pain, Ty's indignation made Darien grin.

"I just gotta get along better with my fellow man," he said. "Especially when the sonofabitch has a gun."

John grinned, too.

Ty said, "This isn't funny. You could've been killed. Don't you guys know how much you mean to me?"

"War isn't funny, Ty," John said simply. "It's killing and dying, shattered lives and broken hearts."

He turned away from the outraged boy to disinfect and bandage Darien's hand.

When he was almost finished, John said, "Ty, we've got to get Darien to the hospital. I want you to go with him."

When Ty didn't answer, both men looked up.

The boy was gone.

Tran practically had to insert his gun barrel into the hoodlum's rectum to move him forward. But move they did. Deeper and deeper into the labyrinth of the tunnels. Through two trapdoors, past three booby traps, and around numerous turns. Tran was sure that he could find his way back to the point at which they'd entered the tunnels, and he was equally sure that the gangster was hopelessly lost.

Feigning anger, Tran hissed at Jimmy Giap to move faster. The next time his gun bumped against the hoodlum's backside he would open a new drain for him, he threatened. Jimmy scurried ahead, and Tran let him go.

He'd leave him to the Americans. They could kill him. Or a booby trap could do the job. Or he could just wander through the tunnels endlessly until he went mad and starved. Of course, there was a chance the young hoodlum might actually find his way out, but Tran seriously doubted that Jimmy possessed either the wits or the strength of character for that.

In utter silence, Tran reversed himself with the suppleness of mercury. Within seconds, he had left Jimmy behind.

He was on his way back to the world above when his curiosity overcame him. These tunnels so resembled the ones at Cu Chi he could scarcely believe that they had been dug by Americans. The memories they evoked in him were vivid to the point of being painful.

He had to explore them for just a little while before he fled. Thirty minutes later, Tran had to admit to himself that there was one important difference between these tunnels and the ones in his homeland.

In his own tunnels, he would never have gotten lost.

Gil slogged through the storm and couldn't find a goddamn dink anywhere. And they should have stuck out like a sore thumb, because there sure as hell wasn't anybody else on the streets. He thought maybe the rain had made them bivouac somewhere for the night. Although, in the old days, the VC had loved to move through the monsoon; it was perfect cover.

Whatever, there was nobody downtown. Gil considered the possibility that Charlie had decided to look for an entrance in Riverfront Park. Maybe the SOBs felt that was the closest thing to a jungle environment they'd find in town.

He didn't want to admit that he didn't know where the hell the enemy would turn up next.

Soaked to the bone, he searched the park. The only thing he saw out of the ordinary was how damn high and fast the river was running. He'd never seen it like that, and, man, the rain just kept making it worse.

In the distance, the church that John's grandpa had built was all lit up like Christmas. CR, chamber number two, lay directly beneath it. Gil couldn't see any way Charlie would know that, but he had nowhere else to turn, so he made his way toward the church.

As he came to within fifteen meters of it, he spotted someone fucking around outside the building. Even through sheets of rain, he could see the guy was way too big to be a dink. But he might as well have been once Gil realized what he was doing.

The sonofabitch was placing an explosive charge against the wall. He was going to bring the place down.

.   .   .

Standing at the back of the church, Jill was increasingly restless. She couldn't seem to get into the spirit of hope and renewal. She tried to join in the songs, but after a few notes her attention drifted.

She looked at the banks of lighted candles at the side of the church. Every one of them had been lit by the time she arrived. She hadn't had the chance to light one for John.

She said a private prayer and hurried outside.

It occurred to Gil that maybe this asshole setting the charge was working with the dinks, that he was their cover man. After all, in the Nam, the VC could hide among their own like fish in the sea, but here, in the middle of America, they'd need help to bring them in and get them out. If that was the case, Gil thought maybe a little interrogation was in order.

He took out his knife and crept up on the guy. With all the racket from the rain the big man never even heard Gil coming. But he finished placing his charge and had started to turn just as Gil arrived. Neither man hesitated.

The bomber lashed out with a backhanded blow, but he was a big man, and Gil had a lot of experience ducking the blows of larger opponents. With one slashing sweep of his knife, he severed the tendons at the back of the man's right knee. The guy went down like a chainsawed tree.

But the fight didn't go out of him. He clawed inside his coat for a gun. Again, Gil and his knife were too fast. The tunnel rat lashed out at the man's wrist, slicing through muscle and severing a vein. The bomber forgot all about his gun. He clamped his left hand around his right wrist, trying to stop his blood—and his life—from flowing out into the mud.

Gil knew he wasn't going to make it. He'd die where he lay. The cut was too deep, and his weakening fingers too inadequate a tourniquet.

And the sonofabitch wasn't going to be answering any questions, either. He was getting old, Gil thought. In his glory days, he never would have been so clumsy that he had to kill a guy before he questioned him. Almost as an afterthought, Gil plucked the detonator from the plastic explosive.

He looked back at the guy, and sure enough he was dead, had died looking straight up into the rain.

And then Gil realized that he wasn't alone. There had been a witness to the killing. Standing on the path that ran alongside the church, not forty feet away, looking at him with his knife in his hand and the corpse at his feet, was that woman lawyer. Tommy's shyster, John's squeeze.

Gil thought for a second that he should explain that he'd just saved the church and everybody in it, but he saw it was more than the stiff in front of him that was bothering her. Somehow she knew he had more blood on his hands.

At the howl of an approaching police siren, Gil returned to the world where he did his best work. Where he was a superstar.

Turning and running, he used an entrance in Riverfront Park, and as he closed the trapdoor, the rain-swollen river climbed over its banks and pushed toward the church . . . and the tunnels.

82

Highway 98 was flooded. The creek running alongside it, fed by the Elk River, had reached flood stage an hour earlier. The overflow had turned a low-lying stretch of road into a small but growing lake.

Hunt considered trying to drive through it—until a fork of lightning lit the sky. Then he saw the cab of an abandoned pickup truck that had tried to make the crossing: the bed of the vehicle was underwater. He shifted his Lexus into Reverse and brought it around the way he'd come. But by that time there was water on the road in that direction, too.

Hunt didn't hesitate. He floored it, and the Lexus shot forward. He'd come down the road only moments before, and he knew the water ahead couldn't be as deep as what lay in the other direction.

Still, his knuckles whitened on the wheel as the road dipped and the car lost contact with it. Suddenly, Hunt had a $65,000 hydroplane. Water rushed over the hood of the Lexus as if it were the bow of ship. When the wave hit the windshield, it overwhelmed the wipers utterly. He had no idea where he was going.

But he got there with a bang. The impact was hard enough to activate the airbag. His hands were blasted off the steering wheel and he was smacked with a faceful of plastic pillow. He couldn't see a damn thing.

But he felt the wheels bite solid ground again, still moving. He jammed on the brakes, hoping the ABS would keep him from spinning out of control—and that he was clear of the flooded area.

As the car shuddered to a remarkably straight stop, Hunt flung the deflated airbag aside. The heavy car's momentum had carried it through the trough; hitting the road's upgrade on the far side had activated the airbag. He was still on the road and hadn't been hurt. But the engine had died, and it wouldn't turn over. Too much water had gotten under the hood.

Hunt looked out his rear window. The body of water from which he'd just extricated himself was sweeping forward to reclaim its prey. With a sharp curse, he snatched his gun from the glove compartment and pushed open his door.

Bent against the downpour, he started back toward town on foot. He thought he might soon need gills to survive . . . and that was when the idea struck him. It was childlike in its simplicity.

If your car won't float, steal a boat.

Orville Leen sat in a patrol unit at the corner of Lincoln and First. His engine was running and the windshield wipers thunked back and forth trying to clear away the rain, succeeding for only the blink of an eye with every pass. The sheriff, having the advantage of a police radio, knew all about which roads were flooded, which was basically all of them. Every one leading out of town, at any rate.

That meant Hunt was trapped in Elk River, unless he'd gotten lucky.

A bolt of lightning split the sky, making the air dance with malignant yellow diamonds. The accompanying clap of thunder never came. Leen found that disturbing.

It made a man wonder about unpredictable circumstances. Especially a man who'd had murder on his mind—and then minutes ago changed his mind.

When Ron Narder had brought Hunt to the morgue to view the remains of his henchman, the bastard had had a nasty little surprise for the sheriff. Hunt had shown the sheriff copies of account deposits totaling almost two hundred thousand dollars. The accounts were in the name of Orville Leen.

Not that these funds had been left to linger at Riverman Savings. No, wire records showed they'd been transferred to a bank in the Cayman Islands.

The signatures for all the transactions were genuine.

There was no reason why they shouldn't be. Orville Leen had banked at

Riverman Savings for years. The institution had several legitimate copies of his signature.

Hunt had informed the sheriff that he could claim he'd been framed, of course, but he'd still have to defend himself in court, and he'd be lucky to get acquitted.

Because it wasn't unheard of for cops to take money under the table. And with the kind of figures involved here, who wouldn't believe that Hunt hadn't owned Leen, down to his dental fillings, all along?

Certainly not the people at Local 274. Which in turn would raise the issue of what role Leen had played in Tommy Boyle's murder and the cover-up thereof.

For an hour or two, the sheriff had mulled the possibility of breaking into Riverman Savings, doing a black bag job, and removing all the forged evidence that he'd been in Hunt's pocket. He knew he could gain entry to the building, could probably find any paper records with his name on them, too. But computer records were another matter entirely. If Hunt had been thorough, he'd used the institution's database to build his frame, and pulling phony numbers from a computer was beyond Leen.

The sheriff gave far greater consideration to the idea of just plain fighting Hunt's setup in court. If it took every last cent he had, so be it. But if it impoverished him, and he wound up in jail anyway . . . well, to hell with that!

The thing was, he could see it happening that way. He might have been only the sheriff of a hick county in the Midwest, but he'd seen more than enough of the justice system to know how it worked. Money and politics determined the outcome of a trial far more often than right or wrong.

But if Tony Hunt died before he could hang Leen out to dry, that would be the end of it. Leen didn't see anybody coming out of the woodwork to pick up Hunt's blackmail scheme. Which meant Orville Leen could retire in peace, and that was the only thing he wanted. He'd had enough of sheriffing to last him the rest of his life. He wanted to go somewhere warm. Someplace where it didn't rain.

But even the prospect of retirement had been bittersweet for Leen. It galled him that Hunt's coercion was going to turn a decent man, a career law enforcement officer, into a killer. But he hadn't seen any other way out . . .

. . . until a half hour before, when Ronnie Narder had radioed him with the news about Hunt's having left his plant in a big hurry. Then two very basic questions hit the sheriff squarely between the eyes: Why was Hunt on the run? And why now?

He couldn't have known that Leen intended to arrest him. The sheriff hadn't told anyone of his plans except the chief deputy, and the Chicago

Cubs would win the World Series—several times—before Ron Narder would sell out.

So, what had made Hunt take off right when Leen had wanted him the most? Maybe the man had troubles of his own? The very thought brought a tight grin to the sheriff's face.

He grabbed his radio microphone and called his chief deputy.

"Ron, call City Electric and see what other power outages there are besides the plant. Over."

"Did that, Sheriff. WABE is off the air, but that's because their tower took a direct lightning strike. Otherwise, the grid's holding up like a champ. Everyone's got power. Over."

"Everyone except Hunt," Leen mused aloud. "Well, let's keep looking for him, Ron." And then the sheriff amended his previous order. "But if you can, try'n bring him in alive. Over."

There was a static-filled pause on the sheriff's speaker. Then Ron Narder replied. "That's my general inclination, Sheriff. Give 'em a chance before I drill 'em. Over and out."

Leen let the chief deputy have his little dig. He was busy entering new factors into the equation that would ultimately decide his actions.

Hunt's plant hadn't lost power due to the storm or by accident. No, somebody had turned the man's lights off, and that had scared him. Enough to make him run.

Make him run for good?

Leen chuckled grimly. He'd run himself, as fast and far as he could, if he had John Fortunato after him. Especially if he'd killed Tommy Boyle. And the sheriff had seen in Fortunato's eyes that he knew who Tommy's killer was. Hunt? Why else was he leaving his business behind—and who else beside Fortunato could have sabotaged Hunt's plant like that?

The sheriff would surely like to know how a man who made his living taking pictures could do all the things Fortunato had done, but right then it was enough that he was giving Leen an unintended helping hand.

If Hunt were still in town, Leen would find him. He'd let Hunt know that two could play the frame-up game, tell him what he had in store for the bastard regarding Billy Shelton's death. If that weren't enough to get Hunt's hooks out of the sheriff—Leen would then tell Hunt he'd let Fortunato have him. Maybe he'd truss Hunt up like a sacrificial lamb somewhere and let Fortunato cut him to pieces.

The sheriff was *sure* that would persuade the sonofabitch to light out for parts unknown and never look back. In fact, once the roads cleared, Leen would even make certain Hunt got out of the county safely. He'd do it because he'd come to respect Fortunato and didn't want to see him go to prison. Not for killing a shit like Hunt. Bastard wasn't worth a murder rap. Not if you had any choice in the matter.

Leen put his car in gear. Staring intently through the storm, he headed up to Oak Crest to see if he could find the man at his fancy house.

He wanted to get this damn thing over with.

"Damnit, Bill," the deputy shouted over the downpour, "this isn't the Red Sea here, and you aren't about to part it like Moses."

Bill Deeley refused to leave his church.

Everyone else had been evacuated. Including the stiff the deputies had found. And the bomb they'd found next to the body. Who could worry about preserving the crime scene when the crime scene, the church, and everything else along the river was about to go for a swim?

All the soaking-wet cop had to do to complete his job was get this one last madman the hell out of there, but Deeley wouldn't be budged.

"You go, Joe," Bill told the deputy. "I have a few more prayers to say."

The deputy was struck speechless. Water streamed down his face and into his open mouth. What did you say to a man who believed so much in the power of prayer that he wasn't afraid to die?

He shook his head. "I hope one of those prayers is for you, Bill. God bless you."

The deputy left at a trot, raising a splash of water with each footfall.

"May God bless and keep us all," Bill Deeley murmured. Then he turned and walked to the front of the church. Here the sounds of the storm were muted—by the work of a master artisan or the grace of God, Deeley couldn't say. He knelt before the altar and bowed his head in prayer.

He was utterly convinced that this church embodied the town's faith in itself, as well as its faith in God. He was sure that if the Church of the Resurrection was lost, the ability of the town to survive would also be swept away.

John went back into the tunnels. To get Darien to go to the hospital, he'd had to promise that before he did anything else he'd find Ty and force the boy to go above ground. So Tommy's killer would have to wait a little while longer. John could live with that. Saving lives came before taking them.

Besides, the extra time would let his hearing clear up some more. He felt that it was halfway back to normal. The ringing was fading.

Crawling noiselessly through the underground blackness, tracing a passage where man was never meant to be, much less fight, he felt an old familiar feeling come over him: fatalism. You did your best to stay alive and to protect your buddies. Sometimes your efforts were good enough, other times you were left grieving, and one inevitable time it would be your turn to go.

There was no rhyme or reason to the selection process that anyone could discern; the best you could hope for was that there would be some answers when you got to the finish line. That, as much as anything, was why there were no atheists in foxholes.

John had promised to get Ty out of the tunnels, but Darien had understood implicitly that he'd meant only that he would do his best, die trying if necessary. There was no guarantee, however, that anyone who was under the earth of Elk River that night wouldn't remain there permanently.

Ty made his way cautiously toward the tunnel leading to Oak Crest. He moved without a light. At intervals of one meter, he stopped, listened, sniffed, and waited to feel any kind of vibration that would indicate the presence of another human being, especially a hostile human being.

When he'd first left Darien and John he'd moved with far greater speed; he knew the tunnel system cold by now, and Gil had briefed him and Darien on all the positions where he'd be placing booby traps. There had been no reason for delay. He'd been so damn angry that Darien had been shot, all he'd wanted to do was hit back.

Then reason asserted itself. His intellect doused his emotions. Whoever shot Darien hadn't known he was Ty's friend, and certainly hadn't shot him because of that friendship. Darien had been shot because the other guy had been afraid Darien would shoot him if he got the chance.

War wasn't personal. Only survival was.

Which made Ty remember, chillingly, that there were men with guns nearby who would kill *him* at the first opportunity. He also recalled Darien's telling him that VC sappers had sometimes turned the GIs' own claymore mines on them so that firing the devices had become acts of suicide. Who was to say that Charlie wasn't busy right now screwing with Gil's booby traps? Or that he hadn't set some of his own?

So Ty moved very carefully, because things could change without your knowing about it. And then he stopped moving entirely, because suddenly, and with complete certainty, he knew how Doolan had disappeared.

He'd vanished through the hole that wasn't there.

. . .

The tunnels beneath Elk River were occupied by five men with guns: John Fortunato, Gil Velez, Ty Daulton, Tran Chi Thanh, and Jimmy Giap.

Among them, they occupied four different tunnel segments on two different levels over a distance of slightly more than a kilometer.

All of them heard the sudden huge roar.

Followed by the hiss of rushing water.

Deputy Joe Carney couldn't have gotten any wetter running through a car wash than he was right now. He stood a block to the east, upstream, of the Church of the Resurrection, staring through the endless torrents of water at the lights of the building. Joe just hadn't been able to abandon Bill Deeley to the consequences of his faith. He was also more than a little curious as to what the outcome of such fervid belief might be.

If the river ate away the foundation of the church and the building collapsed, there would be nothing he could do. But if the water just pushed through the building, well, he'd had two years on the University of Indiana swim team before he'd had to leave school, and . . .

Jesus, there it was!

It wasn't so much a wall of water; it was more like a dam somewhere had been broached, expanding a little creek into a real river. Except the Elk River had averaged sixty feet across to begin with. Now the surge of water racing southwest, downstream, looked twice that wide.

The wave hit the church with enough force to send spray flying four stories high into the night air. Then the damnedest—no, the most miraculous—thing Joe Carney had ever seen happened.

The water started to disappear.

Just like someone had pulled the plug in a bathtub. The flood still covered the church grounds, to who knew what depth, but, in the light from the church, he could see a whirlpool in the water where it was being sucked into the ground. All that incredible overflow was actually draining.

The deputy looked the other way. The pavement and asphalt glistened in the rain-gauzed light of streetlamps, but the floodtide that should be racing across Riverfront Drive toward businesses and homes—and him, for that matter—never got past the park. And he'd swear he could hear it draining into the ground.

It was as if someone had dug a secret flood-control system.

But, hell, that was nuts.

Jill Baxter hadn't said a word to the cops at the church about the murder she'd seen or the man she'd seen standing over the dead body with a bloody knife. She'd allowed herself be evacuated with the others. But she hadn't gone very far.

She, too, saw the miracle that saved the church. Unlike Joe Carney, however, Jill knew exactly what had happened. She also knew that John was most likely still underground—she'd sent him there to sabotage Hunt's plant—and her heart lodged in her throat. The thought that the man she loved, the man who'd saved her from death, would drown in darkness because of her was more than she could bear.

She started to tremble when she realized what she had to do. She had to find John . . . she had to warn him . . .

She had to go down in the tunnels.

The covers to the tunnel entrances in Riverfront Park had been unable to withstand the tremendous power of the Elk River's surge. A force strong enough to uproot trees had ripped them open as if they'd been made of papier mâché. At that point, the tunnels had indeed acted as a giant drainage system.

The clay soil through which the tunnels snaked was sufficiently porous to withstand the initial inundation by letting the water filter directly through to the subsoil. But that stratum was already near saturation point from hours of heavy rainfall.

Army engineers might once have tried to flood VC tunnels with water from the Saigon River at the rate of eight hundred gallons a minute without result, but now, every second, nature was pouring huge multiples of that figure into the tunnels of Elk River.

The result was inevitable. When the soil beneath the tunnels could absorb no more water, the inflow began to bubble up from the subsoil like a resurrected river and began a slow but inexorable spread throughout the system.

The flood above had abated.

The one below was just beginning.

83 Tony Hunt wasn't home. Orville Leen knew that for a fact because he'd shot the lock off the man's front door and searched the place from top to bottom. As he stepped out of the huge house and back into the storm, the sheriff thought maybe the bastard had gotten away after all.

He tried to decide if that was good or bad for him. Good, if Hunt just kept on running. Less good, but not so bad really, if he came back and tried to pick up where he'd left off. Then the sheriff would just put his plan into effect.

Splashing back to his patrol unit, Leen slid behind the wheel, cranked the engine over, and turned on the wipers. He was tempted to go home and just fall into bed. He had things figured now. He didn't have to put himself to any more bother.

But then he thought how that would look. He'd ordered everybody else back to duty. How could he just ignore an emergency situation? Sheriff Orville Leen had become much more sensitive to the way his actions appeared to people after making such a mess of things with Tommy Boyle.

He sighed with fatigue, then made his way carefully down the hill to Elk River.

As long as he had to be out, he might as well keep looking for Tony Hunt.

By the time Hunt reached Riverfront Park, he was waterlogged. But finally, across the rain-drenched park, he saw his destination, the marina.

Somehow, its lights were still on. Several craft had been swamped right in their slips, but a dozen others still tugged against the restraints of their moorings. He didn't know shit about sailing, but Krieger had showed him once how to hotwire an ignition system. He was sure he could start one of the powerboats and pilot it to St. Louis.

The last obstacle between him and freedom was the expanse of the park. The ground looked like a giant, sucking mudhole.

He took off his shoes, peeled off his socks, and rolled up his pantlegs. He was just stuffing his socks into his coat pocket when he saw the flashing light of a sheriff's patrol car approach. He took his gun out of the pocket he'd just put the socks into and slipped the weapon inside the shoe he held in his right hand.

Then he turned to see Sheriff Leen getting out of his car with his gun in his hand.

The ruins of the Fortunato house were a pile of jutting, blackened timbers. The rain had washed away the stink of charred wood but added to the atmosphere of despair. Nothing would rise here again that was half so grand as what had been lost.

As she ran toward the site, Jill felt a pang in her heart. She'd spent only a few nights in the house, but all of them had been memorable. Talking the night through with John, making love beside the fireplace, fighting their way out of an inferno . . .

She scrabbled across the debris as quickly as she could, making sure she didn't impale herself on any sharp projection of wood, metal, or glass. She cleared the wreckage and went directly to where John had told her there was an entrance to the tunnels. It took her a moment to push the shrubbery aside and locate the trapdoor. She barked a knuckle getting it open.

She heard water moving below.

Attached to the underside of the trapdoor was a flashlight. She removed it from its brackets and shone the light into the tunnel. Directly below her, it was still dry. But she could hear the water coming closer, boiling up from the lower elevations.

With her heart beating like a trip-hammer, she remembered the words her father had spoken to her in the dream: "Any troubles you face, I'll be right there with you."

"I need you now, Daddy," Jill Baxter said, drawing on all the courage she had.

Then she lowered herself into the blackness.

Gil moved with the speed of a rat through a long-ago-mastered maze. Of all those in the tunnels, he'd been the closest to the river when the system had been breached. He understood intuitively what had happened and immediately sought the higher reaches. He slipped past the booby traps he'd set with the ease of a combat master.

Ahead, he heard the hysterical clawing of a kit. The young fox was frantically trying to escape the ambush cage Gil had built for it. Along with every rat, mole, and other burrower in the tunnels, the little fox wanted to flee the oncoming water.

Normally, Gil wouldn't have given a second's thought to saving the animal, but now he realized he could use it. He plucked the whole cage from the tunnel ceiling, turned the opening to face uphill, and let the kit make its escape.

The little fox would be his point man. If the VC were in the tunnels, as Gil hoped and prayed, they wouldn't know what the hell to make of the desperate creature dashing its way out of the darkness. The dinks'd open up, pinpoint their position for Gil, and, *boom*, he'd light 'em up like clay pigeons.

But there was no yelp of anyone taken by surprise; there was no gunfire. That was okay, too. It told Gil that the tunnel ahead was clear.

A damn good thing, actually, since the water behind him was getting closer.

Jimmy Giap thought he was going to lose his mind. He didn't know which way to turn, which way to go. All he had was a flashlight and a gun, and neither was going to do him a damn bit of good when the water got to him. He was going to drown, trapped like—

Rats!

Hundreds of them. And other animals, too. Fucking things he couldn't even identify. They'd just come around a curve in the tunnel at him like a herd of stampeding cattle. Jimmy screamed in terror. He flung himself flat on his face and covered his head with his arms.

A horde of rodent feet raced over his head, back, and legs. He tried to lie still while the nightmare tide rolled over him, but a muscle in his leg twitched and needle-sharp teeth immediately bit into his ankle.

Jimmy screamed again. Fortunately, he was bitten only once as the pack's terrified momentum carried it swiftly along.

Unfortunately, the furious mass of vermin set off an explosive booby trap several meters up the tunnel . . . and the crazed survivors came racing right back at Jimmy.

Though the explosion had been thunderous, Jimmy's eardrums had been saved by the fact that he'd had his arms covering his ears. But he still heard the pack's panicked shrieks as it returned.

It ran over him again.

And once more, as the rodents realized the water still threatened them from below, they reversed course. Making Jimmy their doormat a third time.

Wailing under the frantic scurrying of a thousand sharp claws, the former gang-banger and terror of his neighborhood wondered in self-pity: What? What have I ever done to deserve this?

The other four men now in the tunnels beneath Elk River had unknowingly crept close enough to each other to hear the explosion set off by the rats.

Tran listened intently, hoping to hear the Americans move in the direction of the blast. He was still lost. He needed to find someone who could lead him out of the tunnels. When he didn't hear anyone else, he crawled off in the direction of the explosion. He reasoned that if any of the Americans had been near the detonation they would be deafened, easy for him to capture. He could also easily envision that young cheeseburger-eating fool he'd abandoned setting off the booby trap; he would have to thank the young hoodlum's spirit if he caught the Yankees by surprise as they examined his remains.

Gil's thinking proceeded along remarkably similar lines: One of the dinks, a cherry, had set off the mechanical ambush. Who knew how many of them it'd got? But he'd bet that Mr. Badass, the genuine VC who'd returned his fire, was still alive. That's why he wasn't going to risk a direct approach to the point where he was sure the booby trap went off.

There was another way to get behind them, but it meant doubling back, going *toward* the water before he could turn around. Gil didn't hesitate for a second. This was a better game of Charlie 'n' Joe than he ever could have imagined.

. . .

John, too, assumed that the intruders had triggered the blast. He thought
he knew where any survivor might be going, and he definitely knew how to
get there ahead of him. But he had to go through the U-shaped water
trap.

When he emerged dripping from that vile immersion his ears no longer
rang. They sloshed. And the water in his head was the only thing John
could hear.

Ty knew where the dinks had to be going: uphill. Any idiot, much less an
experienced tunnel fighter, would know that if you were threatened by
water from below, you looked for higher ground.

That meant Oak Crest. It was the highest point in the system, and even
if they didn't know the name of their destination, or just how to get there,
that's where following the upward slope of the tunnels would lead them.

They'd soon intersect the main tunnel to Oak Crest, keep going uphill
till they found the exit in the woods of the exclusive enclave . . . and
would they wait there to ambush anybody else who had to use the same
exit to escape?

Ty had given up the notion of avenging Darien. After all, his friend was
still alive, and he just didn't have it in him to be some kind of berserk
killing machine. Maybe he wasn't cut out to be *any* kind of a soldier. But
he wasn't going to let the dinks get to Oak Crest and set up an ambush.

He was going to get there first.

Jimmy Giap figured maybe all those furry little fuckers who'd run over him
knew something he didn't. After all, this was their turf. If the shit started
flying back home on his turf, *he'd* know which way to run. So, it only stood
to reason that they knew the way to get the hell out of this mess.

Trying to ignore the pain from the bites he'd suffered, Jimmy crawled
off in the same direction the pack had fled. Some of those fuckers were
wounded, too. They'd left a trail of blood to follow.

Jimmy hadn't gone very far before he felt his gorge rise. He saw that the
floor and walls of the tunnel, lit by the beam of his flashlight, were plastered with blood, guts, eyeballs, bones, and all sorts of shit.

Jimmy held his breath and plowed through the mess. Stuff squished
between his fingers; a jagged shard of bone jabbed his left palm. He could
no longer control his gag reflex: He added his vomit to the muck.

But he made it through. And beyond the site of the explosion there was still a trail of blood for him to follow.

Goddamn, he thought giddily, I'm going to make it.

Seventy seconds later, having unknowingly followed Jimmy, Tran saw the remains of the vermin and realized that they had set off the charge. No human had been responsible, but . . .

Tran sensed someone coming up from behind him, just around a curve . . .

And he heard a trapdoor being thrown open ahead of him. He knew without question that neither the man behind him nor the one ahead was his former lackey. They were Americans.

He was trapped.

Jill poked her head into the HQ chamber in the slim hope that John might be there. He wasn't. She was about to withdraw when her eye settled on a handgun that somebody had left atop a crate. It was a revolver, the kind she'd seen John use.

She knew how to use the weapon herself. Like many urban professional women, Jill had been to a shooting range to take target practice. She'd even considered buying her own handgun. She never had, but a strong visceral impulse told her not to pass this weapon by. She grabbed it, and just holding it in her hand reassured her.

But what happened next terrified her.

The beam from her flashlight dimmed. She looked down at the bulb in disbelief. Its power was fading right before her eyes. Her eyes darted around the chamber at the stacks of crates, but none of them was marked "batteries." Or "flashlights."

There was the electric lantern, but that was too big and clumsy to carry while crawling, and, ironically, it would throw too much light. It could make her a target.

The sibilant roar of the flood grew louder, closer.

Jill had no choice. She shoved the gun into her waistband, turned out the flashlight, and crawled out into the tunnels.

84 "Come along, Mr. Hunt," the sheriff said. "I'll put you in the back of my car where it's nice and dry. Then we'll have a little talk about you, me—and John Fortunato."

Hunt didn't need to hear another word. As a blinding bolt of lightning tore across the sky, he shot the sheriff with the gun hidden in his shoe.

Sheriff Leen lay on his back in the mud with the rain beating down on his face and no earthly idea of what had happened to him. It didn't matter, though. Everything he'd ever known was going away, slipping right past him . . . and a whole new consciousness swept over him in a rush.

Hunt looked down at the sheriff. Now he'd killed two men. Then he glanced at the shoe he held in his right hand. It was no good to him any longer with the bullet hole in it. Well, he'd have to make do. He stole the sheriff's shoes.

He only hoped they would fit.

The moment he flipped the trapdoor open John knew he had someone just downhill of him. A second later his nose told him it was nobody whose scent he knew . . . but there was something familiar about the odor nevertheless.

The man nearby was Vietnamese.

Charlie.

John stayed where he was, crouching in the entrance to the lower level. The intruder wouldn't be able to shoot John from where he was, and if the guy rolled a grenade toward him, John could slam the trapdoor shut.

If he heard it coming.

After a moment, John realized that Charlie wasn't moving. He wasn't advancing, he wasn't retreating, and John was damn sure that the guy was aware of his presence, too.

Which meant . . .

"Gil, you back there?" John called out.

"How about this for a game of Charlie 'n' Joe?" Gil responded from the darkness.

Caught between the two Yankees, able to see neither of them, armed only with a pistol, Tran waited. He told himself to stay calm and listen to the Americans. If they were foolish enough to talk instead of strike, he might learn something to his advantage.

But this time it was very hard to be patient.

"Whaddya say, man," Gil asked, "whoever dings the dink wins?"

"I'm more interested in you than him," John replied.

"Why's that?" Gil asked.

"We need to talk about why you killed Tommy."

Jill crept forward through the blackness. She fought back panic as the din of the rising flood hissed louder in her ears. If she lost control, she would drown for sure. She forced herself to think of her father. He was down here with her: He wouldn't let her die.

John told her he used all of his other senses as he moved through darkness. So she tried to overcome her sight dependency. She tried to hear something besides the goddamn water. She brushed her fingertips along the clay as she crawled, hoping her sense of touch might reveal something. She sniffed, trying to notice something more than an undifferentiated stench.

She smacked headfirst into a dead end.

She hit hard enough to see stars, and instantly the fear welled up in her that she was trapped. To backtrack would mean going right into the flood-waters. And she wouldn't have to go far, either.

She pulled her flashlight out of her coat pocket. She had no choice but to *see* if there was any way out. Even if it meant using the last of the batteries' reserves. She switched the light on.

The beam yielded the illumination of a dying firefly, and a second later it expired irretrievably. Still, it had been enough.

Jill had seen the trapdoor above her and the intersecting corridor to her right. She could have discovered either merely by reaching out, but that idea had never occurred to her. She was hopelessly dependent on her eyesight, and now she was deprived of it.

She took the uphill choice; the water would first have to fill the branching tunnel and then climb to get her. She eased open the trapdoor, climbed to the higher level, and gently lowered the door behind her. With the hatch in place, the sound of the torrent diminished.

Which let her hear something else. Somewhere up ahead, there were voices. They were too far away for her to understand the words or identify the speakers. But the muffled sounds gave her a point of reference, a destination, the hope that one of them might be John.

As she crept closer, she recognized who she was hearing. It was John . . . and Gil.

Gil was saying, "You know, man, I've wondered ever since the Nam who'd be better if we really went at it, me or Johnny fuckin' Fortune. So what I think maybe we oughta do is smoke the dink and not care who gets credit for him. Then, once and for all, we settle who's the best down here, you or me. How's that grab ya?"

As quietly as she could, Jill slipped the .38 out of her waistband and inched forward.

85

The rain seemed to wash the very pigment from Tony Hunt's skin; his fierce gray eyes stood out like tombstones against a chalk-white skull. He was covered with mud up to his knees from crossing the quagmire that was Riverfront Park. His impossibly sodden suit clung so closely to his body it looked as if he wore a layer of bark.

But by the time he made it to the marina he was smiling.

He saw just the boat he wanted. For one thing, it was berthed at the end of the dock, pointing outward. He wouldn't have to try backing up. Just take it right out into the river.

It was the right size, too. Twenty feet or so. Big enough to feel safe, small enough to maneuver. It even had a spotlight so he could see where the hell he was going.

Hunt bent and unsnapped the tarp. He hopped down into the boat and went straight to the driver's console. He reached underneath a panel to find the ignition wires, and located something even better. The key. He put it in the ignition and turned it. The motor roared. He looked at the fuel gauge. Full. He snapped on the spotlight and a cone of brilliant white light illuminated the roiling waters of the river. He was ready to go. Good-fucking-bye, Elk River.

Except he couldn't free the lines. The wet nylon ropes that held the boat to the dock were slippery as hell, and they'd been knotted thoroughly.

Hunt laughed. If that was Fate's idea of tripping him up . . .

"You'll have to do better than that, motherfucker!" he shouted fiercely at the sky.

Somewhere in this marina, in one of these boats, was a knife, a pair of scissors, a piece of glass he could break, something he could use to cut through the lines. He *was* going to get away.

He returned quickly to the boat's control panel. There was a drawer directly below the ignition switch. The drawer was full of all sorts of crap: charts of the river—sunscreen!—first aid kit, a water-safety manual . . . and a utility knife. Just what the doctor ordered. Didn't even have to search another boat.

Hunt returned to the lines and sawed his way through them. As soon as the last fiber parted, the boat bobbed free, heading out into the swollen river and downstream as if it had a will of its own.

He scuttled back to the steering wheel, seated himself, and hit the control to lower the motor into the water. The small boat shot forward. Squinting against the rain, he pointed the bow toward the Mississippi. Free at last!

Fortunato would never get him now.

He tossed the gun he'd used to kill the sheriff overboard. That took care of the murder weapon. There'd been no witnesses. He'd get rid of Leen's shoes as soon as he bought new ones.

True, he had failed here, but he'd dipped into the Riverman Savings till to the tune of five million dollars, and that money he *had* wired to a Caribbean bank. He'd sit in the sun somewhere and reflect on all the things he'd done wrong. He'd consider how to get back at Fortunato, or whether that would even be worth his while. Whatever, he wouldn't make the same mistakes again.

And before you knew it, he'd be back on top.

Jimmy Giap couldn't believe it.

Those fucking rats had screwed him. He'd followed them and followed them, making certain that he never lost the blood trail, absolutely sure that the little fuckers were going to get him out of this, and now look where he was.

Stuck in a dead end.

Oh, there was a way out for the rats and their four-legged friends. It was a shaft about four inches wide that ran on a slant to the surface, which had to be a good fifteen feet up. He could see the sky and hear the rain falling; he could even feel a sweet-smelling breeze on his face. But no way in hell he could get back to the real world from where he was.

Worse, he was more lost than ever and had no idea of what to do next.

Jimmy Giap howled in torment.

He shot off his gun, and that made him feel better. He kept shooting until some instinct told him to save his last round. He might need it for something practical.

Buoyed now by the joy of exercising his trigger finger, he crawled off to look for a way out. He didn't know it yet but the vermin had led him uphill, and he wasn't far from the Oak Crest entrance to the system that he'd been forced into at gunpoint.

Outside of which, Frank Murtaw still huddled, armed with his father's semiautomatic.

Tony Hunt did just fine while he was on the Elk River, but once he got to the Mississippi he knew immediately that he was in trouble. The Big River wasn't just rolling along a mile wide, it was roaring, and for all Hunt could tell it was as wide as an ocean. The current seized his boat as if it were a wood chip in whitewater.

He was trying to maintain a sense of control when a huge three-forked flash of lightning showed him that while he was the only boat in sight, he was far from the only traffic on the river.

The raging waters had swept everything within their reach into the Mississippi, and, eerily lit by the lightning, the image was one that Bosch might have painted: the stainless steel sarcophagus of an Airstream RV bobbed along upside down; cows, drowned and swollen, passed by, the macabre parody of a livestock show; and a forest of trees, large and small, whole and shattered, coursed through the churning water more sinister than crocodiles.

Tony Hunt knew that if he hit *any* of those things his boat would sink and he would drown.

The sky and the river returned to blackness, leaving him to be guided only by the slender beam of his spotlight. Now the deadly water hazards were reduced to fantastic dancing shapes, each barely glimpsed before it disappeared, each more incredible than the last.

Hunt gasped as he saw that he was bearing down on a white horse. The animal was swimming with all its might, struggling to reach the invisible shore. The horse turned its head toward the boat, its eyes rolling insanely. Hunt knew he must swerve, but he was riveted by the animal's plight. The horse disappeared under a foaming wave seconds before the boat would have struck it.

Hunt's hands were slick on the wheel, and not just from the rain. Fear extended icy fingers through his guts.

All right, he told himself, just hold on. If the river's a fucking nightmare, get the fuck off the river. Get to shore and take it from there.

He angled obliquely for where he thought the near bank of the river should be. He hadn't gone far before something clawlike reached out of the darkness and ripped the flesh off his cheek.

A new jolt of fear surged through him, and he hastily veered back toward the river's middle. He swung the spotlight around to see what had cut him. It was a tree. Several branches, stripped of their leaves, stuck up out of the violent water like great grasping claws.

He shifted the spotlight forward, thinking maybe he could get ahead of the downed tree, but another raced along in front of it. And another in front of that.

Hunt swiveled the light to the other side of the boat. There was a line of trees on that side, too. This was madness.

In desperation, Hunt tried to come hard about, but the current slammed the boat broadside, nearly knocking him off his feet. The craft took on water as it tilted crazily. He reflexively jerked the bow around, once more heading downstream.

There was nowhere to go but straight ahead.

There *had* to be a way out. . . some new tactic . . . some . . .

Then he heard the singing. Above the wind and the rain and the roar of the river, he heard a smooth, crooning baritone that froze his soul. Unable to help himself, Hunt directed the spotlight forward.

He saw an island, a spit of mud flooded until it was not much bigger than a manhole cover, but big enough to support a storm-ravaged tree thirty feet high.

Krieger stood in the uppermost branches, staring at him, grinning ear to ear, and singing. Singing to Hunt.

"Should old acquaintance be forgot . . ."

Hunt frantically cranked the wheel hard left, hoping to push one of the barrier trees aside. But the limbs held him at bay, reached out and pushed the boat back on course. The same thing happened when he tried to break through on the right. He cut the motor, but the rushing current drove him relentlessly onward. There was no escape.

When he looked back, Krieger was at the base of his tree helping someone out of the water. The sheriff! Krieger said something to Leen, the two men looked at Hunt, and both threw back their heads and laughed.

Hunt screamed.

And kept screaming right up to the point where his boat hit bottom, flinging him headfirst into Krieger's tree and instantly snapping his neck. Thus, Hunt joined Krieger and Leen in death, and for eternity.

Tran knew he'd made a terrible and possibly fatal mistake. He never should have lingered a minute more than necessary in these tunnels. He never should have mistaken them for his own.

These tunnels hadn't been dug to support a liberation movement, they were the work of madmen, a warren for insanity. For the first time since he'd been a child, Tran felt fear at being under the soil. He feared that the madness might be contagious, that he could lose his mind, too.

The American who had been behind him was gone. Tran's instincts told him this as certainly as if he'd seen the man walk off across a sunny field. What bothered him was that he hadn't felt or heard the Yankee withdraw; he had simply stopped being where he was.

And now there was someone else in his place.

Tran considered that the departure of the first American and the arrival of the second might have been masked by the gunshots he'd heard. There had been several, but none of them purposeful, merely a spastic reaction to emotional turmoil. Which told him his young hoodlum survived.

Tran knew that there was someone new behind him because his nose told him a man had been replaced by a woman. Tran had fought and lived with female comrades in the NLF for years. He had met his wife in a tunnel, and they had been married and spent their wedding night under the earth. He knew the scent of a woman.

And storming past this woman would be the way he would free himself from his immediate predicament, being caught between two Yankees. After that, he would find his way to the surface.

He eeled his body around, and with gun in hand headed in the woman's direction.

Something was happening, John could feel it. Gil had stopped talking to him, and people were moving through the tunnels. That was the part that confused him. He felt someone creeping toward him, and, at the same time, someone was moving away.

The two bodies in motion seemed to be moving past each other on parallel tracks, and that was what he couldn't understand. A tunnel was a one-lane road. It left no room for two men with guns and hostile intentions to pass each other by. Not without contact and conflict.

But that was just what was happening. Unless . . .

. . . his uncanny ability to sense movement in the dark had gone haywire. The thought made his mouth go dry with fear.

Jill heard the softest rustle of somebody moving toward her. John? Or was it Gil?

She held her gun with two hands and remained perfectly still. She sniffed the air and was surprised that she could distinguish the man approaching her from the background stench.

It wasn't John. She knew his smell. She tried to remember Gil's smell.

The man crept closer. Even though she hadn't made a sound, she knew he was aware of her, too. Now he was close enough that she was sure he wasn't Gil, either.

There was something *foreign* about his smell.

Jill extended the gun in front of her just as a sudden bright light stabbed her eyes.

She fired blind, three shots without hesitation.

As soon as she squeezed off her third shot, Jill flung herself flat on the tunnel floor . . . and a protracted sigh, a mortal exhalation not just of breath but of life, cleaved through the ringing in her ears.

Then she realized that she could *see* the man she had shot, the man she had killed. He'd dropped the flashlight and it had come to rest shining on his face. One of her shots had caught him directly over his right eyebrow.

He was a small man with a hard Asian face frozen in an expression of terminal surprise. Jill had never seen him before. He had a gun in his right hand. She had no doubt that this stranger had intended to take her life.

But that was the past.

What mattered now was that she still had to help John with Gil. She crept forward and took the gun out of the man's hand. She put the safety on and pushed the gun several feet down the tunnel.

Then she turned the flashlight off and waited next to the corpse, waited to feel at ease in the dark again. She'd considered taking the light but decided against it. Look where it had got the last guy who'd used it.

John heard the three shots as muffled pops. His ears remained partially blocked. But he was certain that the gunfire had to have happened dozens of meters away; he couldn't smell any cordite yet. He crawled out of the lower level, easing the trapdoor shut, and moved forward two silent meters, hoping to hear—

A ripping noise hissed just behind him, as if someone had torn a linen sheet. Then someone jammed a gun barrel into the back of his head.

Gil said, "You just nail Charlie, Johnny Fortune? Good for you. Now we can have our little talk."

86

Ty tripped over the body of Vinnie Vinh as he came out of the Oak Crest entrance to the tunnels. He sprawled facefirst into the mud. Then someone turned a flashlight on him.

A voice called out, "It's me, Daulton."

Frank Murtaw!

Ty rolled over and kept rolling. He grabbed his gun and scrambled behind a tree. He was past the idea of taking revenge on Frank, but if he had to defend his life . . .

He peeked out from behind the tree.

Frank stood there with the flashlight pointed at his own face. "I'm on your side now," he said.

Frank had a gun stuck in his waistband, but when he saw Ty looking at it, he threw it down into the mud. "I'm unarmed. Okay?"

Ty asked, "What do you mean you're on my side?"

Frank shone the flashlight on Vinnie's body. "I figure it's your guys against those guys. I want to be with you."

"Did he just come out of the tunnel?" Ty asked.

"Yeah."

"And you shot him?"

"He shot me first."

Frank put the light on his flesh wound. Ty stepped forward and took the flashlight from Frank and bent to look at the body. He saw that the dead boy was only a few years older than he. The terrible stillness of death was on his face. He could imagine the rain dissolving the boy's body. Soon there'd be nothing left at all.

He stood and turned to Frank.

"Pick up your gun," he said. "We've got to find a place to hide. There may be more of these guys popping up any minute now. Let's try to take them alive."

Jimmy Giap figured he was actually going to find a way out.

Moments before, someone moving very quickly, crawling fast and making a lot of noise, had passed by not far from Jimmy. He'd been able to track the sound. Using his flashlight, he'd found the trapdoor leading up a level.

His first impulse was to pop right up and hightail it in the same direction. That thought died swiftly when he considered who he might've heard.

That crazy old gook. He'd waste Jimmy as soon as look at him.

Well, Jimmy still knew which way that fucker had gone.

So, he'd wait as long as he could. Then he'd make his getaway.

"You think you got it all figured out, don't you?" Gil asked.

John didn't answer immediately. He felt another presence nearby. Jill was somewhere just in front of him, no more than a half dozen meters away. *She'd* nailed Charlie, and Gil thought John had done it.

He had to do whatever he could to keep Gil from becoming aware of her. He had to keep Gil focused on him . . . until the time was right.

"Yeah," he said. "You killed Tommy because he was seeing your ex, Rayette."

Gil gave a harsh laugh.

"*Seeing* her? They were *fucking* each other's brains out. Leavin' me out in the cold."

A missing piece of the puzzle clicked into place for John. It fit perfectly with Bobbi Sharpes's comment about men coming by to comfort her.

"You tried to make it with Bobbi, didn't you?"

"That was the whole idea, man. It all started one night when Tommy 'n' me were at this bar talkin'. How we both liked tough broads, but the ones we had were always bustin' our balls. So we thought we'd try swappin', see how that'd work."

"Who brought up the idea?"

Gil didn't reply, but John felt the pressure of the gun against his neck increase.

"You did, Gil. It was your idea. Tommy had his own reasons to be angry at Bobbi, so he played along, but she didn't want any part of you."

"That's right, goddamnit! And I told Tommy, too. So he should've laid off Rayette. But he kept on." Gil's voice dropped to a dispirited whisper. "He made her fall in love with him . . . when I loved her."

"Maybe Rayette was the one who kept on with Tommy."

"Maybe she was," Gil answered bleakly. "Maybe she thought she was sparin' my feelings sneakin' up here from Texas and bein' careful to screw Tommy only at his place 'n' crummy motels. But I knew . . . I knew every time that bastard had her."

"Sure. You probably spotted them one time. After that, you followed Rayette on a motorcycle she didn't know you had. The one you stole. When you couldn't take Tommy being with her anymore, you killed him. Then you killed her. You used the C-4 to burn down the motel and try to hide the murder. Jesus Christ, Gil, are you sorry about any of it?"

The force of the gun against John's neck diminished slightly.

"I didn't kill Tommy."

"You're lying. Hunt was hit with a round from a 16. That was you."

Gil's gun cut into John's flesh again. "That's right, I hit Hunt. I was *tryin'* for Tommy, but I got the wrong guy."

"You dug a line extension outside the plant, brought it up in that storage yard, didn't you? And you dug a bypass that you used to get behind me just now."

A note of triumph entered Gil's voice.

"That's right, motherfucker. When you 'n' Darien stopped for good, I kept diggin' anytime the two of you were away. I kept at it because I'm the only professional around here. And, hey, my little secret bypasses gave me an edge playin' Charlie 'n' Joe. Like just now."

John didn't respond to the taunt. He could feel Jill edging closer. He wanted to keep Gil distracted a little longer. "So who killed Tommy, if you didn't?"

"Can't you guess, man? *Rayette* did. That dumb fuck Tommy, he finds out he's going to be a daddy and right before he gets turned loose from jail he calls Rayette up at the motel and dumps her. 'So long, baby. Thanks for the lap action. See ya around.' You think she was gonna sit still for that shit? Fuck. She got right in her car and dinged the bastard."

John was stupefied. But he *could* see it that way. Except for one thing.

"If Rayette killed Tommy, why'd you kill her?"

Gil went through another mood swing. The anger was still there, deeper than ever, but now it was hard and cold, had a surgical edge.

"I'll tell you why, man. I found her at the motel, and you know what she was doin'? Cryin' her heart out for Tommy. Cryin' that she killed him. Said she . . . she loved him. Not me, him. I told her I'd help her. I'd fix it so the cops'd never pin anything on her. So we could go away, start over."

Gil lapsed into silence. When he resumed his voice was as barren as if it had come from a microchip.

"She said she was going to turn herself in. Confess. Ask for the death penalty. She told me if she couldn't be with Tommy in life, she wanted to be with him in death. Right then, I wrapped my hands around her throat . . . strangled her."

Gil concluded, "She didn't even fight it, man."

"What's wrong?" Ty asked.

"Nothing."

"Okay."

Ty waited. He could almost feel the words stacking up in Frank's head. When the pile got too high they'd all come tumbling out.

"I keep telling myself that I didn't have a choice," Frank began. "But the truth is I feel like shit about killing that kid, and I don't know if I'm ever going to feel any better."

"You said he shot at you first. He *hit* you. *You* could be the one who's dead right now."

"I keep wondering if that wouldn't be a relief."

"What choice did you have?"

"The choice not to pick up a gun," Frank lamented. "The choice not to be where I was. When I walked out my door with a gun, *you* were the one I thought I should kill. Then I figure out how stupid that idea is, and look what happens anyway."

Ty heard Frank start to cry.

"Fucking guns," he sobbed. "Fucking guns!"

Frank scrambled to his feet and flung his father's handgun deep into the darkness of the woods. "I'll wait with you if you want," he told Ty, "but I'll die before I shoot anybody again."

"No problem," Ty said.

. . .

Jill edged close enough to hear Gil's voice descend to a whisper.

"That's it, Johnny Fortune. You want to turn in your ol' bro for murderin' the woman he loved? I'm afraid I can't cop to Tommy's death, even though I made the attempt. You tell me, Johnny. We'll do what's right."

"All I wanted, Gil, was to hear you say you're sorry. But what the hell's the point? Where your soul is right now, sorrow would be a ray of sunshine."

"Ain't that the fuckin' tru—"

Suddenly, the gun was removed from John's neck.

"Dink!" Gil yelled. He'd finally sensed Jill's presence. "Duck, man!"

There was no time to explain. All John could do was rise to his knees, turn, fill as much of the tunnel as he could—and take the bullet. The round hit him high in the chest.

In the light of the muzzle flash, Gil saw that he'd just shot his friend. He was horrified. He couldn't understand why Johnny Fortune had used his body to shield a dink.

Then he heard a guttural female cry of rage: "You *bastard!*"

Gil was around the nearest curve before Jill shot at him.

Jimmy Giap was about to make his move when he heard the gunfire. Then someone else was hauling ass his way. If the first one had been the old gook, who the hell was this guy?

He didn't know and he didn't care. All he wanted was to get out of these miserable rat holes as fast as he could; the fucking walls were closing in on him. So as soon as this sonofabitch whipped past . . .

. . . but whoever it was didn't whip past. He came to a dead stop. Jimmy could hear him breathing hard but not moving. What the fuck was he waiting for?

Gil came to an abrupt halt. There was someone waiting under the trapdoor just ahead. He could feel it. It wasn't Darien. Gil knew him in dark or daylight. He thought it could be the kid, Ty.

Yeah, had to be him. Now that he was paying attention again, Gil could smell the cheeseburgers on the kid from here.

Just to be sure, so the little guy didn't get excited, or Gil's reflexes didn't get the better of him, he whistled a few notes of a song.

Ritchie Valens. "La Bamba."

•   •   •

Los Lobos. "La Bamba."

Somebody up there was whistling the song. Jimmy Giap didn't know what to make of it, but something told him to whistle it back. So he did.

Right after that, a voice he'd never heard before said, "It's okay, kid, you can come up."

The guy sounded all right. He wasn't that fucking gook, that was for sure. But Jimmy wasn't taking any chances. He went up with his gun ready.

The kid came up with his flashlight on . . . but it wasn't Ty. It was a dink with a gun in his hand. Or was it? Gil had thought John's woman had been a dink. Maybe he was seeing dinks everywhere now, going crazy. Shit, how could a dink know "La Bamba"?

He'd almost fired on the kid—the dink?—by instinct. But he held back. Even though the kid was raising his gun at Gil.

Jimmy didn't know who the hell this guy was, but he shot him anyway—and made it count. He had to, once the guy put his own gun on Jimmy. Funny thing was, though, Jimmy got the feeling that the guy had waited for him when he could have shot first.

His mistake, the dumbass.

Jill had John's head in her lap when she heard the shot ring out. It came from up the tunnel. She didn't know who had fired it or what it meant. What she knew was that John was still breathing and she had to get him out of there.

Her only choice was to head off in the direction Gil had gone and hope he was heading toward an exit and that she could follow his trail.

Then she heard something that gave her a great sense of urgency. She heard water. It had filled the lower level and was coming after her once more.

She gently laid John's head down, scrambled over him, took his feet, and started to drag him forward. Hunched over in pitch blackness, tugging inch by inch, it was backbreaking work. Heartstopping work when she imagined the water advancing faster than she could retreat.

They moved uphill. She prayed that the water would stop rising before they did. Prayed there was a way out.

.   .   .

Jimmy Giap pushed the trapdoor open and felt a rush of sweet air and rain on his face. He thrust his fist into the air and gave a shout of joy. The shout turned into a squawk when the rest of him rose into the air along with his hand.

Someone was lifting him. Then a light went on in his eyes.

Squinting through the beam, Jimmy saw that he was being held by a humongous white kid. He didn't try to squirm free. Because a small white kid held a gun on him.

"What's your name?" the kid with the gun asked.

Jimmy gave it at once.

"What're you doing here?"

Jimmy said that he'd been kidnapped by a crazy old sonofabitch and forced to go down this hole.

The big kid nodded. "I saw it. Some old fuck made these guys go down at gunpoint."

"What's happening down there?"

"Shit, I don't know. It's dark," Jimmy said. He sure as hell wasn't going to tell them he'd killed that guy.

"You have a flashlight. And you can *hear* in the dark."

The small kid pointed his gun at Jimmy's head.

"I heard a lot of shooting," the gang-banger volunteered quickly. "And the fucking place is filling up with water." Then he remembered something else. "I heard a woman scream, too."

"And you didn't try to help her?" the big one asked.

"Hey, I'm not from around here."

The big kid dropped him in the mud.

The little one kicked him.

"Hey!" Jimmy Giap yelled.

"You better get out of here while you still can," the little one told him.

"How'm I gonna get home, man?" Jimmy whined. "I'm from *California*."

"Try surfing."

Jimmy was about to mouth off some more. Then he noticed Vinnie's body, not five feet from him. He scrambled to his feet and fled down the hill.

"What're we going to do now?" Frank asked Ty.

"I'm going to go back down."

"What about me?"

"Pray. Hard."

· · ·

Jill bumped into a body. In the dark, she had no idea who it was. But when she put her hand out to keep from losing her balance, she felt a prosthetic foot. Gil.

Unmoving at her touch.

She pinched his leg—hard—just to be sure. No response. No sound of breathing, either. So who'd killed him? Some crazy sonofabitch waiting around the next curve with a gun? She didn't have her own gun anymore; she'd left it behind after she'd emptied it.

She also didn't have any more time. The water kept coming relentlessly. She rolled Gil as far as she could to one side of the tunnel, and she found *his* gun. By touch, she could tell it was loaded. She stuck it into her pants.

She dragged John past Gil. And John moaned—almost sounding as if he were saying something to Gil—scaring the hell out of her. Jill kept tugging. She had no time for supernatural conversations.

She worked her way uphill until she heard someone approaching fast. Gil's killer? She stopped and let go of John's legs. She took out her gun and turned to face whoever was approaching.

Whoever it was froze. The tunnel was quiet. Except for the water, coming inexorably closer. She had no time for this impasse.

She extended her gun.

Ty knew there was someone out there. He even knew who it was. Jill. Some aspect of her presence had imprinted itself in his mind. But she wasn't alone . . . and she was afraid.

He also felt a gun was somehow involved. Did someone have a gun on Jill?

Ty heard the water approaching, too. There was no time to dick around here. He lay flat on his stomach. He held out his gun.

He tried to find the saliva to moisten his lips.

And hoped Jill knew about recognition signals.

Jill's finger was tense on the trigger, almost ready to fire—when a hand grabbed her ankle.

She screamed.

Ty yelled, "Jill, get down! Give me a shot!"

.   .   .

Ty! And she'd been about to kill him. Jill felt weak.

But she spoke quickly. "Ty, I have John with me. He's wounded. We've got to get out of here. Do you know where there's an exit?"

He did, it wasn't far, and he had a flashlight to guide her. A flashlight! It almost made Jill throw up. If he'd turned it on before he'd called out, she would have . . .

Wait a minute. Who had grabbed her?

John? But he'd given no sign, before or since, that he'd regained consciousness.

Still, somebody had definitely grabbed her ankle—just before she would have shot Ty.

Who?

Then she remembered her father telling her he'd be there for her.

"Daddy?" Jill whispered.

Ty and Jill couldn't get John out of the hole. The angle was too steep, and neither of them possessed the strength to lift him. Frank, who waited above in the rain, was strong enough, but he couldn't get more than one arm and a shoulder into the hole, couldn't reach John.

"This is crazy!" Ty shouted.

Jill took Ty's flashlight and pointed it down the tunnel. She could see the water, not more than thirty feet away. It was filling the shaft steadily, like a pipe being fed by a garden hose.

"A rope," Ty said, thinking aloud. "Or a vine. We've got to get something to make a harness." He looked at Jill. "I'll be right back, I swear to God."

Ty scrambled out of the hole. Jill heard him give frantic instructions to the boy above. After they left, she held John close. Held him from behind, so his head was slightly higher than hers.

If the water was going to take them, it would have to take her first.

87 Ty hadn't gone ten feet before he came up with the solution. They had no rope, and even if they knew what to look for, there was no way he and Frank were going to find a *vine* in the dark and the rain. Not in time. He quickly explained to Frank what they should do, and they stripped off their pants and belts. They threaded their belts through two loops at the sides of Frank's pants. Frank would use these as handles. Then they tied the pantlegs together. When they were done they had a harness that would reach John.

Ty slid back into the hole. The water was already lapping at Jill's feet. Together, Jill and Ty got the improvised harness around John. With Frank pulling and the two of them pushing, they got him out.

Jill went next. Ty was the last out.

They carried John on the run to the nearest house. The homeowner who answered their furious banging saw the desperation on their faces and John's mortal need for swift medical attention. He ushered them inside. Without prompting, he called 911 and handed the phone to Jill.

She told the emergency operator she needed an ambulance immediately: a man had been shot in the chest. When the operator asked her location and heard Oak Crest as the response, she informed Jill that the roads were out. No ambulance would be able to reach them for hours.

Ty, who'd been listening in, grabbed the phone from Jill. "We need a dust-off," he yelled. "Get a helicopter into the air immediately!"

He might have been only a boy, but the emergency operator didn't argue with him.

"The nearest medevac is at Quincy General. . . . I'll patch you right through."

A moment later, a phlegmatic male voice told Ty that the rain in Quincy, forty miles south, was too heavy for him to take off.

Ty took the only shot he could think of; the guy sounded about the right age. Through gritted teeth, he said, "Our gunshot victim will *die* without urgent medical attention. He's a former Eleven-Bravo, Twenty-fifth Infantry, Tropic Lightning."

"Served at Cu Chi?" the guy asked, surprised.

"Yeah."

"You better not be shitting me, kid." Then the pilot asked for an LZ.

Ty got the address, and a few helpful suggestions for visual landmarks, from the homeowner. He told the pilot all the lights in the house would be on, there was a cul-de-sac right outside where he could land, and there'd be people outside shining flashlights at the sky.

Fifteen endless minutes later, the helicopter descended out of the rain, skimmed the tops of the trees, and set down perfectly. Within seconds, John was strapped on a gurney. The paramedic and the flight nurse loaded him into the helicopter and gave the pilot the signal to take off.

Nobody had tried to tell Jill or Ty they couldn't go, too.

The medevac flight had alerted Elk River Community Hospital en route to Oak Crest. A surgical team and an operating room were waiting. The hop down the hill took only minutes. The ER staff was on hand in the parking lot. They raced John straight into the operating room where the surgical team stood ready.

Jill and Ty had to remain outside in the waiting area. They'd done all they could. They sat side by side, holding each other's hands and praying in silence.

Inside the operating theater, John was given general anesthesia. As soon as he was under, the surgeon opened John's chest. The assisting nurse whispered, "Dear God."

The surgeon allowed his emotions half a beat to absorb the damage this patient had suffered. Then he snapped to his team, "Let's go, people! We've got a lot to do if we're going to save this man!"

.   .   .

Despite everything, or perhaps because of it, John was aware of his surroundings. Conscious of the doctors and nurses covered up to their elbows with his blood. Cognizant that his chest lay open and his heart was exposed.

None of that interested him.

Because as he looked up Doolan hovered there above him.

Doolan hadn't changed at all. He was as young and lean as ever. His red hair was rumpled. His grin was just as crooked. He still wore his boonie rat fatigues.

The only difference was in his eyes: They no longer flashed with blue fire; they glowed with a profound sense of peace.

"Good to see ya again, bro," Doolan said.

"Jamie . . . Am I dead?"

"Not yet, Johnny Fortune."

"Am I going to die?"

Doolan laughed. "Everyone does."

"I mean now." Suddenly, John burned with shame. He finally had the chance to see Doolan again, and just like the last time he could think only of himself. "Jamie, I'm so sorry I got you killed. So damned sorry you'll never know."

"I know *exactly* how sorry you are, Johnny. That's why I'm here. Listen, man, have you ever figured out what happened to me?"

John nodded. "Just a little while ago. Gil ambushed me, came out behind me from a hole that wasn't supposed to be there. I felt him nearby, but I didn't know how to respond. My mind kept telling me he couldn't be where he was. I didn't know Gil had kept on digging—just like Charlie did."

"That was it, all right," Doolan told him. "Our little friends from the NLF were connecting up a new line with the tunnel we were in. They were just about ready to break through when we went by. That's how come I got so nervous. At some subconscious level, I *heard* 'em coming."

Doolan shook his head. "Of course, I didn't know that until *after* I was caught. Anyway, they grabbed me. And when they heard me yell for help, they threw that dimestore grenade at you. It looked like it was going to do the job, though. So they moved your body up the tunnel, ahead of where they had just broken through. That's where Gil found you. In the meantime, they got busy patchin' up the entrance to their new hole."

"Why?" John asked.

"Because if you'd followed the line they'd just finished digging—and it was beaucoup klicks, believe me—you'd have come up right inside of COSVN."

COSVN was the Communist Office of South Vietnam, the enemy's headquarters for the war in the south. American forces had never found it, though years had been spent trying.

"Those were some upset little comrades, thinking that we might finally be onto them. They planned to do some serious interrogation on yours truly. Of course, they never got the chance."

John asked hesitantly, "How come?"

"No need to BS, Johnny, not now. We both know how come. When you were evacked, you told the brass about those arty pieces you saw. Pretty soon after that, the B-52 raids started. One of those blockbusters they dropped spared me and my new pals a real nasty game of Twenty Questions."

"Oh, Jesus, Jamie, I'm sorry. Some intelligence guy at the hospital started talking to me and I was pumped so full of drugs, it just came out before I thought of the consequences."

Doolan put a hand on John's shoulder.

"Bro, I was dead once the little people grabbed me. And our brass were going to bomb anyway." For the first time, *Doolan* seemed a little sad. "I got something to tell you, Johnny. Something maybe you never thought about. You know why those VC were able to grab me, why I wasn't waiting for you right at that water trap?"

"No."

"Because after you left me I got too scared to hold my position. I didn't know if you would ever make it back, and I couldn't stand being down there alone. I just had to *di-di*. I deserted you, bro. I'm the one who owes *you* an apology."

John wasn't ready to concede his guilt. "But if we'd stayed together, the way you wanted, we could've fought those motherfuckers off."

Doolan shook his head. "Shoulda, coulda, woulda is all a lot of crap. You do what you think is right and face the music. Which was just what I had to do. Because after you die, Johnny, you got another hump ahead of you. Up this mountain path. Just above the crest, you see this amazing light. And you know right away what it is."

"God?"

"A lot of people'd say that. For some reason, I always thought of it as the Source. Where we're from, where we return."

John waited a long moment, then asked, "Is it hard, Jamie? That last hump?"

Doolan nodded. "Yeah, it's hard."

"But you made it, right? That's why you're here."

"I made it, Johnny. I had help staying on track. There was this guy who kept lighting all these candles."

Doolan's smile took away all of his friend's fears, eased all of his pain and doubts.

At that moment, John recalled the night so very long ago when Grandma Sophia died—and Grandpa Michelangelo had come for her.

"It's my time, isn't it, Jamie?"

Doolan extended his hand, and he walked point for John up the mountain path.

88

Two days later, Jill walked along Riverfront Drive alone. She was dressed in black and on her way to John's funeral, but hadn't yet found time to grieve. She'd been too busy. She'd kept herself too busy.

When the surgeon had finally emerged from the operating room, both she and Ty had seen immediately that the news was bad. Ty broke down, demanding to know, through his tears, how this could have happened. They had done everything they could. Goddamnit, they'd gotten John to the hospital *alive*! He'd looked at the haggard surgeon and had been about to lay the blame on him when Jill put her arms around the boy and led him away, somehow giving him comfort from a heart that was bereft of solace for herself.

She'd taken Ty to the hospital room where Darien was recovering from his wounds. There, Ty blurted out the news and fell across his friend's chest. Darien put his arms around the boy.

He looked at Jill and asked, "Gil?"

"He's dead, too."

Darien bit his lip so no sound could escape, but tears formed in his eyes. He was able to tell Jill that the only family John had left were two elderly aunts, one in Oregon, the other in Colorado. He didn't think they traveled much anymore. He gave her their names and the names of the towns where they lived.

Jill left to make the funeral arrangements. At the Church of the Resurrection, she found Bill Deeley cleaning up the church grounds. She told him what had happened, and he put his arms around her. Still, she wouldn't let herself cry. There was too much to do.

From Deeley, she got the addresses and phone numbers of Sid Tomlinson and Harry Waller, the remnants of the Local 274 executive committee. The three of them drove to Chicago later that morning and Jill introduced them to Toshiro Yoshihara, the inventor on whom Hunt had based his whole plan. After Jill outlined her plan, and Yoshihara made only slight changes, they called Carter Powell, Hunt's erstwhile banker, and Yoshihara's father in Japan.

Jill proposed to use the Elk River plant that had already been prepared for manufacturing. Financing from Carter Powell's bank would now be guaranteed by the Japanese company of the elder Yoshihara. Thus, the enterprise would be financially sound, the Yoshihara family honor would be preserved, and business could go forward without delay. This would be possible because New MicroCosmic, Inc. would assure itself a loyal workforce by agreeing to employee ownership.

The details provided that the workers would own 50.5 percent of the company. They would be represented by a company union, to remain unaffiliated with any outside union. The workers would pay for their part of the ownership from their part of the company's profits until the debt was retired.

Ownership of the remainder of the company would be divided among Toshiro Yoshihara, Carter Powell's bank, and the elder Yoshihara's Japanese company.

Now, as she walked toward the Church of the Resurrection in the morning sunshine, Jill looked around her. The park was still a muddy bog, but the rest of the town, perversely, looked renewed. Saved from inundation by the tunnels, downtown glistened in the sunlight. Brick, stone, and mortar had been washed clean. The streets had been swept of storm debris by the sanitation department and looked neater than ever before.

Elk River looked like a place with a future.

In the new spirit of consensus, Oak Crest would be annexed by, and become part of, Elk River. By unanimous agreement, those in town who found out—or were informed—about the tunnels of Elk River decided to keep them a local secret.

The Church of the Resurrection was standing-room-only for the funeral of John Fortunato and Gil Velez. When the water had receded, Darien had gone down into the tunnels and, with Ty's help, had recovered all the bodies. He'd persuaded Jill that the two former comrades-in-arms should be buried together by reminding her that Gil had once gone down a hole to save John's life.

Unable to effect a meaningful reconciliation with his father, Ty sat next to Darien, who wore his old army uniform. Without a word, the boy and the man adopted each other.

The sun shone down through Michelangelo Fortunato's stained-glass Jesus and bathed the two flag-draped coffins. Bill Deeley spoke a simple eulogy of forgiveness, reconciliation, and salvation.

After the service, Jill Baxter remained seated, the only person left in the church. She felt no need to go to the churchyard. She felt the need to grieve . . . and to hope.

She looked up at the figure of Christ in the window. And she looked within her heart to address a man she'd never known. "He finally found you, Jamie Doolan, didn't he?"

Before she left the church, Jill honored John's final request of her and began a habit she'd continue every day for the rest of her life.

She lit a candle for him.

About the Author

Joseph Flynn is the author of *The Concrete Inquisition* and *Digger*. He lives in central Illinois. He is currently working on his next novel for Bantam.